Two Wolves

By Hugh Darby

Humo and Espejos Publishing
Austin, Texas
© 2010

Copyright © 2010 by Hugh Darby

All rights reserved. No part of this book may be reproduced, scanned or distributed in any printed or electronic form without the express and written permission of the author or publisher.
Please do not participate or encourage piracy of copyrighted materials in violation of the author's rights. Purchase only authorized editions.

This book is a work of fiction. Names, characters and incidents are products of the author's imagination. Feel free to use a little of yours as well. Flights of fantasy while reading are encouraged. Serious consideration and analysis should be taken at your own risk. Any resemblances to actual persons, living or dead are entirely coincidental. Further, the author nor the publisher have any control over and does not assume any responsibility for third-party websites, blogs or comments made by the media.

Acknowledgements

Cindy L., Yvette Y., Justin L., Adam L., Yuen Y., Rebecca C., James D.

Cover art and design by Justin

Prologue

"The charm of history and its enigmatic lesson consist in the fact that, from age to age, nothing changes and yet everything is completely different." — Aldous Huxley

* * * * * *

The following is a precautionary tale of a society yet to come in the not so distant future. Although the vision is simplistic, the principles are, nevertheless, valid.

Not long after the turn of the new century, the majority of the North American continent was consolidated into one sovereign country — the United Authority. This historical transformation didn't occur overnight; rather it was a gradual metamorphosis — skillfully planned and executed over several decades.

Travel and to a lesser degree trade to and from the United Authority were gradually controlled to the point of virtual suspension. It became widely accepted that an isolationist posture would create the objective of improved safety and security for this new nation. In addition, many new and constricting internal controls were also deemed necessary to achieve the ultimate goal. All citizens, in order to be considered UA

Citizens, were required to register with the newly formed United Authority. Registration was electronic and controlled by a combination of implanted microchip and hand-held, multifunctional data devises known as Tel-Cards. Citizenship was completely voluntary. Most people appreciated the standardized benefits of membership, which included: virtually guaranteed employment, medical assistance, mandatory electronic banking, purchasing privileges, and a retirement opportunity. Those not registered, on the other hand, were considered non-Citizens or Plebeians, commonly referred to as Plebes, and no benefits were forthcoming.

Many businesses and industries were consolidated in an effort to conserve energy and to create a more equitable pricing structure. As a result, the majority of research and development was deemed no longer cost effective. Most advances in science and technology had slowed or were discontinued all together due to the downturn in markets, increased regulations and the steady decline in consumer demand.

Looking back as an average Citizen, most of the preceding years, with but a few exceptions, had seemed otherwise unremarkable. The changes made were gradual and for the best. The Citizens were satisfied. Everyone was finally equal.

And then the calendar turned to 2084.

Bizarre

1

"The mass of men lead lives of quiet desperation." — Henry David Thoreau

* * * * *

2083 had come and gone with seemingly little or no notice. Life on our planet seemed more or less the same as it had been for the previous one hundred years. And yet, changes were taking place on every level, and affecting every aspect of life as well. Regimes came and went — as did the ebb and flow of power. Societies were mutating around the world. But then, they always had. With the exception of the effects that major wars have on civilizations and cultures, societal evolution has always been a dilatory process.

At least that's what Austin had read and had been told — what he thought he remembered. He didn't know first-hand because he wasn't born until 2047. An elite and select few knew it as the year of the Spider.

Looking back, if it were possible, one could begin to see how Orwell's prophetic words were coming to fruition in his novel *1984*, albeit more slowly than he predicted, but just as deliberately nevertheless. Life and living had changed dramatically in the hundred years since — and yet, few seemed to have noticed or remembered.

There were multiple methods and levels of changes required to transform an entire society's perception of reality. The vision and execution was a carefully guided metamorphosis. After all, the most innocuous control over a society is one that is progressive.

In the words of the United Authority, "Life is now balanced." The Registered Citizens of the Great New North American Continent, known as the United Authority or UA, lead their lives in analogous satisfaction. The State administered benefit programs provided life's required essentials. What more could one ask for? It wasn't a perfect system. Everyone knew there was no such thing as perfection. But, everyone also regarded his or her homogenized life as fair, if not routine. There was no longer a need for change. Most considered each day to be more or less the same. There was so much satisfaction in consistency and the new equality.

Austin Llanoc's life, on the surface and by most measures, seemed as unremarkable as everyone's. His thirty-seventh birthday came and passed — and there was little reason to notice. There just never seemed to be much of a distinction from one day to the next. Yet privately, Austin believed, he felt, that he was somehow different from other Citizens in a number of ways, and in ways in which he was unable to express. Aspects of his memories were not always consistent with accepted truths. He was secretly confused and there was no one with whom he could confide. Although his life had been mostly unremarkable, he frequently sensed a difference. Often he considered his condition as a dichotomy or aberration.

In the end, Austin endured the reality of his existence. His feelings were muted out of necessity. After all, most Citizens, seemingly lived in a never-ending present, combined with the all but bleak prospects of future. Plus, without having an accurate knowledge of the past — most could only feel trapped in a constant state of limbo. Their consolation was equality.

That was until today.

* * * * * *

A series of violent explosions woke Austin from a particularly sound sleep — briefly shaking his condo on the level of a magnitude seven, or larger, earthquake.

"What the hell was that?" He blurted. *The ground is shaking!* He thought while bringing himself to a state of semi consciousness. *Earthquake.*

Austin's body was frozen as he lay on his back staring at the ceiling. *Where am I?* His eyes had not yet focused. *What time is it?* He sensed a pungent odor. *Something's burning!* His small bedroom flickered from lights reflecting past his balcony's sliding glass doors. *What the hell is going on?* He thought as he sat up in his bed.

Quickly glancing at the time-meter on the bedside table Austin thought it remarkably bright outside for 3-am. The Pacific was glowing. He quickly slipped from his bed yet cautiously approached his balcony.

"Geeeee-zus!" — Was the only word he could manage as he stepped out onto his private balcony overlooking the ocean.

To the south, he could see the United Authority's Continuity Building burning out of control — what was left of it. Within a few minutes Austin thought he heard, and possibly felt, more distant explosions in the Los Angeles basin — or was it his half conscious imagination?

Looking down to the street below from his fourth-story perch, he watched people running erratically, up and down the street — screaming, yelling, pushing, shoving — some throwing on various articles of clothing — all of this in spite of the fact that the Continuity Building was more than two miles to the south, with very little evidence of damage in between. Then there were the sounds of sirens in the distance. They were approaching. At first only one or two could be heard. Soon, more joined from multiple directions. Their cries were unique and growing louder by the minute.

What the hell is going on? His state of confusion was heightened and stirred from the sights below. *I don't recall ever seeing people this animated. But then, nothing like this has ever happened before.* Austin rubbed his eyes in an effort to bring clarity to his vision and force his mind from its still groggy state. *Maybe things like this have happened elsewhere — just not here.*

He stood at his balcony for a number of minutes — mesmerized by the sights, the sounds and the unique sensations he was experiencing — frozen from action or reaction. He felt in a haze — as if he was dreaming. Suddenly, if this insanity wasn't enough, he came to the realization that something was missing. Walking back inside he glanced around the small room. His eyes stopped at the wall in front of his foldout bed. His Tel-Com was dark — and silent. He slowly walked across the room and touched the cold, glass screen attached to the wall — yet nothing happened. There couldn't be a power outage because the red, Apple power light was still glowing.

The Com-Center is always on. Tel-Coms were ubiquitous. Every Citizen had at least one. The law required one for every room. Citizens never understood why this luxury had been placed into law. *What the hell? This too has never . . . Without the Tel-Com, how in the hell can I find out what's going on? I may not even be able to call anyone.* He stood for several moments staring at the blank screen. *My only choice is to either stand here and wait until the Tel-Com initializes, or get out on the street and start asking others — What the hell is happening!? As if anyone would know.*

Austin just stood quietly staring at the blank Com-Center his eyes fixed on the cold black screen. There was little reason to dress for work. The Continuity Building — the building in which Austin had spent so much of his recent life, was burning out of control. Thankfully there wasn't a night shift. The building's security was fully automated and off-site, so there shouldn't have been any casualties. Plus, all of the electronic data was stored off-site as well, in an underground UA data farm somewhere in New Mexico. The only real loss would be that of the building and equipment — other than the down time.

"Gotta admit it, this is a hell of a way to get a few days off," he laughed out loud. "On the other hand, cleanup and rebuilding is going to be a real bitch," muttering as he slowly backed up to sit on the edge of his bed, while continuing to stare at the ominously black Com-Center. *Oh well, great job-security*

— at least for those who care. I'm just not sure I do anymore. Thoughts he could never speak.

Austin had become increasingly cynical regarding the United Authority, and therefore more skeptical of the Regional and Central Authorities as well — especially as it related to the Continuity Bureau. In fact, he'd become increasingly skeptical if not down right cynical about virtually everything relating to any authority. This was incredibly frustrating due to the fact that he couldn't let anyone know his feelings. After all, that could be very dangerous for someone in Austin's position. As a matter of fact, it would be dangerous for anyone in any position.

Let me think. Maybe I should go to the office anyway. Maybe I should at least give the appearance of concern. I might even find out what is happening. Austin alternated speaking out loud and thinking to himself as he paced the small condo like a caged animal. "But then, my office doesn't exactly look like the safest place to be at the moment either." *Bull shit! If I don't show up — what is Klaud going to say?* "Where were you? You should've been here! I tried calling you!" *Never mind the fact that communications appear to be completely out. Besides, nobody is going to get the scheduled workload out today anyway. How could we? The farging building is destroyed!* The pain behind his eyes throbbed with the cadence of his heart. Rubbing his temples with both hands had but a momentary soothing effect.

Austin cautiously walked back to the balcony. *This has to be a dream.* He thought. Maybe he wasn't fully awake. Maybe he didn't really see what he thought — what he knew he had seen. But there it was. He was observing the same chaotic milieu. *Should I show up? — Or not?*

He stood in silence staring out at the Pacific from his balcony, scratching his head while consciously trying to understand the solution to his not so simple dilemma.

"Damned if I do – damned if I don't."

That's when the thudding intensified inside Austin's head. Frequently just the thought of Klaud would precipitate the pain. But, this time, it seemed even louder, more pronounced than usual.

Klaud! — The boss from hell. He thought to himself.

* * * * * *

The truth was that Austin had headaches most of his life — even before Klaud Akakios — and before his current position as Continuity Vice-Director. As a matter of fact, his Klaud headaches had become less frequent with his new position. Thankfully, Klaud had begun to treat Austin in a slightly different manner of late.

It was somewhat fascinating looking back from his college days to present. Although Austin's life seemed, essentially, the same as that of most Citizens' — there clearly were differences — opportunities had presented themselves to him almost mysteriously over the years. He had risen through the ranks to manage a team of researchers, copywriters, editors, artists and producers to ostensibly control all national advertising. But it wasn't called advertising — rather, "clarification documentation" or "affirmation promotion." And yet, he had so little absolute confirmation about most of the products or services he promoted. Frequently he even had doubts about his own past for that matter — especially the early years. In fact, Austin fully expected a complementary head pounding just trying to remember details of his own past — not all of the past, mind you, but specific pieces of his past. It was very confusing at the least. On occasions, it felt as if he had duplicate, albeit somewhat contradictory reoccurring memories. There were moments in his life that sometimes seemed more than déjà vu. As ridiculous as it may seem, Austin often believed he had memories of 1984 and events before his birth. Was he unique? Did others suffer from the same malady? There was but one person, an exception whom he had limited knowledge of. This was not a topic to bring up in public conversation. And, therapy was completely out of the question.

He tried not to think about it — not just to rid the headaches — but to keep from being caught, or detected. The gods forbid that should happen. Detection could be very dangerous. And yet, there were moments that Austin felt as if "they" might already know. *But how could they?* He would wonder. *The microchips implanted at birth are for identification purposes only.* As far as he or anyone knew the UA-ID chips that were lodged under the skin, beside the brain didn't mean they could actually read one's mind. There had been talk of research conducted in a Texas lab — but no published reports that he could remember or that he was aware of.

Unfortunately, the throbbing occurrences had increased over the years along with his growing cynicism. Not long after this morning's pounding commenced, it seemingly began to echo in his head. *Great! Double-pounding! Now I'm getting stereo headaches.* Austin tried to put a slightly humorous spin on the duplicate pounding, which he quickly determined was coming from his front door.

* * * * * *

"Yes! I'm coming! Hang on!" He shouted — and then muttered under his breath, "I really would rather not deal with anyone at the moment. Please don't let it be Klaud – anyone but Klaud – well, *almost* anyone."

As Austin cautiously pressed his thumb to the lock sensor, and the door began to automatically slide into the wall, he could hear a familiar female voice.

"Austin. Are you there? You *are*! Good! You're here! Thank the gods. Are you OK?"

"Diana. Yes. I think I . . ."

"You look as disoriented as I feel. I mean . . ."

"Yea, well — That makes two of us then doesn't it?" Austin rubbed his temple. "And throw in a bit of a headache maybe — how about you? Are *you* OK?"

Diana Akira had been one of Austin's condo-neighbors for about a year. She wasn't his body-mate — at least not yet. But he thought about it regularly and was slowly working on it. Although he'd known and seen much more beautiful women in his lifetime, Diana's contemporary, attractive Asian looks had made their impact on him. *She's not hard to look at,* as his father would have said. Diana's age was the same as his, and they did share a few common interests. But there was more to it than that — each of them just seemed to mentally connect from the moment they first met.

* * * * * *

Austin thought back about that moment many times, trying to remember exactly what the connection could be. It was partially physical — for sure. But it was more than that — something else — something almost intuitive rather than cerebral. They were discovering that they each shared many of the same thoughts and feelings — at least those they dared speak of. She *was* the exception — the exception to all of the other women he'd met — the exception to whom he could cautiously share a few of his guarded thoughts. And Austin was her exception as well. The two had discreetly talked about a few of their shared sensations on more than several occasions — trying to make the connection. The phenomenon was in many ways similar to that of reincarnation. Not that either believed in the possibility. There was no known research confirming the existence of life after death — or anything after death for that matter. These types of conversations were reserved for their frequent Sunday walks on the beach.

There were few areas remaining, free zones, where Citizens could speak freely without the possibility of UA monitoring — not that monitoring was necessarily a bad idea. Over the years, the UA determined that it would be in the best interest of all Citizens to have the ability to monitor communications in public and private locations — strictly on a random basis. It was thought that monitors were not installed along beaches or the remote and rural countryside locations. There were other surveillance methods for these areas; though, their effectiveness was somewhat questionable. Most Citizens appreciated the additional safety and security afforded them in spite of the occasional breach of their privacy. It wasn't as if Citizens were required to make a sacrifice. After all, this small inconvenience was just a sign of the times.

Sex was also on Austin's menu with Diana — he just hadn't quite gotten past the appetizer portion of the menu. They both seemed to be making progress in that regard, however. It had just taken a pre-cautiously long period of time to establish a level of complete trust between one another. One simply couldn't choose a body-mate too carefully these days.

* * * * * *

"I'm OK, Austin, except for the sinking feeling I had in my chest thinking about you. Oh yes, and along with *my* usual headache too. I was frozen at my window for it seemed forever — watching — mesmerized. I stared at the Continuity Building in flames, and suddenly, I came to the realization that you frequently go to work early. And — and I ran to your door. I was worried, frightened. Do you have any idea what's happening to . . ."

"No — not even a hint. Your Tel-Com's out too?"

She nodded, and then, while looking up into Austin's brown eyes, she slowly wrapped her arms around his waist. He placed his palms on the small of her back, pulled her closely, and they embraced more tightly and meaningfully than ever before. Their bodies came alive. This moment was clearly four octaves higher than their more typically friendly embraces in the past.

"I feel better just knowing you're alright Austin. What should we do?"

"I don't actually know, but this feels like a good place to start." Tightening his hold on her, they stood in each other's arms as if to realize their lives might never be the same again.

Within a few moments, Austin's Com-Center began to flash and low-level-audio static sounded for a few seconds — then nothing. After waiting a few more moments in silence, the Com-Center didn't restart. Austin guided Diana to the kitchen and started a pot of Coca-Coffee.

"I've got to have a cup before we do anything else. It'll help me get my brain into gear and out of the pounding mode. How about for you?"

"I haven't had coffee, breakfast, anything. Coca would be great. I haven't even thought about makeup, or dressing, or . . ."

"Oh. You're *not* wearing makeup — are you?" smiling as he clearly stared below her neckline. "I hadn't noticed." He gazed through her translucent nightshirt. It didn't hide much and at the same time it didn't reveal everything. It was most apparent that she led a very healthy lifestyle. All the right curves were in all the right places. Her silky, streaked-blonde hair had always caught his attention as well. Each time Austin gazed at her, a few of his lost memory fragments would materialize.

"So — coffee, and let's see what I have for a quick bite. I'm not accustomed to entertaining at this time of the morning. Come to think of it, I guess I'm not really used to entertaining at all. Maybe I should work on that."

"Maybe *we* should work on that," she said softly. "Coca-Coffee will be enough. Thank you."

* * * * * *

Austin and Diana took their Coca-Coffees to the balcony and watched the day slowly begin to break.

Within the hour the fire subsided. There were fewer frantic people running below, no doubt due to the Central Authority's Protection, Raptor- Cruisers patrolling. They sat drinking their coffee and discussing possible explanations to this unique event — an earthquake, gas line rupture, terrorist attack, or possibly an aircraft collision — all the while they were feeling caught up in a surreal tableau. Their conversation turned to quiet contemplation. Diana wondered why there was no media streaming on the Tel-Com. Austin couldn't stop thinking that he should be doing something. He just wasn't sure what that something should be. After drinking an entire pot of Coca-Coffee, the two were not only wide-awake but also energized to the max.

Diana was first to break the silence. "Austin, we really have to do something. I mean we're just sitting here, having a casual coffee, calmly discussing the most bizarre day of our lives as if it were routine — as if we were just watching a program on the Tel-Com."

"You're right. You're reading my mind — again. We *should* be doing something. We shouldn't be just sitting here. I'm not sure which is more bizarre, this morning's events or our ultimate reaction to them. I keep trying to apply logic to my, to *our* next move. But as my dad always said, 'You can't get logic from illogic.' There's still a lot of missing information, missing data to act on. What we've been watching isn't logical. We keep asking the same questions. Has there been a major utility disruption? But there's still power and lights. Are we being attacked? — And, if so, by whom — and where next? Besides, even if we are under some type of attack, we aren't in the Authority's Protection Service. The United Authority employs me, and you for that matter, but we haven't been trained for military action. I mean, I'm simply a Continuity Vice-Director and you're a Senior Programming Producer. Plus, if it was an attack, why hasn't it continued?"

* * * * * *

Diana's thought process was much like Austin's. She was a reporter at heart. And her professional rise had been as stellar as his. She had been hired as a field reporter for the United Authority's News Network and Multi-Media Bureau. The former Central News Network had been consolidated with the remaining news and entertainment networks thirty-two years earlier. Advertising sales had continued to decline shortly after the turn of the century. In 2057, the United Authority stepped in to save the sole existing national news organization.

"Do you really think this has not been the result of an earthquake? I realize it didn't exactly feel like any in the past. But, isn't it at least possible, Austin?"

"Possible but unlikely. Think of the quakes we've been through over the years, Diana. This event didn't have any of the same motions. And the results seem to have been different than previous quakes of this magnitude as well — at least from *this* vantage point. And have you noticed any aftershocks?"

"No. Good point."

"There just has to be something else going on."

They sat again in silence staring out across the street and the glowing ocean beyond. After a few moments Austin gently grabbed Diana's hands across the table. He stared into her deep, dark eyes. A vision was slowly emerging in his mind. If his thoughts were true, even if they were only partially true, not only might their lives never be the same — there would definitely be some new challenges in front of them. He just needed to put some missing pieces together. Diana was staring back into Austin's thoughtful eyes, and after awhile she once again broke their silence.

"What are you thinking?"

The thoughts in his head were too bizarre to contain. He recalled a text he had read a few months back. If only he had access to his network files to check the details.

"Diana, I'm thinking that we have to investigate! I have some ideas — something I remember reading a few months back. It could be nothing. On the other hand, it just might be the foreshadowing of today's events. Besides, sitting here will get us nowhere."

"Very profound, *Austin*," she said with a big smile.

"It's my job, you know. Like you, I'm a professional writer. It's the curse of a vivid imagination," he smiled back. "You're welcome to tag along. Unless you think you should try and make your way to the Multi-Media Bureau?"

"Why should I? All communications are down and I haven't been able to get in touch with anyone at the MMB. Besides, Com-Centers still aren't working anyway. So, just try and shake me — at least until I'm able to talk to someone at the network. Tell me what to do, Austin."

"You can start by going back to your place and getting dressed. Meet me here when you're ready. I'll leave the door unlocked."

* * * * * *

No sooner did the door close behind Diana — the Com-Center came to life with a short flicker then a bright blue glow. At first there was an ear-piercing tone for three to five seconds, followed by the familiar United Authority's Anthem with the traditional montage of patriotically soothing images and the ubiquitous graphic message:

"United Security and Safety is *your* Safety and Security."

While keeping one eye on the Tel-Com, Austin began throwing on his color-coded uniform.

A larger than life-size, still-photo of the President of the UA appeared on the screen, and a voice-over message from President Gates began.

"My good friends and loyal Citizens — good morning. Please don't panic. I can assure you that everything is under control. A series of slightly catastrophic events occurred this morning at approximately 4-AM Mountain Authority Time. Very few details are available at this time. However, all respective Bureaus are rapidly conducting investigations. Make no mistake, your United Authority, Regional and Central Authorities are regaining all services, with the exception of some of your Tel-Com functions which should be restored by the end of this broadcast, as will your multi-channel selector and other personal Tel-devices."

Gates' voice was calming and deliberate. And, as usual, the broadcast was being simulcast on adjacent channels in English, Spanish, Mandarin and Arabic — the four dominate languages remaining in the world.

All other languages were ever so slowly fading with each passing generation. There were but a few remaining language-cults preserving some dialects from their ultimate demise.

"As I previously stated, investigations are underway to determine the cause and extent of these events," Gates continued. "All investigative data have yet to be filed at this time, but there is some evidence that foreign, militant-cult forces have attempted to disrupt Authority harmony. Complete details are not available at this time, but it is believed that *no* Citizens were involved. I can assure you that your safety will be best served if you remain calm and continue your daily Citizen obligations and routines as best you can. Please continue to monitor Com-Centers for updates from the official United, Regional and Central Authority News Network channels. If you are an Authority-Employee-Citizen, please report to your duty station at the termination of this broadcast."

"In the meantime, let me be clear, you can feel proud . . ."

At twenty-five, William Jefferson Gates had become the youngest vice-president in the UA's history. Six months after the election he was thrust into the position of president due to the tragic death of then President elect Thomas Setag, whose shocking demise was attributed to an apparent suicide. Less than four years later, Gates was elected to lead the country for another term. Although most voters viewed Gates' previous few years as on-the-job-training, his knowledge of twenty-first century technology, superior logic and his great wealth made him the most viable candidate for the position. And yet, he only received a slim fifty-one percent majority vote, no doubt due to his otherwise lack of political experience. Gates' post-college resume was thin and consisted primarily of bringing community organizations and events together. It was thought by many that he won the election due to his youthful and vibrant appearance. An elegant orator, Gates rallied the youth and minority voters with his campaign slogan, "Change is the Way." But the "Change" didn't happen in quite the same way people had expected — in *more* ways than one.

It was said that just a few months before the end of his second term, there was a nuclear attack on the country. There have been so many revisions and remedial editing corrections to the preceding years that it was difficult to understand much less remember all of the details. Presumptively, it was as a result of that event, Gates issued an executive order to modify the twenty-second amendment to the Constitution of what was then the United States of America. It effectively allowed an elected president the option of additional and unlimited consecutive terms. This was entitled the "Courage to Continuous Presidential Leadership Amendment, number XXXVIII." During his third term, Amendment XXXIX was also introduced and passed, changing the names of Canada, Mexico and the US to the United Authority, due to their consolidation in what some considered to have been a peaceful coup.

As President Gates continued his broadcast giving direction and assuring the Citizens that everything was back to normal and under control, something seemed abnormal to Austin — as if everything might not be *exactly* under control. It wasn't just what the President was saying necessarily — rather it was the *photo* of the President. Austin realized the President wasn't on-camera. Instead, his smiling, youthful election portrait filled the screen.

That never happens. Austin thought to himself. He also noticed a different element to the photo.

Suddenly, in mid-sentence, the Tel-Com went dark again.

"I *knew* it." Austin spouted.

He turned to his entry table and grabbed his Tel-Card, and almost as a second thought snatched his battery pack just as Diana opened the door.

"Did you see *that*?" she blurted incredulously. "Something is definitely not kosher about this entire ordeal. I mean the Com-Center comes on — no live video-feed of Gates — Then he says, 'be calm because everything is under control, report to your duty station' — a second later, the Com-Center goes dark again? This is *so* bizarre."

"I agree. But, I am still going to check-in at my office."

"Because of Klaud. I understand."

"You've got it. Depending on how long that takes, we can head to the Multi-Media Center next. Since we furnish all communication outlets with their certified copy and ad production, I'll just tell Klaud that I need to investigate their status. I think he'll go for that."

* * * * * *

Not wanting to wait for the elevator, they sprinted down five flights of stairs to the underground parking garage. Austin quickly pulled the plug from the car's power-port — and since the top was down on his GM Hydro–Z, a popular albeit difficult to attain roadster on the West Coast, he jumped over the door. No sooner than his butt hitting the seat, the automatic shoulder and leg-straps snapped into place. Touching the starter-sensor the engine spun and the turbine whined to life. Diana, on the other hand, was a little too short for the jump so she opened her door and carefully stepped in. Once seated, she tilted her head and stared at Austin with a lady-like smile. Pulling from the secured underground parking, he drove up to the street in front of the complex.

Diana was first to speak. "What do *you* make of the President's communication?"

"The same as you. Obviously no live video. The audio and video quality was poor. And then I noticed something odd about Gate's photo? Even though I've seen that photo a hundred times. It was enlarged greatly and I think I recognized something extraordinary about it for the very first time. I'll explain later."

"You can't tell me now?"

"We should locate a sharper, digital-photo enlargement, if possible. I need to be sure. Then I'll show you."

Clicking the Z roadster into power mode, they quickly turned south towards what use to be Austin's office building. Traffic was a little heavier than normal but about the same degree of speed and maneuvering required. Most days Austin walked to the office. Today's five-minute drive to the office didn't reveal any obvious or additional damage to other buildings or streets. In fact, everything seemed to be almost back to normal on the surface — with the exception of the still smoldering Continuity building.

"Did you try your Tel-Card again, Diana?"

"Yes. Nothing."

"Would you give it another shot, please? Try calling your office."

Diana pulled her Tel-Card from her bag. She tried several different numbers. Each time she placed the card to her ear, she would give Austin the same puzzled look and shrug her shoulders.

"Nothing. I tried calling my boss from the condo, my office, your number and the Authority's Com-Service number. All I get is the same series of short tones and then silence. It's obvious. The entire system is down."

"I can't imagine that we will learn much, or for that matter, spend much time at my office — unless we run into Klaud. In that event, I'm not sure how long it could take before I can get you to the MMB. But, regardless, there should be time to drive into LA. Besides, there are a couple of other locations I may want to investigate while we're downtown. If you don't mind, keep your Tel-Card out and just give it a try every few minutes. I may need to make a few calls when it activates."

"Sure."

"Do you recall your Tel-Card ever not working, Diana. I mean, not working like today. You know — dead?"

"Never like this. I've had the usual and frequent dropped calls, dead zones, and discourteous reps when calling to talk to customer service. You know, the usual. And yet today, we're supposed to believe things are under control — and everything is back to normal? I don't think so. By the gods, am I becoming more cynical? You won't say anything, will you Austin?"

"I won't if you won't. Diana, I need to confide in you. I hope — I believe we can trust each other . . ."

"Of course."

"But this isn't the right time or place. Let's spend a little time investigating today. Maybe later this evening we can take a walk on the beach."

* * * * * *

The streets were barricaded about a block or so from the United Authority's Continuity Building. The fire department had the blaze mostly under control, but the building appeared to be totaled. Only a smoldering steel skeleton frame remained. Austin parked as close as possible and approached the Central Authority Protection guard on the perimeter. He flashed his UA-ID card. The guard allowed them to pass with a warning to be careful and keep a respectful distance from the emergency people.

"Officer — has the cause of the explosion been determined yet?" Austin asked in passing.

"Nothing official at this point, but an isolated gas leak is suspected."

"What about the other explosions we heard closer to LA? Were they isolated gas leaks — and at specific locations as well?"

The guard's face immediately swelled as he came to attention. "I don't know what you're talking about. Stand down, Citizen! What's your UA number?"

Diana and Austin continued to briskly walk past the guard, "I need to check in, officer. I'll be back later with that number." He said over his shoulder. Diana quickly placed her hand over her mouth to hide her grin.

The security officer tried to get them to halt but he was manning the barricade alone and was unable to leave his post. As Austin glanced back, however, he could see the guard was attempting to communicate on his Tel-Card. Hopefully his was working as well as Diana's.

There was a small gathering of people about thirty meters in front of what was remaining of the main entrance to the United Authority's Continuity Building, so they walked cautiously in that direction. Austin could make out a few familiar faces the closer they got. Within moments he spotted a couple of department heads from the research department talking with Klaud.

"Well, Diana, you're finally going to have the opportunity to meet Klaud. He's been a United Authority Citizen, of position, since the very beginning. I'm not sure where his connections came from, but, connected he is."

At about the same moment, Klaud spotted Austin.

"Austin! Over here!" Klaud yelled and raised both arms over his head while furiously waving. *"Where have you been? Who is this?"* He bellowed above the surrounding clamorous racket, while pointing to Diana.

Austin placed a protective arm around Diana and guided her to within normal hearing range.

"Good morning Klaud. I would like to introduce you to Diana Akira."

Continuity

2

"Who controls the past controls the future. Who controls the present controls the past." — George Orwell

* * * * * *

What can I say about Klaud? Austin thought to himself. Not that Austin would ever utter anything remotely disparaging about Klaud out loud. From a personal standpoint though, Austin knew he had to give Klaud credit — credit for hiring him, appreciating the quality of his work, grooming him through the years, and ultimately raising Austin to a high level UA-12. But the kudos ended there. It was truly tough love.

At 55, Klaud (Klaudios) Akakios was the first Continuity Director for the United Authority — a UA-15 level. He was the consummate political/bureaucrat. Which is, undoubtedly, how he rose through the ranks to command one of the most revered bureaus of the United Authority — notwithstanding the UA Protection Service (military), the UA Compliance Bureau (all legal divisions and law enforcement), the UA Contribution Bureau (tax collection), The UA Security Service (secret service), The UA Central Bank, the UA Multi-Media Bureau (all mass communications), and the UA Safety Bureau (intelligence). The Continuity Bureau had become what could be considered the national/UA advertising and public relations agency.

* * * * *

Unquestionably, Akakios was a major contributor to Austin's career climb —not to mention his never-ending headaches. He had no known life outside of his Authority duties. His entire living, breathing, commitment in life — 24-7 was work — understandably, his thinking was that his subordinates should have the same tireless dedication. It was only logical and rational.

Austin never thought that Klaud was an inherently evil person; but if there is a Satan — he knew Klaud had his mannerisms. To Austin's way of thinking, Klaud was a micro-manager who was eternally demanding, quick to criticize, short on praise, requires total loyalty (to the Authority and to himself), a pessimist to the first-degree, with an obtuse sense-of-humor and the personality of a stump. He also recognized Klaud to be among the power elite.

Austin's memory may have been a little fuzzy about some aspects of the past, but he did have a perfect recollection about the day Klaud called him into his office the previous month. He was sitting at his desk in the management area of the 6th floor, with close to fifty other coworkers, looking at the daily-final text revisions, and getting ready to break for lunch, when they all heard Klaud yell through the Tel-Com.

"Austin. Got a second? Let's meet."

Everyone knew that "Let's meet," meant come to my office.

Austin calmly saved the work he'd spent his morning laboring over and placed his Desk-Com on the security setting. The Microsoft/Dell logos began to glow and pivot around the screen. He very slowly and deliberately moved away from his desk and started down the long passage to the express elevator. The entire room fell silent. Austin's walk was viewed in slow motion. Every eye on the floor tracked his progress. No one relished the thought of being summoned to Klaud Akakios' office on the top floor.

* * * * * *

This wasn't Austin's first trip to the seventh floor. He'd been there on many occasions — some visits were fairly productive and even somewhat cordial. But, regardless the number of trips, the underlying uncertainty of the request to ascend was always painful. It was the fear of the unknown — and the what if? What if there was a Bureau Director's complaint about the quality of the previous day's work? Was there a breach in the previous week's continuity report? Was the output too slow? Could there be a fault with the research or a dozen other technical issues? Some UA Citizens had even been demoted for not expressing the proper "team spirit" or attitude. And if these infractions weren't enough to consider, there was a UA handbook with over 700-possible Authority-Correctness violations to think about — commonly known as AC.

A number of years prior, a small political sub-group within the UA Compliance Bureau, small but feared legal group, felt that it just wasn't politically correct to use the word "political" in this manner — as in "politically correct." They were offended because being "correct," after all, is *not* political in the least. Therefore, they demanded that "authority" should be substituted for the word "political." President Gates recognized an opportunity and created a Continuity sub-bureau. The UA-AC Bureau became the sixty-second regulatory bureau created since Gates had taken office. This single one-word change and the formation of this new AC Bureau staffing created more than a year of development and historical revision work for the Continuity Bureau. Reams of historical data and digital publications required researching and correcting. Films were reviewed and either edited or simply destroyed. A team of more than one hundred continuity researchers, writers and producers dedicated their time to this one-word change. Ads were either pulled or rescheduled after post-edits. The project also required the part-time efforts of as many university interns working albeit for a quarter of the Credits paid a full-time researcher or producer. In Austin's spare time, what little he had, he calculated the cost to be about $80-million Credits.

Then there was the Political now Authority Correctness Handbook itself, which had to be updated and rewritten. Everyone referred to it as the "Post Correctness Project," or PCP. The original tome totaled slightly over eighteen hundred pages of infractions, definitions of infractions and their penalties. The AC Handbook now toped twenty-eight hundred pages. Needless to say, it was difficult for a Citizen to remember all nine hundred sixty plus infractions; but ignorance was no excuse for committing one. Penalties ranged from rather small fines, to employment demotions, dedicated public service hours in which participants were required to wear pink jumpsuits signifying humility, and potentially all of the above.

* * * * * *

During the short elevator ride, Austin tried to mentally process and prepare himself for every possible Klaud scenario — all the while he was developing a throbbing in his head.

The elevator doors quietly opened to an expansive view of the Pacific and the coastline to the north. It was a fabulously clear view all the way from Redondo Beach to Malibu. Austin took a few seconds to absorb the sight he never tired of. Living many of his younger years in Colorado were breathtaking, but there was something about the ocean and Redondo Beach in particular that made him whole.

As the doors closed behind him, Austin turned to the left and walked down another long hallway — passing a private, albeit empty office and a large conference room to the small opening where Klaud's assistant, Randi, was seated. She was looking down as he approached her desk. Her concentration was focused on her hands — preoccupied with a Tel-Card. He stood in front of her desk, unable to keep from staring at her rather large and healthy cleavage. Klaud had a proclivity for hiring buxom blondes. As a matter of fact, there were several of these hand picked lovelies in the building. But then, this was southern California after all. He tried to refocus his eyes on the Tel-Card while watching her fumble with the devise for a couple of seconds; then he cleared his throat.

"I — um, I'm here to see . . ."

"I know," she said without looking up, "he's expecting you. Go right in. Oh, but first Austin, can you help me change the battery in the Director's Tel-Card? I can never get the . . ."

Austin reached his hand toward hers. It was a simple process — one he'd completed on so many occasions. "Sure. No worries." He often wondered why the most seemingly simple tasks eluded so many people. As he snapped the back from the devise, Austin couldn't help but notice that Klaud's Tel-Card was somehow different than his. That noted, he quickly placed the new battery and put the fleeting thought out of his mind for more pressing considerations. "Your wish is my command." He smiled as he handed back the device.

"Thanks. I owe you one, Austin."

"I'll put it on your tab."

"Good — because I'd rather owe you than beat you out of it." She returned the smile.

* * * * * *

Every Citizen was issued their personal, adult Tel-Card at the age of UA Enlightenment — thirteen to be exact. The memory chip for each future Tel-Card devise was presented at birth. The Citizen's primary information was stored on the chip. This included their name, their parent's name, and date of birth, place of birth; and of course a UA Security number was obligatory. It was a duplicate of that which was implanted in the area behind one's ear. These primary data would never change. They were the essential and unique Citizen identification items. The data on the memory chip of their future and personal Tel-Card, on the other hand, required to be updated every year after. On each of the adolescent's anniversary dates, a parent was instructed to present the Tel-Card chip to a local UA Education Programming office. This process was enforced and repeated each year — for a diminutive fee. At the age of thirteen, the chip would be placed into the Enlightened Citizen's adult Tel-Card and presented to them at a public ceremony. Yet another privilege not afforded to Plebes.

* * * * * *

After handing the device back to Randi, Austin pressed his thumb on the door-sensor to Klaud's office. The large double doors began to automatically slide into the wall and he slowly walked into the Director's spacious office.

"Good morning, Austin. Have a seat. How are you?"

Whether it was or it wasn't, Austin couldn't help but think that Klaud's question was rhetorical — but at least he was smiling — and that was a good sign.

"I'm well, thanks. These crystal clear mornings are what we all live for here on the coast. The view of Malibu, stepping out of the elevator is spectacular — and seeing Catalina from your office is unbelievable this morning," Austin nervously cleared his throat. "But then — I guess you already know that. What can I help you with, sir?"

"Yes. It's clear — very clear. The view of Catalina is nice, but it also gives me concerns these days — security and all that, you know. But, we can talk about that later. The reason for our meeting, you see, I believe you can help me even more than you have over the past few years. But first, would you care for a Coca-Coffee?" And without waiting for an answer, Akakios pressed his Desk-Com. "Randi, have you finished putting that new battery in my Tel-Card? And would you bring us a couple of coffees?"

Austin, nor anyone else for that matter, would ever turn down a cup of Klaud's Coca-Coffee. Unlike the variety available to most UA Citizens, director levels and higher were able to select the finest-grades of merchandise – not to mention they could afford them. In the case of coffee, they bought the freshest, finest quality, Organic-Kona. Although the flavor was much richer, it didn't seem to pack the same punch as the common variety. Regardless, rank truly had its privilege.

* * * * * *

Coca-Coffee had become the preferred national beverage — hot or cold — only mildly sweet but very energizing. Several decades earlier the largest soft-drink corporation had merged with the major coffee supplier in an attempt to increase coffee sales. The merger had produced the proper operational efficiencies, but over the next couple of years it had failed to increase the ever-sagging coffee sales. The United Authority noted the continued losses of their annual Sales Contribution Revenues (SCR, previously known as added value tax).

It was determined by the UA Director of Contributions that this shortfall was due to the Coca Company's failure to recognize the market attrition of their aging population and their ineffective promotion to build a larger youth market for the coffee product. The traditional coffee market was dying and, as a consequence, reducing sales at an exponential rate. Due to their corporate marketing arrogance, causing the steady decrease in profitability, it became the responsibility of the United Authority to take control of the company. The United Authority determined they could not allow this significant business to fail — for the benefit of the employees and that of the Citizens. The Director of Contributions pressed for the dismissal of the company's current president and with the support of the President of the UA, he appointed a UA advisor to control the company.

In less than two weeks after assuming the position, the new advisor presented an action plan he guaranteed would stimulate future sales. He proposed that the United Authority could and should allow the newly formed UA Coca Company to blend a brand new coffee product to be called Coca-Coffee. Although the recipe remained top-secret, he recommended that it include an ingredient of the original and almost two hundred year old soft drink's recipe. By adding a fraction of cocaine to the new coffee flavored drink, the advisor promised, in fact he guaranteed to energize sales of the failing product. The proposal was quickly approved by the "powers that be," but only for a limited one-year test period, with expressly no mention of the added ingredient. Fresh marketing and advertising was rapidly developed, fast-tracked through the UA Continuity Bureau's Advertising/Scrub Departments, and then rolled out to the media.

NEW & IMPROVED
Coca-Coffee — Your Four Seasons Drink
The Same Low Price but with a Distinctive New High
It's the Brew for You!

The desired effect was quickly achieved a few weeks into the campaign's launch. Within the first year, Coca-Coffee broke all sales records for the existing soft drink and traditional coffee product. The SCR soared — as did the clientele.

* * * * * *

"Austin, you may not be aware of the additional pressure I've been under for the past few weeks. As you know, I've been in this position for many years. Every year has become increasingly more difficult. But, the pressure from UA Security changes these last couple of years has been exponential. Not only has Authority Security been ramped up since the attack in Houston two years ago — the Continuity Bureau is expected to spin, rather, get the proper edits of those occurrences documented, produced into a series of edu-ads, and transmit them throughout every region. We understand our charge and our mission statement, *'He who controls the past – controls the future.'*"

"I know," Austin spoke softly, "George Orwell's *1984*. You allowed me to read your copy."

"I shouldn't have. But — I'm glad I did. Austin, I don't care how you came up with the slogan. It was a stroke of genius. That mission statement earned me the largest bonus-Credits in my career and you received a full grade promotion to UA-8 level back then as well. Look — there have been so many updates and rewrites — well I guess I'm preaching to the choir. Don't get me wrong — I'm not complaining."

Austin sat quietly doing his very best to keep his mouth from dropping open. Klaud's litany was completely out of character — and he continued, almost non-stop, for the better part of thirty minutes. He only paused, ten minutes into it, when Randi opened his office door.

"Randi. Good. You take your coffee black, Austin?"

"Sure."

Randi proceeded across the expansive room handing a hot cup first to the Director and then to Austin. She turned back to Akakios, leaned over and slowly pulled a device from her low-cut dress. "Here is your Tel-Card, sir."

Akakios slowly licked his lips as he watched her in motion. "Thank you, Randi. Any problems with it?"

"Oh, no sir." She said, glancing at Austin. "It was so simple." And she slowly and artfully walked out of the room.

The entire exchange didn't take more than ninety seconds, and it was as if Klaud had only skipped one-beat as he continued to summarize the state of affairs facing the Authority and therefore the Continuity Bureau.

"Austin, the minor attack on Houston not withstanding, it has been more than six years prior to that event since we were attacked on our own soil. With any luck, and a lot of effort, it will be much longer before it happens again — hopefully never. We have little control over the luck aspect, but the Continuity Bureau does share some responsibility for the security effort. We are expected to become more proactive rather than reactive with our efforts. We will continue to work on modifying previous productions and historical publications. However, we will *now* be required to create what will be called 'Forward-Documents,' 'Forward Ad Productions' and proactive documentaries. We can get into more detail about these projects later. The President has approved a major budget increase for the Bureau. As a result, we will be adding a new floor and staffing it with a brand new department."

"Another new department?"

"Now Austin, that's where you come in. I can't continue to oversee and progress this expanded bureau alone — especially with this added workload. I need help. I need a Vice-Director."

"Are you suggesting that . . ." Austin began quietly.

"I'm not suggesting anything!" he responded in his typically verbose style, "I'm saying that I'm recommending *you* as my Vice-Director. And of course, you will receive a healthy raise to UA-12 Level. We will need to move you up here to the top floor in an office just down the hall from me. I'll see to it that you get a personal assistant. Would you prefer male or female? Never mind, we'll work that out later. You and I will meet in the conference room between us every morning at 7-am sharp and again at 5-pm unless I'm out of town."

"What about my current work load in progress, sir?"

"No more 'sir' business, Austin. From now on we're on a first name basis. Got it?"

"Yes sir, er, I mean, OK — Klaud."

"Good. What are you working on right now?"

"Well, to begin with, ah, Klaud, we have that priority revision on the President's un-Authority

Correct remarks he made in yesterday's speech about the Prime Minister of Eurostan, and . . ."

"Right, well that's not what he really meant to say anyway. Now was it. Look — how quickly can you find and train your replacement?"

"Maybe a week or so if . . ."

"You've got 48-hours. Keep me posted and let's meet at 7-am tomorrow. We need to get you up to speed right away. You can just work around your other duties. Your promotion goes into effect tomorrow — so move your gear up here this afternoon. Any questions?"

"Only a few hundred."

"Great. Save them for our morning meeting. Now let's get busy. And I'll bring you up to speed tomorrow."

"Yes sir. I mean, got it, Klaud," he said quickly standing.

"Oh, and one more thing, Austin — I expect your full transition plan, in writing, for tomorrow's meeting. Do you have someone in mind for your replacement?"

"Steven Lu."

"Perfect. Lu will do."

As Austin turned to leave, Akakios spoke again, while quietly smiling. "And Austin, your contribution, dedication and attitude are all noted by the United Authority and appreciated. When you next activate your Tel-Card you'll notice additional Credits have been deposited into your account. I retro-activated your raise from the first of the month."

"How did you know I would accept?"

"Austin, you had no choice."

* * * * * *

Walking past Randi's desk in a bit of a daze, Austin glanced her way. "Have a safe and secure day, Randi."

"You as well. And congratulations, Austin."

Austin froze in his steps and tilted his head towards her. "How did you know that I . . . ?" And after a beat, he smiled and quietly said, "Never mind."

As Austin pensively walked down the long hall to the elevator, he decided to stop and take a sneak preview into his new office. He turned to his left at the very next alcove where his new assistant would be sitting. Austin pressed his thumb on the door-sensor, and it began to automatically slide into the wall. *WOW! Rank really does have its privilege.* Looking beyond his new spacious office was a wall of windows facing the north coastline — just like the view from the elevator, only larger. The spectacular scene drew him in for a closer examination. Although Klaud's view was panoramic and even more dramatic, Austin was overwhelmed just to have a view at all, much less one like this. He had worked for years in an eight-by-eight cubical, and his only view was out his door looking into the bullpen of 100 or so desks. Now he had real light, openness, and a view — a view all the way to Malibu. Austin stood mesmerized for a few moments picking out various landmarks in Redondo. He could even see his condo building. *I guess I've arrived.*

* * * * * *

He remembered his first year as a Continuity Junior Producer on the 2nd floor. Even with so many confusing years in between, the first year was a lot like mental chaos. College had not fully prepared him for this working environment. Armed with a degree in communications that included studies in: production techniques, technical editing and creative writing, he believed his only employment options were, state-run multi-media, state-run teaching or state-run media continuity. Although any of the three suited him, the UA's Continuity Bureau intrigued him. His recollection of history was somewhat vague, and he thought the research department at the bureau would help to clarify missing parts of his own past.

Austin had always been a bit of a loner. Rather than socializing, he felt more comfortable observing those around him and he spent much of his time alone, reading. He wasn't shy, but the underlying skepticism in his personality made him a natural voyeur of human nature and logic, or more likely, illogical behavior.

So it wasn't out of character for Austin to understand that the odds of getting hired by the Continuity Bureau might be close to one in a thousand. There were, at the least, hundreds of applicants for the very few new openings with the media, teaching or with the Continuity Bureau. In addition to the numbers working against him, Austin also fully realized that even with his extraordinary talent, his scholastic achievement was fairly average — thus lowering him to the middle of the pack at best.

It was to his utter shock and surprise that he was hired, on the spot, on the very day of his application to the United Authority's Continuity Bureau — and as a Junior Producer at that.

* * * * * *

Austin's four years at the University of Texas were clearly his most memorable. Thinking back, as he often did, they were the fastest four years of his life as well. His entire tuition and boarding had been paid for from the trust of an anonymous donor. It allowed him to concentrate on his studies with no concern of finances.   It was a most valuable benefit because studies didn't come easy and graduating was his personal imperative. His choice of a communications major with additional degrees in creative writing and technical editing had, at the least, given him some preparation for his future career.

The little free time he had during those college years were spent mostly alone. When he wasn't studying, which was how he spent the majority of his time, Austin walked the banks of the Colorado River that flowed through Austin, Texas. The gentle flowing waters helped to sooth his frequent head throbs and soothed his mind for reflection of his somewhat disarranged early life. Even though most of his early childhood and adolescent Colorado memories were pleasant, they were confused with thoughts of another life and others whom he had never met — or maybe he had. They seemed as a chimera, but then, often more real than dream-like. *There are others in my head.* He frequently felt that he was more than just one person — maybe another person all together. It was far too confusing.

Many others walked the banks of the river on clear days as well. There were always a variety of students jogging, Citizens taking a restful break, and no shortage of Plebes fishing or bathing in the cool waters. Individuals smiled but rarely spoke to one another. There were occasional albeit brief conversations. The river was a "free zone" after all. Safety and security monitoring devices had not yet been installed at that time. Austin frequently encountered regulars on his walks. His favorite was a cute Asian student he shared a class with. Another was an older and personable Plebe who seemed to hold a special interest for him. They were the exceptions to the rule. Most only smiled and passed. Austin appreciated their common need for moments of solitude. He held a special fascination for the Plebes. What he never grasped, however, was any rationale for not becoming a Citizen. Although Plebes seemed content — even quite friendly — they were never afforded any Citizen privileges. *What am I missing?* Plebes had no visible means of support, no ability to purchase food or a place to live. *Why would people subject themselves to such a meek and meager existence?* It was a frequent but only fleeting thought.

* * * * * *

Over the years, Austin, Texas had become the second largest and arguably the most significant technology research center in the UA. This was in large part due to the University and the variety of research projects conducted there. The campus housed several separate research buildings; most of which were partially if not totally funded by the UA. Of those buildings, one stood out as rather ominous. It was positioned at the far northern edge of the campus. The Image building, as it was known, appeared to be a misnomer as if it had no distinct image to speak of. It appeared to be a single story brick structure positioned in the exact center of five-acres of bare lawn, no trees and an eight-foot tall, black, chain-link security fence. Unlike the other buildings on campus, security was high and visitors were not permitted. The Image building was originally constructed as the campus infirmary a hundred years prior. Shortly after the new century it was secured by the government, completely remodeled, and converted into a research lab. Speculation was that the lab involved human organ research. At the end of the day, it was a lab that no one really seemed to know much about. Few people came or went, and with virtually no exterior windows, the building always appeared dark — even in daylight.

* * * * * *

As Austin cleared his desk, everyone on the 6th floor assumed he had been fired. It was not an uncommon sight at the Continuity Bureau. At least there were no security guards escorting him. He spoke to no one and no one spoke to him; but everyone watched. Each item from his desk was carefully placed into the boxes he had carried from the storage closet. Many of the items had some small memory attached and he slowly recounted his many years of service as he placed each item. Austin packed each item, occasionally looking up and out of his small office window, gazing into the cavernous bullpen and thinking, *Why me?* Each glance up he would see faces drop down. Looking out at so many talented, and in many cases, more deserving peers. *Why have I been so fortunate? There have been so many years of routine. One day leads into another, yet I get an invisible boost from time to time.*

Senior Producer, Steven Lu couldn't wait any longer. His curiosity had the best of him as he walked to Austin's door. "Hey buddy! Is everything OK?"

Austin smiled as he looked up. "Swell."

"I couldn't help but notice — I mean, I guess we all could see you . . ."

"Moving upstairs."

"No shit?"

"No shit."

"Need a little help, Austin?"

"Thanks. Steven, I'm going to need a lot of your help. And I'm not quite sure where to begin."

The two spent the better part of the afternoon moving Austin's office items to the top floor while talking about the changes within the Continuity Bureau. Once settled, they sat at his new desk admiring the view. After a brief and quiet rest, Austin looked at Steven and thanked him for helping.

"Anything else I can do for you?"

"As a matter of fact — this was just the beginning, Steven. I'm promoting you to Executive Producer."

"You're joking."

"You asked if I needed more help. Steven, you have no idea."

The Event

3

"Instead of an army, a small leak can sink a great ship." — Benjamin Franklin

* * * * * *

While major explosions were being felt in many of the major UA cities, the vast majority of the continent was sleeping this winter's morning.

It was 4:30am Mountain Time in Aspen, Colorado when his Chief of Staff, Carey Dunstan, gently awakened Gates. The time wasn't a problem for the president who had always been an early riser. What was troubling was who was bringing him into a semiconscious state. He wasn't used to anyone telling him to wake. And no one was more aware of this than his old buddy Carey Dunstan.

Dunstan and Gates met their freshman year in law school. Although different in so many ways, they shared a lot of common ground. They were both about the same build, equals in intellect, they had several common and influential friends, had no intentions of ever being married, each was bothered by chronic headaches, they were the same age to the day, and both believed in a socialistic version of Manifest Destiny. When Gates became President, his first appointment was Carey Dunstan.

Dunstan knew that Gates' routine, especially when he was on retreat, was to be awakened by the music on his Tel-Card at 5am sharp, regardless of time zone. He would then spend the next fifteen minutes, exactly, lying in bed reflecting on the previous day's events and then organizing his thoughts relating to some of the duties of the day ahead. After another fifteen minutes of calisthenics, he allotted thirty minutes for bathroom activity. Once dressed, his long workday began with a breakfast-briefing meeting. It was a constitution that served him well. This particular morning was the exception to the rule, and Dunstan realized that his breaking Gate's routine would not be pleasant — to one degree or another.

Once touched on the shoulder by Dunstan, and hearing the words, "Mr. President," Gates slowly opened his eyes. Looking into Dunstan's troubled eyes was a definitely disappointing break from his well-established routine. There was just one thing he could think of saying.

"Now what?"

"Bill, I'm sorry to report, we have a situation," Dunstan began.

"Well?"

"There have been multiple explosions in most of the major cities throughout the United Authority. We don't know . . ."

"Any nukes?" Gates asked calmly.

"To the best of our knowledge — no."

On this, Gates went into his well-known hyper-state. Almost levitating from the bed, his feet landed a foot or so in front of his Chief of Staff. *"What do you mean, to the best of our knowledge?"* he screamed, "That's *NOT* what I want to hear."

Dunstan knew this would be the wrong answer to his question, but it was the best he could do under the circumstances. He also knew that today would be a double-headache day.

"Bill. Please. Give me a chance . . ."

"I'll give you a chance, a chance to give me the facts —*NOW!*"

"OK. OK. The facts. Just the facts. Don't get your testicles in a knot! Here are the facts we know at this time." Dunstan took an extra beat; quickly organizing his thoughts while smiling inside that the President of the United Authority sleeps in the nude. Walking away from Gates and trying not to stare, he reported. "Just thirty minutes ago, or so, we began receiving intel from our UA Safety Bureau field offices. The reports were almost simultaneous and consistent with each other. United Authority buildings were exploding.

"Which buildings?" Gates demanded.

Having been snapped at once for the wrong answer, Dunstan carefully considered his next remark. "Bill, within a minute or two of getting the reports, all communications went down."

"Impossible!" Gates blurted.

"You're absolutely right, Bill. We have every available resource working on the problem as we speak. In the meantime, might I suggest that you, ah, get dressed quickly," Dunstan tried hard to keep from smiling. "Your plane is being prepared to transport us to the Springs. I'm sure, once on board and in the air, communications will be restored and we will get the intel we need for an action plan. I will begin writing your emergency address to our Citizens."

As Gates marched to his bathroom, his mind began a myriad of calculations. He had the ability to expertly quantify multiple scenarios and calculate odds, almost simultaneously. There were side effect however, with throbbing that would last for hours — headaches that he had been assured were incurable.

* * * * * *

Surrounded by a score of UA Security agents, President Gates' body-double was being rushed from the front door of Gates' mountain home and winter retreat to the Aspen airport. Almost simultaneously, Gates exited through his back door and quietly boarded a nondescript GM armor-clad, Hydro-Drive SUV with Dunstan who was working feverously on his Tel-Tablet preparing the presidential response to, well, to whatever could be learned once communications were restored.

On the circuitous drive to the airport, Gates pounded on his Tel-Card. "Nothing! This is *completely ridiculous! UN-believable!*" Gates moaned and threw his Tel-Card from the back seat to the inside windshield, shattering it into a dozen fragments. The driver and shotgun ducked. "Carey, do you recall your Tel-Card ever not working? I mean, not working like today? You know — dead?"

Dunstan just shook his head. "Never like this. I mean, I've had the usual and frequent dropped calls, dead zones, and discourteous reps when calling to talk to customer service. You know, the usual," Dunstan said without looking up from his notes. *You know, brother Bill, we've had numerous discussions about these types of problems. You simply never make it a budget priority.*

"This is ridiculous!"

"Agreed." — *For the hundredth time.*

Gates' driver parked behind an extension building to the Aspen main terminal. As the president stepped inside a UA Secret Security agent handed him a pair of coveralls and a ball cap. He then stepped into a catering truck and was driven to UAAF-2, one of two almost identical aircraft. The aircraft were matching in type and equipment — but UAAF-2 had an exterior look of a standard military issue. UAAF-1, and Gates body-double had departed fifteen minutes earlier.

Gates carried an empty cardboard box on each shoulder as he rose up the plane's rear steps. Dunstan followed a couple of minutes later using the same type of disguise.

Before everyone could be seated, the captain was notified that the aircraft doors were secure and ready for departure. The jet was slowly backed away from the gate and was given immediate clearance for take-off from Aspen control.

* * * * * *

The weather was clear and ordinarily it would be a short flight to the new Capitol of the United Authority in Colorado Springs. But with the relatively recent bombing of petrochemical plants in Houston, and now this morning's attacks, additional precautions were warranted. Today, it was going to take a little longer to get to the Springs than usual.

While UAAF-1 headed directly to the massive underground Capitol of the UA in Colorado Springs, UAAF-2 managed a heading due north and over sparsely populated wilderness at almost forty-thousand feet — the concept being that there was less opportunity for detection.

Approximately thirty minutes into the flight, military and safety channel communications were restored, if only temporarily, it was long enough to begin to get some basic intel. UA Safety agents began to file reports from all UA regions. Intel came in back-to-back from the tip of the southern border of what was once Mexico to Alaska and most United Regions in between.

The President's Chief of Security, Stanley Bates, approached Gates and Dunstan who were both enjoying a filling breakfast of grilled Colorado Elk backstrap, two poached eggs, and fresh blackberries topped with New Mexico piñon nuts in crème. The private dinning area of the aircraft was quiet except for the low decibel hum of the engines.

"Excuse me sirs for interrupting your breakfast, but we are beginning to get reports from the ground."

"How bad is it?" Gates calmly but sternly requested slowly tilting his head, while wiping his mouth with a monogrammed, linen cloth.

"Very bad. Very different. Somewhat confusing. But not as serious at it could have been."

To look at him, Stanley Bates was not what one might consider the typical head of security would look like. He stood a mere five-foot six and had the appearance of an accountant or librarian. Bates was balding, wore glasses, spoke with a slight lisp, and had an IQ of 180+. His attitude was, you can always hire muscle for protection — but you hire intellect for security.

"Let's begin with very bad," Gates said, looking up from his plate while continuing to blot his mouth.

"It's very bad in that multiple UA buildings have been totally destroyed in most of our UA Regions — thank the gods not all, but many. The attacks were obviously well planned, and perfectly timed despite the distances involved and the number of targets." It's worrisome in tha*t* . . ."

"Worrisome? *Worrisome*? Gates blurted. "We've taken control — and we're *not* giving it back. We will do anything and everything necessary to keep control of this country and stay in power."

"You bet it's worrisome! How could this happen with security as tight as it is?" Dunstan questioned. "There will be no delays in finding these criminals and bringing them to swift and public justice."

"That's just it! Our security is extremely tight. It's worrisome that in spite of the tightest security standards possible, there are plenty of additional targets available with the same security standards, and they were untouched. Part of what's confusing is that even more buildings were not brought down. And unlike the attack on Houston's petro-plants, where the enemy was obvious and easily brought to justice, we have zero intel on possible perpetrators or real motives of the current attacks."

Bates had been appointed to the top-level position by the president several years back. As a lower level security analyst he had single handedly decoded and identified the perpetrators of the horrific New York City destruction. Gates was so impressed with Stanley Bates' discovery and confirming detail; he retired the former head of security. *"I want this man on my "A" team."* Gates had demanded.

"And this is where it gets somewhat confusing," Bates continued. "The Houston attacks were in broad daylight where hundreds were killed and even more injured. The current attacks, on the other hand, were obviously planned for a specific time of day, or rather night, when there would be little or more probably, no human casualties — which is why I say the attacks were not as serious as they could have been. Plus, none of the targets were infrastructure — with the exception of our communications network. Which was almost coincidental. This leads us to believe that the perpetrators have contrary motives. They are, more likely, motivated differently than those who attacked Houston. It goes without saying, we have our total assets in place and we will get to the source or sources."

"It also goes without saying, that you will keep us posted as soon as you get additional Intel." Dunstan stood and walked to the coffee pot. After a short pause, he turned and walked directly to within a foot of Bates. He sternly looked down on Bates from his six-foot vantage point. Bates' head was tilted back farther than he thought possible, squinting quietly up at Dunstan. "Nothing, I repeat *nothing* is more important. Do I make myself clear?"

"Of course." *But you don't intimidate me in the least — you sophomoric ogre.*

"Feel free to interrupt us with all important updates whenever you receive them." Gates slowly looked up from his plate of organic fruit and stated very quietly to Bates and Dunstan, "Gentlemen, you understand that regardless of what we ultimately learn about today's events, we have experienced a massive failure, a catastrophically massive failure." He paused for dramatic effect, calmly picked up his knife and began sliding it slowly back and forth across his fork. "Heads *will* roll. And they may begin to roll even before we understand completely what has happened, how it happened or even why it happened. I will be sharpening my ax."

* * * * * *

While Gates finished his breakfast and a second or third cup of Kona Coca-Coffee, Dunstan finished writing the emergency, Presidential address to the Citizens and to the powers that be. There simply was no time to consult with the Continuity Bureau, especially in light of the lack of communications. Due to the lack of details, the speech was short yet reassuring that the UA was in control, and a personal presidential promise of safety and security. He handed his draft to Gates and suggested they walk to the on-board studio to prepare for the first broadcast. Gates read over the script and made a couple of minor changes — looked at Dunstan and said, "Let's do this thing."

Gates took his place in the over-stuffed leather studio chair while the media director quickly began to type his speech into the teleprompter. Moments later, as the director adjusted the camera in front of Gates, Dunstan quickly suggested that instead of a live video feed, a still shot of the president would be recommended with a live voice-over or VO. Gates was confused and asked Dunstan for clarification.

"Mr. President under the circumstances, I think it would be unwise to give away your location. We don't have the ability to CG a different background from this studio, and everyone will recognize it as your aircraft studio. Plus, I'm not sure how long we'll be in the air or when our next broadcast will take place. I have already talked this over with Bates and he is in complete agreement."

"That's why I keep you around, Carey." Gates yawned. "In that case, I don't need the teleprompter. Give me the damn pages to read and let's get this show on the road."

The director sat behind the small control console, adjusted his headphones, made a few control changes and asked the president for a mike-check. Gates cleared his throat and began to read the first couple of sentences. The level was set and the director called for a satellite up-link and a network cue. He turned to Gates and asked, "Are you ready Mr. President?" Gates nodded and the director continued. "Cue the music. Bring up video open. Super the UA slogan. Dissolve to the President's photo. OK we're live, in 5 – 4 – 3 – 2." Then he pointed directly at Gates.

"My good friends and loyal Citizens — good morning. Please don't panic. I can assure you that everything is under control. A series of slightly catastrophic events occurred this morning at approximately 4-AM Mountain Authority Time. Very few details are available at this time. However, all respective Bureaus are rapidly conducting investigations. Make no mistake, your United Authority, Regional and Central Authorities are regaining all services, with the exception of some of your Tel-Com functions which should be restored by the end of this broadcast, as will your multi-channel selector and other personal com-devices."

Gates' had acquired, or more likely achieved the voice ability of a professional actor. He had never required public speaking or speech tutoring. The President was considered, by most, to be a natural orator, one of his many attributes. He intuitively knew the basics of how to work a mike and camera at an early age. And his confidence level when speaking to an individual or group of any size came as natural as a seasoned thespian. His inner circle thought of him as "one-take Gates."

"As I previously stated, investigations are underway to determine the cause and extent of these events," Gates continued. "All investigative data have yet to be filed at this time, but there is some evidence that foreign, militant-cult forces have attempted to disrupt Authority harmony. Complete details are not available at this time, but it is believed that *no* Citizens were involved. I can assure you that your safety will be best served if you remain calm and continue your daily Citizen obligations and routines as best you can. Please continue to monitor Com-Centers for updates from the official United, Regional and Central Authority News Network channels. If you are an Authority-Employee-Citizen, please report to your duty station at the termination of this broadcast."

Gates continued for an additional fifteen or so minutes, not realizing that ground broadcast transmissions had been cut once again. "In the meantime let me be clear, you can feel very proud of the brave UA Security Citizens who are tirelessly working to keep you safe and secure. And due to their advance training, they were able to not only control the damage to less than half of what it could have been, but they were also able to make sure that events like these, should they happen, could only happen at night eliminating the possibility of casualties. I can assure you, the United Authority Security and Safety is your safety and security. Good day, and let the United Authority stay with you."

On completion of the president's speech, Dunstan suggested that he and Gates walk back to the private lounge to try and relax while waiting for additional updates. "If we have to sit around in this flying tin can, we may as well get some relaxation. It's going to be a long day. I think a Bloody Mary is in order and maybe a Cuban," Dunstan smiled.

"Carey, you were reading my mind — again."

Now that Cuba, as well as the other isles in the Caribbean were all members of the United Authority, Cuban cigars were available — well, they could be had for those who had means. But, needless to say, they were available to the president at no charge from "friends" of the administration who made sure a fresh stock was always available in every presidential location.

As Gates and Dunstan relaxed, they put aside the morning's events and reminisced about the good old days, the days of future visions they both shared, the days of planning, and their fortuitous introduction to individuals who not only recognized their vision but also had the where-with-all to make things happen. Sometimes it all seemed like a dream — and yes, a dream come true. For the next couple of hours they were able to relax like the couple of old chums they were and appreciate that, "Change is the Way."

* * * * * *

While UAAF-2 was flying jumbo circles around the country, UA Protection Service squads and UA Safety Bureau teams were sparing no energy in their investigations. Obstacles small and large were quickly removed while taking total control of all areas affected by the attacks — even if that meant that a few Citizens and Plebes were dealt with a little harshly and some detained for questioning. All department heads were forewarned that these areas would be secured and brought under total control immediately — period. They were warned by the administration that there would be serious, personal consequences if investigations and arrests were not completed before sundown.

Some of the first reports radioed to department heads described how, within only a couple of hours or so after the explosions, the initial shock to the Citizens had surprisingly worn off. The Citizens, by and large, became very calm and compliant. A lot of force wasn't required at any of the locations. As a matter of fact, within a brief time, people were sitting at sidewalk cafes having Coca-Coffee, shopping or back at their workstations. It was as if the morning's events were just another distraction in their otherwise routine day — and Citizens, by in large, really didn't seem to care.

All of the buildings attacked were cordoned off and Central Authority fire crews were controlling the blazes. It was being reported that in each location the UA building targeted would be a total loss — while surrounding buildings suffered little or no damage at all.

The UA's Safety Bureau was operating at full speed gathering Intel from all directions and all locations. Satellite images were being reviewed as well as local video surveillance from each location. They began with the current day's footage, and then carefully studied each day at specific times preceding the events. Undercover Safety Bureau agents were canvassing the areas and asking a lot of people a lot of questions. Known informants were interviewed with generous offerings of Authority Credits for any useful information leading to the arrest of those responsible. Plebeians were all but totally overlooked by the authorities with a few exceptions. However, there were a select few Plebes who looked on with great interest.

In Denver, the UA's Contribution Bureau headquarters was still burning out of control. The Director of the bureau, Jasper Belial Foley, was meeting with the heads of his various departments and local UA Safety agents a block or so upwind and to the north of the burning building. Foley was giving the agent in charge his theory regarding the event.

* * * * * *

"I don't know if any other Contribution Bureau buildings were destroyed today, but what I do know is that people in general don't like the bureau. We may have millions of enemies for all I know. Let's face it, contributions to the United Authority are voluntary. Even so, some believe that just because the contributions are automatically deducted from the Citizen's accounts each month that it's mandatory taxation. It's ridiculous. Everyone has a choice. I mean, let's face it, people could simply choose to be reclassified as Plebes. There are those who think that we are taking credits away from them. They never stop to think about how much it costs to run this country and the expense required to keep them safe and secure. They truly believe the Credits are theirs, which of course is misguided. Credits belong to the United Authority and the UA Central Bank. They never stop to think that we allow them to keep twenty-percent of all earnings. As I said, they do have a choice. Plebeians pay no taxes. Now, that's not to say that terrorists from outside the country aren't trying to disrupt our Credit supply." Foley paused, and then he directed a question to the agent in charge. "Speaking of Credit supply — are you aware if any of the Central Bank's regional buildings were targeted?"

The agent continued writing notes and without looking up and calmly stated, "We aren't at liberty to discuss any details of an on-going investigation — even with you, Director Foley. I'm sure you appreciate that?"

Foley froze and glared at the agent yet remained completely composed. *Why, you little twerp. You have no idea who you're fucking with.* "I fully understand, agent." Foley continued politely. "However, I'm expected to file a detailed report to the President this afternoon. So if you would care to give me your UA-ID number, I can let him know how cooperative you are. And, I'm very sure *you* can appreciate that."

The agent slowly looked up at Foley and smiled. "What would you like to know, Sir?"

* * * * * *

UAAF-2 had been in the air for little more than four hours with the ability to continue aloft for four to five more without refueling. Intel calls were beginning to come into Stanley Bates in rapid succession. He quickly compiled a detailed outline. Within a matter of a few minutes, he was walking to the President's private dining room, status report in hand.

Opening the cabin door but without entering, Bates cleared his throat and interrupted quietly, "Excuse me sirs."

"*What?* Bates — can't you see the door is closed and the President and I are meeting?"

"Sorry sir, but you said to feel free to interrupt at any time that . ."

"Do you have information for us?" Dunstan blurted.

"That's why I'm here," Bates said sheepishly.

"Then why didn't you say so? Don't just stand there. Come in. Have a seat. Would you like a drink, or something?" Dunstan smiled.

"Well, I wouldn't mind a Coca- . . ."

"What do we know Bates?" Gates interrupted.

"Well sir, we are beginning to get a picture of who, what, where and possibly why. We know that all eighty-seven plus UA Contribution Bureau buildings have been destroyed including Contribution headquarters in Denver."

"That's crazy! Are you sure? How is that possible?" Dunstan steamed.

Bates continued, "As crazy as it sounds, we're sure of that much and we're working on how it was possible and by whom. In addition to those buildings, there were a few other UA buildings targeted."

"How few?" demanded Gates.

"Just four others are destroyed that we know of — the UA Continuity Bureau in Redondo Beach, the UA Commerce Bureau in Atlanta, the UA Entertainment Bureau in Toronto, and the UA Labor Bureau in Mexico City. There weren't any UA Protection Service installations, Embassy buildings, or UA Safety Bureau buildings targeted. In addition, we've determined that there were no Regional Authority nor Central Authority buildings targeted either other than Contribution Bureau buildings. As you can see, there is an emerging picture. We know the 'where' and the 'what.' Now, as a result, the 'who' and 'why' can be narrowed down," Bates paused, "Would it be possible to have that Coca-Coffee now, sir?"

"Sure. Help yourself," Gates smiled. "I have another question. What was used to bring down the buildings?"

Walking to the coffee bar Bates continued, "Until the fires are brought completely under control it's almost impossible to say. Forensic fire inspectors will begin when it's safe to enter the buildings to gather evidence. Unfortunately, that may not be until tomorrow. I know you wanted to have this solved by the end of the day today, but these fires were intense." Bates returned to the table joining the president and Dunstan.

"If you're sure that's the best you can do," Dunstan stared at Bates.

"Needless to say, investigation of the 'who' is in full swing, and as quickly as we get qualitative Intel I'll give you that update." Bates took another sip of his coffee.

Gates stared at his Chief of Security. "What are your thoughts?"

"My thoughts about 'who?' Sir, you know how I feel about conjecture?"

"I'm not asking for a wild-ass guess! Hell, a Plebe could give me a WAG. Sometimes you have to go with your gut, man. What is it telling you? I have no intention of holding you to it."

Sweat was beginning to seep from Bates forehead. He pulled a tissue from his shirt pocket and carefully blotted it. He carefully walked to the waste container and dropped the tissue while carefully gathering his response. Clearing his throat, "Excuse me, sir. My gut tells me we're either dealing with paramilitary or rogue UA military individuals."

"Citizens in other words."

Bates slowly removed his glasses and began polishing them with his clean linen hanky. "Yes, sir."

"I would like — no — let me rephrase, I must go back on the air with another report to the Citizens no later than 6pm Mountain Time. So I expect your up-to-date report at least an hour before. Understood?" Gates stood signaling that the meeting was concluded. "Now it's lunch time. I would ask you to join us Stanley, but I know how busy you are and I wouldn't want to interrupt your work."

"Well sir, I need to stop for lunch myself, so . . ."

"Thank you, Bates. And keep up the good work." Dunstan dismissed him.

As Bates left the room, Dunstan turned to Gates, "What's for lunch?"

"I think you're going to like this — hot dogs and beer." Gates smiled.

"You're joking, right?"

"OK. Maybe you would prefer a second choice of avocado stuffed with Gulf shrimp and a dollop of Russian dressing over a bed of mixed organic greens and tomatoes, corn-fed venison medallions in red wine sauce, steamed organic asparagus with a touch of béarnaise, and for dessert . . ."

LA

4

"I am willing to believe that history is for the most part inaccurate and biased, but what is peculiar to our age is the abandonment of the idea that history could be truthfully written." — George Orwell

* * * * * *

"So this is Diana. Austin has spoken of you. My dear, you are as lovely as I imagined." Akakios smiled as he reached his hand towards her.

"And Austin talks of you frequently as well, Director." Diana put her hand out to Akakios expecting a firm grip. Instead, she received a soft and rather warm caress.

He held her hand for several seconds staring into her dark eyes then quickly turned to Austin. "I repeat Austin — where have you been?"

"Klaud, as you know, I can see our building from my condo balcony. It was quite obvious that the entire building was engulfed in flames after the explosions. I felt that for all of our safety, it would be wise to stay clear of the emergency vehicles and to monitor the Com-Center for information and whatever details possible. When the Tel-Com never came up, and the traffic calmed down, I got here as quickly and safely as possible. How long have you been here?"

"Oh, I just got here about ten-minutes ago myself. But I tried calling you and got no signal," Akakios confessed.

Austin looked at Diana and just smiled. *I wouldn't have expected anything else from Klaud.* There were few surprises after spending so many years with him. And, in many ways he was the most predictable person he knew. He often wished he knew as much about his parents as he knew about Klaud. His adolescent recollections had mostly faded over the years due in part because his parents had mysteriously disappeared his second year of college. He had but a few fleeting memories of his mom and dad.

"So Austin, please tell me that you confirmed all department data back-ups before we left last night."

"I did." *Give me credit, Klaud.* "You know that I always secure the daily data. Everything was secured — as usual. The data is safe. But the real question now, is just how are we going to access it? We obviously have no building, no equipment — not to mention, there's a really good chance that we won't be getting any new documents today or maybe for the next several days depending on how bad things may be elsewhere."

"Leave that up to me for now. For all we know, this may be an isolated attack." Akakios turned to Diana, "You work for the UA Multi-Media Bureau, correct?"

"That's correct, sir."

"How are things over there?"

"I really don't know sir, since all communications are still down."

"Why are you here then? Why haven't you driven there?"

"I was hoping that Austin . . ." Diana began.

"We were hoping, Klaud, to drive over there together. It's not only a safety issue for Diana, but I need to do some reconnaissance to determine what news or information they may have and their progress bringing back communication systems. I'm sure their engineers are working on it." Impromptu speaking was another skill he had honed over the years. Speaking extemporaneously had never been one of Austin's strong suits in his early years. His real communication skills were formally confined to the written word and creative production abilities. Once he understood the value and power of speaking with authority and conviction, he concentrated his efforts to master this deficiency. The results amazed him. "This will be time well spent for us. I'll report back to you ASAP."

"Good thinking, Austin. That's just what I had in mind for you today as well." Akakios boasted. "In the meantime, I will be working with the department heads to determine how we can locate another building and jerry-rig some data-ports. My guess is that the President is going to need our help very soon. We're talking multiple layers of damage control."

* * * * * *

Austin and Diana took their leave and walked to the east of the Continuity building and past the security barrier on the opposite side to avoid the guard they had confronted on the way in.

On their drive through Redondo and to the 110, they couldn't help but notice everything seemed all but back to normal, as if nothing had happened — it was business as usual. In fact, their entire drive into downtown LA was quite uneventful. Traffic was about the same as any weekday, except for the one burning building in the distance and just to the west of downtown.

The closer they came to the multi-media center, the better they could discern that the only other building burning in the LA Basin seemed to be the UA Contribution Bureau. Austin thought this odd — for several reasons. He spent most of the drive looking, observing, organizing his thoughts — trying to make sense of everything. Diana utilized her time taking in the sights and continuously trying to get her Tel-Card to operate. She wasn't looking forward to working today. She had rather wished it were the weekend with more time available to spend with Austin — especially after the morning's events. Diana had grown very close to Austin in the recent past. It was almost fortuitous that she had moved to the condo the year prior. She noticed magic between them from their very first meeting. In her mind, it was kismet. *I believe it was our destiny to be together.* She told herself many times. *There is a reason we are supposed to be together. I wonder — I wonder the purpose?*

After a long silence, Austin suggested, "Crazy, but it's turned into a beautiful day for a drive. How about some lunch after we check in at the MMC? I know a nice little sushi place on the beach in Santa Monica."

"Yes. Yes. *Yes.* I'm getting hungry already. Would we have time for that walk on the beach afterwards?"

"Diana, you're reading my mind — again. How do you do that?" Diana just smiled and shrugged her shoulders.

"Is your headache any better?" Austin asked.

"A little, but maybe the ocean air and the beach will be the cure. How do you feel?"

"Much better. A day with you and away from Klaud is my cure." Austin smiled back.

* * * * * *

Everything appeared normal to Diana as they approached the UA Multi-Media Center. There were a few cars missing, but otherwise there didn't seem to be any drama. Austin stopped at the security guard gate while Diana flashed her credentials, and they were swiftly waved through. Austin pulled into Diana's reserved parking spot close to the front door.

As they entered the first set of doors and into a small secure airlock, Austin noticed the same security features were used here as in his building. Diana asked Austin to insert his Tel-Card into the slot beside the door to his right. She then inserted her Tel-Card and quickly pressed her thumb to the door sensor. Within a few seconds, there was a buzz and the double glass doors slid into the wall.

They stepped into a large and nicely decorated lobby area. About twenty feet or so in front of them was a contemporary counter, manned by two typical looking southern California beauties — one male, the other female. The male was clearly security.

To the left of the entry there was a large stylish Network logo sculpture and a flowing, stylized fountain. To the right Austin stared at a wall-to-wall, floor to ceiling bank of huge flat-screen Tel-Coms — all of them operating. Austin stopped in his tracks staring at the wall.

"Diana, it looks as if communications are working here."

"Unfortunately, no. They're just running previously recorded video."

"Interesting."

They continued to the front counter and Diana greeted the guard and receptionist.

"Hello, Sam — morning, Peggy. When did you guys come in?"

"My usual time. Why?" She remarked casually.

"Just curious. Is everything OK?" Diana queried.

"I don't know. I guess so. Well, except I can't watch the Com-Centers. I mean, I can but I've already seen all of the programs they're showing this morning." She sighed. "It's so boring."

"Yes. I can see that. Would you please buzz us through?"

She and Austin walked to the left of the counter and towards a door that was already sliding into the wall. The elevator sped them to the management offices on the fifth and top floor. Once there, they stepped into a smaller, but just as nicely appointed lobby area facing yet another counter. Diana waved, said hello to the executive receptionist as they walked to another door already sliding into the wall.

She and Austin continued down a long, wide hall to a corner alcove in front of the Regional Director's corner office. Diana asked his assistant if the Director was available. The rather well built young man said he would check and to please have a seat.

A couple of minutes later, Diana was summonsed into the Director's office. Austin waited in the alcove reading their in-house organ. After flipping through the pages a few times, he sensed something amiss. Quickly, it dawned on him what was missing. *This publication had not been certified and approved by the Continuity Bureau.* He was well aware that this was a capital offense. It would be his duty to take this copy and report it to the proper UA authorities, even if the publication had no UA objectionable material. Now he was faced with a serious dilemma. Austin flipped through the pages once again. *I know that there is always a hidden security camera in these rooms.* He forced himself not to look up. He knew that a camera could be recording him reading this magazine. Should it be found out later by the Bureau that the publication wasn't certified — if Austin didn't report the offense, and it was, in fact, found out later that he had failed to report, he too could be locked up for dereliction of duty. But, *if I turned the publication over to the authorities, someone, maybe even Diana would be locked up for this serious offence.* Austin's headache began all over again.

Now, instead of thinking about what Diana may be going through in the Director's office, Austin was forced to consider how this situation should be handled. Finally, and just before Diana and the Director walked out, he decided to make his discovery more obvious. So he stood up and walked over to the assistant's desk.

"Excuse me. My name is Austin. I'm sorry, I don't know your name."

"I am Sergio." He smiled.

"Sergio?"

"Yes. Sergio!"

Sergio didn't have to look up at Austin because he had been staring at him virtually the entire time he had been seated.

"And, can I help you, Austin?" He said with a very big smile.

"Yes. Ah, Maybe. Sergio, do you think the Director would mind if I borrowed this copy of your in-house publication?"

"Heavens *no*! *Please*. Don't be *silly*." And he winked. "Would you care for an Espresso?"

"Oh no. No. But thank you very much, Sergio." He turned and started to walk back to his seat.

"It's really very special. I make it myself — with a little twist of lemon."

"I'm sure. Maybe next time — thanks." *Now it is even more obvious that I have read the rag, and asked to take it. I will stash it in the trunk of my car. Then, should someone in the future ask me why I didn't turn it in? — I'll just say; oh, thank you for reminding me. I forgot it in my trunk — and at that point I'll just pray that Diana won't be involved.*

* * * * * *

After a brief period, Diana and the Director walked from his office. Both were lightly laughing. She was very fond of the Director. Among other things, he was responsible for her hire and rise through the ranks. He had mysteriously taken a special interest in her from the very beginning. Unlike the stories Austin had told her of Klaud's overbearing ways, Director Benton had always been very kind to her — almost fatherly to her. Why, he was even responsible for finding her new condo and helping her to arrange it's financing.

"Austin, I would like for you to meet Regional Director Benton. Director, this is my friend Austin."

"Pleasure to meet you, Austin. Klaud speaks very highly of you — as does Diana, of course."

"My pleasure, sir. Would it be possible for you to give me an update, for Klaud that is, on getting communications back up and running?"

"Not at all. We hope to be up and running later this afternoon and certainly no later than tomorrow morning. All of our engineers are working overtime with the folks at UAT&T and Oracle." Benton said confidently.

"Great. Would you mind if I took Diana to lunch since the systems are still down?" Austin smiled.

"Fine. And, Diana, why don't you just check in throughout the day with your Tel-Card — that is, when it's working again. There's no reason to be here until we get back on-line." He said patting her on her shoulder. "Austin, be sure to give Klaud my regards."

After Diana gave Austin a quick tour of the facility, they headed to Santa Monica — about a twenty-minute drive — just enough time for a quick and private conversation while in route.

"Thank you for the tour back there. That is quite the operation, and much more interesting than our plain old, boring Continuity offices. Now I have a picture of where you spend your days when I'm thinking of you."

"Sure." She smiled. "And do you think of me often?"

"More and more every day." Austin smiled back. "I have to ask you though, did everyone at the MMC seem to be in a trance? I mean no one seemed to have any energy. Not at all how I expected to see people working at a multi-media center."

Diana thought for a moment, "No, not really. No more than usual, I think. You know Austin; most people just don't get excited about much of anything — even at a multi-media center. We just do our jobs like everyone else, go home, then start all over again the next day. It's mostly routine. I don't think people really care. I mean - it's just a job after-all." She sighed.

"It just seems to be the prevailing attitude everywhere. I guess my expectations were a little different, especially under the circumstance. Let me change the subject. While I was waiting for you, I looked over your in-house magazine. Are you involved with that publication?"

"Well — I don't know. Do you like it?" She laughed.

"Sure. It's very professional."

"In that case, yes — and no. I actually have very little to do with it. Occasionally they ask me to submit a piece — but that's the extent of it. I have way too many other things to fill my day. It's actually a regional publication online. We only print a few copies for our lobby areas so that visitors have something to keep them occupied while they wait for their appointments. Now, changing the subject on you. I'm really getting hungry!" She said as she reached over and touched his leg.

"Keep doing that and I just may drive off the 10 and right into the Pacific!" He laughed.

"OK. Maybe I'll just keep it up a little later then." She said coyly. "I think I may be ready to do even more, Austin."

Now this, Austin thought to himself, *has been a very remarkable day. And it's not even over yet.*

* * * * * *

After their delicious and relaxing lite lunch, Diana excused herself for the ladies room and Austin asked for the check. He reviewed it for accuracy. *If this is what a light lunch cost, I can only imagine the price of a not so light lunch!* Moments later Diana returned to the table just as Austin stood up from the table. "I'm ready for that walk on the beach now," and placed her arm around Austin's waist.

Austin smiled and they walked to the front counter. The cashier took the check and said, "That will be $137 Credits. Would you like to add gratuity?"

"Yes. Twenty-percent please."

"Fine. Please insert your Tel-Card into the Central Bank dispenser." She said with an automated tone.

"Wow. This place is a real bargain." Diana remarked.

"I know, especially these days. A couple of sushi rolls, some edamame, and a couple of cold green teas almost anywhere else would be closer to $200 Credits.

After pulling the Tel-Card from the dispenser, Austin noticed that there was still no signal. He looked up at the cashier, "The Tel-Card dispenser isn't working."

"No problem. Your data has been stored on our local system and when communications are restored, your data will be transferred and your account debited." She smirked.

"How do I get a receipt?"

"A receipt? You *need* a *receipt*? Grabbing a small pad, she impatiently scribbled a few quick numbers. "*Here!*" She forced her hand towards him with a crumpled piece of paper. "Will this work for you?" She demanded.

"Works for me." Austin gave her a big friendly smile, "Have a 'safe and secure day!'"

* * * * * *

It was a perfect day for a walk on the beach — a few scattered clouds but otherwise a crystal clear sky, 76-degrees and a slight ocean breeze. Other than a few seagulls and even fewer people, it was the ideal place to have a totally private and secure conversation. There were no Com-Centers or any other type listening devises on the beach that they knew of.

"Is your headache better, Diana?"

"Much. Thanks. And yours?"

"I think you and the sushi made it disappear." He laughed. "Seriously, I've been thinking a lot lately, even before today . . ."

"Thinking of sushi or about me." She smiled.

"About you. And you can be sure of that. I've thought about our becoming body-mates." He said quietly. "And I know you understand the amount of trust that requires. I believe you have the same feelings and trust in me."

"Yes. I do." Diana stopped, turned and put her arms around Austin's neck. They embraced as two lovers, kissed, then continued their walk, holding hands for the first time and letting the cold sand squeeze between their toes. "This makes me very happy."

"I've been thinking about how we are so perfectly matched." Austin continued. "It's uncanny and even serendipitous that we were brought together. I could spend the next few hours talking about our past — we've talked about most of it before — born in the same hospital just a few days apart, the same pediatrician, we both lost our parents, went to the same university, some of the same classes. You know we think a lot alike and even share headaches. Too bad we didn't actually meet way back then."

"But we did, Austin."

"I know, I know. But we didn't really realize we were meeting. I mean, you know . . ."

"I know. They were just close encounters." She laughed.

"Right. But I also wanted to talk about my concerns about the future — concerns for our future. I need to confide in you."

"You can. And we should." She said.

"Good. OK. Here goes. I have become increasingly skeptical about life —my life, including much of my past. I have these mixed thoughts and emotions. I see so many people, not unlike the people back at the multi-media center, and others I work with, just going with the flow. There seems to be so much vacuity, so little emotion. People, present company excluded, just don't seem to care or notice what's going on around them. Even with the catastrophic events of this morning — you know, with explosions, people running helter-skelter through the streets, and Security Forces patrolling with guns armed, Raptor-Cruisers with loudspeakers blaring — the majority of Citizens, that is people outside of the power elite, average Citizens — they just seem to be coasting through life. Within a couple of hours after the event, everyone reacted only with resignation. It's as if

Citizens are in the quicksand of denial. It's as if people won't or can't fend off their paralyzing anxiety — provided they even have any lasting anxiety. It's as if they are resigned to the understanding that there's nothing they can do to change anything. They seem to be artificially satisfied. It's as if everyone is just doing their time, before they reach 60 and will be put in transports and sent to mandatory retirement camps in either Cuba or Baja." Austin skipped a beat. "I wonder if we get a choice?"

"I understand, Austin . . ."

"I hope — I think you do," he continued, "I feel guilty and more than a little confused. Because I think I'm beginning to recognize things even more. I'm also concerned because we aren't supposed to think or feel this way — in fact it's dangerous just to be talking about this." Austin stopped again and rubbed his forehead. "Diana, I know things. I read things. Then I get confused and can't remember what was real, what is true and what is accepted as truths. Do you actually know what I do?"

"Sure. I think so. You are Vice-Director of the UA Continuity Bureau."

"Right. That's what I am — not what I do. I oversee hundreds of people who correct history, fabricate public relations releases, produce video ads, documentaries, infomercials, and video textbooks. And it's much more than mere production. We are charged with altering history and then destroying earlier versions of every source." Austin paused a moment and caught his breath. "Some of what I remember isn't what is widely accepted today. For example, I remember getting Ameros as compensation for employment. Now, we have this electronic Credits system. Do you think it is really fool proof? Do you truly trust it, I mean, not having physical control of your Credits?"

* * * * * *

Decades earlier, the three North American country's governments were consolidated. A new union was established and renamed the United Authority. Much of the foreign import/export trade was discontinued. The value of the Amero plummeted and was no longer used as a standard around the world. The Central Bank called in all printed and coined money. Holding gold was illegal. The new United Authority, or UA as it came to be called, legislated that the new Central Bank was to establish a distinct monetary standard of digital Credits. Citizens had thirty days in which they could take their Ameros to a branch of the Central Bank and exchange them one-for-one. At that point, digital UA Credits were placed into Citizen's individual accounts, less a 10% transaction fee, of course. From that point forward, all purchase transactions were made using the universal Tel-Card that included a 1% bank transaction fee with every purchase. Other transactions like, rent, utilities or large purchases for example vehicles or homes required an automatic monthly withdrawal from their account. Citizens were told this system was superior because it eliminated the possibility of counterfeiting. And the government said everyone would be "safe and secure," knowing that Citizens no were no longer required to carry Ameros — and that it would be impossible for someone else to access a personal account due to electronic safeguards. On the surface, this seemed too be a safe and secure system.

* * * * * *

"Well, sure. It's always worked for me." Diana said quietly.

"You don't see any problem or potential problems with this?" Austin responded quickly.

"OK. I suppose there could be electronic problems. I guess there is the potential for some privacy concerns." She looked puzzled.

"You're right. But, how about control? Control by the UA — and your *loss* of control?" Austin demanded. "Maybe it's just me. Maybe I'm paranoid.

Maybe it's because I vaguely remember our old system, or maybe have read about it — I don't know. But this definitely has at least something to do with my increasing cynicism. I have read so much. I think I remember things. I know it's more than just déjà vu. And I'm certain you've experienced at least some of this too."

"Yes. I have — and frequently — although, maybe not all of the same issues. It's almost as if there was another lifetime. Austin, do you believe in reincarnation?"

"Diana, I'm not sure what to believe in anymore. I have some belief in me — and mostly, I believe in you." He reached over and gave her a kiss on the cheek.

They walked silently for a while — Diana deep in thought — and Austin organizing his. She had compelling emotions running through her mind and body. At the same time, Austin was processing a hypothesis. It was as if he had been presented a giant jigsaw puzzle. And it was his mental quest to find the corner piece. The couple's common denominator, however, was the feeling that they were in another world — a parallel universe.

"Sometimes I would like to believe in reincarnation." She spoke softly.

"And sometimes I think there may be even more to our odd memories than reincarnation." Austin became almost breathless. "Remember earlier this morning at the condo when we were talking about the President's photo being used during his address on the Tel-Com? I said I noticed something odd about Gate's photo. And even though I've seen that photo a hundred times, I noticed something extraordinary about it for the very first time?"

"Sure. I almost forgot. You said you would explain later. I only thought it odd that a still photo was being used in place of live video. But, you think there was something more to it?"

"No doubt. If everything were under control, why wouldn't Gates be live on camera as he has been on every other single televised address?"

"I know. But Austin, it could have just been a band problem or a satellite video malfunction. The reception wasn't that clear. It's odd but under the circumstances there could have been . . ."

"You're right. It could have been any of those problems. That's my point. The President said everything *was* under control. Don't you see? He had to know otherwise. Look, be that as it may, Diana — one other thing struck me. Gates photo was enlarged from earlier photos I had seen — much larger. I wish it had been sharper. Regardless, I noticed a mark. It appears that Gates has a tattoo — a tattoo of a spider just like mine on the side and to the back of his neck just below his left ear — just like me." At which point, Austin pulled back his hair exposing a discreet spider.

Diana stopped cold and stared. "My gods Austin! So do I!"

* * * * * *

Austin stared back in disbelief and touched her small spider tattoo. Now his mind raced with a combination of confusion, and angst with the presentation of this new discovery. *Why hadn't I noticed this before?* Now he was more certain than ever before that he was not unique. That somehow this could be a corner piece in the puzzle of his life. It also seemed to be a corner piece in Diana's as well. Just as importantly, how did the two of them connect with the President of the United Authority?

"Diana, I've known that you and I have many similarities — it seems now even more so than we knew before. And it appears that we also share at least one connection with Gates. Could there be more? What are the odds? What the hell does this mean?"

"You're right, Austin. This is more than just a coincidence."

"Exactly. Plus, you and I are the same age as Gates."

"We are? He is?" She said in almost disbelief.

"What else?" He asked himself out loud. "Let me think." Austin stared out to sea for a moment.

"Diana, I remember you telling me once that you had pretty good grades at the university."

"Well, they were OK. I graduated just shy of the top ten-percentile."

"Right. And didn't you tell me how surprised you were getting hired at the UA Multi-Media Bureau? I mean there was considerable competition as I recall."

"True." She remembered her shock and absolute joy the day she was chosen. She could hardly believe it was possible. "In many ways mine was just like your experience."

"And, we both rose through the ranks faster than our contemporaries — faster than what we thought was possible — you are UA-10 and I'm a UA-12 level. Right?"

"Correct. But I don't see where . . ."

"Stay with me now. Did you know that Gates also shared this almost meteoric ascension?" Before she could answer he continued. "I've heard or read that he came from a modest and somewhat questionable background, and although he has an IQ near genius, he didn't finish at the top of his class. Yet, somehow he secured a relatively powerful position shortly after graduation, and rose to the position of Vice-President of the UA in an astonishingly brief amount of time. There has to be some type of a connection. As you said, this is more than coincidence. Diana, I'm beginning to believe there are no coincidences."

"This is fascinating and a bit frightening. How do we learn what this all means?" Better yet, how can we investigate if there's more?" She asked with a puzzled look on her face.

"Very good questions. I have another. How do we investigate without raising suspicion? We both know very well that just having this conversation could have serious consequences for us if overheard. Thank the gods we're on the beach and there are no monitors..."

Before Austin completed his sentence, they were interrupted by the deafening sound of an approaching turbocopter racing down the beach behind them at a very low level. They all but simultaneously looked over their shoulders to see it speeding closer with incredible clamor. Austin and Diana stopped in their tracks to watch the fly-by. But, suddenly it began to slow, as it came closer, until it hovered almost overhead. Sand swirled in every direction around them. Their eyes were squinting in the direction of the aircraft. They could barely focus on the dark-blue, unmarked aircraft barely recognizing it to be of a UA Security variety. Over the wind from the blades and wine of the twin-hydro turbine engines, they clearly heard its loudspeaker,

"Citizens! Stand down!"

Discovery

5

"The more corrupt the state, the more it legislates." – Tacitus

* * * * * *

It was obvious to the Director of the UA Safety Bureau, Hector Deimos, that the morning's attacks had been skillfully planned and flawlessly executed. Although it was still too early into the investigation to determine who was behind this obviously well coordinated effort to disrupt the safety and security of this country. There had been no chatter preceding the attacks, no rumors, no advance reconnaissance or intel of any kind — and so far, no credit taken.

Make no mistake, this was a massive failure of his department, and he knew it. The only reason he hadn't received a more immediate call from the President was due to the fact that all communications had been down for most of the morning. He understood very well, maybe more than most, that the buck stopped here — more so than the UA Security

Bureau, the UA Protection Bureau, and even more so than with the President himself. Deimos was the person responsible for the country's covert intelligence gathering. His Bureau was the very foundation of the safety and security for the entire country. This time the "buck" would be heavy, and it would land squarely on the top of his head.

There had been no attacks in Colorado Springs on that morning. In fact, Director Deimos would have never known there was a problem had he not been awakened from a very sound sleep by a decidedly loud, "Code-Red," emergency alarm tone. He reached over, shut off the UA Safety alarm and grabbed his Tel-Card to check in. It was dead.

His wife rolled over and sleepily said, "Your emergency alarm went off dear."

"You've *got* to be kidding, Doris!" Deimos blurted while sitting straight up in his bed.

"Why did the emergency alarm go off, Hector?"

"How *in the hell* am *I* supposed to know? I just woke up too! And now my Tel-Card isn't working!" He almost screamed.

"Would you like to use mine, dear?" She said sweetly.

"*No!* Can't you see the Com-Center is not working either? Nothing is working!"

"Don't be mad at me. I was just trying to . . ."

"Just try and go back to sleep!" He said sharply. "I'm going to headquarters to check this out."

Deimos didn't take time for all of his usual bathroom duties. Hopefully, once he checked out whatever malfunction had occurred he would drive home to finish those duties and then grab a leisurely breakfast. His office wasn't that far away.

* * * * * *

UA Safety Bureau headquarters was buried deep inside Cheyenne Mountain and only a few miles from the Director's home in Colorado Springs. It had been a real feather in his cap when the President accepted his suggestion to relocate the UA's Capitol from the east coast to the Springs — not to mention a quantum leap in his political and financial capital.

Years earlier, Deimos had made a simple case for the relocation of the nation's capital born out of potential security concerns. It may have been a somewhat simple case on the surface, but the reality was a logistics and political Rubik's Cube. The then present location of the Capitol in Washington DC had served its purpose for the better part of three hundred years. But times had changed. The UA Safety Bureau had gathered increasingly credible intel of plots to attack East Coast cities — specifically New York and Washington DC. Based on these potential threats, Deimos submitted a comprehensive report and action plan for the President's consideration. This "Top Secret" proposal came to be known as "The Peak Project." If it met with Gates' and the Senior Board's approval, Deimos requested that the President hold the news regarding the Capitol's relocation for at least a year. A massive public relations multi-media campaign would be required of the Continuity Bureau to better prepare the public for news of the transition. The President agreed.

Deimos had an ulterior motive for the one-year delay. It would buy him the time he needed. He quickly hired a real estate agent in the Springs upon the plan's approval. The agent's charge was to sign purchase options on any and all available real estate within a 5-mile radius of the center of the city. He also asked the agent to canvas the city's commercial building owners to determine who might be motivated sellers. Deimos also wanted to capture every piece of vacant property available, all potential commercial building bargains not listed, and as many up-scale residential properties as possible.

Deimos had some leverage over the Director of the Central Bank. He knew the Director could be persuaded and agreeable to a friendly line of credit. A few months later his Realtor called him with a list of properties available and the amount of funds needed to secure them. Deimos called the bank and arranged for the funds to cover the options and/or earnest monies. He sweetened his capital request with an offer to cut the Director of the Central Bank in for 10% of all future profits gained from the ultimate sale of all properties. The deal was done.

There was little traffic at this hour in Colorado Springs. Driving at breakneck speed, Deimos made it to headquarters in record time. *What in the hell is the emergency? And — double why the hell are communications down?* After sailing through security, he was greeted by the duty officer in charge. Deimos was quickly filled in regarding the multiple UA building explosions in various regions, but wasn't given much detail other than an "All Hands On Deck" — "Code-Red" alert had been sent out immediately to all Regional field agents, as per protocol. During the briefing, an aid offered the Director a cup of Coca-Coffee. Deimos quickly accepted and asked if the morning's Krispy-Kremes had been delivered yet? Within seconds of the briefing and after giving his action orders, his Tel-Card rang.

To his utter shock and surprise, the first call he received, albeit a brief one wasn't from the President, rather from UAAF-2 and the Chief of the UA Security Bureau, Stanley Bates. Deimos had not been looking forward to getting a call from the President, but getting a call instead from Bates? — this was a slap in the face. *Just who in the hell does he think he is?* Deimos thought to himself. *Bates can't treat the Director of Safety as a subordinate.* Luckily the call was brief and Deimos assured Bates that he had just put out a "Code- Red" alert to all of his field operatives — 100% of his assets were taking charge in every region. If all communications hadn't ceased at that moment, he would have also given Stanley Bates something else to think about — something very personal as well. *I'll deal with Stanley later.* Hector Deimos had a very long memory. This infraction of decorum would not be forgotten.

* * * * * *

Later that afternoon all UA emergency radio channels were restored. UA Safety Bureau Agents were utilizing every tool and contact available to them. And they were not above taking special liberties in each of the affected regions. This would go down as the largest investigation and shakedown since the majority of New York City was wiped off the face of the map.

Unlike the current attacks that had come out of left field, information preceding the attack on New York had been gathered and tracked for several years in advance. The ultimate and final attack was nevertheless a shock due to the fact that no one could predict exactly how it would be orchestrated, when it might actually take place or how severe it would ultimately be. And the Citizens never knew how the bureaucratic maze, political positioning, and to some degree government complicity allowed this horrific event to happen years earlier. Deimos and his Bureau were additionally frustrated by the prevailing policy of the administration; which was to handle informants and captured enemy sympathizers with kid gloves. Interrogations were to be treated as polite conversations.

Citizens had been lulled into a false sense of prosperity and safety those years preceding the attack on New York. And it was determined by the "powers that be" to not unduly alarm the population, which would have had a detrimental effect on the economy and the stability of the current administration.

About two years prior to the event, based on increasing intelligence, the government covertly prepared for the very real possibility of a major, potentially catastrophic attack. Director Deimos's action plan, "The Peak Project," to relocate key people and organizations from New York City and the total governmental relocation of the Capitol worked like a charm.

The first order of business was to move the Central Bank and the headquarters of all major financial institutions to Denver over a one-year period. This was presented and publicized as a major budget savings effort due to the high cost of conducting business in New York City. Needless to say, national political representatives, local and state politicians were not keen on the plan. The "politically favored" amongst them received attractive incentives to help soften the blow and to garner their support. The incentives were not only of a major monetary nature, but additionally included a very strong recommendation for these individuals and their key personnel to relocate somewhere farther up state or west of the Hudson River for potential safety concerns — in fact as far west as possible. It was additionally suggested that personnel promotions be given to the "less favored" leaders (less favored by the administration that is) to entice them to stay in the city. Or, as an option, the current elected officials could simply resign their positions and allow the political succession process to take over.

The other power elite and top tier of UA Citizens, those who were strong supporters of the administration were also discreetly contacted. It was suggested that they place their NY City properties up for immediate sale at "fire sale" prices — no pun intended — and to relocate to one of their many other homes as soon as their real estate listings were placed.

The migration from the city was mostly quiet. It was a transition that took place over the better part of a year or so, and consisted of a relatively small percentage of the total population. The vast numbers of remaining Citizens were not in the "know" and were left unsuspecting in the city.

The ultimate attack seemed to come from out of nowhere.

There was no warning that day. In fact, business appeared to be pretty typical. People were into their regular routines. Some were just waking up, others on their way to work, and many on their way home from night shifts. Trains were running, traffic was beginning to increase; coffee shops and restaurants were getting their usual morning customers. It was life and business as usual in the Big Apple.

The day was particularly calm and clear; in fact, it was a beautiful fall morning. The air was cool and crisp at 6-am on this mid-September day. It was the time of the year and the time of the day that always seemed the most pleasant, especially in the city. Even with the typical morning activity, however, the city seemed unusually quiet — and then, very loud.

There was an ear-shattering explosion the likes of which no one had ever heard before, except for the people around 39th Street and 6th Avenue who never heard any sound at all.

* * * * * *

It took many weeks for any accurate damage assessment after the 10-megaton nuclear blast. Much of Manhattan including about a ten-mile radius from the blast area was laid fallow from that day forward.

There was no effort to rescue or extinguish the fires due to their scope and intensity. No one could imagine the major scale of destruction in the affected area. Even after the flames had subsided, relief from the outside never came. The UA Protection Bureau cordoned off the entire area. No one was allowed past the barriers or into the blast zone for any reason. Days after the blast, there were few diplomatic condolences sent from Eurostan, Asia, and Suramerica, but no relief was offered.

Needless to say, the rest of the United Authority became either catatonic with the fear of another attack; or enraged, demanding answers and swift retaliation. The fear was natural — the retaliation, impossible. No one took credit for the attack.

Director Deimos and the UA Safety Bureau, however, had gathered a considerable amount of data in the few years leading up to the attack. All of that information could now be analyzed in retrospect. Deimos was privately advised, to his pleasure, it was time to take off the gloves. Any interrogation method could and should be used as long as it was completely discreet. With that, and in combination with the method of the attack now known, a definitive perpetrator or enemy could begin to be identified.

The blast was from a single missile.

In the very early morning hours before its launch, a nuclear powered submarine had swiftly made its way to within 60-miles of the East Coast. Its crew stealthily navigated up the Hudson Canyon, came-about 180-degrees, launched a single missile, then headed for the deep open waters of the Atlantic — all of this taking place in less than two hours. There was little time to be detected and close enough to insure that the missile would reach its target without the possibility of any counter measures being taken against it even if discovered.

The Hudson Canyon was the perfect launch site.

The Canyon, just off Long Island, New York, is not unlike most of the continental shelf sea canyons on the East and West Coasts for that matter. It begins at the very edge of the landward side of the continental slope. From there it extends to the seaward in an almost straight line and in a classic "V" profile with steep walls and rock outcroppings. The axis of the canyon trails down the continental slope for a distance of approximately 50 to 60 miles with a depth of more than 4,000 feet.

It was the perfect venue for an attack.

Unless the sub had been hijacked prior to the attack — and none had been reported — there were only two other world powers that had a naval vessel, armed with weaponry of this sophistication. Due to the fact that no one or no foreign power had taken credit for the attack, the UA Safety Bureau resorted to what might be considered "old-fashioned" detective work focused on Eurostan and Asia.

* * * * * *

The investigation lasted less than a year. At the end of which time, Deimos presented the administration with conclusive proof that either Eurostan or a radical element of their culture was culpable. It came as no surprise to anyone, least of all President Gates. It had long been understood that Eurostan harbored a great anger toward all infidels. Their ultimate goal had always been either conversion to their ancient beliefs or eradication and their eventual world domination.

Following his briefing, President Gates contacted the Supreme Leader of Eurostan, who quickly condemned any attackers and disavowed any knowledge of the perpetrators. He told the President, "The gods willing, those responsible will ultimately get what is coming to them." He vowed that no stone would be left unturned to help find these alleged radicals and bring them to justice.

President Gates made his official "State of the United Authority Address." He reported the findings of the investigation and assured the country that the criminals would eventually be found with the help of Eurostan and brought to justice. Although justice should there be any, would have to wait until their afterlife. Convictions never came.

During his hour and a half speech, he spoke of his personal resolve and his personal dedication. He spoke of his years of personal service and sacrifice. He offered his sympathy to the poor underprivileged individuals who could have sunk so low as to perform such an unwarranted deed. And he did mention briefly the sadness in his heart for New York City. But then he made it very clear that he and the United Authority would always be vigilant to the on-going "Safety and Security" of the Citizens. The next morning he flew to one of his several homes, this one in Acapulco, for a much-needed 2-week vacation.

* * * * * *

The Director was now receiving almost constant reports and updates on today's multiple attacks from most areas around the United Authority. It was a massive undertaking. The New York City attack was massive on a different scale yet carried out with a relatively small number of individuals. Although it was a surprise attack, there were many months of intel forecasting the event. Today's attacks, on the other hand, numbered ninety-one or more. That meant there were at least ninety-one or more people involved with a minimum of ninety-one weapons or devices, and absolutely zero advance warning. With this information and some, shall we say, stern interrogation conversations, Deimos was ready to make his call to the President.

"Good afternoon, Mr. President." Deimos began. "I have a preliminary report in hand. Is this a good time for . . . I mean, do you have time for me to report our initial findings?"

"Yes please. Your timing is perfect." Gates agreed.

"As you may know by now, there were ninety-one known targets — all ninety-one are a total loss. Eighty-seven of the targets were United Authority Contribution Bureau buildings. The perpetrators didn't miss a single one. Based on the facts that these particular buildings were the primary targets, the time of day in which they were orchestrated minimizing the potential for human casualties, and based on our initial interrogations; we understand the perpetrators to be potentially our own Citizens. Some Plebeians may have played a roll as well." Deimos sadly reported.

"Was this in anyway an Intelligence failure on our part?" Gates asked.

"Sir. No sir."

"Director, how could this happen? Who in the world could these people be? What is their issue or issues with the United Authority?"

"Sir. We strongly believe their issues are a fundamental objection to the amount of contribution required from Citizens, and possibly the methods used in the collection of UA contributions. Although we have no absolute affirmation, it has all of the appearances of a tax rebellion."

"If that's the case, then what is the reasoning behind the other four buildings targeted? None of those are Contribution buildings. And why were all of our communications taken out? Do you think that was tactical?"

"We have no clear reconnaissance at this time, so it would be conjecture or educated guessing on our part at this time, sir."

"Give me your best WAG, Deimos. There are plenty of other UA buildings out there that could have been targeted and weren't."

"Sir. You know I don't deal in wild-ass-guesses, but I'll give it my best shot. The UA Continuity Bureau building in Redondo Beach — This department basically controls all of the national advertising and much of the news content in the media. Excuse me sir, but they may have the opinion that Continuity is the mouthpiece of the administration."

"Do you believe that, Director? Gates asked sternly.

"Please don't shoot the messenger, Mr. President. You asked for my WAG and I'm trying to second guess criminals."

"Point taken, Deimos." Gates softened.

"As for the UA Commerce Bureau in Atlanta — Even though 80% of the economy is controlled by the UA, a strong 20% is free market, or private enterprise. Disrupting commerce has the effect of stopping most personal services and a major portion of the food business. If Citizens can't get the services they've become accustomed to, especially those of us in the top tier, well, and a disruption of food? Well, that goes without saying."

"I'm with you. But how does entertainment figure into this?" The President asked.

"This one is a little more difficult. You're referring to the UA Entertainment Bureau in Toronto?"

"Correct."

"I can only imagine that this is thought of as an extension of the Continuity Bureau since all scripts are required to be certified by that department of the UA. Additionally, some entertainment may be thought of as a powerful propaganda tool." The Director continued. "And that would bring us to the UA Labor Bureau in Mexico City."

"Bring labor to its knees." Gates interrupted. "I think I've got it. Labor unions control the vast majority of the workforce. Put that department in disarray and the UA engine grinds to a halt."

"Correct."

"This is certainly all plausible, Director. But none of this explains what happened to our communications. The UA Communication Bureau headquarters or UA Data Farm in Albuquerque weren't targeted — were they?"

"Sir, that seems to have been a fluke. Albuquerque was not attacked, however our communication systems are all tied together. When so many UA buildings were destroyed and all of them basically at the same time, it may have created an overload of the systems. And there was a domino effect that . . ."

"How is that even possible?" Gates interrupted.

"Between the automatic failsafe systems in our UA building's communication systems, the overload of emergency responders and such, plus the huge scale of the attack, well, we believe that all of these factors created a chain reaction — a domino effect, if you will. Allow me to remind you, respectfully Mr. President, our communications systems have needed updating for many years — at least 15-20 years. And every year that we have proposed Credits to not only upgrade but to build in needed redundancies to the systems the budget was denied and reallocated to other areas or projects. Just last year, the budget was reallocated to GM-Boeing to replace our aging fleet of government and executive jets. The current aircraft in service must be at least 4 to 5-years old." Deimos said almost condescendingly.

"Point taken. This is clearly an area that needs to be studied. Maybe we can address this in next year's budget request."

"If I can be of any help in that regard, Sir?" Deimos suggested.

"What else do you have for me?"

"I will have more for you very soon. My people and I will be working 24/7 until we get more definitive information and hopefully the Intel that leads to a resolution."

The President quietly put the Tel-Card in his pocket and picked up his glass of Kinclaith single malt Scotch whisky, 36-years old when it was bottled in 1975. He looked out of the UAAF-2 window as it banked and changed its heading to the most direct course to the Springs. After a few moments of silent consideration, Gates turned to his Chief of Staff. "Carey — it seems that we have some serious malcontents in our midst."

* * * * * *

Director Deimos turned to his assistant, "I want you to contact all of our department heads here in the Springs for an intel update meeting one hour from now. If we still have communications, alert the regional department heads to give their reports via the Tel-Com at the same time. Oh, and let the Vice-Director know that he should dust off last year's communications systems budget request and bring it to the meeting as well."

Deimos walked over to a hidden built-in wall cabinet to the left of his desk. He pressed his thumb on the security button below it. As it slowly slid open behind the wall, he stared for a long while at his small collection of automatic weapons and his rather large selection of premium Tequilas while trying to decide which of the aged 100% Agaves he required. "Ah. Voodoo Tiki Tequila." His mouth watered as he slowly pulled the bottle from the cabinet and gently fondled it. He poured two-fingers into a snifter glass and swirled it around for a full minute before raising it to his nose, taking in the pure essence and then wetting his tongue. It was almost a religious experience.

He had acquired the Voodoo Tiki Tequila from a private family collection during the time he was also acquiring real estate in the Springs. Although fine Tequila had always been one of his few indulgences, Voodoo Tiki was the crème de la crème. This extra-aged Añejo, 100% Blue Agave Tequila had been originally aged for three years in white French Oak brandy barrels. Only 1,000 bottles were released each year in their unique 2-foot tall, hand-blown signature bottle weighing almost 9-pounds. This particular bottle was hand-etched with the date of 2009.

Deimos then walked over and sat behind his large executive desk, and called his wife to inform her of his meetings that would be stretching much later into the evening.

She smiled and sweetly said, "So then — will you be home for dinner, dear?"

The Springs

6

"Cynical realism is the intelligent man's best excuse for doing nothing in an intolerable situation." — Aldous Huxley

* * * * * *

Flying fast and low over the breaking waves, the twinjet, GM-Boeing Bull-Bat drowned out all other sounds in its cabin. It was hard enough just to hear one's self think over the more than 120 decibels created by the turbocopter's engines and mechanical gears. What was even more difficult for Austin and Diana was the fear of the unknown — being mysteriously located by the UA while innocently walking on the beach in Santa Monica, quickly and quietly getting picked up by UA Protection Guards, and now being flown to the gods know where — and for only the gods know what reason. Austin tried to ask the Protection Guards, as they were stepping into the vibrating cabin, the reason for their apprehension. But, other than being asked their names, no other conversation was exchanged. And to make matters worse, they were quickly seated between two armed guards — seated and squeezed that is. Another guard rode shotgun up front beside the pilot. Not only couldn't they talk to one another, due to the pulsating engine noise, they couldn't talk to or ask any questions of the guards. Even if it were possible to ask questions, Austin and Diana wouldn't be able to hear the answers because they had not been given headphones.

They sat shoulder to shoulder — looking forward — holding each other's sweat soaked hands — thinking — fearfully anticipating their final destination and the ultimate consequences. The two turned their heads and gazed into each other's eyes, as if on queue. Diana's high, round cheeks glistened from her quiet tears. Austin's lips began to move — "Don't worry." She couldn't hear but she answered with a sad smile.

It was Austin's second nature to psychologically prepare several possible defensive strategies in advance of any confrontation — provided he had the time to do so. Taking a mental inventory of his actions that day wasn't yielding any reason or combination of reasons to be in this situation however. *I simply refuse to believe that they, anyone for that matter, could overhear our conversation on the beach.* It was frustratingly impossible to prepare a defense without at least the hint of a possible infraction. *The gods know I'm not entirely innocent. But what could we have done to warrant this level of apprehension by the authorities?* There would be no way that he could remotely know that the questions in his mind were only going to multiply exponentially upon the arrival to their destination.

Thankfully the flight was short.

* * * * * *

Austin and Diana didn't recognize the unmarked building at LAX where they were descending. For one thing, it was on the opposite side of the field from the main terminal buildings. They were setting down beside a large unmarked, UA Executive jet that was parked and taking on fuel at the building's south side. The chopper had barely touched the ground when they were grabbed by their guards and rushed to the security doors of the unidentified matte gray building. Diana was struggling to free her captor's painful grip from around her upper arm. She felt as though she was being dragged.

"*Hey*! Take it easy with her!" Austin yelled. Not that anyone could hear him over the whine of the turbines. The mirrored double doors automatically slid into the building wall as they approached.

Stepping inside the lobby, Austin and Diana looked up in shock to see Director Klaud Akakios standing in front of them. Simultaneously — they thought, *Aw shit!*

Although still confused, Austin decided to take the lead with some rapid-fire questions. "Klaud! What's happened? Why are you here? How did you find us? And what's the ..."

"Never mind how we found you. We have to leave — now!"

"We? What the hell are you talking about? We just got here! And now we are going?"

"You and I are going out to that executive jet sitting outside the doors just as soon as they finish fueling it. I'll explain once we're on board. No time now." He turned to the UA Protection Guards from the turbocopter and barked. "Take Diana back to Austin's car. Diana, I want you to drive back to UACNN and check in. Director Benton is expecting you. Austin should be back by tomorrow night — provided things go right."

* * * * * *

The executive jet was rapidly ascending on takeoff from LAX over the Pacific and beginning to bank to the north and then back to the east. Klaud was waiting until the aircraft leveled off before briefing Austin on their mission. This could be the most important assignment of their lives.

There is nothing like being left in suspense — again. Austin thought. *But at least I'm not in shackles. So, I've got that going for me. And I'm flying first class for the first time in my life. That's a good sign. I could even get use to this.* In fact, Austin had only flown on two previous occasions with no chance of first class accommodations, let alone on a UA Executive jet. This experience was better than first class, more like he imagined, flying in a luxury yacht. Based on his limited previous experience, flying could only be thought of as a necessary evil. It was expensive, aggravating, humiliating, boring, and often dangerous — at least being squeezed on United Authority Airline's Commercial flights. *This,* He thought on the other hand, *is incredible — just the two of us in this huge aircraft. I'm beginning to have a very good feeling about this.*

The only positive aspect about flying commercial these days was that there was only one airline to choose from, United of course. At least that made things a little less complicated. Many years prior, there had been a dozen or more competing airlines. One by one, over the past couple of decades or so, most airline companies began to consolidate. United Airlines had always been the nation's largest, prior to its fairly recent bankruptcy. Gates could not allow the nation's largest air carrier to fail. There were simply too many jobs at risk from the failure of this important business. It was decided by a unanimous vote of the UA Senior Directors that the Central Bank loan United Airlines the Credits needed to stay in business. United's name was changed to UAA (United Authority Airlines). With the backing from the Central Bank, UAA was now able to help the Citizens by lowering their airfares and making it much more affordable to fly. It did however make it difficult for the few remaining airlines to compete against the lower fares. The decision to rescue and subsidize United resulted in the beginning of the end for the other airlines. One by one, the others closed down or they were purchased by UAA at a very attractive price.

There were countless reasons for the commercial airline failures. Their hardships were eating away profits like a growing cancer attacking multiple organs over an extended period. Labor costs and employee legacy benefits grew disproportionately from year to year due to powerful UA Union strength. Fuel prices had skyrocketed as a result of the national exploration moratorium and the discontinuation of importing oil. Also adding to the cost of doing business for the airlines were the supplementary security measures required by the UA after the attack on New York. Mysteriously and shortly after that attack, aircraft accidents also began to happen on a somewhat regular basis. Many, if not most of the accidents occurred in good weather, baffling investigators. Several of these were later reported to have been as a result of pilot error or mechanical failure. But others were attributed to terrorists, according to intel collected by the UA Safety Bureau. The new security measures also greatly added to the hassle-factor of flying. Although an additional expense for the airlines, most Citizens accepted and even claimed to appreciate the extra security measures.

Booking and paying for a flight had remained the same and simple enough, albeit increasingly expensive. The ticketing process could now be handled on an individual's Tel-Card from home or various other locations at anytime. Ticketing agents at the airports were no longer needed. Baggage handlers were additionally relieved of their positions due to the banning of all checked baggage — only a single carry-on was allowed. The real aggravation, however, commences once arriving at the airport.

The traveler's first step begins by walking up to the now fully automated check-in counter and placing a carry-on bag in the x-ray sizing cabinet. Once a Citizen's Tel-Card is placed into the counter's insert-slot, the flight verification is approved and a UA coded luggage sticker is printed. It's then required to wrap the sticker around the luggage handle. Once the Tel-Card is pulled from the counter insert-slot, the luggage conveyor is activated and sends the luggage to the appropriate aircraft departure gate — most of the time that is — awaiting the traveler to retrieve it just before entering the aircraft. Occasionally, on the bag's journey to the gate, it may simply disappear. A ticket or boarding pass is no longer required due to the Tel-Card insert-slots at each of the remaining checkpoints.

    The next step after check-in is to proceed to the appropriate changing room. There are several rows of benches and three unique automated dispensers inside of each large changing room. The dispensers require activation and payment using the Tel-Card. The first wall mounted machine issues, by size, a mostly translucent pair of coveralls made from a white synthetic, thin yet durable nano fabric. Each opening can be fastened by small pieces of Velcro. The loose fitting coveralls' price is $150 Credits. Undergarments are strictly forbidden. In addition, a pair of open Flight-Flops™ can be purchased for $50 Credits since no shoes are allowed. The third dispenser issues a standard-size clear plastic flight bag with an attached plastic handle for an additional $50 Credits. No purchase is required if a passenger has flown before, and remembers to bring their previously purchased coveralls, Flight-Flops™, and bag. All clothing items are required to be placed into this bag including shoes and any clothes worn to the airport. Only one carry-on bag and flight bag are allowed for each passenger. The UA "Safety & Security" (S&S brand) coveralls are also required to be worn for the entire flight.

In the year 2003, officials of the National Aeronautics and Space Administration (NASA) reported to the current President of the US that the agency was developing brain-monitoring devices in cooperation with a commercial firm. This Space technology could be adapted to receive and analyze brain wave and heartbeat patterns, then, feed that data into computer programs to detect passengers who potentially might pose a threat at the nation's airports.

NASA wanted to use "noninvasive" neuro-electric sensors that would be imbedded in all security gates and throughout airport common areas, to collect tiny electric signals that all brains and hearts transmit. Computers would apply statistical algorithms to correlate physiologic patterns with computerized data on travel routines, criminal background and credit information from hundreds to thousands, if not millions, of data sources.

UA-NASA Bureau acquired the commercial firm holding the patent in 2079 for the benefit of the Citizens. The systems were finally approved, budgeted for, and installed in each of the nations airports in the year 2080. UA-NASA Bureau's Director retired the following year to his estate in Jamaica.

After clearing the changing room, it is now a relatively short walk to the fully automated security gate. The passenger places his or her flight bag onto a conveyor belt and inserts a Tel-Card. Once the Tel-Card is pulled from the insert-slot, the conveyor is activated. After the Citizen walks through the sensor portal, their flight bag may be recovered from the opposite end of the conveyor. The only person stationed at the security gate is an armed UA Protection Guard. Should the security alarm go off at this point, everything comes to a complete stop faster than a rollover on the 405 — and neither one is a very pretty sight.

Walking to a departure gate is a very eerie hike with the new security requirements. All restaurants and shops are closed and removed — sealed automation units have replaced them. Purchases are made by a Tel-Card and the machines are stocked with food or UA approved gift items from behind. Bathrooms and common areas are cleaned only after-hours. The only people who are allowed in open spaces and past the security gates are passengers, UAA flight crews, airport employees, UA Protection Guards and local airport security personnel.

Check-in at the unattended departure gate is a relatively simple process. Again, the Tel-Card is slipped into the counter insert-slot. Once removed, the Tel-Card is activated, glowing bright green, and a bar-code sticker is automatically placed on its back. At which time an automatic door slides into the wall allowing a single passenger to enter the gateway at a time. Simple enough. Simple enough that is until the final step.

UAA had improved their on-time record the several years prior. The 20-30 minutes LOA (late-on-average) was reported to be a very positive improvement. In fact the UA considered this to be a remarkable scheduling record, awarding United a UA Triple-Star rating and commending the UA Director of the Transportation Bureau a personal 7-figure Credit bonus for the year.

It was only slightly annoying for the traveler to add 20-30 minutes to the already boring 3-hour advance check-in requirement. But it did allow for some relaxation in front of the omnipresent Com-Centers while watching the latest information from UACNN.

Once the flight arrives and docks at the Jetway, the appropriate arrival-gate door automatically slides open and into the wall. All arriving passengers exit the aircraft and proceed to the exit changing rooms.

Now it's time for the departing passengers' final step. After walking to the end of the Jetway and just before entering the aircraft door, the Tel-Card is slid into a slot, which is built into the side of the aircraft. Upon removal of the Tel-Card, its face begins to pulsate bright green flashes and the posted UA Protection Guard allows entry into the aircraft. After finding a seat, one's journey finally begins — more or less.

But it's here at this final step where things can go terribly wrong. According to UAA, in the unlikely event an aircraft gets a last minute gate reassignment and there hasn't been sufficient time to reprogram the previous gate's check-in computer — well, obviously the wrong data is downloaded onto the passenger's Tel-Card, and an incorrect bar-code sticker is attached to it. Unfortunately, none of this can be detected until the Tel-Card is actually pulled from the aircraft insert-slot. It's at that "fail-safe" moment that the Tel-Card's face would pulse a bright red flash and sound a rather shrill alarm.

Due to the fact that there is no one to talk to about this slight inconvenience, one is left to wandering up and down the halls, looking for posted gate-change information. With any luck the proper gate can be located in time and before a flight is missed. But then — what are the odds?

* * * * * *

As the unmarked executive jet leveled to cruising altitude, an attractive flight attendant made her way to the only two passengers on board. She smiled and handed them each a menu for the evening's flight. It may have been Austin's imagination or possibly the cabin lighting, but the attendant's flight uniform seem more translucent than the standard issue. It was then that he also realized that he and Klaud had not been required to change into S&S garb.

"Good evening, gentlemen. I will take your meal orders whenever you are ready. In the meantime may I offer you a beverage?"

Klaud didn't hesitate. "Dear, would you happen to have a vintage Laphroaig Single Malt on board?"

"We do."

"Austin — name your poison."

"Klaud, I really don't get to drink often. I'm not sure that . . ."

"Dear — make that two. I'll have two-fingers neat in a snifter."

"Uh, make mine on the rocks with a tiny splash." Austin quickly added.

"Coming right up. Would either of you care for an appetizer?"

"Sure," Klaud snapped. "What's our choice?"

"We have a wonderful smoked salmon with . . ."

"Perfect. Bring enough for two, dear."

"Back in a splash —" she smiled at Austin, "— with your splash."

As she turned to walk to the galley, Klaud began to undress her with his eyes, what was left for him to undress.

"Austin, I'll bet you don't see that kind of talent flying commercial?"

"Well, I've only flown a couple of times, and I can honestly say I haven't experienced anything like any of this before — period."

"Could you get used to it?"

"I'm ready."

"You are going to get your chance — believe me. Now I'm sure you're wondering just what in the hell this is all about."

Austin gave Klaud a puzzled look and nodded his head yes.

"We have been summoned to meet with the President and his Chief of Staff at the Capitol in Colorado Springs."

All Austin could think to say was, "No shit?"

"No shit. They wanted to personally meet you and for the two of us to work with them on writing all of the media releases and video productions for the next, what they consider to be, critical 24-hours of this national emergency."

"I guess I'm flattered."

"Flattered hell! This could be fantastic for the both of us. If we pull this off right, we will be sitting pretty for the rest of our lives. Just think about it, Austin, I'm 55-years old. I only have a five more years to make enough money to maintain my lifestyle for the remainder of my life. Someone will need to replace me when I retire — right?"

"Right."

"That puts you in the logical progression to take over — with my recommendation of course — well, and with the approval of the President as well. Now, you know that when a person reaches UA-15 level they no longer are required to retire at one of those retirement camps in Cuba or the tip of Baja. Right?"

"I see." But, really, Austin had no idea. It seemed he was learning plenty now, however. This day had truly been an educational and eye-opening experience — eye-opening in so many ways.

"Look Austin, I already have my retirement home built and furnished in Puerto Vallarta. So, with the sale of my home here in Palos Verde, plus the Credits I will continue to put away in my Gold Account, and the retirement income I'll receive from the UA, I'll have a sweet and stress free rest of my life. We can make this work for you as well. Do ya follow me?"

"I think I'm with you all the way, Klaud." *Diana is definitely not going to believe any of this!*

"Great!"

At that moment, the flight attendant arrived with her cart. "I hope I'm not interrupting, gentlemen?" She smiled. "Here are your drinks and refreshments. Have you had a chance to look over the menu? Or would you like a little more time? I would be happy to make a suggestion."

Klaud smiled and his eyes gave her the once over — again. "And what would you recommend, my dear?"

"I've had the opportunity to tempt my tongue around the bacon wrapped filet mignon and it is extremely tender, extra moist, and very succulent." She whispered as she licked her lips. "Young meat is always tasty," then starring into Klaud's eyes, "but sometimes I prefer a little age on my beef — if you know what I mean?"

"Sold. Make that two." Klaud smiled and winked.

"Excellent. Coming right up. And gentlemen, be thinking about a special dessert for later."

* * * * * *

The meal was one of the finest Austin had ever had. It was not only a special treat, but also one that was served in private at thirty thousand feet. After Klaud had long finished his meal and excused himself to the rear of the cabin, Austin continued to savor every bite. He took his time considering this unexpected pleasure.

As the aircraft began its descent into Colorado Springs, Austin watched Klaud appear from the private rear cabin, combing his hair, followed closely by the flight attendant. Klaud took the seat once again facing Austin. The attendant stopped momentarily, smiled and said, "It's time to buckle up, gentlemen. We are beginning our descent. If I can be of further service, please ring for me. Otherwise, I'll see you on the ground."

"Are you OK, Klaud? You look a little flush."

"As you get older, Austin, it happens sometimes when you get your pipes cleaned."

Austin tried to keep a straight face, but the vision of Klaud with that knockout flight attendant . . . he tried to put it out of his mind. "While you were in the aft cabin, Klaud, I was thinking about doing some prep work before we meet with the President. You know I like to be as prepared as possible on any new assignment."

"Good point, and good timing. Unfortunately there wasn't a lot of information before we took off. But, I was just about to hand you the communiqué I received just before your arrival at LAX. You'll have plenty of time to read this over before we land and arrive at the White House." He handed the file over to Austin. "We should still have time to put our heads together and craft a starting outline. We need to stay flexible, however, because there's bound to be new intelligence once we meet with the President."

"I understand. No doubt this is going to be a fluid process."

"Very fluid, flexible, challenging, as I'm sure it will be surprising." *And most of all, it should be rewarding!*

"You've met the President before, Klaud?"

"Several times. And as you know, not many people have."

"What's he like?"

"In what way?"

"In every way."

"He's sharp. He's extremely resourceful and decisive. And he's a man of very few words."

"Just like me." Austin said jokingly.

"Well, you two are the same age. There may be a couple of similarities I suppose. I think you two will hit it off just fine."

"I think I should read over this brief now."

There was little substance to the report. Understandably, there had not been enough time to gather any conclusive intel for the initial report. What frustrated the investigators most was the lack of eyewitnesses. It was as if the ninety-one presumed perpetrators were all ghosts.

Little did Klaud and Austin know, but they could have accurately guessed, their entire flight had been caught on video and audio — digitally recorded and transmitted real-time to the White house. Upon landing, the back-up memory card would be express couriered to the President. Gates had already spot-reviewed their flight preceding his meeting with them.

Carey Dunstan and Stanley Bates, on the other hand, would watch every frame in the very near future.

* * * * * *

There was no longer a stately capitol building or any prestigious monuments at the new Capitol of the United Authority in Colorado Springs. In fact, the city looked much the same as it had for the previous 100 years, albeit with a larger population. The former Capitol in DC had been transformed into a city-sized museum.

Instead of the numerous buildings and monuments displaying the historical architecture in Washington DC the new capital view was the grandeur of two prominent mountains west of the Springs — the 14,115 foot (4,302m) high Pikes Peak and the 9,565 foot (2,915m) high Cheyenne Mountain. The majority of the critical UA governmental functions currently take place in one of the most unusual installations in the world. So unusual because it is housed 2,000 feet into the side of a mountain on the southwest side of the city.

Halfway up Cheyenne Mountain, in North Cheyenne Park, is the Shrine of the Sun Memorial, erected in memory of Will Rogers. It consists of a 100-

ft (30-m) tower, the interior of which is decorated with frescoes; there is a bust of Rogers by Jo Davidson. The headquarters of the North American Air Defense Command (NORAD) and other defense facilities were once located deep inside the mountain.

The Cheyenne Mountain complex proposal dated back to 1956, when the then Continental Air Defense Command proposed construction of a new underground combat operations center. The mountain was an ideal site due to its location in the center of the continent and lack of earthquake activity. These were just a couple of the same reasons utilized in Director Deimos' outlined proposal to the President as the rationale for the ideal location for a safe and secure UA Capitol.

The original excavation for the facility began in 1961, and was completed in May 1964. An Operations Center (OC) was built deep inside the mountain. A main tunnel was bored almost a mile through the solid granite heart of the mountain. The original conception and construction of the Cheyenne Mountain facility was during a period of history known as the "Cold War." There was a prevailing fear that the, then, two great world nuclear powers, the USA and the USSR could decimate each other's countries due to their escalating quantity of atomic weapons. The only possible survivors from such a holocaust would be those who could be ultimately protected from the initial blast and shielded from the many years of ensuing radiation. Therefore, the Cheyenne's deep center complex was designed to withstand up to a 30-megaton blast from 1.5-miles of its entry portal.

The entire complex was well thought out and engineered for survivability, protection of its occupants and contained all of the high-tech equipment it required therein. Emphasis on the design of the structure was not only to provide protection; it also afforded the occupants self-sufficiency for long periods. The entire underground facility included redundant power supplies, backup communications, closed-circuit audio and video, commissary, a large food storage area, dining facility, barber/beauty shop, two physical fitness centers with a sauna, dental office, and a state of the art medical facility that was stocked with plentiful quantities of supplies and drugs. The food supplies and drugs were completely rotated each year in a quarterly cycle.

The metal walls of the tunnels served to attenuate electromagnetic pulse (EMP). Water for the complex comes from several natural springs and an artesian well that are deposited into four major excavated reservoirs. Backup diesel generators provided emergency electric power. And protection against fallout and biological or chemical warfare was handled by a massive filtered air intake supply system to remove harmful pathogens and radioactive particles. All of that was before.

Director Deimos' plan for Cheyenne Mountain and the new Capitol of the UA not only brought the facility up to twenty-first century standards in every way, it required expanding the underground complex by a factor of ten.

The one remaining addition he proposed to the President was the construction of a full-scale replica of the "White House" to serve as the single historic image for the new Capitol. The new "White House" was built at, and backed up to the base of Cheyenne Mountain. The entire structure was fabricated as a solid steel-plate shell with an architectural façade of stone. It was replete in every detail to the original building in Washington DC on its exterior. However, unknown to the masses, there was no interior at all. The building was a hollow shell, not unlike a large movie facade with the exterior appearance of a conventionally constructed building. In actuality, it covered one of the several portals leading into Cheyenne Mountain while protecting a replica of the Oval Office and the President's opulent underground quarters.

* * * * * *

Klaud Akakios and Austin's chauffeured limo passed thru the security gate at the new "White

House" and around the horseshoe drive to the President's front steps. Waiting to greet them was non-other than Chief of Staff Carey Dunstan accompanied by two UA Security agents. The agents opened the limo doors and as Austin stepped out, Dunstan extended his hand. "Welcome to the White House. I'm Chief of Staff Carey Dunstan."

"Austin Llanoc — it's a pleasure to meet you, sir."

"No sir is required — just Carey, we are all friends here," Dunstan turned to Akakios "Klaud — how was the flight?"

"No problems — delightful as usual, and many thanks for the special treat."

"I thought you might enjoy that." Dunstan smiled and winked at Klaud.

Entering the front door, the entourage walked through a beautifully historic looking and expansive foyer and a forty-foot long entryway. A second set of doors opened into an almost cavernous room, with massive twin, winding staircases and an open balcony. The group walked between the two staircases to a waiting elevator — Dunstan and Akakios chatting small talk all the while.

Austin was silent and for the most part experiencing an all but complete sensory overload as he peered up and around. He was simultaneously impressed and nervous. His thoughts ran the gambit. He was remembering the events of the past 15-hours, the anticipation of meeting the President of the UA, the incredible responsibility that was about to be handed to him, not to mention just exactly how he would be able to describe all of this to Diana. The one thing he had not realized was that he hadn't experienced a single headache since the executive jet leveled off on the flight to the Springs. Although there was and is a level of stress during this timeframe, there hadn't been any pain. *This is all too good to believe.*

It was suddenly, and at that very moment, that his heart dropped. In fact, his entire body dropped. He was shocked to realize the elevator was descending rapidly rather than ascending.

* * * * * *

President Gates was waiting to meet the group as they entered the Oval Office. Austin's first impression was that the President seemed somewhat smaller than he appeared on the Com-Center — not that he was short.

"Welcome gentlemen." The President spoke first.

"Mister President, I would like for you to meet Austin Llanoc." Dunstan said as he guided Austin to Gates.

"Pleased to meet you, and very pleased you are able to join our team. I've heard a lot about you, and I must say I'm impressed."

"My pleasure, sir."

Gates turned to Akakios. "Klaud — you know it's always good to see you. Are you two ready to roll up your sleeves?"

Simultaneously they responded with, "We are."

"Good. The first order of business is to bring you up to speed on the latest developments. Why don't we sit over here?" As he walked over to a comfortable seating area on the other side of his office, he asked if anyone would care for a drink or a Coca-Coffee.

"Carey has prepared a detailed and updated report for each of you here on the table. You will need to study this information later. But first, I would like to talk to you about the highlights in this report and give you some of my initial thoughts about how we should handle the release of the information to the Citizens."

As coffee was being served, Gates turned to Austin who was seated in an antique chair to his left.

"Austin, I have been following your career for some time and I am sincerely impressed. You seem to possess all of the attributes the UA looks for in it's future leaders. Klaud tells me you've refined your leadership skills over the years and that you are, arguably the finest wordsmith and producer he's ever had the pleasure of working with."

Austin modestly smiled. "Thank you, sir. But, I'm sure Klaud would agree that he has a propensity to exaggerate."

"You may not realize it, Austin, but you and I have a number of things in common. In fact, I may be able to tell you a few things about yourself that you don't even know. Once we put this nasty business behind us, I would like for you and I to spend some time together — mano-y-mano — that is if it's OK with Klaud," Gates looked up to a smiling Akakios, "Do you like to downhill ski, Austin?"

"I've never had the opportunity to try, Mr. President."

"From now on it's Bill when we are together in private, you can drop the formalities. And you know that goes for you too, Klaud. We're all friends here and in this together."

With that, Gates put down his coffee and picked up a copy of the bound report.

"Now, let's get down to business. To begin with, does the name Alexander Conall mean anything to you?"

Liberty

7

"... By bringing the whole of life under the control of the State, Socialism necessarily gives power to an inner ring of bureaucrats, who in almost every case will be people who want power for its own sake and will stop at nothing in order to retain it. The only salvation lies in returning to an unplanned economy, free competition, and emphasis on liberty rather than on security." — *Homage to Catalonia* by George Orwell.

* * * * * *

There are between 8,000 to 10,000 caves in the state of Texas. They cover about twenty percent of the state due to the geologic formations known as karst regions. Karst is a terrain formed by the dissolution, by water, of bedrock over many thousands of years. Most of this bedrock is easily shaped due to its soluble nature. Typically, the underground karst formations are composed of a carbonate rock such as limestone or dolomite. And many of these caves channel water underground, which are generally characterized by sinkholes. A multitude of these caverns were explored over the centuries — yet, the majority were not. Some of those discovered were long since lost and forgotten — while others were so remote, they may as well have been on the moon.

Texas caves and caverns had long served many diverse needs over hundreds, if not thousands of years — from their use as primitive shelters for prehistoric hunter-gatherers, cool storage areas for early Native Americans, hide-outs for desperados, fountains of fresh spring drinking and irrigation water, and home to various types of wild life including 100 million Mexican free-tailed bats.

Sorcerer's Cave in West Texas had seen them all. And at 558 feet down, Sorcerer's Cave is the deepest known cave in the state. It also became a home to Los Salvadores.

* * * * * *

Several weeks prior to the multiple attacks of UA buildings, Alex Conally was standing in front of and slightly above a group numbering roughly one hundred. The cave was cool and welcoming from the extreme West Texas heat. The gathering represented a mix of races, genders, and ages — from 18 to 66. Dr. Norm was not only the oldest of the group he was also the only former Citizen. He had escaped the forced retirement camps in the Baja. Of all the Plebeians, the youngest were the children of the middle-aged couples and there were less than a dozen or so who were exactly thirty-seven. Alex couldn't help laughing to himself, looking out over this motley crew — *If this isn't what they used to call Politically Correct, well then I don't know what is.* Although they all appeared to be very different on the surface, and many of them were, each of those present had a common cause — the desire to take their country back.

Alex was a striking leader. At a lean six feet, his healthy physique and hardened good looks were archetypal of a movie adventurer. His thirty-seven years had been dedicated to self-sufficiency. He was unique in many aspects including the fact that he was currently the only Citizen of Los Salvadores.

* * * * * *

"I think we're all here." Alex began. "Everyone that is, with the exception of 'The Wolf,' and I assure you, he is here in spirit."

"When do we get to meet Alexander the Great?" Yelled one of the elders in the back of the group.

"Maybe soon. Maybe never. I don't get to see my, well, my ah, our father as often as I would like to either. And I too believe he is great." He laughed. "But then I'm biased. Whether he's great or not, he prefers to be thought of simply as, 'The Wolf.'"

"Everyone here must realize that there is a rather large price tag on his head. His stealth is his salvation and longevity. Very soon, and after our first attack, there is the very real possibility that— should things not go well — there might be a price on all of your heads as well. Never forget for one moment that stealth is your deliverance as it is his. Your suppression must be acted out daily in speech and actions. We must be unified by this fact as one of our fundamental principles. To use an old English colloquialism, 'If we don't hang together we will all hang separately.' So 'The Wolf' must remain a ghost, as he has for the last half of his life — at least the last half so far."

"Long live 'The Wolf!'" A yell came from the group.

There was an immediate round of applause and cheering that echoed through the cave chambers like thunder. Alex stood silently allowing the revelry to continue until there were only whispers. He could feel the energy of the group. Their attitudes fueled their dedication. And their dedication was paramount.

"OK Alex, what's next? Has he finalized our first plan of attack yet?" Another asked.

"Yes. He has."

And again, a short burst of applause and cheers erupted epitomizing their spirit.

"So when do we begin?"

"We already have." Alex stated firmly.

* * * * * *

Alexander Conall, a.k.a. "The Wolf," had spent the majority of his life patiently preparing, precisely planning for his destiny as the father of the resistance. Now, at the ripe age of eighty-five, he fully understood what he had known for so many years — that he would not live to witness the total rebirth of what was once a great nation. At least, that is, he would not be witness to it in this timeworn body. But then, like his entire life, he was well prepared for that as well. At some point, others would have to continue the struggle. And he was wise enough to understand that, not unlike a game of chess, many future moves would require his contingency engineering in order to achieve an ultimate checkmate and the final victory. His later rewards may come vicariously.

Conall was born and raised in Texas. He was an only child to a mother who was a high school history teacher and a father who was a successful engineer at NASA in Houston. It was at a time in which the country was vastly different. The entire world was vastly different for that matter. It wasn't obvious to the majority — it was simply life. But, Alexander was being groomed to understand the metamorphosis that the country was experiencing. He was taught the differences. Great freedoms that had been enjoyed by people in North America were slowly being stripped away and all the while carefully being replaced with the illusions of freedom.

His had become a lifetime experience that was slowly dying with the passing of each generation. He was educated with real books; and he had the good fortune and ability to study the more accurate historical accounts of this young country's history, not to mention its place in a very old world.

Blessed with a superior intellect and an often-misunderstood, "can-do," Texan spirit, Conall was fortuitous in each of his early business endeavors. He had amassed several fortunes during his younger years. He used his profits for only what he needed to benefit his cause — then, one by one, he donated the remainders away in the form of various trusts. His life's motivation was not that of personal wealth. Wealth was only a means to an end.

Every year, as he aged, he was more and more acutely aware of his country's transfiguration. He witnessed the loss of people's power and the deprivation of their personal freedoms — stripped away one by one. He saw the increasing greed of the patricians and the infectious entitlement attitude of the proletariat. He watched the collusion of large government and big business corruption. It was the complete and total rape of a once great nation. And the infection spread to the adjacent countries, their people — and it saddened him. Yet it gave him a resolve, a predisposition to dedicate his life to the salvation of his own country.

The once guaranteed principles of "Life, liberty and the pursuit of happiness" had all but vanished. And as a remembrance of another time, he carried a battered copy of the US Constitution. Its haggard state was as a result of his repeated reference, ultimately to the point of his total memorization.

In addition to his commercial achievements, Conall was conjointly successful at masking his growing discontent. He learned to fly under the radar and convincingly blended in with average society while meticulously planning every day of his future revolution.

He slowly collected a cadre of loyal followers — most of whom he never actually met. The meticulous assembling of his followers could be compared to the craftsmanship and the precise workings of a fine timepiece — many parts never touching a common part yet all working together in synch. Conall's dedication and resolve were absolute.

Even before the passing of his parents, he understood that his life would have to be one of personal isolation. He was not inclined to even consider having children as a part of his future. That was until 2046 when he fully reconciled the fact that he could not outlive the struggle. Alexander Conall would need a successor — a prodigy.

* * * * * *

"Please be patient. I have been looking forward to this day as much as you all — or, ya'll as they say here in Texas." Alex continued. "In a few moments, we will break for an early dinner. Afterwards, I will meet with each of you privately in the back chamber. The plan is complex and multi-faceted. Each of you will play a totally unique part. I will need for you to completely focus on your scene in our play. There are more than ninety scenes that are critical to the first act. 'The Wolf' and I are the only two people who know the entire production. Each scene and every respective actor is autonomous. By not knowing the full extent of the plan, should one or more of you get captured, God forbid, the remainder of the plan will not lose its integrity. Are there any questions so far?"

"Do we all get a part in the play?" One of the 18-year olds asked.

"Yes. There are only a few your age, however. Our plan is to team each of the younger members into several pairs, consisting of one older and one younger actor. There are four scenes in which two actors are required."

"How many attacks and when are they planned for execution?" another asked.

"There will be a total of about 91-scenes in the first assault — what we are referring to as Act 1. It is critical that each of these scenes occur simultaneously — to the day, and to the exact minute. The time will be 4am Western Time on April 15th of this year — just four weeks from today."

"*Tax day?*" Dr. Norm yelled out.

"You got it! What used to be known as tax day, that is."

At that point, the entire room broke out in laughter for the better part of several minutes followed by jokes and crosstalk. Alex knew this would help to lighten the otherwise somber mood.

"*I guess I don't need to file a tax return this year.*" A voice yelled from the back.

"Sam, you've never filed a single tax return in your entire life!" His wife responded.

More laughter ensued.

"Alex, you say the first assault. There will be others?"

"Yes. There will be several others following the first wave, all within relatively close proximity."

"What about casualties?"

"None if possible. Please understand that we wish no one any physical harm. Personal injury or termination by extreme prejudice could only be justified as a result of someone placing our plan in jeopardy or in self-defense. The only individuals with whom we have a beef are our government leaders and fewer business titans — and we wish them no harm either. If our play goes as directed, they will ultimately acquiesce."

* * * * * *

In the years preceding the formation of the United Authority, corruption and political scandals had become so common in all of the former North American countries that citizens had simply grown not to expect much from their lawmakers. Major "Pork Projects" were lining the pockets of the upper tier of the population. Petty and not so petty scams were also uncovered in their Congresses. In the beginning, many were reported in the media on a weekly basis. Scores of legislators admitted to using taxpayer money to fund phantom employees, to pay for vacation homes, their rampant tax evasion, government bankrolled airfares, exotic vacations, and lavish parties — just to name a few. Much of what wasn't reported in the media found its way into public gossip from second-hand conversations.

Major corruption and scandals involving labor unions, large corporations and special interests groups, grew like plagues fueled by the greed of the few while forsaking the majority. In fact, it was the majority who were picking up the tab for the runaway spending. Taxation was out of control. Ultimately, citizens were paying 80% of their wages in taxes. Inflation took its increasing toll on the remaining 20%, little by little every year.

Initially, the public became incensed by the discoveries that their representatives had lost all consideration of moral sensibility. And they were equally frustrated that the problems were so systemic.

Under the newly revised and complex electoral laws, voters had little direct representation in their Congress; meaning legislators had no specific constituencies that could hold them responsible other than the special interest groups. And the lack of clear campaign financing rules meant that legislators frequently bent the rules to pay for campaigns.

Polls had shown that fewer than 10-15 percent of the combined UA countries' populations trusted their leaders. More than half of all citizens favored closing down their governments all together until they could regain some common sense in their leadership. But with the passing years, it appeared there simply wasn't any cure. North American governments were out of control. Eventually people lost all hope for the "Change" that would help them, and settled for a somewhat false sense of safety and security instead.

* * * * * *

"Before I begin the individual meetings, let's break for some nourishment. As usual, it isn't fancy. We have liberated several pallets of K-rations and bottled water from the UA Protection warehouse in Nuevo Laredo. So, let us give thanks to Gates for our nutritious meal and dig in." Alex stepped down from the rock ledge he had been standing on and walked directly to Maya. "I would like to begin with you after our meal, if that's OK?"

"Sure. I hope you have something special for me."

"I do. As a mater of fact, every single one of our scenes is going to be very special. Let's eat. We'll talk later."

Not only was each scene special, every actor was unique as well. Maya was no exception. This thirty-year-old Latin lady was a five-foot tall bottle rocket. She was born and raised with eight brothers and sisters in Guadalajara. Her father was the Governor of the state of Jalisco when she turned eighteen and entered the University of Mexico. She had political aspirations as well. That was until her senior year when her future took an unexpected change of course. Her father was assassinated. It was during the period in time of negotiations to join the newly forming United Authority. Carlos Sanchez Ortiz de Domingo had been a staunch supporter of the sovereignty of Mexico. His opposition had been uncompromising and far too vocal. Fearing for their lives, the family went into hiding. Myra's new resolve was born the day she witnessed her father's death.

Each member of the group took their turns collecting rations and finding rocks or clear spots on which to sit and enjoy their meal. No one complained about the food. In fact, they appreciated a good meal when they could get one — and the price was right, too. There was quiet conversation throughout. People were getting caught up to date with their friends and current events. They exchanged survival tips and talked about close encounters with the authorities.

The younger members of the group were quietly listening. They were learning many skills including the salient and difficult discipline of patience. The elders engrained the vital understanding of strategic thought and action that they themselves had learned through the years. Some of the elders were being asked about their recollection of history and were prompted to tell stories about the old days. The tradition of communicating history had been used by many civilizations throughout the ages. Long before there were books and formal schools, history was passed along through the art of songs and storytelling.

The group was in good spirits. In spite of the dangers, they were truly looking forward to their missions — even without knowing exactly what those missions entailed. Los Salvadores placed their trust in the 'The Wolf.' Collectively and individually, they understood that this would only be the beginning. But at least, they would be a part of making a positive impact on the future for all Citizens and non-Citizen alike. Only time would tell of their ultimate success — failure was not an option. And they were all willing to invest their lives, if required, for this noble cause.

* * * * * *

Day to day survival required a critical thought process. Their lives, not unlike Alexander Conall's later years, could not be conducted as typical Citizen's lives. They had to master an almost invisible existence and one of self-sufficiency. It wasn't completely impossible to blend in. There was literally thousands of what were considered "Plebeians." The majority of these were homeless vagabonds with no visible means of support. As a result of all currencies being converted to digital Credits, these nomads could only beg or scrounge for food and necessities. Due to their "Plebeian" status, they were not registered with the United Authority and therefore unable to get medical aid or have the ability to take advantage of any typical Citizen privileges. They were simply, survivors.

Los Salvadores, on the other hand, were not survivors. They were survivalists. There was no need to beg for food and necessities. Each had learned unique skills and educated their ranks about living the life of "The Wolf." The land provided a bounty of food.

The skills of hunting had been all but forgotten after the banning of all firearms many years prior. Los Salvadores built traps. Game meat and fish are good sources of protein and fat. Fishing not only provided nutrition but entertainment as well. And depending on the season and geographies, their menus included a potpourri of vegetation.

The sea berry shrub, also known as sea buckthorn, became one of the mainstays. The up to 8-foot tall shrub has gray-green, almost silver foliage with clusters of small, oblong-shaped yellow or orange, edible berries. All but unknown, yet it has been growing in North America for hundreds of years, from parts of Canada and the Northwest states of Washington, Oregon, Alaska, to areas of New Mexico, Texas and Mexico. It's berries are packed with high levels of antioxidants including vitamins C, A and E and cholesterol-lowering phytosterols. Most agreed they have a desirable flavor. People describe the fruit as a mildly tart pineapple taste.

Nopales cactus, also known as nopalitos or cactus pads became a favorite vegetable. The crunchy texture also becomes a bit sticky (not unlike okra) when cooked. This cactus proliferates in the southwestern states and much of Mexico. It tastes similar to a slightly tart green bean, asparagus, or green pepper. Nopalitos contain beta-carotene, iron, some B vitamins, and are a good sources of both vitamin C and calcium.

Other staples included nuts, wild berries, dandelions, wild onions, and mushrooms to name a few. The more daring of the group added some protein rich insects, snakes and alligator meat. Food presented no problem for the skilled.

Communications, on the other hand, were Los Salvadores' biggest challenge. They were spread over hundreds, even thousands of miles with no ability to use Tel-Cards. Even if Tel-Cards were available, they wouldn't be able to risk the tracking and reconnaissance capabilities the units provided the UA Safety Bureau.

Conall spent years devising a coded language in combination with, the all but forgotten, Morse code. The complex language mixed elements of Navajo, Aztec and Acadian pidgins. Handwritten notes were posted in predetermined and strategic locations or delivered by bike for short distance communications. Friendly cargo haulers, motorcycle gangs, and even carrier pigeons were utilized for long distance. It wasn't a perfect system, but it had served the purpose with amazing accuracy.

The final skill of these survivalists was to blend in. It was vital that they appeared to be vagabonds, people of no value. They used the legions of other "Plebeians" as human camouflage. Los Salvadores were ghosts.

* * * * * *

Alex and Maya walked to the edge of a pre-dug pit and discarded their food and water containers. Alex picked up a small lantern and they carefully moved to a secluded section in the back cave.

"Maya, I've chosen to start with you because of the difficulty of your mission. Also, it will require your teaming up with a younger member."

"You have someone in mind no doubt?"

"Jorge."

"Why isn't he here with us for the briefing?"

"Two reasons. None of the Youngers will have any prior knowledge of their mission. You will not divulge a single detail to Jorge. Understand?"

"I do."

"Good. I know that this will be very challenging because he'll want to know. He will feel left out and possibly demeaned. But, his age is the first issue. The Youngers are simply not mature enough nor prepared for the difficulties posed."

"And the second reason?"

"Should the two of you become separated, he could not pull this off by himself — period. You, on the other hand, have the ability to get the bulk of the mission accomplished alone. You can also explain to him that only one person on each team can know the target and the plan for security reasons."

"He will go for that?"

"I believe you will be convincing."

"Puedo sí."

"Bueno."

"You've already told us the date and time. What is the target?"

"Your target is the UA Contribution Building in Mexico City."

"No shit?"

"You know the building?"

"¡Sí! Yes, yes. It's close to the intersection of Paseo de la Reforma and Avenue Insurgentes in La Zona Rosa. I know it well."

"Good. I thought as much. So a map isn't required."

"No. But why this building?"

"Simple — Mexicans have been taxed to death. The Contribution Bureau is the scourge and a symbol."

Life for the majority in Mexico had never been easy. But there was a time when it was all but free from an overbearing government and painful taxes. Even the majority of poor people could lead useful, albeit modest lives with little interference from their government. Although the ruling party in power and a minority of elites controlled the greater population, it was almost a benign grip. There simply had been little opportunity for the Mexican people. Over time, the country began to experience a growing middle class. As the upper class became even greedier, they followed the example of their neighbors to the north and slowly instituted increased taxes on their small middle class and larger poor population. Once the UA consolidated Mexico, the UA Contribution Bureau became the symbol of repressive taxation and totalitarian rule in Mexico.

"Es la verdad. The people feel they work for the government rather than for their families. So I take it, we are going to strike a blow at that symbol?"

"Bingo."

"And the method?"

"Hand-launched rockets. This will allow you a respectful distance from the target. At no time come closer than within 2-blocks of the target building. Like every UA building, it is surrounded by video surveillance. Don't sketch it in advance or any of the surroundings — and no note taking. Commit to memory everything just as a skilled racing driver mentally memorizes the course before an event. Watch the activities and the people around the facility. You must commit every detail to memory. And this should be accomplished not more than 2-days in advance of execution. This is when you can divulge the plan to Jorge — not before. The two of you must use your ghost-like skills while studying the subject."

"We've had plenty of practice."

"Find an attack vantage point not more than about 300-yards or roughly 274 meters from the target. This location should give you a clear view yet also provide you good cover as well.

"I think I already know the ideal location."

"Good. As you know, 'The Wolf' has been very resourceful in gathering equipment and supplies for our revolution. When you leave in the morning for your mission, you will be issued two Speed Hawk incendiary shoulder fire missiles. They are short and fit inside small canvas bags. The firing instructions are simple and located in the bags."

"What if we're spotted before the attack?"

"Simple. You can claim that you found these weapons beside the road and were en route to turn them in to UA Safety forces in the area."

"In other words, we act innocent."

"Don't over act. Just tell them you're trying to do the right thing."

"I'll offer them a bribe if necessary. After all, they are military — if you know what I mean?"

"Only do what you have to do. Just try not to linger. You may be hassled, but there will be no reason to hold you for long. Let the authorities know that you were just tying to do the right thing. Then, disappear as fast as possible."

"Got it."

"On the appointed day and time, make your way to your firing point no sooner than five to ten minutes prior to execution. Be sure and wear black or very dark clothing — no hats. Fire your Hawk through a window at the second to top floor. Jorge should take aim for a window in the center of the building. After execution, lay the weapons down gently and slowly walk away — then disappear. Do not run. Don't do anything to call attention to yourselves. Your next instructions will be posted on the lobby bulletin board at the Hospital de la Mujer on el calle Salvador Diaz Miron 374, on April 16th."

"The very next day. I like it."

"As usual, do not take the instructions. Just scan over all of the postings on the bulletin board, read your message and then walk away."

"We've prepared and waited a long time for this. It's hard to believe the time has finally come."

"Just remember, this is only the beginning. The ultimate victory will take much longer."

"Sí. Es la verdad."

* * * * * *

Alex spent the remainder of the evening briefing each member of Los Salvadores. Although the majority of the targets were the same type, each one was also unique in directions and execution. And due to the expansive distances, every member of the team had to be on his or her way the following morning. Ninety-one UA Contribution buildings, plus the UA Continuity Bureau in Redondo Beach, the UA Commerce Bureau in Atlanta, the UA Entertainment Bureau in Toronto, and the UA Labor Bureau in Mexico City were detailed for destruction. It was a massive undertaking for such a small gorilla force. But, Alex and 'The Wolf' knew they had the element of surprise on their side — at least for Act 1.

"Ninety down and one to go." Alex spoke softly to himself as he stood up and stretched. He slowly walked to the main chamber of the cave. He rubbed his eyes and stared at the sole remaining member. *Eugene — my man!*

Eugene stood to greet Alex as he approached. "Sheee-it man! You finally getin' round to me?"

"Eugene — don't you know we always save the best for last?" Alex smiled.

"Hey. I'm just happy you didn't forget about me!" He said laughing. "Naw man. It ain't no big thing. I actually been takin' a nice nap while you been workin'."

"Well, since it's just you and me, Eugene, we don't have to go to the back of the cave. And I was serious about saving the best for last."

"Good. I'm ready to do my part."

"Eugene, how would you like to go to Southern California?"

"Aw man! I like it already."

"Have you ever been to the Island of Love?"

"Say what?"

"You know — Santa Catalina Island."

"You gotta be kiddin' me, man. You're sending me to go to battle at a resort?"

"Yep. But you're gonna have to leave your surf board at home."

Ocho

8

"Evil requires the sanction of the victim."
— Ayn Rand

* * * * * *

It was a productive flight back to LA. Director Akakios and Austin buried themselves in the task at hand — writing the President's next speech and official press releases. Their deadline was 24-hours. As the Executive jet made its final approach to LAX, Austin handed over his final draft to Klaud. "Done — take a look." Austin offered his text to the Director for his thoughts, merely as a professional courtesy.

"Excellent. But there's no need for me to read it. I'm sure it is, in fact, just excellent. Let's meet at 8am tomorrow morning at the front of what's left of the Continuity building. We can assess the damage and plan our rebuilding. I'll communicate your text to the President from my home tonight."

"Don't you think that you should quick-proof my...?"

"The only thing, I think, is that we run this by the President."

"You're the boss."

Austin had no doubt that Klaud wouldn't be able to resist reading the text before filing it with the White House. If nothing else, his curiosity would get the best of him for sure. He only wondered if there might be a few Klaud touches added for good measure. Either way, it didn't make a lot of difference. It was solid.

"Correct. I am your next link in the chain of command. And while we're on the subject, Austin, that applies to Gates and Dunstan as well. They are the big guns. However, even they are not the leading links in the chain. There are others."

A small group of elite men formed a stratum overseeing the true control and direction of the country. They were the Senior Directors most of whom were never revealed to the Citizens. They had arrived at their positions from birth and a very long linage of powerful families.

"Of course. I know that."

"Just don't forget it. That business back in the Springs about, 'We're all friends' should be taken with a grain of salt."

"But — they said that . . ."

"I know very well what both of them said. But you need to understand that what they said, and what they meant . . ."

"You're saying they meant the opposite? And what does a grain of salt mean?"

"OK. It's time for politics 101. First, let me explain a grain of salt. This is a very old term in common parlance for the Latin, cum grano salis."

"Klaud — I didn't know you spoke Latin."

"I don't. Well, I don't anymore that is. Many years ago, Latin was taught in schools."

"Really?"

"A lot of different languages were taught back then, not like now. Anyway, I've forgotten most of it from non use."

"Fascinating." *This guy never ceases to amaze me.*

"So, hundreds of years ago, cum grano salis meant that a grain of salt was required in any antidote to poison — or so it was thought and stated. Of course this didn't work. But people thought it was possible, so they would prescribe it to anyone thought to have taken poison. When the person didn't die, it confirmed the myth. They never considered that what was ingested probably wasn't poison in the first place — or if it was, the dose was too small to be lethal anyway."

"And that means?"

"It simply means that you should carefully consider any communication from a politician. In other words, you should use a copious measure of skepticism. Don't blindly accept or believe everything as stated. Take it with a grain of salt."

"They were lying?"

"No. Look — it's not unlike what we do at UA Continuity — only in this case it's spoken rather than in writing and producing. Think of it as, well, embellishment. Get it?"

"I think so. Yes."

"Good. My point is to always consider a hidden meaning in what is stated. And, you must never forget your place in the chain of command. There is so much more that you need to learn in order to advance. It will happen over time. Now would be a good time for you to begin. I would like to further this conversation over dinner tomorrow night. Would you and Diana be available?"

"Absolutely."

"Perfect, Austin. That's the right answer."

* * * * * *

Rather than walking directly to his condo unit, Austin stopped first at Diana's door and quietly knocked. He waited a minute and knocked once again.

"Yes. I'm coming."

As her door slid into the wall, they greeted each other with open arms and big smiles.

"Surprise!"

"Austin. You have no idea how worried I've been!" She said as they embraced and kissed. "You're OK? Is everything all right? What happened?"

"I'm fine. It's a long story for such a short trip. Are you OK?"

"Yes — except for worrying about you."

"No worries. Things are good."

"Tell me."

"Where do I start?"

"Would you like to start with a Coca-Coffee or a glass of wine?"

"Sure. Either. Both will go good with a little something I brought you." And he handed her a small, silver box with the Presidential seal engraved on its top.

As she reached for it her face turned to a frozen state of shock. She could only cradle it in both hands and stare for what seemed to be minutes.

"Austin! You've been with the President?"

"Yes."

"You're not joking — are you."

"No."

"Well? Are you going to tell me?"

"Sure. But aren't you going to open it?"

"What is it?"

"Just open it, silly."

Diana carefully lifted the lid as if the contents might be fleeting.

"Oh my gods! Is this what I think? I mean are these . . .?"

"Tim Tams."

"*Austin*. I have only dreamed of eating these." She stood frozen, staring into the tiny box of sweet delicacies. Her mouth filled with moisture in anticipation. "They are so expensive. I could never afford, I mean I could never justify spending — you know."

"Exactly. And they are as delicious as you have imagined. They seem to be, well basically, a chocolate cream biscuit sandwich enrobed by yet more chocolate. But when you taste one, it's like a little slice of heaven."

"Oh — Thank you. Thank you!" She lifted her petite frame on her tiptoes and reached both arms around Austin's neck — almost spilling the treats.

"You're welcome. But you really should thank the President. I'm just the delivery boy. He asked me to offer you this little present."

"I'll put the coffee on. Have you already tried them?"

"Yes, but not yours. Klaud and I had some with the President and his Chief of Staff yesterday."

"Austin. What is going on?"

"Plenty. And you're not going to believe what I'm about to tell you. Hell, I'm not sure I believe it myself!"

In many ways the previous twenty-four hours seemed like a dream. His former confused state of mind was now compounded. He tried to collate his thoughts into a semblance of order and logic. Austin wanted to believe that he had finally found his place — at last an understanding and order to his life.

"And it's all good?"

"It is. And, I think it's going to get even better. I'll tell you all about it over our coffee and Tim Tams. You also need to catch me up on your life for the past twenty-four plus hours too."

"I'm afraid you will be bored after what you've gone through."

"Not at all. By the way, what do you have planned for tomorrow night?"

* * * * * *

Following his 8am meeting with Klaud, Austin spent the bulk of the next day contacting Steven Lu and the other Continuity senior staff members, while Director Akakios talked to various UA Realtors who had been canvassing the area for a new headquarters. The previous UA Continuity building was a total loss and the Director scheduled it for demolition later in the week. The Central Authority Fire investigator and

UA Safety agents determined that the building took a hit from one of two missiles. A Speed Hawk was fired from a high cliff vantage point in Palos Verdes. A rather sophisticated Terrier Hawk surface-to-surface missile was also fired from Catalina Island. It had missed its mark however, and landed on Redondo's south beach leaving a crater the size of a city electro-bus.

It had been a long day, but a productive one. Austin met with the key department heads and detailed their responsibilities during the interim period of finding a new building location. His only break was for a quick, lite lunch. He would have never thought that a simple and inexpensive lunch at Maki-Sushi would present him with his next big surprise.

"Holy UA!" He spouted out loud.

"Is there something wrong with your check sir?" The Maki cashier said in a worried tone.

"Yes! I mean, well NO! That is, it's all good. Thank you."

Austin pulled his Tel-Card from the card-reader, placed it into his pocket and walked out the front door shaking his head.

"WOW!" Was about all he could say. This would put a smile on his face for the rest of the day. This new relationship with Klaud was paying off in more ways than one. Not only had the frequency of headaches decreased, but also there were some additional monetary considerations added in their place. *Not bad,* he thought. *This is getting better every day. I could really get used to this.*

Klaud Akakios had a fruitful day as well. A multi-story high rise was located in Long Beach that might be an even better fit than the previous building. There was no time to search for vacant real estate, plan and design a new building. The timing was critical. An existing building would have to do. Akakios was pleased that one of his realtors had so quickly responded and found a possible fit. The Director was also quick in letting the realtor know his service would be duly noted by the UA.

It was a newer building located on East Ocean Boulevard with a great view of the Pacific and more than enough square feet to accommodate the Bureau — with room to grow. Akakios thanked the realtor and said he would be back in touch tomorrow to make an offer on 331 East Ocean Boulevard.

The location was conveniently located and mostly set up to fit their needs — as is. Very few modifications would be required. The only small difficulty was that it was privately owned and had an approximate ninety percent occupancy. *This small encumbrance shouldn't be that much of a problem. All of those people will just have to relocate somewhere else.* The Director thought to himself. *I'll just make a couple of calls to the right people.*

* * * * * *

At the end of the day, Austin met with Akakios at the appointed time to go over their respective progress. Both were pleased to report to each other the details of their assigned duties. They understood that there would be several days required before the possibility of resuming their normal schedules and continuing their routine workload. In the mean time, they outlined the next day's events and reminded each other to be in front of their Com-Centers for the evening's speech by President Gates.

"Since the President will be speaking at 6pm Pacific-time, why don't we meet for dinner at 7:30?"

"Perfect, Klaud."

"Do you know where the Crystal Ocean Beach Club is located in Redondo?"

"Sure. But that place is really expensive. We don't have to . . ."

"Don't worry about it. The UA will be picking up the tab. I take it you've never been to the . . ?"

"I've never had the, ah, you know, the well . . ."

"Occasion?"

"Not one where I could justify spending that amount of Credits. No. Although — it would be a little easier for me now. Thank you again."

"OK. This will be a nice treat for you."

"And Diana?"

"Of course."

"I just wanted to make sure you hadn't changed your mind."

"I'm assuming you two are body-mates?"

"Not quite. But soon I hope."

"How long have you known her?"

"About a year now."

"And you're not hooking up already. You've been using the UA Service girls in that case?"

"No. Not really what I . . ."

"I give up. What's the hold up?"

"Nothing — well actually, I've just been waiting for the right body-mate. Once I met Diana it seemed prudent to make sure we were, you know, simpatico."

"So you're close?"

"Tonight could be the night."

"Excellent. Then, I believe that this will be a night you both will enjoy and remember for a very long time."

"I'm having the same thoughts, Klaud."

"Fine — very fine," Klaud smirked. "So we will meet at 7:30 at the Crystal. Enjoy the rest of your day. Go home and have a drink — watch the President — relax. I need to make a call to Director Deimos regarding an eviction notice."

"Head of the UA Safety Bureau — Central Intelligence? You know him?"

"Sure. He and I go way back. I could tell you stories that you wouldn't believe about the escapades we had together in college. Looking back, it's a wonder we survived some, and others — well, let's just say we've lost contact with those girls — if you know what I mean. You and I can bend an elbow some evening and I'll tell you some war stories. At any rate, there's just a small matter of securing our new building that I need to discuss with Deimos tonight."

* * * * * *

Austin and Diana walked through the oversized, stained glass doors and into the lobby of the Crystal Ocean Beach Club at 7:30 sharp. Akakios stood from the over-stuffed leather sofa and greeted them.

"Perfect timing, you two. I just sat down. Our table is ready. Diana, you look good enough to eat tonight. Austin, I don't know if you will need to order any dessert if I were you, young man." He winked at the two.

Diana and Austin forced a smile and followed Klaud to the hostess — a beautiful, well-endowed, and very healthy young lady in her early twenties.

"Good evening Director Akakios. It's always good to see you. But it would be even better to see you more often."

"Good evening Angel. And, it would be very good to see more of you too, my dear — and as often as you would allow me."

"Your table is ready — if you will please follow me." She smiled and turned to the main dining room.

Klaud looked her up and down as she walked away. After a moment he tilted his head toward Austin and almost whispered. "If my mother looked like that, I'd still be nursing."

Austin and Diana could only stare back at Klaud in disbelief. When he turned to follow the hostess, they both shook their heads at each other.

Walking through the main dining room was a wonderfully new experience for them. The combination of seeing such opulence combined with the fragrances of fine cuisine, much less actually being a part of it was all but sensory overload.

Angel guided them through a wondrous dining maze to a small, totally private dining room, with an expansive view of the Pacific sunset. Once seated, she presented the Director with a wine list and the evening's menu to each.

"Alfredo will be your server tonight — and he will join you momentarily. May I help you in any way?"

"Dear, you could help me in *so* many ways — but not right now, Angel. Thank you." He raised an eyebrow and smiled first at Angel then to Austin. Opening the wine list, he thought to himself, *now, let me see here. How else may I be tempted tonight?*

There was a long silence at the table as Akakios seriously studied the list of fruity libations. There was little reason to do so. Every wine on the list was an award winner. And, he had enjoyed every single bottle at least once if not on multiple occasions.

"I'm sorry Austin — Diana. I guess I should ask what is your favorite wine?"

"We don't really have many occasions to splurge on fine wine. So, our experience has been somewhat limited. We will defer to your choice."

"Red or white?"

"We would enjoy either." *The problem is that we may not enjoy our usual selection after this evening.*

As if by magic, a waiter seemed to appear from out of nowhere.

"Good evening. I am Alfredo and it will be my pleasure to serve you this evening. Have you selected a wine Sir Director?"

"I have, Alfredo, and if you can guess which one it will be worth an additional $50 Credits on your tip."

"Let me think, Sir Director." He placed the closed wine menu to his forehead and closed his eyes. "I would have to guess the 55' NAPA Chateau Louis."

"Right on, Alfredo. I don't know how you do it."

"Excellent choice, Sir Director. I will prepare it immediately for you and your guests."

He turned and all but disappeared quickly and without a sound.

"It's a little game Alfredo and I play."

"Then you come here often?" Diana asked.

"At least once a week — for a number of years — and Alfredo always wins. Let's just say, he helps me to acquire additional high-quality and, how shall I put it, hard to find items from time to time."

* * * * * *

The wine and fabulous dinner was served and the three spent their time in mostly small talk. Klaud gave them some selective information about his UA background. He was curious about Diana's interests and history. They chatted about the President's evening address and the important part the two of them would be playing in the shaping of Citizens opinions in the future. There was no hurry. Dinner was a leisurely experience. It was merely another test.

As the dinnerware was being cleared from the table he asked Diana if they might enjoy an after dinner libation and if Austin would care for a cigar.

"That would be very nice, Klaud. But I thought it was against the law to smoke in public places."

"Rank has its privilege." Klaud smiled.

"I'm beginning to understand that much more than what I thought I knew. It all seems so intoxicating. And while we're on the subject, thank you for the raise. I had the opportunity to check my Central Bank account at lunch today and noticed my base pay had increased by another $10,000-Credits per month."

"Don't thank me, Austin. You deserve it. That will put an additional $2,000-Credits into your spending cash every month."

"I understand. And believe me I can use it."

"Austin — you're smart enough to know that Citizens need to be cared for. They are the machinery that pays for our great country. It's the masses that keep our economy in motion. And like any collection of good machinery, they require proper organization, management and leadership. Without these fundamentals, they would never have the ability to function. We, management that is, keep the machinery operating at maximum efficiency. Therefore, higher compensation is required for this important guidance."

"You said we?"

"Yes. I am including you, and my hope would be for Diana as well, to continue to be groomed for higher positions of authority within the UA political structure."

"Continue to be groomed?" Diana almost whispered.

"Surely you recognize that your careers have been extraordinary in many ways — in fact, from the very beginning. And, you've been given many tests along the way. I'm not alone in your consideration either. You both have a destiny of leadership. You've exhibited your skills and loyalty to the United Authority. You have been carefully guided to where you both are today. My only question is — are you ready for the next level?"

"Until now, Klaud, I had never given it any thought."

"Nor have I." Diana added.

"I'll be blunt. Yes? Or no."

"Based on what I'm hearing now and what I've experienced, especially the past couple of days, I would be a fool to say no."

Diana agreed even though her desire had been mostly heightened after Austin's return from The Springs and his enthusiastic revelations. She, not unlike Austin, had always seemed to just take their rather rapid promotions in stride over the previous years. But, at the same time, she couldn't help but remember their conversation while walking on the beach only a couple of days before. And her enthusiasm was somewhat tempered by the nagging skepticism that Austin seemed to have lost.

"Good. Now, to get to that next level you will have to continue to perform, of course, as you have in the past with the same level of competence and dedication. In addition, you will be required to better understand the principles of politics and The Octadic Tenets of the UA."

* * * * * *

Once again, Alfredo seemed to appear from nowhere. He stood patiently waiting for the table to be cleared, cleaned, and the bus boys to walk away.

"Sir Director, I trust everything was to your approval this evening?"

"Alfredo, The Crystal has outdone itself once again, — as have you. "

"Wonderful. I will relay your kind message to the kitchen. Would you care to see the dessert tray this evening?"

"How about it, you two? Shall we indulge a tad more?"

Diana looked at Austin with an accepting smile. Austin glanced at Klaud and straight to Alfredo.

"What do you have in the way of chocolate?"

"I recommend our signature Death by Chocolate, sir!"

"Fine. Make it three, Alfredo. And we'll have a couple of your best Cubans. Diana, do you smoke?"

She looked directly at Alfredo.

"Yes. Alfredo, would you happen to have an organic Kona Gold Cannabis?"

"Of course, madam."

"Thank you, Alfredo."

"And Alfredo, we would all enjoy a nice KORBEL V.S.O.P. Gold Reserve Brandy," Klaud added, "In fact, bring the bottle."

"Right away, Sir Director."

Alfredo turned and seemed to disappear once again.

"Now where were we?" Klaud continued. "Ah yes, your continuing education for the evening — The Octadic Tenets of the UA. I have prepared these cards for you two." He reached into his jacket pocket and handed them over the table.

Austin and Diana each seriously studied their small card. Printed in black ink on white linen stock — they read:

The Octadic Tenets of the UA

#1 *Universalism*
#2 *Harmony*
#3 *Collectivism*
#4 *Dispassion*

#5	*Egalitarianism*
#6	*Authority Correctness*
#7	*Moral relativism*
#8	*Societal tolerance*

"You may keep those. Carry them with you. Study them until you know them by heart, and can recite the tenets in your sleep. The Octadic Tenets of the UA is the foundation of the 'Change' that President Gates has used to rebuild our great union. We must all deeply believe in their absolute truths. And we must hold these truths as self-evident."

"That Universalism is something that should be applied throughout the *entire* universe. Any and all property, which is distinguished from a particular individual, can and should be possessed in common."

"That Harmony must be maintained at all costs in accordance with a consistent, orderly and pleasing assurance of safety and security."

"That Collectivism will maintain the foundation of centralized social and economic control, especially pertaining to all means of production."

"That Dispassion is advocated throughout the United Authority promoting a constant emotionally uninvolved populace."

"That Egalitarianism must be encouraged and nurtured as the fundamental truth in the equality of all Citizens."

"That Political, rather Authority Correctness is the fairness that all Citizens respect their fellow Citizens regardless of race, gender, sexual affinity, or ecology."

"Moral Relativism holds that there be no absolute, concrete rights and wrongs — rather, intrinsic ethical judgments existing as abstract, differing for each perception of an ethical outlook."

"And, that Societal Tolerance will stimulate more of a fair, objective, and permissive attitude or understanding toward those whose opinions may differ slightly from what some might consider the accepted truth." Akakios recited the Tenets in order, without hesitation and without looking at a card. They were ingrained in his memory from the very day he crafted them for Gates decades earlier. "If you fully understand and believe these tenets, you will place yourself into a high position of leadership — and all of the justified rewards it brings you."

Akakios picked up his brandy and held it out to the couple.

"Will you join me in a salute to the United Authority?"

Although Austin and Diana were spellbound and almost speechless, they managed to hold up their snifters in front of them. They all inhaled the sweet yet pungent fragrance as they sipped the nectar of the gods.

Durango

9

"The price of anything is the amount of life you exchange for it." — Henry David Thoreau

* * * * * *

At an elevation of just over 6,500 feet above sea level, the small mountain town of Durango, Colorado was much the same as it had been for the past two hundred years. It's location in the lower Animas River Valley, close to the southwestern corner of the state, made it as out of the way as so many of the other small mountain towns in this state.

Some of the area's earliest inhabitants were the Anasazi, or "Ancient Ones" — a rather large Indian civilization, for it's time, which built their complex homes high in the overhanging cliffs and caves. The wide, deep openings into the mountainsides were favored building sites for simple shelters to the more complex and multi-room adobe structures. Each was tucked away, protected from the elements and predators. Archaeologists still debate when this distinct culture appeared, but the consensus suggests their emergence around 1200 BC, during the archaeologically designated Basketmaker Era. It is not entirely clear why these Ancestral Puebloans may have migrated from their established homes in the 12th and 13th centuries. These "cliff dwellers," as they came to be known, had mysteriously disappeared from the area more than a thousand years earlier. Factors examined included: regional climate change, prolonged periods of drought, de-forestation, or possibly hostility from new arrivals. Their intricate cliff constructions survived. Several hundred years after the departure of the Anasazi, the Navajo, Apache, Ute, and Ute Mountain Ute tribes began to flourish on the surrounding mesas and valleys due to the area's climate, abundant fresh water and wildlife.

Because of its bountiful natural resources and secluded location, the area also became the perfect hideout for some of the most famous desperados and bandits of the "Old West" period of the United States. The most infamous of the bunch was the Dalton gang who ended their nefarious careers becoming respected ranchers in the rich Animas Valley just a few miles north of the city.

The city of Durango itself was founded in the late 1800s as a mining support community, supplying food, coal, building materials, houses of ill repute and other staples to the gold and silver miners in the surrounding La Plata mountains and San Juan Range of the Rocky Mountains. Much of the ore was transported by the narrow gauge railroad from the mountain mines to the large smelting operation at the base of Smelter Mountain just south of town. Many years after the mines played out, the city prospered as a result of the numerous farms and ranches established in the late eighteen hundreds and early twentieth century.

In the later part of the twentieth century, Durango had become a popular four-season tourist destination known mostly for it's scenic beauty, narrow gauge railroad, downhill skiing, mountain biking, hunting, and fishing.

The town's population fluctuated very little over the previous couple hundred years to its current 9,600 Citizens or so, which was about average for the little town. No one ever bothered counting the Plebeians — there were few. They came and went with the seasons — some died, others simply disappeared. But then, it had always been that way.

Zander was one of those — he was also one of them. The Citizens thought of him as a native to the area, even though he was a Plebe, because it seemed that he had always been there — at least for as long as anyone could remember. No one knew where he lived or much cared. In many ways he was just another hopeless Plebeian who wandered the streets and occasionally asking for a handout of food or clothing. His short white beard was always neatly trimmed even though his clothes were tattered — he seemed to like it that way.

Zander differed from the other Plebeians in many ways. He was everybody's friend in that he seemed to know everyone's name. He always had a smile on his face and appeared to be in the peak of health. An old character that everyone liked, and many town folk seemed to think was just a little smarter than he let on.

* * * * * *

The air was Rocky Mountain crisp at nine that morning. Although it hadn't snowed for a couple of weeks, there were still piles of the white ice on the north sides of the buildings downtown. The sky was a perfectly deep Colorado blue and there wasn't even the hint of a breeze.

Zander had wandered into town about a half-hour earlier taking his usual, morning stroll down Main Street. He stopped just outside the door of the Durango Coca-Coffee Café for a few minutes blowing warm air into his hands and rubbing them together. Trying to keep the chill off, not withstanding, and the current state of the country, he couldn't help but count his blessings. There were few places on earth he'd rather be — and he'd been to many. Not long after he arrived at the cafe, Sam Dalton walked out. He was carrying two steaming cups of brew — one for him and one for Zander. Dalton was a local rancher. And he too was an old timer — a Citizen who wasn't required to relocate to one of the forced retirement communities due to his exempted profession.

"Mornin' Zander. A tad bit nippy this mornin'." He handed a hot cup to Zander.

"And top of the mornin' to you too, Sam. Thanks for the brew." He said as he carefully pored the steaming coffee into his thermos.

"I see your still sportin' that cowboy hat I gave you."

"Yep — it keeps the weather off, I guess. Headed back to the ranch?"

"Not for a while. Naw, I'm goin' over to the Central Bank to straighten out my account again. Sold a calf a couple of days ago for $1,000 Credits, and those idiots credited my account for $10,000 Credits." They slowly began to walk down the sidewalk, just a couple of blocks towards the Central Bank building. "Didn't even know there was a problem till I paid for my breakfast this mornin'. I'll probably spend more time and energy takin' care of this bank problem today than fixn' the north fence line this afternoon."

"No doubt. Need any help with the fence?"

"Thanks, Zander. I just might take you up on that, my friend. I've got about a hundred yards that got washed out a couple of days ago. Most likely I'll get several hombres to help out — what they call Plebes these days."

"Well it's mud season after all. Spring run off sure can make a mess of things."

"Yep — mother nature and, well, of course the government could screw up a wet dream."

"Now there's a couple of topics we could spend the next few days talkin' about." Zander grinned.

"No doubt. Speakin' of which, what's the weather going to do this weekend?

"Now, Sam, you know the only two people who say they can predict the weather in the mountains are new comers and fools — I'm neither."

They both laughed as Sam opened the bank door.

"I'll try and catch up with you before I leave town."

"And I'll be watchin' out for ya, Sam."

* * * * * *

Zander raised his cup as a salute and continued walking down Main. The remainder of his morning was spent wandering the streets and talking to anyone who would take the time to do so. There were so many topics he liked to talk about — fishing and hunting were his favorites; but then there was also the on-going small town gossip, tales of the 'old days,' catching up on current events and the weather. Every conversation included talk about the weather.

He eventually walked down to the river around lunchtime to check the rising level and throw a few small branches and stones into the rapids while quietly pondering. In a couple of months the river would rise to the top of its banks and create white-water caps three to four feet in the air — beautiful yet dangerous, and as loud as the constant roar of a jet turbine.

Today is a good day — a Colorado perfect day. He almost felt at peace sitting there on the small boulder, inhaling the fresh mountain air while listening to the rushing water. *If only it was a true peace.*

Sitting on the opposite side of the river from him were a couple of Plebeians who were fishing, no doubt for their lunch and maybe dinner too if they were lucky. Pan seared rainbow trout was one of Zander's favorites, and one of the many, many reasons he chose to live here in God's country.

He spent the bulk of the afternoon sitting on that rock, staring at the water and remembering how things used to be. The past wasn't perfect, but it was better than the current alternative. There had been a cultural, political and power evolution over his lifetime. His world had changed for the worse over the years and he wanted nothing more than to change it back — back more closely to the way it was — back to a reality of common sense, personal responsibility, honesty, and real personal freedoms. The failed ruling of the statists needed to end.

Zander was deep in thought that afternoon, pretty much like every day, planning the rest of his life. He still had a lot of things to do before it was over. Today was a good day to think about it.

The afternoon was short and the shadows were getting long. The sun was well below Perins Peak now and the temperature was dropping fast. It was time to walk back up to Main Avenue. He wanted to get to the Central Authority building on Second Avenue to watch the public Tel-Com and hear the President's speech at 5pm.

* * * * * *

Carey Dunstan and Gates were being driven in the Presidential golf cart through the tunnel maze beneath Cheyenne Mountain from the "White House" area to the UACNN studio complex. The two were more than satisfied with the press release and script that the Continuity Bureau had provided them. Virtually no edits were required. Gates had only added a few personal comments.

It was only mildly annoying to the two of them that neither the UA Safety Bureau nor the UA Protection Bureau had any substantive leads regarding the recent attacks. Fire investigators determined the cause of each explosion — that part was actually easy. Left behind at each location was the spent rocket cartridges. One of the major questions remaining was, where the hell they came from. But not a single witness or clue had been uncovered as to the source of the weapons or the identity of the perpetrators. There only seemed to be conspiracy rumors circulating about "The Wolf" and a mysterious group of renegades — but no hard evidence. Gates and Dunstan knew, however, that it would only be a matter of time. The combination of superior UA forces and the mistakes ultimately to be made by these renegades would eventually come together.

Both Gates and Dunstan were in good spirits anyway, despite the lack of progress. After all, they understood an earlier axiom; "You never want a good crisis to go to waste." It's an opportunity to do important things that you might otherwise avoid. They were well schooled in the principles of opportunity. Plus, they were looking forward to the evening's meal with friends, following tonight's broadcast — good friends, great food, powerful libations and UA Service Girls and Service Guys brought in from Vegas. The very thought brought heady, happy images to their minds — work hard and play hard. It was a motto that served them well.

During his ride to the studio, Gates couldn't help but think about how convenient information dissemination had become since the "Pulp Conservation Act" that he had signed into law a couple of decades prior. Plus there was the added "PCA" benefit of true UA budget savings. Several years later, the "Electronic Media - Fair Play and Consolidation Act" had also been signed into law. The result of those two acts in combination with the establishment of the UA Continuity Bureau, formerly known as the FCC, allowed for a much more unified stream of information.

Those who were in power, long understood that the bulk paper and publishing industries had been in decline since the turn of the twenty-first century. Newspapers, magazines and books were very old technology — obsolete. All of the Citizen's libraries, both public and private, could now be converted to digital media. Citizens appreciated this massive relief to their environment.

It was a colossal undertaking. Printed books and periodicals were slowly gathered and recycled into more practical paper goods. Plus the expense of maintaining a current digital library was much more cost effective — not to mention, many of the previous titles were no longer regarded to be in the Citizen's best interest, so they were simply eliminated.

Publications were conveniently and instantly available from all data ports and personal Tel-Com devises.

Over a short period of time, public libraries were consolidated into one central location in the new UA Capitol. It was restocked with digital editions that were first filtered through The UA Continuity Bureau for accuracy and Authority Correctness. There was no longer a need to maintain hundreds or even thousands of library buildings and staffs. Citizens were able to access all available titles from their homes, businesses and even their Tel-Cards electronically.

Most all Citizens cooperated with the "Pulp Conservation Act's" book drive. They fully appreciated the importance of recycling and conservation. After all, this would be good for the environment in so many ways. Everyone was invited to turn in their books for the digital replacement edition, when each edition became available to download; or instead, their Central Bank accounts could be issued Credits of a more or less equal value — Citizen's choice. Most simply chose Credits. It was more than fair, and in many of the Citizen's opinions it was a true win-win arrangement. Most had little time to read these days anyway. Of course, anyone caught after the turn-in date, with even a single printed edition, could be fined up to $1,000 Credits per book, and/or be sentenced up to five years in prison.

The "Electronic Media - Fair Play and Consolidation Act" was another bonanza for the

Citizens. Now, not only was all of their programming virtually free, everyone also received a large wall-screen Tel-Com Center for each room just by trading in their obsolete televisions, radios, and/or multi-media player units. There was only a small recycle-service fee to be paid for each unit. The small programming fee was equally shared by a slight one-percent increase to the Citizen's annual UA Contribution withholdings. This was more than fair and equitable compared to their previous monthly programming charges.

The decline of all commercial radio and television media had begun a decade or so after the publishing industries descent and ultimate failure. Their demise, not unlike that of the publishers, started as a gradual erosion of advertising sales. One by one all broadcast, cable and Internet companies were forced to consolidate, thereby increasing cost efficiencies and effectively creating operational economies of scale.

Eventually however, the cost of doing business was simply more than the three remaining communication behemoths could sustain. Rather than face bankruptcy and probable failure, the UA determined it was in the best interest of the Citizens to subsidize these companies. The President and his "EMFPCA" consolidated them with a massive bailout in 2065 for the public good.

* * * * * *

At promptly 5pm Mountain time, the UACNN main studio lights came up and cameras were switched on to a smiling President Gates.

"My good friends and loyal Citizens — good evening. As you are aware, a series of catastrophic events occurred at approximately 6am Eastern Authority Time on April 15th. Your United Authority, Regional and Central Authorities have since regained all services due to the diligent and tireless efforts of the UA Emergency crews."

"Initial investigations began within one-hour of the attacks by the combined efforts of the UA Safety Bureau's special investigators reporting to Director Hector Deimos and with the UA Protection Bureau's elite, regional strike forces reporting to Director General Gunther Borghild."

"Now, many Citizens have realized that the majority of these attacks were made on UA Contribution Bureau buildings. And, many have considered the irony of the attacks being made on April fifteenth. A date that a few may recall as previously associated with 'Tax Day.'"

Income tax day was a thing of the distant past. Since the digitizing of the monetary system, all taxes were automatically withheld from all income and electronically transferred to the UA Contribution Bureau as were other required Citizen fees to their appropriate Regional and Central Bureaus. Paying taxes was no longer an annual event; it was now a daily function.

"Sadly, I must report the real connection of the date and the subsequent targets was no coincidence. It has been determined that a small band of militant renegades known as Los Salvadores are responsible. I believe that these otherwise good, albeit misguided individuals are culpable. And, that these heinous attacks on you and your United Authority were for the purpose of a misguided tax rebellion. I say misguided because I know that the majority of Citizens share in the belief of equality. The majority of Citizens understand the need for shared wealth. And I know how each and every one of you not only approve of but have supported the 'Change' we've brought together."

"Make no mistake; our investigations will root out these individuals in short order. I can assure you that they will be brought to justice. Let me be clear, we will treat them with respect and rehabilitate them back into civil society."

"In addition, I promise you that there has been no financial risk to the United Authority as a result of their efforts. I can also assure you that this event will have no effect on your personal accounts either. The UA Contribution Bureau has worked hand-in-hand with the UA Central Bank to insure that all of the on-line systems are safe and functioning. Your Credits are safe."

"Of course in the unlikely event a Citizen notices a discrepancy in their personal or business account, it will be their personal responsibility to bring it to the attention of the Central Bank or UA Contribution Bureau."

"I can also assure you, that this administration has always had and will always have the best interests of its Citizens foremost in our considerations. And, as always, let me be clear, United Authority security and safety is your safety and security. It is the cornerstone of the 'Change' I promised you. This has been proven over many years by the peace, harmony and the equality our Citizens have enjoyed. Make no mistake; your United Authority will always remain vigilant in protecting you and the many privileges you enjoy."

As usual, Gates' mellifluous voice was calming and deliberate. His only deviation from Austin's script was the remaining forty-five minutes in which he interjected his many personal sacrifices and contributions to the whole of the United Authority. Finally he summarized his personal feelings in his final remarks.

"Make no mistake, I have proven through the last few years that this administration is capable of tackling our toughest challenges. We have made greater changes and progress than at any time in history. The wealth of the collective regions comprising the United Authority has been redistributed and shared equally among all Citizens as I promised."

"There is now but one class of Citizen. UA Citizens no longer require the former trappings of 'imagined success.' Citizens are now truly free to enjoy a stress free life. The 'Change' I promised has made a profound and positive difference in the lives of all Citizens. The status quo and societal divisions of the past will never return. There is no going back."

"And, I can personally assure you — we will prevail in short order, despite the misguided beliefs and efforts of any who would try to undermine our great United Authority."

"Good night, and rest assured — the United Authority will always be with you."

* * * * * *

Gates was right. This was a simpler time in many ways. Individual ingenuity, innovation or the amassing of personal wealth was no longer a measure of progress. Advancement as it had been measured in the later nineteenth century and through the twentieth century had all but ground to a halt within the first few decades of the twenty-first century. Time had all but frozen exploration, invention and entrepreneurship. Most incentives had been stripped away from people's desire to innovate and bring to market new ideas and concepts because of national isolationism, constricting regulation, heavy taxation, and reduced market forces.

* * * * * *

At the end of the President's speech, Zander stuck around for the free Coca-Coffee made available to those gathered at the Central Authority complex. He talked with a few of those gathered to get their reactions to the President's speech, and filled his thermos with hot Coca-Coffee for the long walk back up Wild Cat Canyon Road.

Most of those gathered had little to no opinion. They were only there because; well, because there simply wasn't anything else better to do — and to get their fill of the free coffee of course.

There was one young man; however, who stayed to chat with Zander after everyone else had left to find a relatively warm place to spend the night.

Young, Alfonso Sandalio was a Plebe who spent most of his time in Albuquerque, New Mexico. He occasionally ventured up to Durango after visiting with his Navajo friends in Northwestern New Mexico and to report to Zander.

"You've been very quiet tonight, Alfonso."

"Yes. Deep in thought, I suppose."

"Its good to see you again, mi amigo."

"You as well."

"Would you care to take a walk?"

"Let me fill my thermos first, Zander."

The two slowly ambled down Second Avenue toward the centuries old narrow gauge train station, stopping occasionally to take a sip so as not to burn their lips on the steaming liquid.

"Did you have a good trip from Albuquerque?"

"No difficulties."

"And our friends on the reservation?"

"They are well and send their regards. Peter Begay said that Esdzanadkhi spoke to him in a dream. He's worried about the future." Peter Begay was a Navajo elder — one of several tribal leaders and the head of his clan. Although Navajos, like the other Native Americans on reservations were considered Plebeians; however, they were also treated to a unique form of citizenship. Their unique affiliation with the UA offered them the same advantages of those granted to farmers and ranchers, including limited educational and medical privileges. Their reservations remained sovereign nations.

"Is this dream something I need to know about soon?"

"I think not."

"Still, I must get down that way in the near future."

"They all would like to see you, Zander."

"Have you finished writing Act Two of our play, Alfonso?"

"Most of the code is composed."

"No problems?"

"None that can't be worked out."

"And the Houston and Albuquerque access for the production?"

"I should have access to the facilities within a few days. Have you decided on a production date, Zander?"

"Would Cinco de Mayo be possible?"

Alfonso laughed. "The United Authority will not be celebrating."

"No. I think not. But, Los Salvadores will have reason to."

"Sometimes I think your name should be Sandalio, Zander."

"Oh — but it is my friend."

"True — El Lobo y el Sandalio. I noticed that our friend in the White House decided not to credit you in his speech tonight."

"True — He may be saving me for a special occasion."

"When they catch you?"

"Maybe — or maybe if they kill me — whichever comes first?"

"I'll pray that neither happens."

"Thank you my friend. I do the same on a regular basis."

They stopped walking in front of the almost two hundred year old train station and Zander put his hand on Alfonso's shoulder.

"It was good seeing you tonight. Good luck with our next act. Are you leaving town tonight?"

"I will. My ride will be waiting for me somewhere south of town on the highway."

"Is Michael Begay driving you, back to the Navajo reservation?"

"Yep."

"He still driving that beat up, old Ford pickup that belonged to his father?"

"Yep — same one."

"Good for him. Tell him, Yah-Ta-Hey!"

* * * * * *

Zander was deep in thought that evening as he slowly walked west of town on Highway 160. But just before he made it to the Wildcat Canyon Road intersection, a Central Authority cruiser stopped him.

All he could think of was, *Thank God he stopped me before I reached the intersection.* There was nothing more vital than maintaining the complete secrecy of his secluded retreat.

"Evenin' officer."

"Zander! What in creation are you doing walking down the highway at this time of night?"

"Nice night for a walk — don't you think, Officer Baker?"

"Are you crazy? It's damn cold out."

"Maybe a little crazy, but I've got my thermos. And that's all I need." He held it up for the officer to see. "Besides, I was about to turn around and walk back to town anyway."

"Well, I shouldn't, but hop in and I'll drive you back."

"Thank you sir, but I'm enjoying the walk. It's only twenty minutes or so back to town."

"Fine. Have it your way. But, you take it easy old-timer. I don't want to cruise by on patrol tomorrow morning and find you laying like road kill on the side of the highway."

"No sir. You can count on that. I'm headed back now. Right now as a matter of fact."

* * * * * *

With that, Zander turned and began walking back towards town. Once the cruiser was out of sight, he turned again and headed back to Wildcat Canyon.

About half way up the canyon road, Zander came to an unobtrusive steel gate. He reached in his pocket and pulled out a small chain with two keys — one for the gate and the other for his home.

Most people had forgotten about the old Breen Ranch. It wasn't that large — about a hundred acres or so. You couldn't see the ranch house from the road due to the thick scrub oaks, underbrush and winding gravel road fifty yards back.

Zander had purchased the ranch forty plus years earlier in the name of Tucker Breen. The ranch was a natural choice due to its seclusion and the small abandoned coalmine on a south-facing hill. He had spent the first two years building a concrete and steel bunker twenty yards into the mine with the construction and material help of his Navajo friends out of Shiprock, New Mexico. It had all of the comforts of home — state of the art power and ventilation systems, fresh water well, galley, large storage area, library, bedroom and an ingenious bath and waste system. He tunneled a short entryway with a well-concealed and camouflaged door. Once construction was completed, he caved in the mine's original portal.

No one in Durango had ever met Tucker. But that wasn't unusual. Many ranch properties were bought and sold in the area through brokers back in those days, and most people never knew who the sometimes-absentee owners were. But, Durango was a small town after all — and gossip was a past time in most small towns. Zander used this to his advantage by leaking the story about an old rancher from the "Front Range" of Colorado by the name of Tucker Breen.

Tucker's story had morphed over the first few years. But the few who talked about it simply believed him to be a widower and recluse. At some point, it was thought that Tucker Breen had simply passed away a few years after purchasing the ranch — yet another part of the story that Zander had carefully leaked to the town gossips.

In reality, Zander hired a tribal law firm as trustees of a perpetually funded Trust in the name of Tucker Breen. It was said that Tucker passed away shortly thereafter. He had become the legend of a legend.

Settled in for the night, Zander once again began his thought process. *Now, where was I? Oh yes, Act Three. There's nothing like a cold night, fresh mountain air and a long walk to stimulate one's imagination.*

Paradox

10

"Achievement of your happiness is the only moral purpose of your life, and that happiness, not pain or mindless self-indulgence, is the proof of your moral integrity, since it is the proof and the result of your loyalty to the achievement of your values." — Ayn Rand

* * * * * *

"Austin — please believe me. I'm enjoying our new-found success as much as you are." *If you only knew just how much I'm savoring the changes.* Diana wasn't feeling the least amount of guilt. Her emotions were high. At the same time she was torn with the nagging logic deep within her soul.

"I know you are — *we* are. That's the only point I was trying to make. We *should* enjoy a little."

"I understand, Austin . . ."

"Yet, I can hear it in your voice, Diana. It's, I understand — but!"

"Yes. But."

"But *what*?"

"It's just that — well — Even though I'm *feeling* wonderful, I just don't think we should completely forget about our talk on the beach, that's all."

"Diana!" Austin said in a whisper, "Not here. Not now."

"OK. I get it. Austin — I love you. You know that."

"I do too. Of course, I love you. That's why we should relax a little — enjoy a little. Sure I remember how things were. I still see everyone around us very clearly. You don't have to worry. I won't forget. Everything hasn't changed — just us. I mean, just our situation." He understood that the very aspect of being unable to speak freely in their own condo was symptomatic of the doubts they both shared about the United Authority and society as a whole.

"So you're not completely closed minded about a discussion? About the idea of taking . . ."

"Diana! *Please.*"

"Austin! If you would just let me finish!"

"Sorry."

"I would like to further our previous conversation in the near future. We haven't had another walk on the beach since before . . ."

"You're so right. We haven't. We should. We will. It's just that we've both been so busy." *If only you knew. If only we had more time to talk openly.* No one had the ability to discuss, to any degree of frankness, the details of issues they faced while working for the UA. Monitoring was random but omnipresent. It was inacceptable to complain or criticize any aspect of ones government — especially if they were your employer.

"I understand, Austin. And it has definitely taken more of your time getting reorganized with the new Continuity building and such. Promise me."

"I do. Look — why don't we make a weekend date. We both have put in the extra hours these past couple of weeks. We deserve a little more time together."

"Sure. A date. We can talk — relax — maybe play a little!" She said with a seductive smile. "We can mix a little personal business with a little — um — how about a *lot* of personal pleasure?"

"Agreed." He smiled and gently kissed her lips. "Sealed with a kiss."

"This weekend?"

"This weekend it is — a long weekend. How bout we start with a romantic dinner Friday night at Chez Zee's on the pier?"

"Oh yes!"

"After all, we can afford it now."

"Perfect. And then?" she said playfully.

"And then, maybe a drive Saturday morning to Newport Beach."

"Oh yes, yes."

"We can rent a sailboat for the day and take lunch on the water."

"I'm loving it!"

"Afterwards, a romantic dinner and evening at the Balboa Bay Resort?"

"Austin, we could be really decadent and have Sunday breakfast in bed."

"I like it — followed by, a very long walk on the beach."

"I accept." She said breathlessly as she wrapped her arms around him.

* * * * * *

At the very top, on the 32nd floor, Austin sat behind his immense new executive desk looking out over the Pacific. East Ocean Boulevard in Long Beach, California was an ideal location for the new UA Continuity Headquarters. He wasn't quite sure how Klaud had swung the deal. Whatever strings he had pulled had gotten the job done though, and in record time. He picked up his fresh cup of Kona-Coca-Coffee, tilted his chair back, placed his heals up to the edge of his desk and sighed. *Equality is a wonderful concept. A little extra equality is even better.*

* * * * * *

The new building wasn't as convenient from his condo as the former location in Redondo Beach, but the extra drive time was a small sacrifice — not to mention a quite enjoyable drive in his brand new Mercedes-Benz SL 9.5-SD. He was pleased that the UA had nationalized the Mercedes plant in Alabama a number of years previously. New car aside, he was considering the purchase of a new condo any way, or possibly a home in Palos Verdes. That would put him a little closer to Long Beach. They could use the extra room now that he and Diana were body-mates and living together. *After all, it was time to start investing more. Life is good.* He put away his doubts about the future — at least for the time being. For the first time in his life he had more than enough Credits than he needed to just barely get by on. He actually had plenty left over at the end of the month. There was even a Central Bank Line of Credits available to him, making it possible to actually budget sizable investments and purchases. Change was nice. Not to mention, his headaches were mostly few and far between as well.

* * * * * *

"Austin. We need to meet." Klaud barked through Austin's Desk-Com.

Amazingly, even the intensity of a 'Klaud headache' was a much lower magnitude these days.

"I'm on my way."

Austin walked by his new assistant, Katy, and mentioned without stopping that he would be in the Director's office if needed. A few short steps down the hall, he sailed past Randi's desk and pressed his thumb on the door lock sensor.

"And good morning to you to — Austin." She said to his back.

"Sorry. Guess I'm a little preoccupied."

* * * * * *

Randi smiled at Austin's backside as the Director's door slid closed behind him. She understood very well. This was her sixth year with Director Akakios. She had met him in the sixth year of her first career selling real estate. There had been a number of buyers like Klaud during that period — smart, demanding, rude, crude, egotistical, loud, and of course with the means to buy. They were all in top-level positions either in major industry or within the upper level of the UA.

A couple of her many successful attributes, not withstanding her rather voluptuous appearance, were her innate sales abilities and a complete understanding of this autocratic personality type. To be successful in sales one is required to have but a few basic proficiencies: adequate product knowledge, a thorough understanding of the market, an almost intuitive reading of the prospect's desires, and the grasp of how to close the sale. But what set her apart as a top performer from those who were less successful was her special skill — knowing how to *position* ones self when asking for the order followed by the ultimate and *intimately* persuasive close. Randi was a pro.

After selling Director Akakios his new home in Rancho Palos Verdes, he was more than persuaded that her adroitness would be of great benefit to the UA Continuity Bureau. She agreed to his offer and negotiated a new condo in Hermosa Beach as a signing bonus for her new position. It was a win-win for them both. Akakios merely buried the purchase price of her entire, new condo complex into his annual capital expense budget. The UA purchased the property in her name, and she and the Director agreed to split the rental income from the four attached condos equally.

Randi was keenly aware that when the Director retired, she would be out of a job and a little to old to start all over. The best she could hope for would be a free and clear condo, some rental income and a much lesser UA Citizen position to help make ends meet until she reached her mandatory retirement age. However, by selling her property, she would be afforded a much more luxurious retirement condo in a Cabo San Lucas Retirement Community when the time came. Life would still be good.

What Randi didn't understand was her peers, the few neighbors she had met through the years and her friends. None of them ever seemed motivated. Unlike her, they lacked any ambition or resourcefulness. She couldn't understand why they all seemed to be satisfied with a mere subsistence. It seemed that their pedestrian existence was their only common denominator.

Why weren't Citizens motivated like herself? How could Citizens not aspire for more from their banal lives? It was true that no one starved. There was always plenty of food available, albeit not much in the way of variety — staples could usually be found. There was an abundance of "Value-Fast" restaurants to choose from. Citizens never had to worry about having a place to live, although the vast majority of residences weren't always in the best of condition or location. Most Citizens didn't have personal transportation, but that wasn't necessary because public transportation was abundant, at least when it was operational. And all Citizens received free medical care in a more or less timely fashion. But to her, it seemed to be a pacified existence — every day bled into the next. It was beyond her comprehension. Randi had always had a burning desire for more — for the better things in life.

* * * * * *

"Austin — I just got off my secure Tel-Card with Carey Dunstan and the President. Dunstan will be calling your office in about an hour."

"New information?"

"Right. They have fresh intel and want you to craft a press release to all media outlets — post haste. The Springs will handle any video but they will wait for our scripts. Needless to say, run your draft back to Dunstan before final release."

"Have arrests been made?"

"Not exactly. I didn't get all of the details, but there has been a significant new development. I would like to read the final draft before you release it though."

"Of course."

"How did the department head meetings go this morning? Are we back under control?"

"We're running at about ninety percent, Klaud. I think all of the new logistics will be worked out by the end of the month — certainly no later than the first week in May."

"Good. Anything you need from me — just let me know."

"Got it."

"No more setbacks! And we need to setup a budget meeting with all of the department heads. We are barely into the second quarter and seventy-two percent of our annual budget is blown!"

"Klaud — I didn't blow up our old building!"

"Careful, Austin."

"OK. Look. I have crews running practically around the clock. That's a lot of overtime pulled from the budget. You know I'm putting in eighteen hours every day myself — with no extra compensation."

"You and I don't require overtime pay. Our extra compensation comes from our position and stature within the UA. No more overtime pay for the staff until we get back on budget. Our people have to understand that a team effort has to be made to stay in budget."

"Great. I'm not sure . . ."

"What's there to be sure about?"

Austin paused and rubbed his forehead for a moment. "Klaud, how do you suggest we get people motivated to work extra hours for less pay?"

"Organize a 'team building' function. In fact, get your managers to 'buy-in' to a 'team building Saturday.' Get the staff's involvement. Build up their team spirit and devotion to making a contribution to the Bureau. Let them know that their efforts will be recorded, remembered and valued for their futures," Klaud thought for a moment, "if that doesn't work — replace them. Get on it right away."

"Right — even more hours with less pay. Is this really an emergency?"

"Perfect. Austin, you're a genius. An emergency — less pay for the cause — I like it."

"Klaud — you think that's perfect?"

"You bet. That's why you're here and they're down there." He said, while boldly pointing his index finger to the floor. "You said, extra emergency hours for less pay. I'll post a memo that due to the current UA emergency, all personnel will be required to not only put in an extra four hours every day, with no additional pay; but, there will be a temporary ten-percent pay cut through the remainder of the quarter. I'll call it our 'Patriotic-Continuity Emergency Contribution Plan.'"

"This is not going to go over very well. I mean there could be some serious repercussions from this if we don't . . ."

"This is the UA, Austin. As I said, those who don't like it can certainly take the option to leave. I'm sure they will find some other kind of employment out there."

"Not likely — and definitely not in their own field."

"Well then, that will be their choice — won't it? A new graduating class will be knocking on our doors next month, anyway. They will be eager to get positions. Hell, we may even be able to pay them less than those leaving the Bureau."

"Klaud, I don't think the UA Writer's Union will go along with this."

"Leave the union to me. That's my responsibility."

"OK. I'll do my best. But this isn't going to be easy."

"Be that as it may — we've got to get back on schedule. And we definitely have to get back on budget. And *that*, young-man, is *your* responsibility. Make up for the down time — get us back on budget. Remember Austin, nothing worthwhile in life comes easy."

"Got it, Klaud — nothing easy." *It seems I remember my father telling me that another lifetime ago.*

"Set up that meeting for tomorrow morning. I want your report by noon."

Akakios had always run from hot to cold and back to hot in flashes — flashes that would run from one of Austin's temples to the other and back again like rolling thunder.

"I want to take a vacation in a couple of weeks. The Bureau has to be running at one-hundred percent or better before I leave."

"Got it, Klaud. But, hold off on putting that memo out. Let me work out the timing on this plan."

"Fine. Just get it done. How's Diana?"

"She's well and looking forward to this weekend. Our first romantic get-away."

"I'm sure she is. You two deserve a treat. You both work hard. I spoke to Director Benton the other day and told him to take good care of that young lady or I would offer her a position over here with us."

"And?"

"And he said he was getting ready to promote her to the position of Vice Director of UACNN."

"You're joking."

"No — of course not. I recommended her for the position. Let her tell you though. We wouldn't want to ruin her surprise — would we?"

"Right. Thanks for your help, Klaud."

"Austin, it's like the President said, 'we're all friends now.'"

* * * * * *

On his way out and as Austin approached Randi's desk, Klaud blared over her Desk-Com.

"Randi! I've got a memo to get out before lunch. I'll need your talent in my office to help me with the finer points."

"Yes sir. Right a way, sir."

"And Randi."

"Yes, Director?"

"Clear my afternoon schedule. I have a very important meeting in Palm Springs this afternoon with at least eighteen holes."

"I'll be right in, sir." She smiled at Austin as she rose from her chair and straightened her skin tight, silk uniform. "Hello again, Austin. Will you be attending the Director's important eighteen-holes-meeting this afternoon?"

"Rhetorical question — right?"

"Maybe a little rhetorical — maybe a little sarcastic."

"Randi — you're worth a million Credits."

"Yes. I know, Austin." She smiled while continuing to adjust the lower area of her dress.

Walking back to his office, Austin couldn't help but wonder how he was going to make Klaud's plan work? He also couldn't help wondering if he was going to get the same pay cut as the rest of the staff.

"Will you be going out for lunch today, sir?" Katy asked as Austin approached her desk.

"No. Not today. Too much to do."

"Shall I bring you something, sir?"

Austin was still having a hard time getting use to being called sir. It made him feel older. In fact, a number of things in his life were aging his thinking these days.

"No. Really — I'll be fine. I have an important call from the White House in a few minutes and I don't wish to be disturbed for the rest of the day — well except for an emergency — and, well, you know, should the Director need me of course."

"It's not good."

"Pardon?"

"It's not good to miss your lunch and work so many hours on an empty stomach."

"OK. I know. What would you suggest?"

"A deli sandwich or some fresh Sushi maybe?"

"Great. Fine. Call down to Maki and give them my card number. Just stop by on your way back after your lunch."

"Perfect. I understand the Director will be out this afternoon, sir."

"How did you find that out so . . .?"

"I can't reveal my sources."

"Right."

"So, I thought I could treat you to a little mid-afternoon dessert in your office later today."

"Katy?"

"Yes sir?"

"Just go to lunch — now."

"Very well. Just let me know if you change your mind."

As Katy walked down the hall, Austin entered his office, slumped into his executive chair, put his aching head in his hands and thought to himself, *UN-believable!*

* * * * * *

Carey Dunstan pressed the disconnect button on his secure Desk-Com after spending the better part of an hour with Austin. He stood and stretched for a few seconds, poured himself a healthy single malt scotch on the rocks and walked into the President's office. Dunstan held his glass of scotch up as to salute the President and smiled. "What do you think, Bill? Were you listening?"

"I heard enough."

"Is he our boy or not?"

"Carey, I've agreed with you since our first meeting with him. Like I've been saying, he's one of us — and he doesn't even know it."

"Not yet?"

"No. Not yet — but soon," Gates took a slow sip of his second single malt for the morning.

"And her too," Dunstan smiled.

"We get a pair. Sometimes ya get lucky, pal."

"Luck has little to do with it, Mr. President."

"That's the way we play the game, now isn't it, Carey?"

"What do you think Akakios will say when we tell him?"

"Fuck Klaud. He'll get over it. He's retiring in five years anyway."

"True."

"Austin will be here at the White House for a few years, then we'll move him back in time to take over the Continuity Bureau. He'll be groomed for that and our next project too." *And Klaud isn't even in the loop on that one.* Gates had been able to keep a tight lid on this formidable project for many years. No leaks and on a need to know basis only.

"Speaking of which, real progress is being made in the research department on the project. There were a few areas where . . ."

"Good. When do the human trials begin?" Gates interrupted.

"They think another week with the chimps and then they can begin with a control group of Plebes. That could take another six months or so — no more than a year tops."

"That should give us enough time to plan the logistics of a roll out. Carey, I would like for you to plan a trip to Austin, Texas — maybe next week. Let's make it a surprise inspection of the lab."

"I still think that we should consider initializing the roll-out with all military personnel — I mean the Protection Bureau."

"Maybe. We need to put more thought into it though. As we get closer, we'll assemble the board of directors and apply some Game Theory to several models. But it does seem logical at this time to have the complete military 'buy-in' before we incorporate the Citizen population at large."

"Agreed. What's for lunch?"

* * * * * *

It had been the week from hell for Austin. Morale was at an all time low at the Bureau — just when he needed the opposite more than ever. He was able to get the verbal buy-in from his department heads on Klaud's "Patriotic-Continuity Emergency Contribution Plan." But it didn't take a UA Mind Reader to know the truth of how his staff really felt about it. And somehow, Klaud was able to convince the UA Writer's Union to go along with his plan — Austin could only imagine how. In fact, this was one of the many things he needed to learn if he would someday take over the Bureau. Klaud seemed to hold certain magic beyond the Bureau. Maybe these techniques would be revealed in the one-on-ones Klaud spoke of having with him in the near future.

Be that as it may, the week was finally over and he was ready to relax. Driving up the PCH from Long Beach, he would try to clear his mind as best he could and make an effort to fully enjoy his weekend retreat with Diana. He only needed to make a couple of stops before picking her up at the condo.

* * * * * *

"Roses! Austin! And a bottle of Champagne?"
"What better way to begin our weekend?"

He was barely able to place the gifts on the entry table as she threw her arms around his neck. This would be a special weekend in many regards. She thought of it as a Honeymoon of sorts. Most Citizens were unable to take additional time off for this antediluvian practice. One week per year was the approved vacation, plus a few sick days. Only UA Level-10 and above earned a full two weeks.

"This means more to me than you'll ever know."

"Oh — I think I have a pretty good idea. Are you packed and ready?"

"Right here," she grinned while producing a tiny silk pouch.

"That's it? This little bag?"

"It's all I need. Sometimes — less is best," she smiled.

* * * * * *

After a superb four-course meal on the pier, they spent a mostly quiet drive south down the PCH to Newport Beach. Soothing music was playing softly in Austin's new Mercedes. They enjoyed the private time together with the soft sounds from the UA's New Jazz station. Driving out of Long Beach, Diana couldn't hold it any longer.

"I'm glad we decided to drive to Newport tonight rather than waiting until tomorrow morning. There is going to be even more for us to celebrate. I have an announcement to make."

"Good news I hope."

"I think so." She said coyly. "I was promoted today."

"You what?"

"Promoted. I'm now the Vice Director of the UACNN. Can you believe it?"

"Fantastic! Great timing. I am very proud of you. You're right. Now we truly have even more reason to celebrate this weekend. Congratulations Diana. I know you deserve it."

"Truthfully — I was shocked."

"You're being modest."

"No — not at all. It came completely out of the blue. No clue at all."

"Makes you feel good, doesn't it?"

"Sure. It also gives me an odd feeling."

"Don't be silly. Enjoy. Right now, our happiness is our highest purpose. We've worked hard and we both deserve the fruit."

There was no conversation for the remainder of the drive. Austin and Diana were each consumed in a myriad of thoughts — some were dream like, a few concerns, plus fresh emotions that would spill over them for the remainder of their weekend.

They would officially be considered "body-mates" now. Each glowed in the warmth of affection that neither had ever known before. They were inspired by a new elation, a joy; a passion unlike their imaginations could prepare them.

A short moonlight walk on the sand felt needed following their romantic four-course meal. It was a cool evening, and they decided a nightcap or two in the Balboa hot tub under the stars would refresh them for an evening's finale in their suite.

Austin awoke first Saturday morning. He rolled over and could only stare at his beautiful "body-mate." Diana was truly a dream come true. She slowly opened her eyes with the sensation of someone watching her.

"Good morning." She said sleepily. "Are we going for brunch now? I'm strangely hungry."

"Gee. I wonder why?" He laughed.

"And then sailing?"

"That's the plan."

"Austin — how decadent."

"We have been — haven't we?"

It was a perfect California day to be on the water — a cool 66-degrees, a brisk ocean breeze and the rhythmic roll of the breakers as they launched their O'Day Sailor.

* * * * * *

Their day of sailing, gourmet dinner afterwards, and playful antics in the luxury suite Saturday night tranquilized them into a deep and peaceful slumber. Upon awaking Sunday morning and after a brief period of disorientation, they savored a leisure breakfast in bed.

"I may never eat again — ever," Diana sighed as she reached for Austin's hand.

"And I may never get out of this bed," he laughed.

"I think we both need that morning walk on the beach we talked about."

Both were reenergized following a frisky half hour dessert in bed, followed by as many minutes of recreational shower time. Afterwards, they teased each other running in the sand to the seaside. The beach was quiet except for the sounds of the rolling breakers. They were alone but for the company of a few sandpipers and seagulls.

"Do you feel as satisfied as I do?"

Austin squeezed her hand as they walked close to the water's edge. "Yes. I do."

Diana stopped, turned and put her arms around Austin's neck. They embraced as two lovers, kissed, then continued their walk, holding hands and letting the cold sand squeeze between their toes with memories of the first time.

"Austin — I wish that life for us could be this way forever."

"But it can."

"I know it could. In so many ways, nothing would make my life more fulfilled. I'm truly happier than I ever dreamed I could be."

"I know how you feel because my life was hopelessly empty before you."

"Austin — that's what concerns me. It wasn't that long a go, we were regular Citizens just like everyone else. Remember our first walk on the beach. We had concerns about our future, but not just our future. Our anxiety was about what we felt our world had become. We had thoughts — maybe memories of a different time, a different world."

"Sure, I realize that I had become increasingly skeptical about life —my life, including some of my past. I guess in some ways I still feel that way. It's just that..."

"And you remember talking about so many people just going with the flow. You said there seems to be so much vacuity. People with so little emotion or motivation — people, that is, outside of the power elite. Austin — we are becoming the power elite."

"I guess you're right. We are."

"Well, they haven't changed — the people. Citizens are still in the quicksand of denial — as you put it. You said that it's as if people can't or won't fend off their paralyzing anxiety — provided they even have any anxiety. There are many who seem to be satisfied. But the others — many — it's as if they are resigned to the understanding that there's nothing they can do to change anything. It's as if everyone is just doing time, before they reach 60 and will be put in transports and sent to mandatory retirement camps. Do we even know what kind of existence that is? Does anyone really know until they arrive?"

"We only know from the promotional videos we've seen. Those camps don't look so bad. But what's wrong with aspiring for something better for us. Maybe this is our calling, Diana."

"Maybe. But I still remember. I still observe. I question so many wrongs that we are told are rights. Ninety-percent of the Citizen population are equal. They will never be nor have any more than their existence. We're on the verge of the upper ten-percent. Look at the difference. Austin, in the deep corners of my mind, I remember a different time."

"And I haven't forgotten — not completely. I'm not sure what to believe in anymore. I still have some belief in me — and you know I believe in you." He reached over and gave her a kiss on the cheek. "Can't we enjoy this for a little longer? We can still keep a healthy skepticism. Maybe we can help to make changes from our higher positions. Who knows, maybe there's something else.

"There is something else, Austin. I was waiting to tell you. I'm not entirely sure what it means though," she frowned and looked down at the sand.

Austin touched her chin and raised it to look into her eyes. "Maybe I will. Maybe I can help you understand."

"When I returned to our condo Friday afternoon, before you arrived, I noticed a small note on our door."

"And?"

"And, it seemed odd. It simply read, 'The Wolf is here and wants to meet with you.'"

"That's it?"

"Yes."

"Do you still have it?"

"I burned it."

"Good. I love you, too."

They walked silently, hand in hand for a while. Each had compelling thoughts and emotions running through their minds. Just as their previous walk on the beach, they shared common denominators. They walked in silence for more than a mile and watched the morning's transition as more Citizens, children and Plebeians began to occupy the beach. There was a feeling that they were living in two different worlds together. Their world had become a paradox. In so many ways they thought they were living in a parallel universe — a universe that had recently become even more complex.

Two Wolves

11

"There are things known and there are things unknown, and in between are the doors of perception." — Aldous Huxley

* * * * * *

Two weeks after the attacks on the UA, Alexander Conall began his more than eight hundred mile trek from Durango to LA at the break of day. He knew there would be little traffic on Sunday, April 30th. First he would spend the night in Shiprock and visit with his Navajo friends. On Monday or Tuesday he could catch a ride with Michael Begay to Gallup and catch a ride on the closest east-west rail line.

Conall knew he could count on Sam Dalton to get him to Shiprock. Dalton had been planning a trading trip down to the reservation for several weeks anyway. No sooner than the front gate was closed and locked, Conall walked a few yards up the narrow edge of Wildcat Canyon Road. Dalton's pickup squeaked to a stop beside him.

"Mornin' Zander! Have you been walking very long?" Dalton yelled out of his open window.

"Mornin' to ya, Sam. No — maybe fifteen, twenty minutes." Conall grinned while settling in his seat and closing the old pickup's rattling door.

"Stopped at the café on the way. Here's a cup of hot brew."

"Just what the doctor ordered. Thanks."

"Looks like my timing was pretty good." Dalton remarked as he pulled away.

"Couldn't have been better if we'd planned it that way." Conall grinned. *He has no idea just how close it was.*

They both laughed.

"Do you mind my asking what's in the back of the pickup?"

"Don't mind at all. I've been tradin' with the different tribes for as long as I can remember — my daddy before me — his daddy before him. It ain't no way to get rich, but it sure beats payin' taxes. This trip, I'm loaded down with a couple of dozen saddles I've collected over the years. Then I'll be takin' back as many sheep as they think those old saddles are worth. I hope to get at least a half dozen sheep or so for em'. Might even stay long enough to grab some Navajo chow."

"Guess I'll be eating some mutton stew tonight, or maybe a Navajo taco, myself."

"Spendin' the night in Shiprock — are ya?"

"Thinkin' about it."

"Mind my askin' where you're headin'?"

"To the coast for a while, Sam. I haven't seen the ocean in a long time."

"I never have — probably never will, Zander."

"It's big."

"So I've heard — but then so are the San Juans."

For the next hour and a half, the two old-timers talked about the "good old days." They reminisced about how things use to be, the changes in people's attitudes over the years, friends they had lost, and girls they had loved.

* * * * * *

Shiprock, New Mexico had taken on the appearance of a ghost town over the previous 50-plus years — not that its appearance had ever been one of a thriving city to begin with. Vandals, weather, the economy, neglect and time had all taken their toll on the town. It had reverted back to its roots — that of a high desert trading post. And there were but a few of those even left.

Dalton pulled up to and parked in front of the oldest surviving building in town, the Toh-Atin Trading Post. Conall thanked his friend for the ride, wished him a prosperous, healthy summer and began walking down a dusty reservation road to the west of town.

About five-miles from town he crossed a shallow arroyo to a small group of adobe houses or Hogan's. It was one of several clusters of the Begay Clan. The Hogan is considered sacred to the Navajo religion. The religious song "The Blessingway" describes the first Hogan as being built by "Coyote," with the help from beavers, to be a house for First Man, First Woman, and Talking God.

A low cloud of piñon smoke rose from their home's fire pits, lowly hovering over the small community. Conall never tired of the sweet smell of burning piñon. Children were running around the houses, laughing, chasing their dogs and visa-versa. A few sheep were mingling with chickens pecking the ground. He stood motionless for a few seconds visualizing a tableau that could have been from several centuries in the past — with the exception of the few pickup trucks parked beside their houses.

Conall approached the front door of the last Hogan, but before he could knock a voice called him from behind.

"No need to knock, my friend. My home is always open to you."

Peter Begay, the Clan's Elder, put his weathered arms around Conall and gave him a brother's hug.

"Peter. It's good to see you."

"It has been too long, Zander."

"True."

"I hear you have been very busy helping the people."

"I do what I can, Peter."

"Come inside. We must talk."

"How are the Diné people and the Begay Clan? Did your people have a good winter?"

"It was long and cold — but we have plenty — and you?"

"Peter — I'm getting tired."

"We worry about you. You carry the weight of another nation."

"I sometimes share your worry, Peter. But now isn't the time to talk of those concerns."

"You're right, my brother. We will celebrate your return to the nation. My wife is preparing our dinner — but first we will drink whiskey and speak of good times."

A couple of whiskies and an hour later, Margaret served them the traditional Navajo meal of mutton stew and frybread. They ate slowly and spoke of many joyful memories.

Peter reminded Conall of their first hunt together so many years earlier, not far from Mesa Verde. It was a good hunt. They had returned packing a large elk cow and a beautiful bobcat. The bobcat hide still decorated a wall inside his Hogan, displayed with other trophies from previous and later hunts. The elk hide was fashioned into a jacket for Margaret's fortieth birthday, and the meat was distributed and shared throughout the clan.

After dinner, Peter suggested the two should retreat to the sweat lodge for a smoke from the pipe and serious conversation.

"There has been much talk of the recent attacks on the government." Peter began. "They say it was a joyful and bloodless coup. This was a good beginning."

"It was only possible with your help, my friend."

"My brothers share our dreams."

"There is more work to do and plans are in motion for the next act."

"We are ready to help again, Zander."

"Thanks, Peter — but not this time."

"Alfonso told you of my dream?"

"He told me of your concern."

"There was a great bear. He appeared from a fog. Two eagles came down from the sky and landed beside the bear. They tried to talk to the bear. They tried to warn the bear of a trap. But the bear could not understand their speech and they flew away. The bear came to a stream where a mountain lion spoke to the bear. It too warned the bear of a danger. But the bear was too thirsty and could not hear the lion. The bear drank from the stream until he was full. Crossing the stream he walked to the edge of a very high cliff where he met a wolf. The wolf tried to warn him about the danger of being too close to the edge. But the bear could not understand the wolf and this made the bear angry. Now the bear turned into a wolf so he might hear his brother wolf. But what he hears makes him even angrier. The bear-wolf attacked the wolf and in their battle they both fall from the ledge — one to its death."

"What do we learn from this, Peter?"

"Zander — you are the wolf. You must be careful not to get close too the edge."

"But I have always been very careful. You know this."

"I do know this. But now I know the dream."

"Should I stop?

"No — you must understand."

"Help me to understand, Peter."

"There is a battle that goes on inside of all people, Zander. The battle is between the two wolves inside us all. One wolf is Evil. It is anger, envy, jealousy, greed, arrogance, resentment, lies, false pride, and ego. The other wolf is Good. It is joy, love, hope, humility, kindness, empathy, truth, compassion and faith. It is a battle to the death."

"Which wolf wins, Peter?"

"The one you feed."

* * * * * *

Austin spent the next few days buried in the all but impossible task of bringing the Continuity Bureau back up to a hundred percent operationally and within budget. Management received the "Patriotic-Continuity Emergency Contribution Plan" as poorly as he had expected. Even though Austin put as much enthusiasm into his presentation to the department heads as he could muster, most could tell his heart wasn't into it. And if there was any "buy-in" by the department heads at all, it could have only been considered lackluster at best. They saw it for what it was. Now their jobs would be to go out, put on their game-face, and try to duplicate as much energy into their individual staff presentations.

The ultimate results were predictable. Morale would drop. Productivity would drop. Within a few weeks, upper management would whip middle management. Middle management, in turn, would then whip the staff. Some would be let go setting an example to those remaining; and those with the most creative passive-aggressive behaviors would remain. Problems would not be solved, but budgets would be saved.

Never the less, like Austin, the managers knew they had little voice and even less choice in the matter. A team-building event was planned for Saturday May 6th when the general staff would be given the news. In the mean time, everyone pushed to get his or her respective departments up to speed.

May 6th would begin with a pep rally including pastries and Coca-Coffee. Lunch would be catered complements of several local restaurants with a full day of activities parked on either side. Each of the Continuity departments would be divided into groups of alternating, competing departmental teams. Each team would be challenged in a series of competitive events. All team members were issued commemorative PCECP Continuity uniform covers for the occasion. Winning teams received prizes that had been kindly donated, at the request of Director Akakios, by the local merchants.

* * * * * *

Austin walked back to his office following the morning's department head meeting. *Well, that went over really well. My head may cave in at any moment.*

"Katy, I can't be disturbed for the rest of the day — with the normal exceptions, of course."

"Yes sir. And your lunch sir?"

"Maybe — I'll let you know. Thanks."

In spite of his throbbing head, he had a full day's work ahead, in fact a full week's work that had to be cleared before May 6th. His first order of business was to write a quick memo to Klaud summarizing the morning's department head meeting. He knew it would require a positive spin. *This is where years of creative writing experience, comes in handy.*

In spite of Austin's concentration on the tasks at hand, he just couldn't put the somewhat cryptic note that had been posted on his front door out of his mind. He had learned of the "Wolf" a number of years earlier. There had been many accounts of this seemingly mythical revolutionist. But it wasn't until his meeting with the President that he learned that the "Wolf" wasn't just a conspiracy tale, rather a real person by the name of Alexander Conall. How much of the stories were true and how many endured as folklore or fabrications were still as unknown as his whereabouts.

* * * * * *

Through the years, Venice Beach had developed a reputation of being a magnet, attracting the most eclectic individuals in Southern California. People from all stripes, colors, sizes, sexes, and flavors gathered daily to enjoy the mild climate, plus the fresh beach atmosphere. They were there to see and to be seen. It had also become a favorite gathering spot for Plebeians. Regardless of class, Citizens or Plebes, everyone seemed to savor the exotic environment and the part they played in this daily extravaganza in motion.

Every day was a party on Venice Beach.

"Nice day for the beach, Eugene." Came the voice from behind.

"Shee-it! You scared the ever lovin' *piss* outta me. Man — don't *ever* do that again! Where'd you come from anyway?"

"Here and there. I've been watching you and the people for about the last hour or so."

"Wolf Man, you almost gave me a heart attack. I was beginin' to think you weren't gonna make it here today. How've you been?"

"Not bad for one of the older models, I guess. How about yourself, Eugene?"

"Good — really good. Livin' the dream in So Cal."

"I can understand that. Wish I could spend more time here myself. The climate's hard to beat. Have you had any problems since the 15th?"

"Naw man — I guess we shook-um up pretty good though. And I'm really sorry my part of the play didn't work out the way . . ."

"No worries — it wasn't your fault. Every now and then you're going to get a dud out of government equipment." *These days you're going to get a dud out of government people as well. Some things never seem to change.*

"Well, I still felt really bad about it. I mean I didn't want to let you down, you know. It's a good thing you planned a back up for me."

"Did you post that note for me yet?"

"No problem. Did it last Friday and nobody saw me comin' or goin'. It was a piece of cake. Stuck it on that condo door — and I was outa there. How bout you — did ya have any problems on your trip out here?"

"Thankfully, the UA freight lines are still running. They are first class travel for us non-Citizens."

"I know *that's* right. Got my quick trip to Texas on a freighter last month. *Texas,*" Eugene shook his head back and forth, "Shee-it, now there's one place you can keep. *Man* — they got too many snakes and weird animals and insects. I don't like it."

"Don't be knocking my state now."

"*You're* state? I thought you lived in the Colorado Mountains?"

"I did this winter. I live where I choose."

"So, how bout the winter? Did ya get any skiin' in this year?"

"Sadly, my downhill days are over — no way to pay for a lift ticket either. But I did get in some wonderful cross-country treks around the San Juan's. I'm not as limber as I once was, but the exercise is needed and the experience is still religious. Have you ever skied, Eugene?"

"Never have and never will. I know that skis and me wouldn't get along. Besides, I got a triple phobia."

"Really — what phobia is that?"

"The bein' cold, fallin' down, and getting' hurt phobia."

They both laughed and began walking down the beach together. The two of them had never had the luxury of being able to spend much time getting to know one another. Eugene was considerably younger than Conall and he wanted to know about the "old days." His curiosity was insatiable and by the end of the day he knew that his life would also be devoted to this great man's dream.

"Are you hungry, Eugene?"

"Man — I was *born* hungry."

"Do you like hot dogs?"

"Sure — who don't?"

"Watch this, and don't say a word."

The two of them walked up to a beach vendor and stood there for the longest time just staring at him. Neither of them said a word while Conall looked into the vendor's eyes and just smiled. After what seemed like forever, the vendor finally broke.

"Are you two hungry?"

"Yes sir." Conall said. "We surely are."

"Great — and how do you propose to pay for the dogs?" recognizing the two as Plebes.

With that, Conall reached deep in his pocket and pulled out a closed fist. "With these, sir." He opened his fist and exposed a handful of rocks.

"What the heck are those? I've never seen anything quite like . . ."

"These are magic crystals, sir."

"My ass!"

Conall calmly smiled and stared deeply into the vendor's eyes. "Reach out your arm and open your hand. You will feel the energy." The vendor stared back into his eyes. After a full minute, he tilted his head back down and reached out with an open palm. *Wow — magic crystals. Today just may be my lucky day.* Conall placed the bright crystals on to the vendor's outstretched hand.

"What kind of magic can they do?"

"All kinds. Carry them with you every day for good luck. And on the evening of May the 5th you will witness your next exciting and electrifying experience." Eugene's eyes bulged as he strained to witness real wizardry. Conall finally broke a long silence with a loud snap of his finger. "Could we each have a couple of dogs and some iced Coca-Coffee?" Eugene and the vendor were startled back into consciousness.

"Well — If you say — OK, sure, why not." And he quickly held out their lunch to them, yet firmly holding onto the sandwiches. "But — Will it be a good experience? The one on the 5th that is."

"Some would say that it would be a wonderful occurrence precipitating the contumacious continuation of the contention."

"Wow! — Way cool. OK, here's your dogs man. Bon appetite."

"Thank you young man. And many days of good luck to you."

"Yea, man. Your safety and security and all that, too."

Conall and Eugene walked to a spot on the beach where they could sit and enjoy their lunch.

"Wolf Man — I ain't *never* seen anything like that before. But, I think the real magic is in your BS. You need ta teach me a lot more before you leave LA. And I gotta get me some a those crystal rock things, too." He took a man-size bite from his hotdog, and before swallowing completely, "Oh, and thanks for the lunch. This is real good!"

"You're quite welcome," Conall finished his dog and enjoyed a cool sip of his Coca-Coffee. "Eugene, imagination is a wonderful thing. That, combined with the power of suggestion and simply asking a question can frequently yield an amazing result."

"I'll remember that. So, let me see — you just look into someone's eyes like this?" He intently stared into Conall's eyes.

"Correct."

"Then ya gotta ask a question?"

"You've got it."

"OK. I can do this." Eugene continued to focus into Conall's eyes for the better part of thirty-seconds. "By the way, Wolf Man, I really like your cowboy hat. Do ya think I could get me one like that someday?" Eugene patiently continued staring into Conall's eyes and just smiled.

* * * * * *

The President and his chief of staff were sitting with the UA's Board of Directors and a quorum of Senior Directors for an early morning briefing. They had spent more than four hours reporting and debating the current state of the UA, recent developments, and action plans required for future management. Gates and Dunstan expressed clear understanding and appreciation of the investments made by all of the directors. And, throughout the meeting, both Gates and Dunstan reiterated their total dedication, commitment and ability to maintain control.

"I think we're all in agreement. Before we break for lunch, allow me to summarize," Gates began. "And please feel free to interject with any thoughts or clarifications needed."

"Our head of Intelligence, Director Deimos, has assured me this recent terrorist attack was an isolated event. As large and damaging as it was, his recon has determined that it was born out of the growing frustrations of perceived high taxation and mass media frustrations. Ironically, they have been unable to identify any Citizens, rather a relatively small and isolated group of Plebes."

"I'm sorry Bill." Stanley Bates interrupted. "I may be a little slow on this issue, but it just doesn't make any since to me that Plebes would have concerns regarding taxes when they don't even work or pay any taxes — not to mention their limited exposure to the media. It seems to me that there's more to this than meets the eye."

"Stanley, you're not slow in the least. As Chief of Security and the Secret Service, it's your job to be suspicious and highly skeptical. Allow me to better clarify this rationale. What we have here is a small, albeit devoted, cult. We've known about their leader, Alexander Conall for many years. 'The Wolf,' as he is known, and by all rights, he should have been one of you — one of us in this room today. He has the intelligence, the skills, and in his early years the financial success required for a position on this executive board."

"Now, I can't pretend to completely understand his motivations. What we do know is that he refused to change his old, antiquated and, shall we say, less progressive ideas about America. He chose to cling to the past and his personal principles of freedom and liberty. Ultimately, it has cost him the experience of new freedoms and a life of luxury. In view of this, how can anyone explain his pathology? As for his few followers, well, it's simply the cult mentality. Together they are trying to make a statement. The statement has been made — and noted, I might add." He turned to Dunstan and smiled.

"Director Foley has assured me that the UA Contribution Bureau is back on-line and running at one-hundred percent, as are all media Bureaus," Gates continued. "Other than the expense of replacing equipment and buildings, the inconvenience lasted but a few days — a couple of weeks at best. Conall's efforts fell on deaf ears and had virtually no impact on Citizens whatsoever. Based on observations and recent polling, the Citizens have few concerns over the entire ordeal and have resumed their normal routines."

"As a final note on this topic, please keep in mind that Conall is most likely in his eighties. Even if we are unable to capture him, his time is limited as is his cult. Director Deimos has determined that he has no clear or known successor. When the head dies — so goes the body."

"The military, rather the Protection Corps will continue to be held on 'Condition Yellow' stand-by for another month. Director General Borghild is in agreement that there have been no signs of civil unrest to date. However, he sees this as an ongoing opportunity to utilize the event as an extended training exercise. We additionally have his full support should we decide to initialize 'Project Arachnid' with the UA Protection Bureau rollout." Gates paused and reached for a glass of water in front of him.

"Do we have a final budget figure and timeline on that project yet?" asked one of the senior Board members.

"Real progress is being made in the research department on the project. They think another few weeks with the chimps and they can start human trials with a control group of Plebeians. That should give us a year or so to plan the logistics of a roll out. As we get closer, we'll assemble the board of directors and apply some Game Theory to several models. We need to put more thought into it. But it does seem logical at this time to have a complete military 'buy-in' before we incorporate the Citizen population at large. As for the budget, final figures have yet to be determined. The ultimate number will fluctuate some depending on our rollout strategy. The research portion is all but complete. We are well within our budget for that segment. Ultimately, I feel confident that the project will come in very close to our original number of 100-million — give or take. This was never a WAG, but a realistic figure based on the research department's estimate and all computer models. But, there are some variables that may come into play as we approach the final deadline. Our 'Project Arachnid' has expanded the original cloning concept exponentially. While the original group from the 'Year of the Spider' was remarkable science at the time, 'Project Arachnid' has taken on an entirely new life — pun intended." Gates smiled and laughter rounded the conference table.

"Most of the original Spiders have been groomed through the years and will be in their leadership positions at roll-out time," interjected Dunstan.

"What exactly do you mean by most of the Spiders, Carey?"

"Sir, with all due respect, I'm sure you remember that the government structure was vastly different in 2047. And, although the original 'Spider Project' was funded and for the most part conducted by the government, the purpose or purposes were somewhat different than how we have incorporated them into our leadership plans. In addition, the original government supervision of that small test group was not that well controlled at the time." Dunstan paused for another moment to quench his throat. "We've lost six of the original thirty Spiders in the test group, either confirmed dead or simply missing. Does that answer your question?"

"Not quite. How can any of these people be missing?"

"It wouldn't be easy," Dunstan interjected, "but we live in a rather large country these days. Even with the latest technology, people can and do disappear. The more important issue is that the majority, the surviving members, are fully trained and under our control. Back to you, Mister President."

"Thanks Carey. And yes we are very pleased with the original 'Spiders.' Although they have and will continue to serve a vastly different purpose with the UA than their original creators imagined. There can be no doubt as to their contribution and value in terms of 'Project Arachnid.'"

"Speaking of Spiders," Dunstan spoke up, "Austin Llanoc is our brightest shining star. He is currently the Vice-Director of the Continuity Bureau. Klaud Akakios has done an exemplary job of grooming this young man through the years. He exhibits all of the right attributes — ambition, creativity, willingness, compliance, and ingenuity. He has learned and believes in the 'Octadic Principles.' In fact, we haven't observed a single fault." *And he's a very good-looking lad, I might add.*

"Carey and I met with him a few weeks ago and we both agree on his future ability to command the Continuity Bureau and later a higher position that we have in mind. Keep your eyes on this one."

"Finally, we've instructed our media writers to begin another round of articles and programs reinforcing the threats of climate change catastrophes, possible energy shortages, and a potentially deadly outbreak of the Hantavirus over the next six or so months. This will serve the purpose of keeping Citizens from focusing on the lack of success we've had in solving the recent attacks; and, of course keep them dependent on the UA for our help and relief from these future dangers. In the mean time, I think you will all agree that everything is under control," Gates paused dramatically, "are there any additional questions or comments?"

Everyone remained seated and looked around the table at each other checking for signs of continuation, while murmuring to one another in hushed tones. After a few moments, one of the Board members stood and said, "Fine job Bill. I think I can speak for the rest of the Board when I say that we continue to fully back your leadership."

There was a short round of applause and Gates raised his hands.

"Thank all of you for your continuing support. Now, before we break for lunch I would like to invite each of you to join Carey and myself for a few rounds of golf this week. I have UAAF-1 fueled and on standby for today's 3pm flight to Paradise Island in the Bahamas. The entire Ocean Club Resort has been reserved and secured for our 5-day stay, retuning quite late on Friday May 5th. We have staggered Tee Times starting at 9am tomorrow. And yes, UA Service Girls, and Service Guys have been hand-picked for us and provided by the resort management."

Revelation

12

"Somewhere, something incredible is waiting to be known." — Carl Sagan

* * * * * *

"Alfonso! — Man! — Where in the hell have you been? We were beginning to think you ran into some kind of serious problem in Albuquerque!"

"Sorry guys — I did. But I finally got the algorithms working with the remainder of the code. Let's face it, 'The Wolf' didn't make 'Act Two' any easier for us than, well, I guess any easier than the rest of the production," Alfonso said while cleaning his wet glasses.

"Nothing worthwhile in life comes easy." Alex grinned.

"No shit — I've heard 'The Wolf' say it more than a few times."

The last week in April, the showers in Houston were finally slowing to at least a drizzle. Alex Conally had spent the better part of the day covering the logistics of "Act Two" with Borislov and Nabhoj while waiting for the critical member, Alfonso, to show. He was very mindful about the dangers of a Citizen lingering for too long with obvious Plebeians. The large public park and to a lesser degree the weather helped to cloak their meeting. He had chosen to meet at a covered gazebo in Herman Park, a relatively dry spot close to the monument of General Sam Houston and well away from the street.

"So — It's done?"

"Finally." *And you guys have no idea!*

"Are you sure?" said Borislov the skeptic.

"Boris — I'm as *sure* as I can *be* under the circumstances — *OK?*"

"Gentlemen," Alex interjected, "we are all doing the best we can — and none too soon if we're going to meet our Cinco de Mayo deadline. So, Alfonso, brief us on the details of the program."

"Right. OK. First — here are your data cards. Load them on to your equipment now to be sure they are compatible. One step at a time."

As the three inserted their cards and began to download their programs, Alex was quietly watching a UA Security Cruiser, drive slowly past, a little more than a block away. It was his second pass. One more pass could signal a real problem. *Timing is everything*

— and now is not the right time. He watched the cruiser turn away, drive a half block in the opposite direction, then spotted the brake lights glow. The cruiser came to a slow stop.

"We may have a small complication," Alex said quietly.

"No. Everything is going smoothly for now," Alfonso confidently responded.

"That's not what I had in mind. Casually look to the northwest."

"Oh great. Just give us a few more minutes," Boris all but whispered.

"Fine. But be prepared to scatter." *I'm getting a very bad feeling about this. That guy is standing on his brakes — for no apparent reason and for too long now.* Alex continued to casually watch out of the corner of his eye. *If I see any revealing motion . . .*

Fortunately, they were about a hundred plus yards away from the street and close to a densely wooded area of the park — chosen for this express reason.

"Should the need arise, does everyone know where to meet?"

They each nodded without looking up from their gear. The program was large and there was simply no method to speed its download progress — especially with such old data units. They were lucky Nabhoj had been able to cobble together the salvaged computer parts needed for the task.

"Alex, we're almost there," Boris sighed.

"I understand — but I don't like the looks of this. There's another CA Cruiser coming in this direction. It just pulled up beside the other . . ."

"Just one more . . ."

"No time. Shut them down — NOW!"

At that moment, the first security cruiser spun its tires, letting out a loud screech as it turned a tight 1-80. Their roof lights began pulsing as they raced toward them, and a loud speaker shouted. "Stay where you are! Don't move! CA Security! Stand down!"

Then, all hell broke loose. As the cruisers screeched to a forced stop hitting the distant curb, the security guards jumped from their units and began to run in the direction of the statue. A CA Security scout-copter appeared from out of nowhere approaching the clearing in front of the galloping guards. The guards in the second cruiser released a dog revealing fangs with every bark. Alex, Alfonso, Borislov and Nabhoj all ran in separate directions and into different sections of the urban forest. Each knew the severity of getting caught. It was critical to escape to their predetermined meeting place. Safety was several miles away. Their other test would be arriving at that location undetected.

With the exception of Alex, each carried a pack with equipment and a change of clothes in which to alter their identities. Alex had another backup plan.

His pack was filled with raw meat. Before running, he reached into the bag and grabbed a handful of meat, scattering it around the ground. He knew of a spot on the other side of the park where a small group of Plebeians regularly camped. As he ran in that direction, he threw down pieces of chuck. Upon reaching the camp, he quickly identified a fellow who was about his size. Almost completely out of breath, he handed the unsuspecting fellow the pack full of meat.

"Here. Take it!"

"Hey, man — what's up?"

"It's a bag full of fresh meat for everyone in the camp."

"Wow! Cool, man. Thanks!"

"Just one thing."

"Sure."

"I was never here. Nobody has seen me. Got it?"

"Yea. Sure, man."

"Good. Spread the word quickly. Oh, and tell the security guys when they get here that you're sorry for running. You didn't want them to take your meat. OK?"

"Yea. No problem. Wait — *security* guards?"

"Don't worry. They'll just start asking a lot of questions."

"OK. If you say so — hey, nice hat too."

"Here — it's yours."

"Thanks!"

"And another thing — tell them you want a reward. You want a big reward, because you heard people talking. You heard there's going to be another bunch of huge attacks coming soon. You got it?"

"Yea, man — no sweat. Are the attacks going to hurt me and my friends?"

"No. Just stay out of the downtown area and you'll all be safe."

"Cool. No problem — and thanks for the meat, man. Good luck!"

* * * * * *

Alfonso, Borislov and Nabhoj had little difficulty getting to the abandoned warehouse close to Buffalo Bayou on Houston's southeast side. Waiting for Alex to show, they continued downloading the data cards with the code needed to mount their next attack.

While they prepared their equipment, large rats the size of small dogs and a score of mice scurried around the building scavenging for their next meal. Glowing spider webs decorated the oversized translucent windows. Grime covered the glass panes from years of weather and neglect — at least the ones still intact. Most webs featured a black, eight-legged silhouette mounted in their centers. The building smelled of decay and rot — but at least it was dry — mostly.

"I hope Alex is OK," Nabhoj quietly mentioned, almost under his breath as he continued working on his system.

"No worries," Borislov whispered a few seconds later.

"We've been here just thirty-minutes or so. Alex can take care of himself," reminded Alfonso, "not only is he from Houston, so he knows it like the back of his hand, he has the most amazing survival skills. You two may not be aware of who he really is."

"Sure — he's Alex — 'The Wolf's' son," one of them commented nonchalantly.

"Not exactly. Have you ever noticed the small tattoo on the back of his neck?"

"No," they both said simultaneously.

"Alex actually *is* Alexander Conall."

"Of course. He's his son," remarked Nabhoj.

"Yes and no."

"What are you talking about? He is — or he is not. Which is it?" Borislov said sarcastically.

"Alex is one of the original Spiders. He *is* Alexander Conall."

"No shit? He's one of those?"

"No shit. And — he has a twin brother. They are both perfect and completely artificial clones of 'The Wolf.'"

Boris and Nabhoj simultaneously froze. "This is true?" Boris asked in disbelief.

"Just before Alex's first birthday, and before he could be implanted with the nano-data device, Conall nonchalantly walked into the cloning lab in Austin, wearing a white lab coat. He picked up one of the twins, placed him into a barrel bag and walked quietly, right back out without anyone even noticing."

"You mean to say he just left his other, well his other, I mean his other son?" said Nabhoj incredulously.

"He did. His plan was to raise one son, with the help of foster parent friends of his in Colorado on their ranch."

"They were Citizens?"

"Right. They were special category Citizens in that they were not required to be implanted with chips — you know — farm and ranch category Citizens. He wanted the other son to be raised in the system — ultimately achieving a high-level government position. That other son is on the West Coast and now in a very high government position."

"That's crazy. It doesn't make any sense." Nabhoj considered this to be completely illogical. *Why would a father want to separate his sons?*

"Makes perfect sense," Borislov said quickly, "he wanted someone on the inside and one on the outside — right?"

"Correct."

"But that would be very risky — in very many ways," Nabhoj remarked.

"True — but it was a calculated risk 'The Wolf' had to make. He understood early on that his struggle would take longer than his own lifespan. 'The Wolf' needed to expand his lifespan. He also knew that if he could be in two places at once — one of those places would need to be close to those in power. Alex, on the other hand, would also become a regular Citizen, but of a special class. He was to become a rancher in Colorado. Instead, after graduating from Texas A&M he would start his farm near Columbus, Texas, which allowed him to maintain his special privileges, and, shall we say freedoms — not unlike the native Americans. It wasn't 'The Wolf's' first major gamble, and it wouldn't be the last. He'll have a few more perils, no doubt, before he dies. Risk should be Alexander Conall's middle name — and may *be* for all I know."

At about that time, Alex walked into and across the large expanse of the warehouse carrying four small paper bags.

"Alex! We were getting a little concerned . . ." Nabhoj began.

"Gentlemen! Did you think I wasn't going to make it?" he confidently said as he sat the bags down on the rusted metal table.

"We really had no doubts," said Alfonso, "but it looks like you lost your hat in the escape."

"Not really — I gave it to someone who needed it more than I. There were also a couple of stops I needed to make along the way. How goes the progress?"

"We just completed the download."

"Great! — Good timing. Now, everyone is clear on the parts they play in 'Act Two' of our little production?"

They each nodded their heads in agreement. It would be a sprint to the end game with the distances required and the deadline facing them. Yet, they were confident of their individual abilities. Alex had reminded them regularly to temper their confidence with a large degree of detailed considerations.

"Borislov, you have the Canadian power grid. Nabhoj controls the US power grid and Alfonso takes care of Mexico. And the day and time will be?"

They each reassured Alex that it would be in the evening, just before midnight on May 5th.

"Good. Now — when you've downloaded the infected data streams, just leave your equipment, and walk away very slowly. You will, once again, become ghosts. Are there any questions?"

"Just one," Said Alfonso, "what's in the bags?"

"Dinner — a few hamburgers, some fries and Coca-Coffee. Is everyone hungry?"

"How the hell did you manage that?"

"You know," he smiled — it's simply amazing what a handful of crystals will buy these days."

* * * * * *

The weeks slowly slipped by not unlike every other week of the year. If there was one thing that the majority of Citizens appreciated it was consistency. May the 5th had begun about the same as any other day. Traffic was as light as usual. And the weather in Southern California was perfectly typical. On Austin's drive that morning from Redondo Beach, he couldn't help but remember the weekend that he and Diana spent looking at new homes as he passed by Palos Verdes. Never in their wildest dreams could they have imagined the possibility of living in such opulence. He thought about the very first home the realtor presented to them and the expression on Diana's face when she opened the front door.

"Oh my gods, oh my gods, oh my gods, Austin! Look at this. Can you believe what I'm seeing?

"Wow!" was the only thing he could force from his mouth.

They slowly explored each room with wide, unblinking eyes. There were so many of them, and they were so large, each with their required wall mounted Tel-Coms.

"Austin — we could live in any one of these rooms."

"True — just pick one."

They slowly explored the possibilities of a completely new lifestyle. The realtor reminded them that there were four more homes scheduled for their tour that afternoon.

"You said you worked with Randi for a few years."

"I did."

"And she told you my position with the Continuity Bureau?"

"She did."

"Do you honestly think these homes are within our reach?"

"No question, sir. I've also looked at your financial data."

"What? How was that possible?"

"Well, at first it wasn't. It should have been routine. What I mean to say is that on my way to the office, I stopped for my usual breakfast at 'Joe's.' Fortunately, I go there every morning. Do you ever eat at 'Eat at Joe's?'"

"Sometimes — we know the place."

"Well, like I said, it's my morning routine — and they know me. So I'm ready to leave and I place my Tel-Card into the slot — nothing happens — nothing! So I pull it out and reinsert it. Now it reads my account is overdrawn — talk about embarrassing."

"So they made you wash dishes for a couple of hours — right?" Austin laughed.

"Very funny. Now, I know about how many Credits should be in my account, so this is just ridiculous. Since I know these people, they said I could take care of it the next morning when I straightened out my account."

"That was good of them."

"No kidding. But it made me wonder about the same thing happening to someone they didn't know. Do you realize the problems that would have caused? In fact, what if it happened to me again at a business I wasn't known at? Do you know what the legal consequences are for that? It's considered a crime."

"True."

"So then I'm walking to my car and my Tel-Card rings. It's my landlord. He says my rent payment was turned down at the bank and there would be a $50-Credit bounce charge — not to mention I had 24-hours to make the rent payment good."

"Sounds like a bad day," Austin said getting a little bored.

"But that's not the end of it. As soon as I hung up there was a message from the Central Bank saying my account was over drawn and there would be a $200-Credit over-draft charge."

"Tami, it sounds like you need to watch your balance more carefully." Diana remarked.

"You don't understand, I keep an additional $5,000-Credits in my account to keep that from happening."

"So what did happen?" Diana asked.

"Well, I knew I would have to drive to the local branch of the Central Bank and work this out. But first I wanted to get to the office to pull your financials and the paperwork for two other clients. I sit down at my desk, insert my Tel-Card, punch in my access code and it is refused!"

"How is that possible? Why didn't you just call the Central Bank?"

"Don't get me started! That's a totally different story — and not a pleasant one I might add. I called them and was shuffled from one department to the next, one person to the next and on hold for more times than not. I got disconnected three times to boot and that's the short version of the story. So I drive to the Central Bank branch in Redondo. About 3-hours later everything is in order — problem solved, extremely frustrating, and almost an entire day wasted. Oh! — And on the way back to the office I got a flat tire!"

"Really bad day — but it could have been worse."

"How?"

"Could have been raining," Austin smiled.

Diana tried to keep from laughing as she walked through the back doors and onto the patio.

"Austin — a pool!" She slowly strolled around the pool admiring the spacious and private back yard, replete with perfectly manicured privacy landscaping. Bending down, she dipped her fingers into the warm pool water. *It's feels like bath water.*

"I'm sorry Tami." Austin remarked. "I shouldn't make light of the situation. Although, I guess I can because we've all had days like that. So back to my original question — this is all new to me. How did you pull my financials?"

"Simple — once my Tel-Card was corrected, I was able to acquire your UA pay level using the limited access and totally secure financial verification records system. You and Diana are more than qualified for any of the homes we look at today. And yes it's a very nice pool, Diana. You and Austin could enjoy some very enjoyable, private moments here — or some pretty interesting parties if you are so inclined," she grinned while wiggling and adjusting her tightly fitting silk uniform.

Austin didn't give much more thought about poor Tami's Tel-Card problem. He was too caught up in the moment thinking about how happy Diana was. Watching her sample the pool. His mental image was the two of them, making love under water. He could see the two of them in this home — now. And, he was ready to live the dream.

"Do any of the other homes we're touring have pools?" Diana asked.

"They all do."

"Wonderful. Don't stop now. Let's keep looking."

Although they didn't end up choosing a home that weekend, Austin had a pretty good idea, which one Diana favored. They could go back for a second look in a week or so and make their offer. After all, there was no hurry.

* * * * * *

Austin arrived at the office as early as usual — always the first. He enjoyed the quite mornings. He was not only more productive, but more creative as well after a good night's sleep. First things first though — a fresh pot of hot Coca-Coffee was required. Within an hour or so the staff began to assemble. It wasn't like the old days when his cubicle office was at the edge of the bullpen with everyone else. These days, he was isolated on the top floor. It remained quiet virtually all day with very few interruptions. His first small disruption however, was always Katy checking to see if he was ready for a fresh pot of coffee — or anything else she may tempt him with. The second would be Klaud.

"Austin! Are you ready for our morning meeting?"

"Ready when you are, Klaud. I'll be right there."

It was no longer a big deal — just routine. After their meeting, he spent the remainder of the morning finalizing plans for the pep-rally with his department heads. Everything was organized — everything that is but their attitudes. He did his best to get them to understand the importance of putting on a good face for the event and the consequences of any negative appearance. It was the best he could do.

Walking back to his office he stopped at Katy's desk.

"How are you this morning Katy?"

"Fine — thank you for asking."

"I apologize for being short and not recognizing you sometimes. I hope you don't take it personally?"

"I don't. I think I understand."

"Good. I really do appreciate your efforts."

"I know, sir."

"Please — remember — no sir."

"I'm sorry. I forget sometimes. It would be easier if you would allow me to do a little more for you though. It would keep me from thinking of you so, how shall I put it? Formally." She winked.

"Don't stop trying. It's very flattering."

"But I'm not trying to just flatter you. I would honestly like . . ."

"OK. Maybe we'll go to lunch together someday. How about that, Katy?"

"It would be a start, I guess. How about today?"

"Sorry. I'm going to lunch now, and I need for you to prepare this data stream by the time I return."

"Early lunch?"

"Saturday is a big day." He handed her the data card. "I'll be back in about an hour or so. That should give you plenty of time and then you can take your lunch."

"Fine. But I'm going to remember your offer."

"And I promise not to forget either."

After arranging a few items at his desk, Austin left the Continuity building and walked a few blocks alone, deep in thought, to Maki Sushi. He could afford to treat himself to lunch anywhere these days, but he simply favored Sushi. Austin was especially happy when he learned that Maki-Sushi had a second location in Long Beach. There were a few remaining items on his to-do list for the afternoon culminating with a final meeting with Klaud before he could go home and relax with Diana. He was pleased that she would accompany him at tomorrow's event. It would keep him somewhat grounded, plus he could show her off to the staff.

Approaching the front of Maki-Sushi, he couldn't help but notice a couple of odd-looking individuals. They were Plebeians based on their attire.

Both were standing close to the entrance. The younger one was wearing a weathered looking cowboy hat. The other was one of the oldest looking people he had ever seen. As he reached for the door, the younger fellow with the cowboy hat said, "Escuse me." And Austin stopped dead in his tracks.

"Are you talking to me?"

"Ain't nobody else 'round here that I can see." The younger man said quietly. "Spose you could spare a couple cups of Coca-Coffee on your way out? You know, help out a couple a Plebes?"

"Well — I suppose I could . . ."

"That would be mighty kind of you, Mr. Citizen."

"Sure. No problem."

"Say — you wouldn't happen to be Austin — would ya?"

"Why yes — yes I am. How did you . . ?"

"Somebody here wants to meet you."

The old timer stepped forward and reached his hand out.

"Hello, Austin. I'm your father."

* * * * * *

Austin stood as a statue, on the sidewalk in front of Maki Sushi, as if frozen in time. His mouth was wide open and his tongue motionless, as he tried in vain to force air thru his vocal cords. The two strangers also stood silently waiting for Austin's shock to wear off. He was sure that his father had passed away after his disappearance — or had he? After what seemed to be minutes, Austin finally blinked and managed a half smile.

"Sure. OK. Right. Now — what do you fellows really want?"

"Austin — It's true. This man really *is* your father," answered Eugene.

"Right. Now if you will excuse me, I'm just going in here for some lunch. I would ask you to join me, but — well, how should I put this . . ?"

"No — we're not Citizens. You know we cannot join you," Conall said, "but I am your father, and we would like a coffee when you finish your lunch."

"Yea. Sure. Why not." *And maybe you'll be gone when I leave, too. Maybe this is some kind of twisted joke — worse yet — a test.*

"Maybe I could just ask for one other small favor?"

"Look — I don't have anything of value on me."

"I only ask that after your lunch, you could spare me just five-minutes of your time. Would that be too much to ask?" Conall smiled.

"Well — no, I guess not." *That is, if you're still here.*

"Good. We will be across the street, sitting in the plaza." Conall pointed to a park bench a few yards into the trees.

Austin rolled his eyes, turned away, and slowly walked into the restaurant. His plan for lunch was to leave the office and try to clear the accumulated clutter in his mind that was beginning to create a monumental headache. Now, his previous concerns aside, his head had an altogether different matter filling it. *My father!? What the hell is this all about?*

"So much for a relaxing lunch to clear my head." He said out loud as he pulled the chair from a table.

"Excuse me?"

"Oh — sorry Susie. I'll have my usual."

"Very good."

"One other thing — when you bring me my check" . . . Austin paused and thought for a moment.

"Yes?"

"Um — would you bring me two Coca-Coffees to go?"

"Hot or cold?"

"Yes — that's a very good question."

"Yea. I know. That's why I asked it?"

"Clever. Yes, you really know your stuff — don't you?"

"Of course I do. I'm an over educated, highly trained, multi-talented, and I might add, consummate professional waitress."

"Well — in that case — what would be your professional recommendation?"

"Cold."

"Ah! — Then cold it is! I will take care of your counseling fee when the check comes."

As she walked away, Austin placed both elbows squarely on the table and firmly planted his head into his open hands. He closed his eyes. All he could think of was, *Oy! Some people.*

* * * * * *

Austin took his time savoring each bite of sushi and sunomono. He had the strangest urge for a glass of Japanese beer. He couldn't understand why. To the best of his knowledge he couldn't remember ever tasting Japanese beer. The oddest thing was, as a matter of fact, not only didn't he know what Japanese beer tasted like — he wasn't completely sure what Japanese was. It was just another one of his many previous puzzle pieces of his past.

After clearing his tab, he carefully walked across the street to the plaza. At first he didn't see the two strangers. Then, twenty or thirty yards back, he could see a couple of figures sitting on the park bench and he walked towards them. *What in the hell am I doing?* Austin casually looked around to see if there might be someone or ones watching him. There were no signs of anyone paying any attention. Not that there were many people close by anyway.

"Here you go fellows — enjoy. I have to get back to work now."

"Wait. Before you go," said the older man, "would you please just spare me a couple of minutes?"

"Look — I don't know what this is all about, but you two . . ."

"And you will never know if you don't sit for just a while. Is your work so pressing that you can't spare a little time?"

"Well — no — I suppose I could. OK, what's on your mind?"

"You are on my mind, Austin. I really am your father — in a way. It's complicated, but it's also very important that we spend some time together so that I may fully explain."

"I don't know how in the *world* you could . . ."

"That's kind of the point. You see, it wasn't exactly in this world."

"This is getting very strange."

"OK. I know this is out of the blue and doesn't make a lot of sense, but I can clear it up for you if we could just spend a little time — not now, but — could we meet somewhere privately on Sunday?"

"You're joking — right?"

"Hardly. What I have to say will be life changing."

"*Life* changing, hey? For *me* — or for you?"

"For the two of us."

"Fine — the only place I know of that's mostly private is the beach."

"Good. How about south of the Redondo pier on the beach? I'll treat you to lunch."

"What?"

"Yea, man. He knows a great way to buy hot dogs!"

"You've got to be kidding me?" *This is getting stranger all the time. A Plebeian wants to buy me lunch.*

"This is hardly a joke. It truly is a very serious matter. I must have your assurance that you will be there."

"I suppose . . ."

"Noon Sunday — on the beach — is it a date?"

"Sure. Whatever you say."

"Good. We'll see you and Diana then."

"*Diana?*"

* * * * * *

Austin's afternoon was less than productive after his encounter. If he didn't already have a head full before, now it was packed to the brim. Tomorrow's event was dominating his thoughts. Now, mixed in were these two non-Citizens and a clandestine meeting on Sunday. *Who in the hell were they? What were they really up too? Why would the old guy say he was my father? I know who my father was — I think. This fellow looks somewhat familiar but not exactly what I remember my father looked like. And, how in the world did they know about Diana?* It was almost too much to digest. He wondered how things in his life could possibly get more bizarre?

On his drive home that evening he may as well have been on autopilot — if there were such a thing. Earlier in the afternoon, for a fleeting moment, he considered calling Diana. On second thought, not only wouldn't it be prudent, but this story needed to be told in person. He did call to let her know he was working late. As his car pulled into the underground condo-parking garage, he shut off the engine, looked around, shook his head and wondered to himself, *I'm not even sure how I got here.*

"Are you home?" Austin said as he walked through their condo door.

"I'm here — preparing a nice, late night, romantic dinner. We can eat on the balcony under the stars. Would you like a drink?"

"I thought you'd never ask!"

At that moment — the lights went out — everywhere.

Cinco de Mayo

13

"Disobedience is the true foundation of liberty. The obedient must be slaves." — Henry David Thoreau

* * * * * *

The first week of May in the Bahamas had seen the typically perfect Chamber of Commerce weather. The UA Executive and Senior Board of Directors, the President and all his men exercised 18-holes most days.

The Ocean Club's course provided an excellent test of Caribbean golf — dealing with wind that can change from moment to moment. In fact, wind and water turn out to be the prevailing threats on this 7,123-yard par 72-layout, and there's plenty of sand, to boot. With the seaside foliage removed, there is nothing to protect the course from gusty breezes off the ocean that play havoc with club selection and shot placement. Large and small lagoons also come into play on many of the holes.

Although Gates was a scratch golfer, he accepted the essentials of senior respect, and consequently lost more Credits than he won. He understood the game in more ways than one. Tempering his competitive spirit was his true challenge. His art was the ability to conceal his true handicap. One must be skillful to lose convincingly. By the fourth day of 18, on the same course, he could have played blindfolded.

Carey Dunstan couldn't have chosen a better venue for their spring retreat. The Ocean Club on Paradise Island dated back to the early 1960s. It was the private enclave of Huntington Hartford II, heir to the Great Atlantic & Pacific Tea Company fortune.

Hartford built the Ocean Club, a luxurious 52-room hotel plus four, two-bedroom cottages, and commissioned architect Dick Wilson to create an 18-hole course for the pleasure of his guests. In the 1960s the Ocean Club was *the* place to be seen with the likes of Orson Welles, Benny Goodman, and Sean Connery to name a few celebrities, plus a host of international ambassadors and royalty.

The ultra private resort had changed hands a couple of times through the years getting extensive upgrades and remodeling along the way. Little was known about the current ownership. The entire Island had been purchased in 2040 by a group of investors who resold it a year later to a private Trust. The Breen

Trust continued to maintain The Ocean Club's five-star status to the current day.

Evenings were spent dining in the hotel's enclosed, yet open air, Courtyard Restaurant. It was an appropriate name for the romantic dinner setting complete with candlelight, fountain, reflecting pool and overhanging tropical plants and waving palms.

After dinner entertainment choices included several varieties and qualities of massages, moonlight skinny-dipping surfside or in the lagoon-styled hot tub. Some gambled at the nearby Atlantis Casino. And, of course, young UA Service Girls and Guys were provided, for both day and nighttime pleasures.

After 5-days of fun and frolic, rest and recuperation, it was time to get back to the business of state. Final notes and commitments were exchanged during the last meal Friday evening at the Courtyard Restaurant. The tables in the restaurant had been arranged in the shape of a large UA for the final ceremony.

* * * * * *

"It was a wonderful week, Bill," said the most Senior Director, David Amir who was seated beside Gates.

"I'm glad you enjoyed it."

"Enjoy would be an understatement."

"Thank you. It means a lot coming from you, sir."

"As much as the board members have relaxed and enjoyed the week, we've also had the time to recharge our batteries, think, and talk together."

"Of course, that was part of the plan."

"Bill, with out a doubt, you've done a fine job to date. I want you to know that we're proud and will continue to support you."

"Thank you, sir. It has been my . . ."

"But Bill — you have also made some mistakes," he continued very quietly.

"Well — sir — I know that . . ."

"Don't get me wrong, Bill. We've all made our share through the years. To stay in the game, you only need to be right fifty-one percent of the time."

"I understand, sir. You see . . ."

"I know you do, Bill. And I know that you understand that anyone can just stay in the game. But, we have to do better than that."

"Correct."

"It's an ill wind that doesn't blow some good. We've managed to profit to this point. But, we've also seen some stronger winds of change lately that, quite frankly, could be very damaging if they continue."

"Trust me, sir. My staff and I are on top of things. We are going to . . ."

"Just stay on top of things. Don't let us down, Bill."

"No, sir."

"As I said, it's been a wonderful week. You can relax on the flight home tonight. But, tomorrow I want you to gather your staff and spend a couple of days preparing a complete and detailed action plan and written report to the Senior Board members regarding your resolution with this 'Wolf' fellow and his band of scoundrels. That's not too much to ask, is it, Bill? Do you think you can take care of this for me?"

"It will be done."

"Fine."

After dinner, Gates and Dunstan walked together to their respective rooms in order to prepare for the long flight back to the Springs.

"What the hell was that all about?" Dunstan said quietly to Gates.

"You heard?"

"Not everything — but I got the drift."

"Enjoy the rest of your trip. I'll explain in detail tomorrow. Send a memo out ASAP to all Department Directors to be at the White House no later than noon Saturday."

"Tomorrow. Sounds like the party's over."

"All good things must come to an end."

* * * * * *

"That's the damndest thing I've ever seen! Did you catch that?" Captain Miller said, almost under his breath.

"No shit! Beats anything I've ever witnessed," answered his copilot.

Jeff Miller and Rod Spiker had been flying UAAF-1 for more than ten years together. Their total, combined flight experience spanned more than a half-century. They had each observed numerous in-flight phenomena ranging from the questionable to the completely unexplainable. This evening's spectacle however, was totally unique from any of their previous observations. Miller opened his mike.

"Good evening, Atlanta control. This is Captain Miller, UAAF-1 flight 69-6-66. Do you copy?"

Miller paused, waiting for a reply.

"Atlanta control. This is Captain Miller, UAAF-1 flight 69-6-66. Are you there?"

Again, he paused, looked at his copilot and shrugged his shoulders.

"What do ya think?"

"Odd."

"Rod — keep trying. I'm going to walk back and report this to the President. I just hope he's not sleeping," Miller said as he unfastened his belt.

"Maybe we should wait until we get to the Springs," Spiker cautiously came back.

"I think not. Just keep trying. I'll be back shortly. Want anything from the galley?"

"Sure — some fresh Coca-Coffee would be great. Oh, and see if there's any of that avocado and conch salad left from dinner."

Miller didn't mind. Spiker would do the same for him — and had many times over. Miller walked slowly and quietly through the dimly lit cabin to the President's quarters. He stared at the door for several seconds. The "Do Not Disturb" light was shining brightly. This was a very clear warning and it patently presented a dilemma. *Now what?* He stood silently for a moment considering his next option.

Miller walked the entire span of the aircraft without finding a single passenger in even a semiconscious state. On his return walk back to the cockpit he hesitated at Director Bates' Cabin. After a full minute of contemplation, he knocked quietly on Stanley Bates' door — paused — then knocked once more.

"Yes?" Bates said sleepily as he opened the door.

"I'm really sorry to disturb you, sir; but I need to report this to someone."

"Yea — Sure — Fine — What. What time is it? What's the issue?"

"Close to midnight. Director, Atlanta went dark — completely dark."

"It's probably a cloud."

"No sir. There are no clouds. It's a perfectly clear night."

"Maybe it was a brown-out. These things happen. Did you radio Atlanta control?"

"Yes sir. There was no response. In fact, we've lost all radio frequencies."

"All of them? You tried them all?"

"A complete scan — and nothing."

"Odd. No lights and no traffic control from nearby airports either — I'm sure it's just . ."

"Sir. You don't understand. The lights went out everywhere — as far as we could see. The only lights are from the stars overhead. The entire country just went dark."

* * * * * *

"Great! Austin said sarcastically, "California Edison strikes again."

"I hope the lights stay out for a while," Diana smiled, "It will be even more romantic. And . . ."

"Yes?"

"And, there won't be any Tel-Com either." *We can say and do as we please.*

"True," Austin smiled. *We just may get carried away tonight.*

"I could feel very free tonight, especially if the power stays off!" she whispered in a sexy tone.

"Maybe go with the flow?" he asked as he gently touched her arm.

"Yes. But dinner and drinks first."

"I hope dinner was almost ready, since the power is . . ."

"Austin — we cook with gas."

"Oh yea — right. I'll pour the wine."

"First, Austin, why don't you slip into something a little more comfortable — you know — a little less confining? — I did."

Austin set down the wine bottle and corkscrew, put his arms around her and grabbed her shapely rear with both hands.

"So I noticed," he said, as he gave her a long romantic kiss.

"*Austin*! I'll burn dinner."

"You can burn something more after dinner," as he licked her lips.

"Change! Go change now — before . . ."

"Before what?"

"Before we decide to skip dinner and start with dessert," she said laughingly.

It was an unusually warm May evening. Austin and Diana enjoyed their candlelight dinner on the balcony. The stars were brighter than ever due to the absence of light pollution from the city. There was no traffic on the street below and the only sound was from the gently crashing waves just yards away.

"Would you care for another bottle of wine?" Austin asked as he rose from the table.

"I thought you'd never ask," she said mockingly, "but I'll be ready for margaritas after dinner."

"I know, that's true," he laughed as he selected a bottle from the wine rack. "How was your day?"

"Routine — and yours?"

"The morning was spent finalizing plans for tomorrow's event. And then I went to lunch at Maki Sushi — very strange."

"Strange sushi?"

"No. I met these two — well — these two characters. They were standing in front of the restaurant waiting for me — as if they knew I would be there."

"That's a little strange I suppose. Maybe they were just hanging out."

"Yeah, that's what I thought at first. But that's not the really strange part."

"Really. Who were they?"

"Now that's what was so disconcerting."

Austin spent the remainder of the dinner and their second bottle of wine relating the bizarre encounter with his alleged father and an odd younger fellow named Eugene — both seemingly Plebeians.

"Your father? Austin, your father was a Citizen. And, I thought your father was dead."

"As did I."

"How can you be sure he really *is* your father?"

"That remains to be learned. What's more — he knows about you."

"What?"

"And he wants to meet with both of us on Sunday."

"Austin — you're not — we're not going to . . ."

"I'm compelled. I think we should."

"We need to talk about . . ."

"I have a better idea. Why don't we have a few margaritas now — enjoy the rest of our evening. We can talk about this tomorrow."

"You definitely know how to organize your priorities — don't you?"

The bottles of wine plus copious amounts of tequila, combined with the absence of the Tel-Com suggested a very long and playful evening. They felt relaxed and free to explore each other as two innocent children playing in the dark — as if they were the only people in the world with no cares. It was during the early morning hours that they finally collapsed, soaking wet, on the living room couch.

* * * * * *

Captain Miller made his way forward, stopping briefly in the galley to fill a thermos with fresh Coca-Coffee and checking the refer for leftovers.

"Any luck? Miller said as he stepped through the open cockpit door.

"Some. Not long after you went aft, communication came back on with air traffic control. Atlanta went on emergency power. Damnedest thing though..."

"What's that?"

"They thought the power outage only affected Atlanta. They've lost all local and outside communication as well. I reported lights out to the horizon."

"Well, as long as traffic control can guide us into the Springs, we'll be just fine. Let's keep her on the same heading until we get further instruction. Since Atlanta control is up, I'm sure other hubs will be on emergency power as well. Get out your charts in case we need them."

Stanley Bates' communication gear was even more sophisticated than the aircraft's equipment. He was pleased to be able to contact headquarters in Colorado Springs within a few minutes after Miller left his cabin. But he was alarmed to discover that the power outage appeared to stretch from southern Mexico to the northern reaches of Canada and all points in between. Before disturbing the President with current events he wanted to spend a little more time trying to gather additional information. After speaking with the Springs he walked up to the cockpit.

"You were right, Miller. It's damn dark out there," he stated as he stepped into the cockpit while looking through the windshield.

Miller felt like saying, NO SHIT SHERLOCK. But instead, he calmly said, "No changes so far, sir."

"I just spoke to the Springs with my gear. They were beginning to get some intel as to the scope of the outage. Do you expect any problem navigating back to the Springs?"

"As long as air traffic control stays up — I mean, on emergency power, we'll be in good shape," Spiker said confidently.

"Good. I'm going to take a little more time collecting as much information as possible before I disturb the President."

"Great idea. He'll be full of questions."

"Oh — by the way, the Springs said it's snowing there," Bates commented as he turned to leave the cabin.

"Great."

"Right. So — keep me advised of any changes. I'll be in my cabin for at least the next fifteen or twenty-minutes."

Occasionally Miller or Spiker would notice a very small cluster of lights as they continued across the country. No doubt there were isolated buildings, like hospitals or UA installations running on emergency power. For the most part, the view was like Bates said, " . . . damn dark out there."

Bates decided to wake Dunstan first. He wanted help breaking the news to the President. Dunstan was used to being engaged as a buffer and completely understood Bates' concern.

"What — in the name of the gods is going on?" President Gates yelled.

"We don't know — a, yet, sir," Bates said meekly, "it's really difficult to gather intel when there is no power and virtually no communication in the northern hemisphere."

"I guess you could say we're in the dark on this one, Bill." Dunstan said jokingly.

"Not funny, Carey!" Gates barked sharply, "What's our ETA?"

"Another three hours or so to the Springs," Bates quickly snapped back.

"Tell Miller to step on it! And, I want a full staff assembly in the war room! NOW!"

* * * * * *

That night, using the cover of darkness, Los Salvadores along with their volunteer army of Plebeians plastered hand painted signs on building walls and posts from coast to coast and border to border. Within a matter of hours, hundreds of thousands of posters appeared. Citizens would wake on Saturday morning in most towns and the majority of cities to learn that their safety and security had once again been compromised. Various signs read:

"No Power — No Safety and Security."

"The People Want Our Power Back!"

"No Power ? No Credit$! No $ecurity!"

"First – No News!   Now — No Power!"

"Power to the Citizens !"

"How's That Safety & Security Thing Working Out For You?"

"UA — No Way!"

Fires were beginning to be lit in the northern communities as people desperately tried to keep warm. Hospitals and UA emergency shelters filled to standing room only. Before power could be restored there would be hundreds if not thousands of fatalities.

It was an unfortunate consequence that "The Wolf" understood would occur. And although it pained him greatly, he accepted the responsibility and the knowledge, which would plague him for the rest of his life.

* * * * * *

"I had a dream last night, Margaret," Peter Begay spoke softly to his wife, "A great eagle will fly across the earth tonight. It is restless and searches for its home. The bird is tired, confused and almost blind in the snow."

"Does it survive?" She asked.

"I think so. But it is also wounded and may not have many years left to hunt."

With that, he put another piñon log on the fire, kissed her on the cheek and they retired.

* * * * * *

"UAAF-1 flight 69-6-66 this is Colorado Springs control. Do you copy?"

"We copy Springs control. Dropping altitude — reducing power. How's your power?"

"Power is fine — weather's not so fine — over."

"Just bring us in as quickly as you can. We have fused cargo on board. Do you copy?"

"Understand and copy. Active runway is 24 right, wind 210 at 15 knots, altimeter is 29.92, 28-degrees, cleared for initial approach to runway 24 right, call at initial for final clearance, over "

"How is traffic, Springs control?"

"All traffic has been cleared for your arrival UAAF-1, over."

"Copy that. What's the outlook, Springs control?"

"Roger 69-6-66, the weather is 1500 ft overcast, visibility is 1/4 mile and blowing snow, you are cleared to initial approach fix to commence a tacan-2 approach on arrival, call Springs approach control on 322.5 mc now."

"Copy that. See ya soon."

"Runway cleared, flight 69-6-66."

"This is Captain Miller. We are beginning our approach and decent into Colorado Springs. Please be seated and buckle up. It's going to be a little bumpy on the way down."

President Gates leaned his head closer to Dunstan's as he buckled and quietly asked, "How in the hell does an entire country lose its power?" And, all at the same time if it's not sabotaged?"

"Bingo," Dunstan almost whispered, "It's got to be 'The Wolf' and his rag-tag Salvadores."

"Look, if we can't catch this guy and bring him and his group to justice; why don't we reach out to him and try to negotiate?"

"Negotiate what?" Dunstan blurted.

"Hell — I don't know — something — almost anything. What does he want?"

"Who knows? What I do know, however, is that we're going to have a lot of frozen Citizens if we don't restore power soon. Most of the country relies on electricity for either heat or fans to push the heat. And speaking of heat, what are you going to tell the Senior Directors when they come to?"

"I'm working on that. Got any ideas?"

"Not yet — but we'd better come up with something — and fast. I don't think power will be restored before we land." *Truth is, I've got lots of ideas. The trick is picking the right one. We aren't exactly dealing with the general public here.* "We should gather the directors for a quick briefing while the plane is taxiing to the terminal. Let them know, only what we know — no conjecture."

"Carey, it sounds as though you think it's going to take some time to get the lights back on."

"Bill — If these people are smart enough to figure out a way to kill the power grids in most of the northern hemisphere, I can assure you it's not going to be easy flipping the switch back to On!"

* * * * * *

"Let me ask you a question, Eugene."

"Fire away, boss!"

The two Plebeians were sitting in the starlight at the end of the Redondo Beach pier. It was a quiet evening but for the sounds of the surf breaking beneath them.

"Have you ever thought about being a Citizen?"

"Nope."

"Never?"

"Nope. Never."

"Why not?"

"No reason to think about it."

Conall paused for a moment and just stared at Eugene in the eyes. "You're serious?"

"Wolf, I'm serious as a heart attack."

"I'd say that would be pretty serious."

"There ya go."

"So, you don't think there would be any benefit to being a Citizen?"

"Hell no! That's no life for me. It's no life for them either. They just don't know it."

"OK, Eugene — why is your life better?"

"Better than theirs? — Because I'm free. Those people are slaves. And, like I said, they don't even know it."

"Do you think so?"

"Think so? Shee-it — I know so! I can see with my own eyes. Man, I can see it in *their* eyes. They have no life. They ain't happy — and you can see *that* in their eyes, too. They get up in the mornin' and put on those silly uniforms. Then they go to work all day, then they come home ta go ta sleep and get up the next day ta do the same thing all over again. They have to! — And for what? Beats the hell outta me."

"They get paid. Don't they?"

"Not enough. Besides, they don't get no real money anyway. They only get those — what ya call it?"

"Credits."

"Credits my ass! That ain't no real money."

"How do you know that, Eugene?"

"I've been told. I know people used ta have money in their pockets, money under their beds and money in something they called a cookie jar — whatever that is. They had plenty of money to spend on things ta make themselves happy and other people happy too. Now what do they have? — Stupid little cards that don't even work some of the times. And then what? Then — well, then they ain't got shit "

"But you don't have any money."

"Don't need it — but I wouldn't mind havin' some sometimes. Wolf, you know, we go where we want ta go, do pretty much what we want ta do. We eat pretty good most of the time. Ain't nobody tellin' us what we have ta do. Shee-it. I'm talkin' free—dum!"

"And that makes you happy?"

"*Hell* yes! — Happy as a horse. How bout you, Wolf? Ever want ta be a Citizen?"

"I was once."

"No way!"

"It was a long, long time ago."

"So, how come you ain't a Citizen now? How's that possible? I thought that once you're a Citizen, you're gonna be a Citizen till ya die."

"That's the way it is now. It didn't use to be that way — not exactly."

"I don't get it."

"Well — there was a time when everyone was a citizen. But, they weren't citizens in the sense you think of them today."

"Citizens was Citizens but they wasn't Citizens? You're talkin' crazy, Wolf."

"A little confusing to understand from today's perspective I suppose. You see, in the old days, the days before the United Authority, people were just people. There were still a lot of working people of course, but those people had the real money you were talking about. Some had a little, some had more than others, while others had abundance. But they also had free spirits. They were mostly, well, almost completely free — because they had the freedom of choice."

"They had ta work ta get their money. How could they be free? Did they have ta wear those silly uniforms too?"

"Some did — most didn't. Eugene, they were free because they had the real money you spoke of — and they got to keep most of it. Plus, they could spend their money almost anyway they wanted to. There were many other forms of freedoms as well."

"But they still had ta work."

"True. But many of the people liked to work. They enjoyed working, to one degree or another. Many people received fulfillment and a great degree of satisfaction from their professions. People were also compensated according to their level of skill. Some made more than others. Not at all like today. The majority of Citizens today are compensated more or less equally."

"They didn't get equal pay back then?"

"No. But that was part of the freedom. People could choose to work as little or as hard as they chose. And they were compensated, or paid money accordingly."

"But they still had ta work though."

"No they didn't. People were free to work or not. Everyone wasn't equal from a monetary sense, but they were free to live their lives any way they chose. Work wasn't a condition of citizenship. Everyone was truly free from that standpoint. And, unlike today, a majority of the people were happy."

"OK. I guess I could go for that."
"Maybe someday you will.

Arachnids

14

"Who we are is who we were." — John Quincy Adams

* * * * * *

No one could remember exactly when it had all begun; but experimental cloning research was thought to have started in the mid-twentieth century — refined in the beginning of the twenty-first.

They were not all completely nefarious endeavors. Much of the early scientific experimentation was conducted in a genuine effort to improve the species. Many researchers believed their work could pave the way to cure infertility. Those who were left sterile by cancer treatment, as an example, might gain the facility to acquire children who would now be biologically their own. It would additionally allow gay couples to have children genetically their own; although a majority of scientists were highly skeptical about whether it was possible to create sperm from female cells, which lacked the male Y chromosome.

It did raise a number of moral and ethical concerns as well. Those included the possibility of children being born through entirely artificial means, and men and women being sidelined from the process of making babies. Opponents argued that it was wrong to play God and meddle with the building blocks of life. They warned that the advances taking place to tackle infertility also risk distorting and damaging relations between family members.

Regardless of controversy, research continued. Most researchers considered their efforts a noble cause. There were, however, a number of isolated groups who sought a much more single-minded, some might say nefarious, result. And although many labs were privately financed, there were a few with partial government assistance. The leading research firm in Austin, Texas had the government's complete attention.

* * * * * *

Austin was the first to wake Saturday morning, with the sound of crashing surf and bright sunlight shining from the balcony — the double glass doors still open from the night before. *What time is it?* The Com-

Center was still dark. He reached for his Tel-Card and dragged it to his half open eyes.

"Oh my gods! It's 10:30! The alarm didn't go off!"

* * * * * *

Continuity staff, writers, editors, managing editors, executive editors, directors, art directors, video editors and producers, close to 400 in all, began staggering into the Long Beach Plaza between 9 and 10-am Saturday morning. No one was on time due to the power outage. Even Klaud was late by an hour, rolling in a little after 10.

"*Where's Austin?*" He all but yelled to anyone close enough to hear. "*Has anyone seen Austin?*"

Klaud walked through the crowded plaza for the next ten-minutes asking about Austin, but no one seemed to know his whereabouts or even seemed to care. He finally spotted the most senior editor and Austin's successor, Steven Lu. "Steve!"

"I don't know, Klaud — haven't seen Austin yet. It's this lousy power outage. None of us were really on time this morning."

"Fine. Well then, I'm sure he'll be along soon. Why don't you assemble the troops and let's get started," Klaud commanded.

Lu quickly rallied the managing and senior department heads together. They all had clear instructions for the day's activities. Management divided the staff into teams and separated them around the plaza for their competition instructions. Each game or activity would become more challenging throughout the day, culminating in a bracketed playoff.

No one noticed the two Plebeians, sitting on a park bench, and watching from the south plaza sidelines.

Austin rolled in just before noon. He quickly located Klaud standing on the north side of the plaza with Steven Lu.

"Klaud. I'm really sorry but my . . ."

"No worries, Austin. Can't help it if the power goes out," Klaud said with a smile, "you've obviously organized things very well. We have an excellent management team working for us. Besides, you know there's plenty of flex for people at the top — right?"

"Right," Austin said staring at Klaud with a degree of perplexity, "sure. Ah, I noticed that the power is out all the way from Redondo to Long Beach."

"I know. I've tried calling you, United Authority Emergency Services, and Pacific Edison. Of course all Tel-Com service is down as well. I even tried a couple of old landline units. Nothing seems to be working in the LA Basin."

"I'm sure power will be restored today," Lu interjected, "Edison has never had an outage for very long. Regardless, it's good we didn't plan this to be an evening event." They all agreed. "Did you two happen to notice the signs and posters along the PCH? What's up with that? Have people never seen a power outage before?"

"I saw quite a few spray painted on buildings," Austin mentioned casually. "You're referring to the anti-UA signs and graffiti?" Klaud spoke up, "fucking malcontents. They have nothing better to do. I thought you were bringing Diana with you today, Austin?"

"That was the plan. Due to the power outage, I decided to let her sleep in." *No reason to make a big deal over her hangover.* Austin was only mildly stunned that Klaud asked about Diana under the circumstances. He wasn't even surprised with his attitude about the graffiti people. But, he was sparingly shocked when Klaud offered to share his pint bottle of single malt scotch with the two of them.

"I think we've attracted an audience," Klaud said with a chuckle, pointing south at the two Plebeians sitting on the park bench.

Austin glanced in the direction Klaud was pointing and spotted two, now familiar faces. They seemed nonthreatening, not that he thought he had any enemies. He was curious at the least. And, he still had mixed feelings about his meeting with the two of them tomorrow. Austin had a nagging thought in the back of his mind. *I wonder if these two characters had something to do with the power outage? Smiling to himself, he quickly put that ridiculous idea out of his mind.*

The final competition ended shortly before sunset, and the trophies were awarded. The party was over and few of the staff was lulled into a false sense of dedication to the Bureau. Moreover, they felt resigned to the certainty that they had no other real options. At least the Bureau's management team felt a degree of satisfaction with the day's events, if for no other reason than they were spared the temporary cut in income. The participants quickly evacuated the plaza to return to their homes before night fell. The two Plebeians stood and slowly walked away from the plaza.

"Looks like it's going to be another very dark night, Eugene."

* * * * * *

President Gates had been assured that by the end of the day power would be restored across the country. But at 8pm Mountain Time Saturday, he and most of his senior staff were still sequestered in the war room far under Cheyenne Mountain and there was no power progress in sight for most of the country.

Even more frustrating was the fact that there was no way to communicate a calming message of progress to the Citizens — never mind the fact that no progress had been made. Gates knew that the more time that passed without power, and with no reassurance of safety and security communicated to the people, his problems would only compound — exponentially. There were already reports coming in from across the country of anti-UA signs in many communities.

"Mister President," exclaimed General Director Borghild, "we may need to resort to Marshal Law soon."

"By all means, General, let's *really* scare the shit out of the Citizens!"

"Mister President — I just mean that . . ."

"I know fully what you mean, Gunther. Yes, we may have to resort to that — but there is no reason to jump the gun — so to speak. Look — just to be on the safe side, why don't you put all forces on "Code Yellow" standby?"

"That's it?"

"Did I stutter, General?"

"No — Sir!" Borghild snapped and turned away. He had never liked nor respected Gates. In fact, he thought of Gates as a snot-nosed, narcissistic, pompous, sociopathic, faggot.

Gates then turned to his Safety Bureau Director. "Great. Now — Deimos!"

"Yes, Mister President?"

"You said we would have power by the end of the day. And?.."

"Nothing, sir."

"I *know* there's nothing, Hector! What in the hell I don't know is *why* or who, or better yet, *when* are we getting power restored?"

"Sir, if I could find the kid who wrote the code that shut down the power grids, I'd hire him today at top salary." *Then, as soon as he solved the problem, I'd take the little fucker out and shoot him!*

"Good for you. I'd have much more creative things in mind for him — the little puke!"

"Mister President, you have to respect his . . ."

"Hector — I wouldn't even respect this insect's mother!"

"You don't understand the beauty and complexity of his code. Our best guys have been working night and day on this virus. In fact, it's not just a virus — it's without a doubt a super virus. This is a Trojan virus of the first order, the likes of which we've never seen before. It's written in a geometric progression that mutates faster than we can duplicate it. Our security experts are warning that it is one of the stealthiest and most pervasive threats ever. Even if we get ahead of it, there's a real danger that it could be used against some of our other UA systems in the near future. Massive modifications will be needed for the future. Respectfully

Sir, we've been asking for budget allocations for upgrades to the system every year for more than ten years."

"Retirement funding and healthcare reform was a priority for our Citizens — especially for the children. You know we had to create a sense of hope and equality. I can't help it if the cost, over the past decade, was more than we had anticipated."

"Do we have a 'power' priority, now?"

"Right. OK. Let's solve the current problem first. Then we can look at the budget. In the mean time, why can't we just unplug the damn systems? Get them off the grid. Take them off-line, then turn them each of them on separately?"

"If only it were that easy. Not to mention the next problem we'll face once we defeat this virus. It's going to require a very careful reboot for a gradual startup to keep the demand surge from blowing out the entire system again. At least there is a glimmer of good intel coming in, however."

"Give it to me."

"Most all areas are reporting restored power within about a 50-mile radius around power plants or hydroelectric facilities. At least there are pockets of Citizens with some of their services restored. Most of the plants, themselves, are operational. The next step is just to get them back onto the grid without creating a blowout."

"Lovely," Gates said all but defeated, "I could really use a good stiff drink — or maybe three."

"Bill?" Dunstan interjected, "may I make a suggestion?"

"Why not."

"Good. Why don't you go and get a little rest? I'll spell you off for a few hours — then you can do the same for me. What do ya say?"

"Fine. Maybe if I clear my head . . ."

"Right. Do that."

"Carey?"

"Yes, Bill?"

"It can't get any worse than this — can it? I mean, well, this has to be their best shot. Don't you think? Once we solve this issue they can't hit us with anything else of this magnitude — can they?"

"Absolutely no way. Once we take care of this — we're going to take very good care of them. That is — once we find out exactly who and where they are."

* * * * * *

"I love Sundays," Diana said as she and Austin walked hand-in-hand along Redondo's south beach.

"Yep — me too."

"Sundays make me feel free and relaxed. I don't have to worry about the time, no requirements, no going to work. Have you ever wondered why most people don't work on Sundays, Austin?"

"Some very old tradition I suspect. I've never really thought about it."

"That brings up an interesting question. What do we do about work tomorrow if there's still no power?"

Before he could answer, he noticed a couple of recognizable figures walking towards them from the south. One was a young, black fellow wearing a cowboy hat. The other, a tall, white-haired fellow wearing a baseball cap with a "MF" patch on its face. Both were obviously Plebeians.

As they continued to walk toward each other, Diana leaned over and whispered into Austin's ear, "That's the oldest person I've ever seen in my entire life! Is he the one who says that he's your. . ?"

"That's what he claims."

There were few others on the beach at 10am, even for such a perfect morning. It was 72-degrees with a slight ocean breeze blowing. Later in the day, an array of Citizens and Plebeians would begin to gather. Beaches had grown even more popular as the ultimate sanctuaries of abandon, especially since there were no monitors or Com-Centers on beaches. And rarely did any Authority Officials patrol. Beaches seemed to be the last bastions of free expression.

"Good morning Austin and Diana. A lovely day for a walk on the beach — don't you think? But, how rude of me — allow me to introduce myself. I am Alexander Conall. And this is my protégé, Eugene."

"Pleased ta meet ya. I been hearin' a lot bout you two," Eugene said as he reached his hand out towards Diana.

"Is this some kind of a joke? — Or maybe a twisted test?" Diana squinted.

"Neither test nor joke — it's the truth. I am Austin's father — of sort."

"Now you're my father — of sort? Why do you say that? Don't you know how crazy that sounds? And you're also claiming to be the legendary 'Wolf,' Alexander Conall?"

"Please, be patient. Let's pick a spot to sit. I have a story to tell. It may answer more questions than you realize."

"Wonderful. We're all ears," Austin said rather sarcastically.

They walked away from the water's edge a few paces and sat in the sand about midway between the cliff and the ocean. Conall was careful to position himself with his back to the ocean. This gave him a clear vantage point up and down the coast, plus anyone lingering from the cliff above.

"Austin, when I was your age, I was a very wealthy man — and the country was a very different place. It was long before the birth of the UA and the Spiders."

* * * * * *

"Let me see. Where shall I start?"

"How about from the beginning?" Diana said almost sarcastically.

"I'm afraid that would take more time than we have today. Although, someday it would be my pleasure to give you a true history lesson," smiled Conall.

"It would be our pleasure to hear it," Austin said under his breath.

"I can't give you all of the details — time doesn't allow — but an overview will give you the big picture. As I said, this country was a very different place almost a hundred years ago. You wouldn't recognize it. To begin with, the UA didn't exist at that time. There were actually three separate and sovereign countries. North America was split into not quite equal thirds — Mexico to the south, The United States of America, where we are now, and Canada to the north. Each country had its successes and failures, but their greatest strength was the fact that they were democracies and their people had mostly real freedoms. They had the freedom to govern themselves, and the freedom to live their lives as they chose within the laws that they made for themselves."

"I'm sure it was more complicated than that."

"You're right, Diana. It was extremely complicated — and wonderful. However, there were those who wanted more power. And in order to gain the ultimate power, they understood that it would require the total control of the majority."

"Why? I mean, what good or pleasure is gained by total control of the population?"

"Good question, Austin. Let me answer by asking you a few questions. Not all that long ago, you were just a junior editor at the Continuity Bureau. You rose through the ranks rather rapidly. Recently, you were raised to one of the highest positions in the Bureau — vice director."

"True, but how . . . ?"

"Do you have more power now than you ever dreamed you would have in your life? And you too, Diana."

"Yes, but I . . ."

"You rule over hundreds of people who have no power. And with your power you now have more freedoms and the finest lifestyle?"

"That's right."

"And you enjoy it — don't you?"

"Of course we do."

"Now multiply that to the power of ruling a country. It is the ultimate."

"Understood — but if the Citizens were all free at one time, and they were the majority, how could they allow a minority to gain that kind of power?"

"Austin, it only required three elements, time — skill — and patience. The seeds were planted in the last half of the twentieth century. I won't confuse you with names and their ideological labels. The names changed through the years to suit the propaganda in order to achieve a growing impact on society. Think of it as marketing at the pinnacle of adroitness."

"Stop. How can that be considered marketing?" Austin asked.

"Well, that's a topic for another lesson — another time, perhaps. Let's just call it highly skilled salesmanship. Does that make sense?"

"Persuasion — right?"

"Yes — a deft persuasion that morphed its message, but not its ideology, over the period of more than a century. There's an old saying that there are two ways to skin a cat. One is to club it over the head — the other, to convince it that chloroform is good for its health. The club is quicker and painfully lethal. Chloroform takes a little longer, but ultimately more comforting. It was a choice between an armed revolution, or a moderately peaceful evolution."

"So, what was the methodology? And who wanted control?" Diana asked.

"More good questions. We will call them the 'Power Elite,' or statist. They worked inside the system. Those who wanted a revolutionary change in the North American societies, and these people understood the need for the preconditioning of the population. The metamorphosis had to be preceded by a passive, affirmative, non-challenging attitude toward change among the mass of our people. The people had to feel so frustrated, so defeated, so lost, so futureless in the prevailing system that they were willing to let go of the past and only hope for future change. This acceptance is the reformation essential to any revolution."

"You're saying that our country was taken over as the result of a bloodless coup spanning decades?"

"Exactly. First, you must condition the people, then increase the size of government, and create more laws, more bureaucracy, more restrictive regulations, more taxes, and the government take-over of major industries. The government could then control the redistribution of wealth, more collectivism, less individualism, and less freedom. The 'Power Elite' had to do more to ensure that the citizens avoid the consequences of their choices. Ultimately, the people wanted safety and security with no personal responsibility — and were willing to pay more and more to attain it. They paid through taxes and they paid with their freedoms. Over time, their losses were all but total. You see, over those decades, the people forgot that each human being must be accorded his or her natural rights, individual sovereignty, and self-responsibility to be in harmony with nature and human nature and to be truly free."

"Based on what you're saying, this so called metamorphosis has been completed."

"So it would seem, Diana, but it continues as the result of scientific breakthroughs in human cloning. You see, what began as mostly altruistic scientific research caught the attention of those in power. They recognized the potential to uniquely homogenize different segments of the population to perform different functions; and for each of the segments to be even more conditioned — conditioned from birth."

"I think I remember reading about cloning, but didn't realize it involved humans, or the government for that matter," Austin remarked.

"I have a source inside the government lab in Austin, Texas who has confirmed the near completion of this top secret project. Once final testing takes place next year, the UA will begin mass production of their first series segment. Conjecture is that it will be augmented by the military. The code name is 'Project Arachnid.'"

"This is sounding completely ridiculous — far fetched. Human cloning? What possible proof can you show us?"

"Austin, have you ever wondered why you are sometimes confused about your past?"

"Yes. But that doesn't mean any . . ."

"Do you and Diana ever share recollections of different life experiences?"

"Well — I suppose we . . ."

"Have you two ever experienced multiple feelings of déjà vu?"

"Yes! — We have!" Diana quickly stated.

"Have you ever wondered about the small spider tattoos you share on the back of your necks? Look — you had to learn eventually. There is no gentle way to break this to you. Austin, you and Diana were among the original thirty prototypes."

"Wait, wait, wait! You're saying — I mean, you're telling us that we aren't who we are?" Diana said incredulously.

"Yes and no. You really *are* who you are. But — you're also, well, you're also someone else."

* * * * * *

Across most of the northern hemisphere, people were beginning to comprehend the seriousness of the extended power outage and just how much they depended on energy. Not withstanding heating and lighting, or the lack thereof, everything comes to a standstill without power. Fuel was trapped in underground tanks, halting most transportation. All businesses were closed. Even shops and restaurants with skylights were unable to function without the ability to access Tel-Card Credit systems. There was no access to food and medicines. Fresh water stopped running due to the electric pumps required keeping it processed and flowing. Citizens living in high-rise buildings couldn't rely on their elevators. Plebeians were also affected due to some of the curtailment of handouts. And, of course, there were no communication services. Citizens remained in the dark, literally and figuratively, both night and day.

As hours stretched to days, people's concerns grew to anxiety, anxiety to fear and fear to desperation. Waiting lines outside hospitals and emergency shelters increased by the hour. Sporadic and minor looting began by the end of the third day. A tipping point could soon be reached for much more serious actions.

There were isolated areas of the population who fared better. Communities within an approximate fifty-mile radius of a power generating facility for example, military installations, plus emergency and hospital locations were spared from most hardships. Only one other group of people managed their loss of power due to advance preparations and their ability to live off of the land — Los Salvadores.

* * * * * *

"How's that 'Safety and Security' thing workin' out for ya?" Alex said sarcastically.

"Ain't nothin' to it, my brother," laughed Alfonso.

"Man! — That was some serious code you wrote. How long do you think before they break it?"

"Can't say for sure, but it will keep them busy for a few days — with any luck. In the mean time, I'm just glad we're here rather than in the city."

"Which city?"

"Any city. Things are going to get really ripe in most cities — and pretty quickly," Alfonso stated as he walked up to the front porch and sat down beside Alex on the porch swing.

"Did you have any trouble getting here? The farm is pretty secluded."

"Naw. It wasn't too tough. Nice place you've got here, by the way."

"Thanks. It serves the purpose."

* * * * * *

The small farm was situated about midway between Houston and San Antonio, and roughly ten-miles north of Interstate-10, in a densely wooded area. Its entire fifty-yard deep perimeter consisted of native trees, thick underbrush including: yaupon, several varieties of cactus, poison ivy, poison oak and sumac among others. It was nature's own security barrier that could only be penetrated by wildlife or men with machetes, chain saws or heavy equipment — with the exception of the single, winding road from the gate to the farm's interior. The center of the one hundred plus acres had been carved out of dense forest and underbrush back in the mid-eighteen hundreds by a Texas settler, where he had farmed it until he died from a rattlesnake bite. Also in the center of the property and sitting on a slight hill was a small farmhouse and barn. About a hundred yards in front of the house was a 3-acre stock tank filled with perch, bass and catfish. The property was home to a few head of cattle, some hogs, chickens, goats for cabrito, and wandering groups of whitetail deer. It was a small farm by Texas standards, which also helped keep it from being obvious. Its name was El Rancho Escondido.

  Alex had the good fortune of being asked to manage the farm for the Tucker Breen Trust fifteen years earlier. Having a farm or ranch designation with the UA offered a number of additional freedoms and benefits. Although they were taxed at the same high rate, barters were frequent and all but impossible for the government to keep track of. Additionally, farmers and ranchers were the only class of Citizens who were legally permitted to own firearms.

* * * * * *

"Lunch is served, gentlemen." Heather said as she opened the front-screened door.

"Alfonso, meet my better half — Heather," Alex said as they walked into the kitchen.

"Pleased to meet you, Alfonso. But please call me Gabby — everyone does. There are those who think that I talk too much. Although, I have been known to talk the ears off of . . ."

"Alright, Gabby — I think Alfonso gets your point," Alex laughed.

"Please to meet you too, Gabby. Lunch smells great!"

"Just a little venison sausage, sauerkraut and spaetzle — nothing special."

* * * * * *

Director General Gunther Borghild stormed out of the White House, his secretary and Chief Aid all but running by his side just to keep up with his stride, and into his waiting limo. It was all he could do to keep from boiling over before he closed the limo door. And then he exploded.

"THAT SKINNY LITTLE TWO-BIT TWERP! I'D BITCH SLAP THAT MOTHER FUCKIN' PHONEY — IF I HAD HALF A CHANCE! IF HE WEREN'T THE CHOSEN ONE — AND A SPIDER TO BOOT — I'D TAKE HIM OUT PERSONALLY — AND WITH MY BARE HANDS! THE BASTARD'S CONDESCENDING ATTITUDE PERSONIFIES HIS HATRED FOR THE MILITARY. ALL THAT ILLEGITIMATE NARSASSIST CAN THINK OF IS HIMSELF — CUTTING NATIONAL SECURITY BUDGETS AND LINING THE POCKETS OF HIS POLITICAL CRONIES. WHY, I CAN'T EVEN HONOR THE LITTLE PRICK BY CALLING HIM A SONOFABITCH!"

No one said a word for a full minute once the outburst stopped. Then, a quiet voice came from inside of the front of the limo, "Where to, General?" his driver said meekly.

"AROUND THE BLOCK — a LONG block — a VERY LONG block — — TWICE! I need to think."

There followed a deafening silence inside of the limo that seemed to create a vacuum in everyone's ears. Later that day his aid had mentioned the experience to his wife and said, he "expected the bulletproof glass to shatter at any moment from the sheer pressure of the General's voice."

Borghild reached over to the limo bar and grabbed a bottle of Black Jack whiskey — poured four-fingers neat — settled quietly back into the leather seat, making a small grunt, then looked over at his Chief Aid.

"Get me Senior Director Amir on the Tel-Com."

"Sir — Tel-Com services are still down everywhere — even in the car."

"Sonofabitch."

"Yes sir."

"He doesn't have a military mobile, does he?"

"No sir. I don't think so, sir."

"Sonofabitch."

"Yes sir."

"We need to get him one, then."

"Yes sir."

"Tomorrow, I want you to arrange a private meeting between me and Hector Deimos — private and completely discrete. Do you understand?"

"Yes sir — and the location?"

"Good question. Have any suggestions?'

"How about here in your limo, sir?"

"Perfect. Let him know it's an urgent matter. Deimos needs to be aware of some intel I have come across in the last twenty-four hours. In my opinion, there's no time to waste on this issue. Tell him that I want to drive him to an area of potentially mutual interest. It could be a location of security risk."

"Can do, sir."

"If he wants more detail, well, tell him the truth. You haven't been briefed as of yet."

"I understand, General."

"In the mean time, I'm going to drop you two off at your homes for the evening and then pay a visit to Director Amir. I need his council on some future planning activities."

* * * * * *

"Delicious lunch. Do you think I could get a tour of your place, Alex?"

"By all means. Rancho Escondido isn't very fancy — nothing too special about it really. But, a nice walk around the property would be in order to settle our meal. We are completely self sufficient here. What we don't grow for food we catch or shoot. Our water comes from a crystal clean underground aquifer about 750-feet down or so. All of our power comes from the sun and wind, and heating from firewood. I'll show you some innovations we've come up with over the years. I guess you could say this is our sanctuary. Would you care to join us, Gabby?"

"Love to. Just let me get my shotgun."

"*Shotgun?*" Alfonso stopped cold.

"Just a little protection from the varments."

"*Varments?* What kind of varments?"

"Oh, you know, bobcats, wolves, feral hogs — but mostly snakes — only on occasion though."

"What kind of snakes? How many?" Alfonso said nervously.

"Not many — I mean, we usually don't see any. But just in case. Let's see, there are copperheads, coral snakes, cottonmouths, or what we call water moccasins, and of course, rattlers," Gabby said as she loaded shells into her Remington pump, "I shot a beauty just last week — must have been a granddaddy rattler. He was stretched out in the sand sunbathing down on the creek side. I'd say he was a little over six-feet and as big around as my forearm."

"Gabby made an excellent rattlesnake stew a couple nights later," Alex added. He smiled at Alfonso as they stepped from the front porch.

"We aren't going to walk down by the creek — are we?"

"Don't have to."

"Good. I've seen plenty of creeks, anyway."

They spent the better part of the next hour walking the farm and discussing the future. Alfonso would again play a critical part in the next event, "Act Three."

"I guess you haven't had much time to work on 'Act Three,' Alfonso?"

"None at all — but I've been thinking about it quite a bit. Some of the new code is already in my head."

"Where do you get your inspiration, Alfonso?" Gabby asked.

"Not sure — God maybe — aliens — although, we do have this idea tree that grows wild down by the Rio Grande south of Albuquerque," he laughed. When ideas are in season, I just walk down by the river and pick a bushel. Actually, I think it must be divine inspiration."

"Why do you think that?"

"Because the ideas are always there when I ask for them."

"Well, you should have plenty of time to work on it, mi amigo. The deadline won't be for awhile yet." Alex stated, "It isn't finalized, yet, and this is only between the three of us, but 'The Wolf' believes 'Act Three' should take place on July 4th."

Rosetta Stone

15

"The urge to save humanity is almost always a false front for the urge to rule." — H. L. Menken.

* * * * * *

"Carey, you were absolutely right. A little rest was just what the doctor ordered," Gates said enthusiastically as he entered the War Room. "Report our progress. Do we have power?"

"You'll be pleased to know we're getting very close."

"Dare I ask — how close?"

"Very," Dunstan said smiling. "Our engineers have a work-around on the software. It's only a temporary fix, but it will get all sectors back on line and buy us some time to install additional firewalls."

"What's the ETA?"

"Mister President," Director of Technology Padma spoke up. "This will be a staged restart of the grids. We will begin with the southern-most grid as a test, you see."

"Why down south first?"

"It's quite simple, actually. If our efforts fail in any way, or don't meet our expectations, fewer Citizens will be affected — plus there will be fewer political consequences. This will effectively be our test grid. Besides, those people down there are still — how shall I put this. . ?"

"Primitive?" Dunstan quickly chimed in.

"Correct," Padma continued. "If it succeeds, we will continue with each of the interconnecting grids to the north — one at a time. This method should also minimize the potential of a serious spike in power, should one occur. Provided everything goes well, all power should be restored within twelve to twenty-four hours."

"Excellent."

"We need to get this info to the Senior Board."

"Taken care of Mr. President."

"Thank you, Director," Gates said as he turned to Dunstan. "Your turn to rest, Carey."

"No need. I took a nap on the couch over there," pointing to a small conference area in the corner of the large War Room. "As a matter of fact, I think we should get some nourishment, now that you're up. We should also prepare a speech. When power comes back online — so will the Com-Centers."

"Another good idea. I want to stay here in the War Room, though. Let's eat in the conference area," Gates said walking towards the corner of the room.

"Works for me. I'll call out for pizza and beer," Dunstan said smiling.

"My sweet ass you will."

"Fine. How about a filet mignon, baked potato and asparagus?"

"And a Laphroaig will do, just dandy."

"Coming right up," Dunstan said as he reached for the Desk-Com-Display.

"Carey, you know we aren't going to be able to reach Austin with the power out."

"No worries. We'll use our staff writers here. You won't need a lengthy script. The fact is, well, there are no facts just yet, we really don't have much of anything to report."

"Good point."

"Remember, all you need is . . ."

"I know — smoke and mirrors."

"As long as you're on the screen immediately when the power is restored. This is most critical. It's important to reassure the Citizens that you're in control."

"Right."

"Let them know the power outage was the fault of the previous administration, and their faulty equipment."

"OK. But, what about Los Salvadores and 'The Wolf?'"

"Hold off on that. Just blame your predecessor. It's not like anyone has actually taken credit for this attack."

"True."

"Tell them it will be your top budget priority to update the entire system."

"It will?"

"No. But it could be close to the top — couldn't it?"

"I suppose."

"Announce that you will be creating 100,000 new solid-paying jobs to create this state-of-the-art system for the nation."

"That's not possible."

"Hell no! But who cares?"

"Another good point."

"And of course remind them that they're safe and secure, etcetera. Hell, we could write this one ourselves."

"I don't think so. The staff writers need the practice," Gates chuckled. "But, how about this Austin?"

"In due course we'll have some time to communicate with Austin. I think we should fly him back to meet with our local staff writers and we'll put together a State of the UA Speech to be broadcast, say, in a month or so."

"Excellent plan."

"Lunch is served, gentlemen," the White House waiter announced as he rolled the food cart to them.

"Just in time," Dunstan said. "I've worked up an appetite."

"Carey — I don't suppose you would have a couple of those Cubans on you — the one's we brought back from the Bahamas?"

"It just so happens," he smiled as he pulled them from his coat pocket, "but, Bill, you know it's against the law to smoke in a public room."

"So turn me in. Besides — I don't see the public anywhere."

"That's true, Bill. But then, you never do."

* * * * * *

Another week had passed. Austin and Diana were intrigued enough to meet with Conall and Eugene the following Sunday during their routine walk on the beach. Their previous meeting with Conall had been brief and there where to many unanswered questions.

"Austin, I truly wish I had more time to spend with you two."

"Wait — You can't leave us hanging!" Diana said franticly. "We have another hour or so we can spend with you today."

"It's not my choice. Timing is critical. I have to return home to plan my next event."

"Event? What event?"

"Like the events before, the blackout, and the event that's gonna come real soon!" Eugene spoke up and smiled while tipping his cowboy hat.

"I'm sure you think this power outage was caused by Pacific Edison — not unusual, no?" Conall added. "It's not like these things haven't happened before. What you will learn is that *we* cut the power. It wasn't Pacific Edison.

"It wasn't?"

"No, Austin. We cut the power to the entire North American continent."

"*What*? I mean — No way — how is that possible? And, who are the *we*?"

"Just watch the Com-Center when the power is restored. I'm sure President Gates will tell you all about it. We are Los Salvadores. Possibly you've heard of us?"

"As a matter of fact I have. But how could you possibly . . ?"

"Forget about Los Salvadores *and* the power outage. We need to know who are we?" Diana broke in.

"I promise Diana, before I leave for home today, you will know."

"OK. Fine. We obviously need to know who we are. Just continue your story before we run out of time. I'm sure there's a chapter in your story about Diana and me. So, exactly who are Los Salvadores? And, how could you cut power to an entire country?"

"Believe me — cutting all power wasn't easy. But then, nothing worthwhile comes easy — does it Austin? How we did this is a very long story in it's self. And, Los Salvadores is a rather large group of diverse followers I've managed to collect over the years. With a few exceptions, they're all non-Citizens with the ability to fly under the radar, so to speak. It is more manageable if one is not plugged into the system — if you know what I mean? But as diverse as this group is, they are individuals with a common goal."

"And that is?"

"We wanta take it back!" Eugene broke in. "We just wanta return the country back to the *people*. The *people* need the power."

"I see. So you blow up buildings and take away their electric power to ingratiate them to your cause?"

"No," Conall continued, "Our goal is to illustrate and to demonstrate the people's lack of safety and security under the current government administration. The Citizens have to be shaken back into the reality of self-government and personal responsibility. The UA leads this country with a collectivist creed, and greed I might add, which denies the existence of personal responsibility; and an amoral dogma, in which all means are justified by an imaginary utopian end."

"The Octadic Tenets."

"Correct."

"And your group thinks that this, this massive re-education and dare I say revolution can be managed?"

"Yes."

"But, that could take years! It may not even be possible."

"Oh, it's possible, Austin — in fact it's probable. But you're right. It may take years — and that's where you and Diana come in. Because, without a doubt, it will take longer than I have left."

"Then why do you bother?"

"Perhaps you've heard of the US Constitution and The Bill of Rights?"

"Rings a bell."

"Sadly, that too is gone. I bother because I remember them all. I bother because I've dedicated my life to bringing them back. I do this for my parents before me — may God rest their souls. Plus, I must live this struggle every day of my life for my own satisfaction as well. I have devoted my life, for those reasons and for your future. I made this commitment

— well — because it's the right thing to do. My hope is that you and your brother — and Diana will . . ."

"Whoa! Wait. My brother? I have a brother?" Austin stood abruptly.

"A twin."

"Yeah! And he looks jus like you, Austin. He's a *fine* man," Eugene exclaimed proudly.

"Yes — you have a twin. And in many ways he's like you. In many ways he's a lot like me as well. I said that I would tell you who you are, but before I do, let me preface by explaining why I've chosen this time to meet you.

"We're all ears," said Diana.

"I want you to join me."

"You what?" Austin's mouth dropped. "You want me to join you? What are you talking about? You're joking. Join you how?"

"I would like for you and your brother — and yes you, Diana, to continue my enterprise. As I stated before, this struggle will out live me. Should you choose to join us, there are two possible paths to consider. The choice — the decision will be up to you. Understand — this isn't a choice that must be made today. You will have time to analyze your course of action."

"What you're suggesting sounds fanciful," Diana interjected.

"Be that as it may, should you choose to join us, your first option would be to carefully continue your rise in the United Authority, ascending to the highest level of power and importance. Learn the inner workings. Determine who the real power players truly are — ultimately positioning yourself to help make changes from within, when possible — perhaps to even take President Gates' post."

"But, he *is* the power. He's the President!"

"And beside that, he's elected," Diana exclaimed.

"There is no doubt that Gates has power; however, he is but the personification of the real power. He answers to an even more powerful UA Executive Board of Directors. His elections have been manipulated — and his power is, at the end of the day, fleeting."

"Interesting — and you know this to be true?"

"Yes."

"All of this remains to be seen," Austin broke in. "But, continue, the second path is. . ?"

"You and Diana escape Citizenship — join your brother and Los Salvadores."

"Right. And once we've made our decision — I mean, if we choose to believe you and take one of your alternatives — how do we communicate that . . .?"

"You won't have to. In time, either your brother or I will contact you. I will be leaving for Colorado tonight."

"Once again, I think we need some form of proof — some verification you're telling the truth,"

Diana said quietly, "I mean, you have told us an incredible story. It's all very fascinating, and you seem to have a lot of details. But how do we know that any of this is . . . ?"

"Any of this is true? You are absolutely right, Diana. I'm not asking you to make a perilous leap of faith. Please keep an open mind, as I know you will. What I am about to tell you will confirm who I am and what I say to be the truth." Conall reached in his pocket and pulled out a small, tattered, paper booklet. "Here is a copy the US Constitution I referred to. It may be the last of two remaining copies. Your brother keeps the other," He said as he carefully handed it to Diana, "I would like for the two of you to read it — preserve it."

Before his departure, Conall spent the next hour or so explicating the origins of Austin, Alex and Diana. It was far from an easy disclosure. He understood the psychological shock that this revelation would have on someone — and had spent years rehearsing his message to minimize the potential trauma. Conall earnestly tried to consider the impact of this revelation and frequently asked himself the question,

How do you tell someone that — he is you?

* * * * * *

Several days later, in the evening or the early morning hours, the power was restored in California and gradually throughout most of the remaining continent. Austin and Diana were awakened from a restless sleep at 6am to the sound of their Tel-Com and the United Authority anthem. Simultaneously, they tilted their heads up to face the wall-mounted screen in front of them. Within seconds, the traditional montage of patriotically soothing images and the ubiquitous graphic message came into focus:

"United Security and Safety is *your* Safety and Security."

The montage slowly dissolved to President Gates seated calmly behind his desk in the Oval Office.

"My good friends and loyal Citizens — good morning. I hope you had a pleasant night's rest."

Diana slowly turned her head to Austin, smiled, and in a whisper said, "Here's Billy!"

Austin quickly covered his mouth with his hand to keep from simultaneously laughing and choking. Once in control, he whispered back, "Quiet!"

"As you no doubt have noticed, we have restored your power. Let me be clear — there is no excuse for this loss. I know the anxieties that are out there right now. Some of you may be frustrated; some may even be angry. Let it be known that this power outage was the fault of the previous administration, and their unreliable equipment. Had I known or been made aware when I took office that these systems were unreliable, I would have taken measures to upgrade our entire electrical grids. But, make no mistake, plans are already in the works to budget the necessary UA Credits to not only bring the equipment and systems up to state-of-the-art levels; I am proposing a massive employment program as well. We can put more Citizens to work today building the infrastructure of tomorrow. The UA will be creating 100,000 new, solid-paying jobs to expedite this historic project. We will be creating a new UA Energy Bureau to oversee the development and maintain the proper infrastructure."

"So we face big and difficult challenges. Despite our hardships, our union is strong. We will not give up. We will not quit. We will not allow fear or minor set backs to break our spirit."

"As we stabilize and rebuild the electrical system, I will also be ever vigilant in maintaining your safety and security. Now let's be clear – I did not choose to tackle this issue. But I also know this problem is not going away. When I took office, I promised change. I've said time and time again, part of that *'Change'* is continuously correcting the wrongs of the previous administrations. And unlike those before me, I have provided real transparency in my administration. I am absolutely convinced that we are better off today as a nation. Citizens are finally equal. Never before in our history have the majority of Citizens possessed the absolute necessities in life. We believe in the common good. We have true and lasting equality. There is meaningful and actual harmony."

"That is the leadership that I am providing you. Let me set the record straight. There is more work to be done. There is more progress to be made. There will be more challenges ahead. We must not look back. The past is over. We must continue to look forward. We must plan for our future. Rest assured, I will continue to budget the required resources to make the changes I promised. But, I need your help. You must sacrifice for the good of the United Authority when called upon. There should be no doubt that we are all in this together. And — at the end of the day, it is your safety and security that will result. Good morning, and rest assured — the United Authority will always be with you."

Gates' video feed dissolved into scenes of children playing and beautiful fields of rustling flowers with the UA anthem softly playing in the background.

As the Com-Center continued with regularly scheduled programming, Diana sat up in bed and said, "Well, that has to be the shortest address on record. What he needs is a better Director of Communication."

"Maybe I should look into that," Austin smiled.

"And Austin, did you notice? There was no mention of — you know who."

* * * * * *

The morning's commute seemed more congested than usual. Both Diana and Austin were on the long side of late for work, as were many others it appeared. Adding to their tardiness was the morning's broadcast and their breakfast conversation. He went so far as to admit that the President did a fine job but he would be able to provide Gates with superior copy. Even though they had spent the better part of the previous evening talking about their last meeting on the beach with Conall, they couldn't help but continue their conversation that morning. It was challenging speaking in the condo. They could only do so in guarded, almost coded language. Each agreed to consider all of their options and to plan another walk on the beach in the near future.

Once they arrived at their respective destinations, they realized there were others who were even later than they were. Both knew that one of their first priorities this day would be issuing staff memos reminding their staffs of the importance of being on time — and the more than severe consequences of the alternative. The UA had a most strict "Three Times and You're Out" employment policy. Being unemployed was one of the first steps to becoming a dreaded Plebeian. UA employment was only guaranteed to Citizens in good standing. The serious infraction of employment standards, anti social or anti UA behavior, and of course, criminal convictions were dealt with the harshest of penalties — Citizenship expulsion.

"Good morning, Katy. I somehow knew you'd be here before I arrived."

"Of course. I can't afford to be late — and who would prepare your morning Coca-Coffee?" She smiled sweetly.

"I hope you know how much I appreciate you."

"I do. And only *I* know how much more you *could* appreciate me."

Austin knew very well. He felt that she might be one of the few women he'd ever known who he could fully appreciate — on a regular basis. Not to mention the fact that her temptation was one of daily provocation.

"I presume Klaud is in?"

"He is, and on a conference call with the President's office."

"Has he asked for me?"

"Not yet."

"Better that way. I'll take that coffee now, thanks." He walked through to his office. "Oh — let Randi know I'm . . ."

"She knows."

"Of course she does," he said as his door was closing behind him.

No sooner had he settled behind his desk, than Katy emerged with his coffee. She walked provocatively to his desk cradling the cup, tightly to her well-endowed chest, with both hands.

"The warmth feels so good between my hands," she purred as she leaned forward across the desk with arms outstretched, "Randi said that the Director would like to see you in his office now."

"Thank you, Katy." Austin stayed seated behind his desk for a few moments, taking mental inventory of all possible topics Klaud may have in mind, while sipping on his hot coffee. It was an old habit that continued to serve him well, albeit less necessary than before. Once organized, he took the short walk down the hall.

"Good morning, Randi."

"And to you, sir."

"I trust you made out well in the dark?" he said as he walked past her desk.

"Very well, thank you for asking, as I'm sure you and Diana have as well?"

"That's not what I . . ."

"I know, sir," she said smiling, "The Director is expecting you."

"Women," Austin said under his breath as he entered Klaud's office.

"Good morning, Austin! Nice to have the power back on, isn't it? Have a seat. Just finished a long conversation with the President's office."

"Did you get more detail than we did from the President's address?"

"An earful you might say. Confidentially, the power outage covered the better part of the entire continent — from the southern tip of what was formerly Mexico to the northern reaches of Alaska. There is more detail we can discuss later, but the real cause was not disclosed in his broadcast."

"No?" Austin asked as he sat up straight and leaned forward towards Klaud's desk. He was already anticipating the answer, which could eliminate any remaining doubt he may have had.

"No. It was those damn Salvadores and 'The Wolf.'"

"They know for sure? And it was the entire continent?"

"Positive — and there's more information as well. In fact, Carey Dunstan is flying out tomorrow to meet with us. He'll be here early, so clear your calendar for the full day. I'll brief you over dinner tonight. Dinner's on me."

"On you, Klaud?" Austin smirked.

"Well — not exactly. How about my favorite restaurant at seven? Be sure to have Diana meet us there. Some of this concerns her, too. Plus, she will dress the table."

"It will make her evening. If there's nothing else, I have a full day scheduled," he said as he stood and began towards the door.

"Good. Oh — and another thing, Austin — you haven't bought that new house yet, have you?"

"No. Why?"

"I wouldn't bother."

* * * * * *

It had been a long and tiring day. Austin mentally replayed the day's events in his head as he drove back to Redondo that afternoon. It was another discipline or habit if you will, that forced him to refocus on the details. He had called Diana upon leaving Klaud's office and suggested they meet at the restaurant after work rather than their condo.

Mixed in with the other details floating in his head was the confirmation to the cause of the power outage. How much more proof could there possibly be? He couldn't wait to relay this revelation to Diana. The question now was how or rather where this conversation could take place — certainly not in the condo. He knew those walls had ears.

Austin and Klaud drove into the restaurant parking lot within minutes of each other. Diana's car wasn't to be seen, so they decided to stand close to the front door to talk and allow Klaud to finish his Cuban.

"I'm sorry, Austin. How rude of me. We've been standing here this entire time and I didn't offer you a Cuban."

"Maybe after dinner. At any rate, I see Diana's car approaching."

"Fine. I think I'll join you with another after dinner as well. Now — to finish my thoughts on the subject, I'm quite sure you now understand the President's wisdom of not placing the blame on 'The Wolf' and his band of outlaws in this morning's broadcast?"

"Clearly. But I'm not sure we should be having this conversation out in public."

"Not to worry. We're outside after all, and the valet is parking a car."

At about that time, Diana stopped in front and Austin opened her door.

"Hello, love." Austin said as he helped her out and gave her a kiss. "How can you look so radiant after a hard day at work."

"Thank you. I love you too. It's because I'm in show biz, don't you know."

Klaud promptly stepped in front of Austin and reached for Diana's hand to kiss.

"Austin's right, my dear. You look good enough to eat tonight. Shall we? Go inside, that is," he smirked.

Standing now behind Klaud, Austin rolled his eyes so that only she could see. Austin slowly shook his head. *No one but a high-level Director could possibly get away with comments like that. It just isn't Authority Correct. Now watch as Klaud walks inside continuing to smoke his Cuban. Unnn –believable! And no one will say a word to him.* They walked to the door, and as he held it open for them to enter, Klaud asked: "Tell me, you two — how do you two feel about living in Colorado for a while?"

* * * * * *

Late in the afternoon, Director Deimos and Padma had been standing in front of the bank of large, wall mounted Com-Centers when President Gates returned to the War Room under Cheyenne Mountain. They had paid little attention to Gates and Dunstan as they talked in the corner conference area. Deimos was calculating his timing to report the good news — wanting to make the best impression, therefore building his political capital. Glancing occasionally at the corner of the room, he waited until they finished their meal. Sensing an opportunity, he tapped Padma on the shoulder and they casually walked to the corner conference area.

"Good afternoon Mister President — Carey."

"Director Deimos — Director Padma! Congratulations on restoring power."

"Yes sir. Good news."

"Great news! In fact, Carey and I will be leaving it in your capable hands shortly. We don't seem to be needed for now. I'm not even sure why you called this meeting, considering the power has been restored for several days."

"We have some new intel to share with you. It's nice to see you in such good spirits, gentlemen."

"I'm feeling a lot better," Gates admitted, "We've all been under a lot of pressure lately. Would you care to join us? — A Laphroaig perhaps, and a Cuban?"

"We accept, sir," Deimos smiled, "and we, in turn, will provide you gentlemen with your dessert this afternoon."

"More good news, I trust?"

"Let me just say," Deimos began, "you may think it sweeter than crème brûlée."

"Wonderful. Join us. Have a seat. You have my sweet tooth throbbing," Gates smirked.

"Well sir, we have been gathering recon recently that has narrowed our search for 'The Wolf' to an area known as the Four Corners."

"I know the area. I've skied Purgatory and Wolf Creek Pass a few times."

"Good. Well, last night we received a tip that 'The Wolf' was spotted just outside of the small mountain town of Durango."

"Do we have a visual?"

"Yes. One of our operatives has spotted a Plebe who perfectly fits his description."

"This was a recent sighting?"

"Most recent, sir. And the tip last night was a confirmation. And it gets better. It seems that either 'The Wolf' lives just outside of town in a small abandoned ranch house, or he visits there on a regular basis. We haven't had time to research the title holder's name of the house, just yet though."

"Good job, Deimos."

"But wait. That's not all. You also get — 'The Wolf' — on a, shall I say, a silver platter — La Plata to be exact, this very afternoon."

"You're joking."

"Our operative has not seen him leave the ranch house yet today."

"Our man is a fixed surveillance?

"Correct. Since he was seen entering the house yesterday, no one has entered or exited the house in the past twenty-four hours since."

"So, what's the plan?"

"I've dispatched three UA Falcon whisper copters. They're en route as we speak. Each Falcon is carrying a five-man UA Safety Commando team. There will be no possibility of escape. We should walk over to the Com-Centers. They should be on-target within a few minutes."

"Excellent."

They stood and walked to the center of the room facing the large wall mounted Com-Centers. Within a few moments, a live video feed began to stream from each of the Falcons.

"Base command — this is wolf patrol-one. Do you copy?"

"Copy, wolf patrol-one," Deimos reported.

"Base command — do you have our visual feeds?"

"Copy that, wolf patrol-one. Visual is clear. This appears to be an affirmative of the target. The description seems to match. Do you have the reported coordinates?"

"Affirmative. Coordinates match our dispatch orders. Do we have a go?"

"Green light, wolf patrol-one. The President is watching — so don't let us down."

"Copy that. Out."

There were smiles all around as everyone in the War Room's eyes were fixed on the three center Tel-Coms. Each Com-Center was receiving directionally unique views of the assault from each of the Falcons. The only audio was from the occasional chatter of one pilot to the others. The War Room was otherwise silent in quiet anticipation of the capture. And then — it all came apart.

"Holy crap! Did you see that?" blurted the President.

"Oh my god! What the hell!" Dunstan yelled at Deimos.

"I don't know! I can't see — I can't tell what. Wolf patrol — *report*! Do you copy? What in the god's names is happening? REPORT — *Wolf patrol*!"

Paroxysm

16

"Wisdom is knowing what to do next — Virtue is doing it." — David Star Jordan

* * * * * *

Mid morning, three stealth, UA Falcon whisper copters were flying fast and low thru the Rocky Mountain Canyon just west of the Continental Divide, heading southwest at -122 degrees from north out of the Springs. Each carried their cargo of a five-man UA Safety Commando team to a target location in what is known as the Four Corners Region.

The highly skilled pilots pushed their whisper copters to the limits maintaining a top speed of 260-knots, or about 300-mph, at just 200-feet above average terrain. They were sleek, unmarked, charcoal gray aircraft cruising in single-file formation. The Falcons were 4th-generation stealth and fully equipped with the latest version weapon systems. Flying time from the Springs to the target would be approximately 40-minutes.

The teams had been called to report for their pre-flight briefing just before lunch that morning. Intel that had been gathered over the previous days had narrowed the search for the UA's most wanted man to a secluded canyon just west of Durango. Their primary directive was to bring this criminal back alive. Their alternative choice wasn't as pleasant. Their mission was simple — to either take, or take out "The Wolf."

It was a spectacularly clear day with no wind or weather to encumber the flight plan. Heavy snow covered the north face of the mountains, and the valley streams were beginning to run from the spring melt. The grazing herds of deer and elk were undisturbed by the all but mute aircrafts as they passed overhead.

Not long after they cleared Durango, the Falcons changed course to the north as they reduced their speed and flew up the La Plata Canyon. A small ranch house was spotted in a field that was tightly surrounded by leaf-less aspens and majestic blue spruce. Although the outer property barrier was large, the clearing at the center and around the house was narrow and only wide enough to accept one aircraft to land.

Before setting down, aerial video was streamed back to Cheyenne Mountain headquarters for target location verification as they hovered a mile to its south. Hector Deimos anxiously stood by the bank of monitors not only to verify the target location, but also to witness the ultimate capture. Within a few minutes, the OK was given to make the approach.

The plan was for the lead Falcon-1 to set down as close to the front of the ranch house as possible with the other two hovering slightly above and to the left and right. From these positions, the two Falcons hovering above could not only cover the ground crew but also scout the area for unfriendlies or possible escape activity. There was no visible movement around the house with the exception of a ranch dog pacing on the front porch and staring above at the approaching machines.

Within a split second of touchdown, the otherwise quiet afternoon broke into a violent volcanic eruption. As the lead Falcon touched the ground, it immediately shot back into the air — this time into thousands of flying jagged metal and human body parts. Flames and burning pieces of aircraft torched the farmhouse. Due to its age, the dried-timbers ignited into an instant inferno. The exploding Falcon's largest remaining rotor section flew into the center of Falcon-2 hovering to its left, creating a second powerful explosion before hitting the ground. No one on board had a chance. The single remaining aircraft narrowly escaped the convulsion of flames by sharply banking to the right. Once stabilized, the pilot radioed back to the base command — reporting the event and awaiting further orders.

* * * * * *

Dunstan's aircraft set down at the Long Beach airport around 8am Tuesday morning. He spent the 2-hour flying time going over his notes for the day's meeting as well as communicating with the Springs regarding the Durango mission developments. His meeting with Director Akakios and Austin would be even more interesting than he had originally planned. With any luck, he could report a resolution to the "Wolf" problem.

A lone UA Security Aid was waiting for him at the gate and standing beside his ground transportation. As he stepped down from the aircraft, Dunstan could only stare in disbelief. He slowly descended the steps while never taking his questioning eyes from the more than disappointing sight. *I truly hope that this is some kind of twisted joke Bill is playing on me.*

"Good morning, sir. I'm Special Agent Fuchili. Welcome."

"Good morning *hell*! Welcome my *ass*! *Where's* my limo? And *what* in the gods name is *this*?"

"It's a hydro sedan, sir," Fuchili answered innocently.

"Hydro sedan my sweet ass! I repeat — where is my *limo*? Is this a joke?"

"No, sir. We had a problem at the motor pool. You see, we only . . ."

"Well — FIX the fucking problem. I'm not riding in that miniature Citizen's car."

"It's the only vehicle available, sir. The limo is waiting for parts. You see we . . ."

"You mean to tell me — we own a car company and *this* is the best you can do? You couldn't pull a limo from. . ."

"*Yes*, sir. I mean, *no*, sir," he shrugged his shoulders, "That one's down as well — same problem. The parts are on backorder."

Dunstan stood in silence for the better part of a minute, staring at the small sedan and shaking his head from side to side. "Fine. Fine! I'll have somebody's ass for this! Just get in. Get me to the damned Continuity building — pronto," Dunstan moaned in complete resignation.

"Yes, sir." All Fuchili could think of was: *Please don't kill the messenger. I'm just doing my job. And I really need my job.*

Dunstan crouched down forcing his six-foot-plus frame into the back seat, as Fuchili held his door. "But when I leave this afternoon, I expect a limo. And I don't care how you get it. Understood?"

"Fully." *I will perform magic and pull one out of my ass if I have to.*

"And another thing, Fuchini."

"It's Fuchili, sir."

"Whatever."

"Yes, sir?"

"Does the Continuity building have underground parking?"

"Yes, sir."

"Good. Use it. The fewer people who see me in this tin can, the better." *Bill, if this is a joke — I'M NOT LAUGHING!* Dunstan spent the twenty minute drive to the UA Continuity building, crouched in the back seat, head tilted from the low ceiling, talking on his secure Tel-Card checking for the latest mission updates and complaining to Gates about the humiliation of riding in, in his words, "This Citizen's POS." Gates' only response was to laugh.

* * * * * *

"Good morning, sir. I am Randi. The Director is expecting you. Please go right in. Would you care for a coffee?"

"Yes please — but only if you lace it with something strong. Make it a double. And of course I remember you, Randi. How could I forget you?" Dunstan said as he stared for a moment at her rather well developed chest rather than her eyes, then he stormed into Akakios' office.

"Carey!"

"Good morning, Klaud. Where's Austin?"

"He's in his office. I'll call him."

"Good. We've got a lot on the agenda and little time to cover it."

"I trust your trip was . . ."

"Let's just say I'm not happy, and leave it at that. I'll explain over lunch."

Austin approached the Director's door at the same time Randi walked up carrying a tray with three coffees.

"Hello, Austin. I prepared a coffee for you."

"You're the best, Randi."

"I know. I hear it repeatedly." She all but whispered.

She served each of the men individually and carefully. Before leaving the room she purposely walked behind the Director's desk, bending over and handing him a note. Standing up straight she provocatively adjusted her rather tightly fitting silk uniform, smiled, and asked if the gentlemen cared for anything else.

"That will be all for now. Thank you, Randi. And no interruptions please." Dunstan exclaimed.

"Of course, sir," she said as she walked slowly out the door.

"Klaud, It's always a pleasure to visit you. You have a real knack for employee recruitment."

"Why, Carey — I always thought you were of another persuasion."

"I am a man of variety, Klaud, a man of variety. And how about you Austin? How's Diana?"

"She's well. Thank you for asking. She's a little apprehensive about Colorado though."

"She shouldn't be. But, I like that. A good woman needs to counterbalance our aggressive natures. Trust me, she is going to fit right in. Now, let's get right to business. There are three items to be covered on my agenda today. Your move to Colorado is one of those. However, due to recent developments, I'm changing the order of priorities."

"New developments about the power outage I presume?" Klaud interjected.

"Better than that. We think we've nailed the 'Wolf.'"

With that, Austin almost dropped his coffee. He grabbed the linen napkin from Klaud's desk and quickly blotted the few drops from the of lap his uniform.

Klaud sat up straight in his chair staring at Austin. "Are you OK?"

"Fine. The coffee is a little hot — that's all. You were saying?"

"Three Falcon whisper choppers with assault teams were dispatched from the Springs yesterday afternoon to the Four Corners Region. You may have heard of the area. It . . ."

"Yes — Yes. I know of it." Akakios quickly remarked.

Austin simply nodded yes with a glazed look in his eyes.

"We had received positive intel that the 'Wolf' was either visiting a small ranch house there or it may have been his safe-house — not sure at this point."

"*May* have been?" Austin asked as he swallowed hard.

"Yes. Well — you see there was a slight problem. The house is totaled."

"Completely?" Austin gulped.

"Burned to the ground — and then some. The logistics of the mission were straight forward — S.O.P. We dispatched the three Falcons to surveile and then capture 'The Wolf' on his escape from the house. The lead chopper was to land as close to and in front of the ranch house as possible, while the other two hovered above. When the lead chopper set down, it immediately exploded, instantly killing everyone onboard."

"*Holy shit!*" Akakios almost shouted.

"That's not all. One of its blades sailed through the air and sliced completely through the chopper that was hovering to its left. It too exploded even before hitting the ground. Again, everyone on board perished."

"Incredible," Akakios whispered. "How about the third copter? Hopefully it was . . ."

"Fortunately it escaped while witnessing flying, flaming parts engulfing the nearby trees and the ranch house where the 'Wolf' was thought to be hiding."

"Was he?" Austin said meekly as his head began to throb.

"Don't know — yet."

"How on earth did this happen?" asked Akakios.

"At first we assumed it was a strategically placed booby trap or land-mine."

"It wasn't?"

"No. I received an update during this morning's flight here. After further investigation, it turned out to be a faultily capped, natural-gas well in front of the house — a terrible and tragic accident."

"What about the ranch house — and the 'Wolf?'" asked Austin.

"We just don't know conclusively. As I said, the house is toast. It is still undetermined whether or not the 'Wolf' has perished in the farmhouse inferno. There was a body found inside — or what was left of one that is. But, it remains to be seen, at this point, whether or not he's our man."

"The corpse is a man?" Austin asked softly.

"We think so. It may take a while, to know for a positive ID."

"It will be a great day if we finally got that outlaw," Akakios interjected.

Dunstan twisted and stretched in his chair, "I could use a bathroom break, and then more coffee — maybe a snack as well." Dunstan suggested.

"Great idea. I could use a snack, too." Akakios agreed.

Austin stared at him as he stood. He noticed for the first time that Dunstan also shared a small tattoo of a spider on the back of his neck. He had remained seated momentarily frozen in thought. His eyes wide open, he felt as if he was unable to blink. The daily revelations were compounding. *Unbelievable!* A dozen thoughts scrambled through his mind simultaneously — most of them were questions.

Klaud stayed behind his desk for a moment to read the note Randi had slipped him. It read: "Katy would like to know if Mister Dunstan will be staying over this evening?" He stood, then slid the note into his coat pocket and grinned as he walked out the door. "Randi. Please call down to the bakery and have fresh pastries delivered immediately. Make it a nice variety." He began to walk away, then turned back to her. "Oh yes, and the Chief of Staff will not be staying over. He'll be flying back to the Springs this evening."

"Too bad for him," She said sweetly, "Maybe next time."

* * * * * *

Upon returning to Klaud's office they passed the time in small talk while Randi served them warm pastries and refreshed their coffee.

"Next on the agenda is 'Project Arachnid,'" Dunstan continued once Akakios' door snapped shut.

"Which is?" Akakios queried.

"Top secret. This information must not leave this room. Perhaps you have some understanding regarding human cloning research?"

"Some yes," Akakios nodded his head.

"A little," Austin repeated. *I've learned a lot lately, though. Please tell me more.*

"Well, our research team in Austin has not only perfected plenary human clones in their lab, but they have also developed a method of pre-programming them and expediting their rapid development as well."

"How's that?" Austin quickly asked.

"They can isolate specific genomes to eliminate all imperfections that would cause future diseases or weaknesses, of course, then add others for distinctive behavioral characteristics while implanting micro-chips utilizing nano technology. Additionally, they will cancel all reproductive functions."

"Incredible. What are these chips?"

"It *is* incredible, Klaud. My understanding is that they have created a form of DNA "origami" for a powerful new generation of ultra-tiny microchips. The real breakthrough however has been in their abilities of mass production. Did you know that female spiders lay up to 3,000 eggs in one or more silk egg sacs?"

"Mass production of the chips?"

"Yes. And — mass production of the clones. In short order, entire classes of Citizens can be replaced."

"Replaced?" Austin asked in disbelief.

"Austin, 'replaced ' may not be the suitable word to use. You may wish to help us better describe this function — you know — it needs to be a bit more Authority Correct."

"So, how much time are we talking about, and what classes?" asked Akakios. "Are we looking at months or years into the future?"

"The lab is working on a deadline that will finalize human trials by the end of this year. Provided those trials are successful, population implementation could begin as soon as next year. We are just beginning to examine the paradigm that will be the most expeditious while controlling Citizen awareness and, at some level, acceptance. Now — as to which classes you ask? Most all classes of Citizens will be replaced over a period of time."

"I don't understand," Austin began. "How do you replace entire classes of Citizens without . . .?"

"It's not how do you, Austin — it's how do *we*?

The next hour was spent reviewing the history of human cloning research and "Project Arachnid" specifically to Klaud and Austin.

"So please understand that you and Klaud will be an integral part of the plan. You see, the UA ruling class, those of us in power, will be exempt from replacement. The answer to your question, Austin, is quite simple. Natural attrition will take care of some in each of the classes — we will take care of the rest. You know, the cranial micro-chip that all Citizens have implanted at birth will simply be turned off — individual by individual — possibly, class by class."

"But that would be . . ."

"Terminal is the word you're thinking of — mostly terminal. Does that disturb you, Austin?"

"As a matter of fact . . ."

"As a matter of fact," Akakios broke in, "what Austin means to say is how will that affect the Continuity Bureau?"

"Oh. I see. Well, that's another reason we are meeting today. The Continuity Bureau will be going away."

"It what?" Akakios blurted.

"Don't worry gentlemen. It won't happen soon. Most likely, Klaud, it will not happen until after you retire to your place in Mexico. Who knows, maybe you will be able to opt for the 'UA Early Retirement Plan.'"

"I wasn't aware we had one." Akakios stated nervously.

"Well then, Klaud, this might be another little project for you to propose to the President and Senior Board.

"Nevertheless — *no* Continuity Bureau?

"But, surely Klaud, you can see the future? At some point, there simply will be no need for Continuity. Memories and life experiences will be implanted at birth. All historical and current information will be a product of the ultra-new media. In the meantime, the Continuity Bureau is more important, dare I say critical, than ever before. 'Project Arachnid' will require a massive amount of information control. That's where you two come in, and the third item on my agenda for the day. But first, I suggest we break for an early lunch. Do you have any suggestions?"

* * * * * *

The leisure two-hour lunch did little to abate Austin's throbbing head. He couldn't help but think back, not that long ago, when life seemed simpler, albeit mundane, when one day bled into another, and there never seemed to be a distinction from one day to the next. He was no longer caught in a constant state of limbo — no longer stagnant. His life was moving now at warp speed. Austin felt as though he could define his current existence in one word — "flux."

"Excellent little lunch, Austin. I haven't had sushi in forever — college maybe. What a quaint little restaurant. And that waitress — she's hilarious! I can't wait to tell Bill. He won't believe it," Dunstan laughed as they walked back down the hall towards Akakios' office.

"That was very nice for a change of pace. I can't believe you never shared your secret with me, Austin. Randi, would you mind — fresh Coca-Coffee please?" Klaud asked as they quickly passed through his office door.

"Austin, that brings me to you and Diana. Maybe you're beginning to understand why we need you at the White House."

"Well yes, I'm starting to get the picture."

"You're a bright guy. Diana's a bright gal. We're glad you two are body-mates because you both have lustrous futures with the United Authority. In a couple of months, we would like for you and Diana to move to the Springs and work closely with us preparing the information required for the 'Project Arachnid' roll out. You two will also be training our staff writers to take over when you eventually return to the Continuity Bureau."

"How long should we plan on working in the Springs?"

"Maybe a year — possibly a little more."

"It will be difficult getting along without you, Austin," Akakios spoke up.

"I'm sure you'll manage, Klaud. Plus, Austin will be available to you on a special needs basis."

"What happens when we shut down the Continuity Bureau?" Austin asked.

"By then, as I mentioned, Klaud will most likely have already retired. We will want you to be promoted to Continuity Director just prior to helping us to shut it down. Of course, we'll also want to make a big production about closing the Bureau. You know, reducing the size of government — saving the Citizen's Credits, etc. Once we shut down the Bureau, you and Diana will then move back to the Springs."

"We can't carry on or duties from here in California?"

"You could — but I have other plans for you as well. And those plans require an eventual and permanent move to the Capitol."

"How about my senior staff here?"

"Good question, and one we have plenty of time to plan. But, at the very least, you may select a few key senior staff members to join us. It would be smart to identify them sooner rather than later. In that way you will be able to discretely groom them for their new positions. That being said, no one — let me repeat and be very clear — no one can know any aspect of our future plans. Even the key people you're grooming must not be given the slightest hint until days before the transition. Understand?"

"Clearly."

Dunstan spent another hour or so asking and answering questions before taking his leave.

Austin returned to his office and spent the remainder of his afternoon organizing his workload for the next day. Although he dutifully told Dunstan that he understood his orders clearly, he was actually quite confused as to which future path he should now choose.

* * * * * *

Dunstan stepped out of the elevator and into the underground parking garage. He immediately spotted Fuchili standing beside a limo — of sorts. It had been a long day and he simply wanted to get on his aircraft and relax — and now this.

"Fuchedi — Fuchedi — Fuchedi. What in the name of UA creation is this?"

"It's Fuchili, sir. You see — our limos are still waiting for those parts, sir. So I rented this from a local funeral parlor. Is it OK, sir?"

Dunstan was all but speechless. He merely shook his head from side to side as he slowly approached the hearse's rear passenger door. "Just take me to the airport, Fuchili."

His flight back to the springs was mostly uneventful. The weather was clear, and a strong tailwind, managed to reduce flying time by a full twenty minutes. He was starving and decided to order a prime rib, baked potato, and fresh asparagus for the return flight. It was an opportune time for contemplation and solitude. Dunstan agreed fully with the Gates' comment about being under a lot of pressure. He was sensing an undercurrent at the Capitol. Events were shaking the stability of control. It was time for him to get a better handle on the situation — before the handle hit him squarely in the back of his head.

Deep in thought and as his aircraft was dropping for its final approach into Colorado Springs his secure Tel-Card rang. It was a rather surprising and completely unexpected call from Senior Director Amir.

* * * * * *

Austin's drive home that evening would take considerably longer than usual. He had already called Diana to let her know that he would be running late and not to hold dinner for him. Driving up the coast a few miles, maybe to Malibu and back could be the solitude he needed to get his thoughts in order. He turned off his radio and lowered the top. The cool ocean air was more than refreshing. It seemed almost medicinal. On his way back to his condo, he stopped at a small bar in Manhattan Beach, hoping a couple of drinks would finish taking the edge off before going home — also providing him a bit more quiet time to think.

"What'll ya have tonight, Citizen — beer or wine?" asked the bartender as Austin saddled up to the bar.

"Don't you have something a little stronger?"

"Very funny! You're joking — right? What kind of a place do you think this is, Pardner? You know that's all they'll let us serve."

"Sorry. I forgot. I'll have a beer — dark beer."

"Comin' right up."

"Thanks."

"Looks like you've had a tough day, Pardner," the bartender said as he placed the opaque beverage in front of him. "That'll be $37-Credits."

"Make it 50. And keep the change," he said as he slid his Tel-Card across the bar.

"Thanks. Got some problems tonight?" The bartender said as he slid the card back to Austin.

"No more so than everyone else." *If you only knew . . .*

"I know whatcha mean, Pardner. We've all got our share."

"I'm sure you hear your share of stories."

"Stories? Yep. I could tell you stories."

"Tell me one," Austin smiled, "tell me a good one. I'll bet you get an ear full. Here, hit me again." He slid his mug to the other side of the bar. The bartender grabbed it, filled it to the brim and slid it back. All the while, he was either deciding which story to pull from his memory, or maybe composing it for maximum effect.

"OK. Here's a good one. You won't believe it. A number of nights ago, I guess it was that far back, I can't remember exactly, it was before the power went out, I don't know, these two Plebes walked in. Can you dig it? — Plebes walking into a bar? Sounds like the beginning of an old joke — don't it? You know: These two Plebes walked into a bar one day, and . . ." the bartender began to chuckle. "You know. They just walked into the . . ."

"You're shitin' me?" Austin said sitting straight up on the barstool.

"Nope. It's never happened before."

"Let me guess — one was an old guy and the other had on a cowboy . . ."

"Damn! You're good. How'd you know?"

"Lucky guess."

"Yep. They wanted a beer. I had to laugh out loud."

"You gave it to them — didn't you?"

"Not exactly." He reached in his pocket. "Take a look at what I got. You don't see these too often, do ya?"

Austin stared at the hand full of crystals. "Nope — can't say I have." *I certainly wouldn't tell you, that's for sure.*

"And that's not all. The old guy says they were some kind of *magic* crystals. He said something strange and meaningful was going to happen."

"And has it?"

"Are you kidding? All the power went out a couple of days later and I didn't have ta go ta work! I'd call that pretty strange — wouldn't you?"

"Amazing," Austin said as he gulped the last of his beer "later."

"Yea. Later Pardner. Stop in again sometime."

Within fifteen minutes Austin was walking through his front door.

"Diana! I'm home!"

"So am I," she answered. "I was just watching the Com-Center. Did you eat?"

"No."

"Would you like to?"

"Maybe later."

"Tough day, Austin?"

"Yep."

"That's why you get paid the big Credits," she said smiling.

Austin walked directly into the small living room, sank into the couch, and cradled his head with both hands. "Diana. We really need to talk."

Peripeteia

17

"It's choice, not chance, that determines your destiny." — Jean Nidetch

* * * * * *

Weeks had passed since the catastrophic accident just west of Durango. The unsuccessful Four Corners mission gave Gates the feeling his head was exploding. To make matters worse, any potential evidence was all but completely lost in the ranch house inferno. It could only be determined that the human remains were that of a male who was roughly the gender, size and age of the notorious "Wolf." There was little cause for celebration, however, due to the fact that an absolute, positive I.D. could not be made. At the same time, it could not be discounted that there was at least an equal possibility that the "Wolf" had perished. That prospect combined with the fact that there had been no new major events or large disruptions since that time were positive indicators that could be used to Gates' benefit. By most measures the mission was a costly failure.

As a result and under the current circumstances, combined with the previous power outage and the growing Citizen unrest, Gates sensed that control was slipping from his grasp on several levels. His political survival required immediate and decisive performance. He fully understood that a personal action plan was now his first priority.

"How soon they forget," Gates said sarcastically.

"They who?" Dunstan smirked.

"Everyone. All of them!" *Every last fucking one of them!* Gates rubbed his forehead trying to relieve the pain that had been throbbing behind his tired eyes. He paced in short century steps back and forth behind Dunstan.

"Well, I guess that pretty much covers it."

"You know what I mean." Gates stopped to spit on the manicured green.

"Hold that thought. This next fairway is 275-yards with a dog leg." Dunstan carefully studied the drive, took aim at his ball and drove it straight and true. It was a long shot that would be hard to beat.

Gates raised his hand to his forehead to shield the sun as he studied the trajectory. "Nice."

"100-Cedits says you can't beat that shot — mister President."

"Let's make it 200." Gates placed his ball. He took a couple of practice swings, positioned his feet, then came down hard but smooth. They watched as his ball sailed down the fairway with little arch. "I think lunch will be on you today, Carey." He said with a smirk.

"Don't count your winnings till we walk the mile — so to speak. Now you were saying that everyone forgets?"

"Hell yes! Look how long I've been at this job. Look at the successes over those years. Sure we've had some recent setbacks — but you'll have to admit they have been few and far between. And there's no way I can be blamed for New York."

"Your point?"

"My point is the rising sense of discontent I feel coming from above — and even from around me." Gates wiped the sweat from his forehead then readjusted his cap as they walked to their cart.

"You're paranoid." *But don't worry buddy. I'll help take care of you — as usual. And if and when the time comes... That's what friends are for.*

"Maybe I am a little paranoid — not irrational. I'm also aware."

Dunstan slowed the cart and placed the brakes. "So you have a feeling. Do you have any facts?"

"Not yet. I don't need facts at this point. What I need is a big score — a really big win — and soon." *Like yesterday wouldn't be soon enough. I've got the lemons. I just need to understand the best method of squeezing them into several gallons of delicious lemonade.*

They stepped out of the golf cart and walked to their balls. Carey bent down to study the marking of the first ball he approached. "Looks to me, Bill, like you may be on your way to a big win today — or at least 200-Credits."

* * * * * *

Gates and Dunstan enjoyed a long lunch at the clubhouse's private, presidential dining room. They kibitzed lightly about their better plays of the day and how Gates was able to pull off a marginal win on the final putt. They relaxed and spoke of good times past and hopefully, better times to come.

Even though the dining room was private, serious conversations of state were not entertained. They did agree, however, to spend the remainder of the day back at the White House analyzing Gates' concerns and formulating a proactive plan. After all, there was always more than one way to skin a cat.

As they walked from the clubhouse to their waiting limo, three distinct shots rang out. Four UA Security agents quickly threw Gates and Dunstan to the ground and covered them. Two Security Hydro cycles launched toward the front gate of the country club with dead aim at an old pickup truck now speeding away. When it was deemed safe the President and his Chief of Staff were helped from their prone position. They watched from their distance as a single individual, the driver of the pickup was pulled from his truck and thrown to the ground. One of the UA Safety officers stood over the man with his foot planted firmly on his back. The other conducted a thorough search of the vehicle. Several minutes later the truck continued on its way. The cycles returned with their report.

"It's a beet farmer, sir. He was pulling away from the red light in front of the club when his truck backfired. Sounded like gunfire to us."

"I thought we outlawed those damned polluting trucks years ago?" Gates said brushing off his slacks.

"Farmers rights," Dunstan laughed. *Other than us, Injuns, farmers and ranchers get the gold.*

They lit a couple of Cubans and climbed inside the limo discussing the perils of holding higher office. It was a short drive back to the White House. As they entered the Oval Office Dunstan suggested they get down to business with an afternoon cocktail.

"Excellent idea. My grey matter needs stimulating." *As if being shot at by a pickup truck wasn't stimulating enough.*

Dunstan walked over to a well-stocked liquor cabinet hidden behind an oil portrait of Gates. "What are your thoughts, Bill? Since this has been on your mind, where do we start?"

"I think it's time to show some type of major progress against the rebels. And, I believe we need to do more to calm the natives. I need a State of the UA address that makes an impact — something powerful — not the usual touchy-feely. I want to create some heavy-duty smoke and mirrors. Combine those items with a comprehensive plan for the Directors and Senior Directors to quickly implement 'Project Arachnid.' All of these elements need to happen fast — maybe within a couple of weeks or so. Any ideas, Carey?"

"Let's start with the last item first. We should communicate to the research team in Austin that they have one week to write a white paper detailing their thoughts on timing and implementation of 'Project Arachnid.' They must formulate an initial protocol and deadline projection. Let them know not to waste time polishing the budget — an educated WAG is sufficient."

"Put some pressure on them." Gates swirled the golden nectar of the aged single-malt while inhaling the ninety proof fumes.

"Exactly. Turn up the heat."

"They do seem to work at their own pace." *But then everyone does.* Gates thought as his tongue touched his medicinal elixir.

"I would agree with that. It's time to ratchet them up to our new pace. Put a little urgency up their collective asses. Then we fly them here to make their presentation to our 'Arachnid' committee. We can spend a few days massaging the details for a presentation to the Senior Directors. And, I think the research team should be in attendance for that presentation as well."

"I like your thinking. Bringing the 'Arachnid' project to fruition, in and of itself, will tie the knot in our future control — total control."

"We should also include our new protégé, Austin Llanoc, in the entire process. It's time for his introduction." Dunstan added.

"Do you really think that's a . . . ?"

"Yes — for a number of reasons. But we can discuss the virtue of this later." Much later would be necessary because Dunstan had not formulated a practical excuse for his suggestion at this time — at least, one he could share with the President.

"Agreed. Overall, the plan has merit. It will quickly instill the progress our directors are wanting. A deadline is important." Gates tilted his glass back. *By the gods, this is truly their nectar.*

"What's in your mind regarding the anarchists?"

"Carey, I don't know about you, but I think, no, let me rephrase, we need to make a momentous point — an event of our own, so to speak, that will make a serious impact on Citizens, Plebes, our Directors and especially the insurgents. I want to put an end to any possible, future disruptions — period."

"In other words, you want to completely kill any future recognition of events that these banditos could be credited for."

"Exactly." Gates squinted as he relit his Cuban.

"Simple — Kill their leader."

"The Wolf."

"Right. Cut off the head — the body dies." Dunstan made a motion across his neck with his index finger.

"How do you propose we kill someone we can't find?"

"You already did, Bill."

"That can't be confirmed as of . . ."

"Can't be denied either. Look, we have the video of three UA Vipers under attack . . ." Dunstan stood, stretched and began to pace around the room.

"But they weren't really under attack . . ."

"Who's to say? And in that video we show retaliation on the ranch house."

"True." Gates stared into the ceiling, pensively rubbing his chin.

"And we have a body to show."

"But what if . . .?"

"What if what, Bill? We have the evidence. We have the media. Even if he *is* alive, who cares — they have shit. You can broadcast to the majority of Citizens a major United Authority victory."

"Good points. But, what if we take it one step farther?" Gates now looking Dunstan squarely in the eyes.

"I'm all ears."

"I want to instill the fear of Gates into the Citizens, as well as those so-called 'Salvadores,' and the 'Wolf' himself provided he's still alive."

"That's the Bill I know!"

"Carey, this will also get Director General Borghild off my back as well. I've never been able to stand for that blown-up, militaristic bully. I get the feeling all too often that he's trying to undermine my authority. So, I'll throw him a bone to keep him busy for a while. I'll call on the UA Protection Bureau to round up a few Plebes in most of the large cities. We can claim that a list of 'Los Salvadores' was found at the ranch. Evidence we found in a safe that was hidden in the ranch house basement. The military, I mean the Protection Squads, can put on a major show of force that will be videoed along with the subsequent trials and public executions of the Plebes."

Dunstan blew a perfect smoke ring across the room.

"Works for me."

* * * * * *

"Now this is something I could get use to," Diana said with a big smile.

"Beats the heck out of flying commercial, doesn't it?"

"No joke. No changing room. No security lines. No Tel-Card checkpoints. No being treated as a potential criminal. No crowded, tight seating." Diana comfortably wiggled in her over-sized, leather chair. All of her doubts were left at LAX — for the time being, anyway. She was enjoying being firmly seated in the lap of luxury.

"Correct. And, we have the entire aircraft all to ourselves — just us and the flight crew."

"Excuse me. Your lunch is ready. Madam, you ordered the grilled shrimp and bay scallops."

"Yes. Thank you."

"And, sir, the brook trout almondine."

"Correct."

"And champagne cocktails for two. Would you care for Jamaican Coca-Coffee afterwards?"

"That would be fine. Thank you."

"If you care for anything else, just let me know. We have an excellent brandy flan for desert, or blackberries and cream — your choice."

"Perfect. Thank you."

"Austin, this would be difficult to give up."

"Careful."

"You're right. I know. What I mean to say is, uh, well, I'm glad we were chosen for this important work. I wouldn't want to go back to . . ."

"Yes. It's nice to be appreciated." Austin grinned as he licked his fork. *I never considered a dilemma could be as compounded as this.*

"And it's nice that once we move to the Capitol, we'll be working together." Diana smiled. "I understand this trip will be only a few days. Did you get a briefing as to the nature of this project?"

"Only that it's very important and the President's top priority. Top secret — hush, hush don't you know. No one gets the details until the meeting tomorrow."

"And a party this evening?" Diana asked.

"When we land this afternoon, we'll be driven to the White House for a brief meeting and tour of the Cheyenne Mountain facility. Afterwards, there will be a small private party and some type of house warming. I'm not sure for whom."

"Austin, when do we get to our hotel so we can change and I can freshen up?"

"I'm sure we will be well cared for. Not to worry, dear."

"Did you notice there is a private lounge and bedroom in the aft section of the aircraft?" She said looking back over her shoulder.

"As a matter of fact I did. Klaud excused himself to the aft section on my last flight. Why do you ask?"

"Well — I was wondering if you've ever heard of the mile-high club?"

* * * * * *

"Welcome to the White House," Dunstan said as he stepped from the front door. "I trust your flight was pleasant?"

"Excellent." Austin and Diana spoke almost in unison.

"It was wonderful." Diana smiled. "We look forward to more, uh, flying that is."

"Don't worry, this is just the beginning. I know you will be enjoying more in the future. For now, the President is waiting in his office. Follow me."

On their walk, Dunstan described to Diana the reason for the long entry way and the movie-style facade of the White House, it's construction, and how and why it was backed up to Cheyenne Mountain.

Moments later, they were lead through the Oval Office door. "Austin — Diana. We're so glad you're here." Gates said as he stood up from behind his desk. "Come over to the sofa and let's get comfortable." He walked around his desk and shook their hands. "Would you care for a libation — a glass of wine, Diana, or perhaps something a little stronger? Please — have a seat."

"A glass of Pinot would be refreshing. Thank you."

"And you, Austin? As I recall, you're a whiskey man."

"I'll have what you're having, sir."

"Remember — no sir stuff in private. It's Bill, and that goes for you too Diana. We're all friends here. Carey, would you care to pour?"

"Certainly — my pleasure."

"Good flight? I trust everything was to your approval?"

"Couldn't have been better, Bill," Austin spoke up.

"And did you take Diana for a tour of the aircraft? I mean a *complete* tour?" he smiled and winked.

"I don't think I missed a single inch," Diana smiled in return. *We are not only members of 'The Club,' we did our part to christen the aircraft to boot.*

"Good. It's just so boring to fly any other way. After we chat about our plans for the week, I would like for you to take a personal tour of the mountain. Unfortunately, I have a busy schedule this afternoon. So, if you don't mind, Carey has volunteered to show you around."

"Perfect." Diana smiled at Dunstan.

"Good. Afterwards, you can freshen up from your trip in one of our guest rooms here at the White House. We'll have dinner at seven sharp in the main dining room. Afterwards, my driver will take us to the party. I think Diana is in for some rare treats."

Gates and Dunstan spent the next hour or so briefing the two on the plans they had outlined the day before and the part each would play in the development of said plans. It would be a serious commitment, plus a further test of Austin and Diana's skills and ability to work with the White House team.

Austin tried his best to focus, but would occasionally lapse into thinking of the meeting with his father — himself — the "Wolf"— whoever. He felt as though he was playing a part, acting in a life-like film — a film within a film. At times it seemed that he was even watching himself in a very odd, out-of-body experience. The sensation was difficult to describe and sometimes mentally arduous to control.

"Don't you agree, Austin?" Gates asked.

"Ah — Yes! Yes, of course. Please continue."

"That's it." Dunstan stared at Austin. "Are you OK?"

"Fine. It's just been a long day, and the whiskey, you know."

"I understand perfectly," Gates jumped in. "I'm sure this is also a bit of information overload as well. We'll be fresher in the morning. Tomorrow, however, will be a full day. Carey, why don't you show them around our mountain?"

Dunstan drove the two on an eye-opening tour of the facility few had ever experienced or ever would. He stopped briefly at various areas of interest explaining the unique function of each. Austin and Diana were full of questions and Dunstan elaborated the details with seemingly full knowledge and understanding. The final stop was at the War Room.

"This is where it all comes together," Dunstan said as they passed through the ultra-high-security entry. "This is arguably the single most important room in the complex."

"Why is it called the 'War Room?'" Diana asked.

"It's what you might call a commemorative name. You see, in the twentieth century this room was constructed to preserve and command the US military forces in the event of a major world war."

"World war?" Austin asked.

"I know it's a little difficult to understand. Our history has been scrubbed for the peaceful benefit of our Citizens. Well, obviously you already know that. But, there was a time when nations, other countries waged war against each other — even against us. Thankfully that time has passed due to our international policies and isolationist posture. That's not to say there aren't potential threats. Let's just say, well, we have taken ourselves out of the game so to speak. However, the room could be useful in the future."

"How's that?" Austin queried.

"You will be fully briefed in the very near future. I have had some recent communication with some of our Senior Directors. There are plans in the not so distant future that involve you — and you as well, Diana."

"Could you give us an idea what . . ."

"I can give you more than an idea — but only in this room — and it will not leave this room — not even with the President. Understood?"

"Got it." Austin and Diana agreed. Although they agreed, both thought it odd that the President would be out of the loop.

"Austin, I want to appoint you to become the UA's next Director of Communication. Pete Barlow, the current Director retires at the end of this year. Diana will be appointed the Executive Vice Director. The President is well aware of this part of our plans."

"I don't know what to say."

"Say nothing to no one. It is but the first step."

"And the next step being?"

"The next step stays locked in the 'War Room.' We want you to ultimately become our next Chief of Staff."

* * * * * *

At nine that evening, the Presidential limo and entourage drove through the entrance of the Flying Horse residential development. The homes in this exclusive gated community were built around a championship-style, 18-hole, regulation course dating back to the start of the 21st century. Although most of the large, luxurious estates had been maintained and updated through the years, others were razed and replaced with even grander homes.

Slowly winding around the serpentine streets the motorcade pulled into a large horseshoe drive and to the front of a sprawling Spanish-style villa. The President's limo stopped under a large, covered portico with a massive fountain opposite a set of grand double doors.

"I believe we're fashionably late," Dunstan said as he held his hand out to Diana exiting the limo.

As they approached the front door Diana asked, "I completely forgot to ask whose house warming party is this?"

"Why — it's yours, my dear." Gates smiled holding her other arm. "Welcome home."

As both doors began to open exposing a luxurious grand foyer, Diana began to feel as though her legs were turning to pudding.

"Mine? Ours?" She stuttered, her feet frozen to the hand-formed tiles.

"And welcome to our family." Dunstan grinned. "I hope it meets with your approval."

"You're joking." Austin gasped as they crossed the polished granite threshold.

"No reason to joke."

"But, our condo . . ." Diana began.

"Of course — you can keep your condo as well — if you choose. It might be valuable as a rental property," Dunstan continued, "We can take a tour of the house later to make sure it meets your approval. Before we join the party, however, let me just mention that your new home is slightly more than nine-thousand square feet, seven bedrooms, each with a private bath. There is an indoor/outdoor pool, hot tub, and you're on the 9th green," Dunstan bragged.

"I'm not sure what to — how to — what can I say?" Austin gulped.

"Oh my gods," Diana whispered as she viewed the entry's richness.

"That's all you need to say for the moment. But I say — we should join the party in the great room. Right this way," Gates proclaimed.

Between thirty and forty couples, not including UA Service Girls and Guys, Security and catering staff had begun to arrive a couple of hours earlier. The party was already in full swing as Austin and Diana were escorted into the great room with President Gates between them. Gates stopped at the large arched entry to the great room and raised his hands. There was an immediate silence.

"I would like to personally introduce to you our newest members, au courant friends, and our next Director and Vice Director of Communications — Austin and Diana. Please welcome them to their new home." A subdued round of applause followed Gates' resonant intro. "Please — each and everyone, take some time this evening to introduce yourselves to our new associates. Help us make these Citizens feel at home, and — let the party continue!"

"I believe the next order of business is to find our way to the bar," Dunstan exclaimed, "Would anyone care to join me?"

* * * * *

Austin and Diana gazed into each other's eyes' secretly communicating with looks of which no one else could know. They stared in a vacuum of their total silence. It was as if the sounds of the party around them had been muted. Complex thoughts were transferring between them to their amazement. The words, if spoken, would have been simply — *Now what?*

So many of the previous weekends had been spent walking on the beach, debating the dilemma of their future. Each was burdened by the clear understanding that the choice remained only theirs to make. Ultimately it was the result of each choice that remained so cloudy. It wasn't as if they faced an aggregate of alternatives — there was but one of only two. It had suddenly become even more difficult to justify the thought of walking away from a life of privilege into an uncertain existence for that of a noble cause.

"Excuse me." Dunstan broke in. "You two appear to be in shock."

Austin slowly swiveled his head towards Dunstan. Diana turned hers in the opposite direction and stared at Gates. After a second's pause, they almost spoke in unison.

"We were considering our options."

"To what options are you referring?" Gates asked.

"Why — our libation du jour — of course," Austin dryly exclaimed.

"The choice is yours."

"So we've been told." Diana smiled as they walked to the bar.

"You may also choose to take a tour now — or we may join the party."

"Decisions, decisions," she said.

"There will be more to come."

"Of that, I'm sure." Austin sighed.

"If you will please excuse me?" Gates asked. "I have some people I must speak with. Carey would you show our new friends around?"

Diana tried to imagine the two of them living alone in this spacious residence as they leisurely walked from room to room occasionally stopping to meet new acquaintances and chatting along the way. Breakout parties of groups in various forms of enjoyment had already occupied many of the rooms. Some of those seemed not to notice the intrusion, while others invited them in to join the fun. Eventually, they found themselves in the quietest room in the home — the library. Austin stood frozen at the door. He could only stare. "Books," Austin said incredulously.

"Yes. This is your library," Dunstan said proudly, "And, I would like you two to meet someone."

Sitting in the far corner of the room sat Gates and an older gentleman in overly stuffed leather chairs. They were smoking Cubans and enjoying vintage brandy in crystal snifters.

"Austin — Diana — I would like for you to meet Senior Director Amir."

Twilight

18

"When the people fear their government, there is tyranny; when the government fears the people, there's liberty." — Thomas Jefferson

* * * * * *

"Butch!"

"What?"

"Quit foolin' around with that Desk-Com game."

"Why?"

"Because it's midnight."

"So what?"

"So it's your turn to make the rounds."

"Yeah sure. I know. Just let me finish the . . ."

"Put the damn thing on hold till you get back, and make your damn rounds." Sammy stood up from his console chair, walked behind Butch and practically pulled his chair out from under him.

"OK, OK, OK. Sammy, I don't know why I can't just . . ."

"Because we get paid to make them on time — that's why. Now move your lazy ass." Sammy looked at his watch, then paced around from behind to the front of the desk and nervously looked out the glass front doors.

"I hate makin' the rounds at night — creeps me out." Butch slowly stood up from behind the bank of video monitors and stretched. "All them dead bodies layin' round in those glass boxes. Every damn lab room looks like a morgue." He picked up his flashlight and flipped it on and off a couple of times to make sure it lit.

"Butch, you know they ain't exactly dead bodies."

"Yeah — Well — That makes it even worse." *If one of those sons-a-bitches rises up one night — I might piss in my pants!*

"Don't worry. They won't bite."

"I know. They just creep me out — that's all." Butch reluctantly started his two-step crawl down the long and low-lit hall. His flashlight flickered off and on a couple of times as he shook it. *Don't you even think about goin' out on me now, you sorry ass mutha. I'll take your guts out and put in new batteries when I get back.* He said to himself as much as to the flashlight.

"Just make your rounds and I'll put on some fresh Coca-Coffee. It'll be ready when ya get back. I'll be watchin' ya on the monitors. Deal?"

Butch looked back over his shoulder. "Yeah sure. I just don't like spendin' the next thirty minutes walkin' through the . . ." he mumbled as he walked down the long, almost dark hallway to the first lab checkpoint.

Sam waited until Butch was out of sight, walked back around the security counter and quickly turned off the master alarm system. It was exactly midnight. Sitting behind the row of Desk-Com monitors, he could observe each of Butch's checkpoints. He also could observe the four figures approaching the building on monitor "A." They were dressed in black, each carrying a small backpack. The small team walked swiftly through the lightly landscaped campus grounds. At about the same time they reached the front entrance, Sam was already unlocking the second set of glass doors. Once inside, he quickly relocked both sets of doors.

"Nice packs! Who brought the marshmallows?" Sam laughed.

"Very funny."

"Hey — S'mores around the campfire are always good."

"Where's Butch? Asked Alex. "Carlos, check the monitors."

"He's in lab three."

Alex turned to his team members. "Good. Right on time. OK— you guys know the drill. Go!"

The first two ran quietly down the main hall to lab three. Carlos removed a cloth soaked in chloroform from a sealed plastic bag. As Butch opened the lab door and stepped into the hallway, the two grabbed him from either side. The struggle was short as Carlos quickly laid the cloth across Butch's face. Still holding him by his arms, they drug him down the remainder of the long hall to a back door and dropped him to the floor.

As Carlos ran back to the main lobby, his partner removed Butch's guard uniform. He then entered lab six and walked to one of the several four-foot by eight-foot glass boxes setting atop various lab tables. Slowly raising the hinged side of the glass cover, he pulled what appeared to be a nude male body out and on to the floor. After closing the container, he placed the guard's uniform on the body. Although the body was warm, it didn't seem to be breathing.

At about the same time Carlos joined the others, Sam returned from the basement stairwell. "Alex, we've got to make this quick. The gas furnace line is disconnected downstairs. I lit a candle on the far side of the room. We may have ten, maybe fifteen-minutes tops — not much more."

"No problem. Gabby has already placed your uniform on a body from lab two and we placed it on the chair behind the monitors. Now, everyone split up and take a lab. Open the gas jets and place a lit candle on the floor of the far side of each room. Sam, take lab one. Don't waste any time getting to the back door. We'll meet there ASAP. Now run!"

Sam ran to the security console and flipped the alarm system switch back to the on position. The others disappeared down the dark hallway. In five minutes flat, Sam was the last to get to the door. They picked up Butch's still limp body and pushed the bar on the automatic-locking back door. The alarms immediately began to blare as they sprinted behind the lab building to a parked black van. As they closed the sliding doors of the van and sped away, the claxon sound of the alarm that had been blaring during their sprint was replaced with a thunderous eruption — one of the largest explosions Austin, Texas had ever experienced.

* * * * * *

"Tell me everything." Amir demanded.

"Pardon me?" Austin responded.

"Please — have a seat. I want to know your thoughts."

"About this house?" Diana asked.

"No — Of course not, my dear. I know this house is more than the two of you could ever dream of. I want to know how you intend to earn it. What are you both prepared to do for the United Authority?"

"Whatever is required of us, sir," Diana quickly responded.

Amir smiled at Diana then turned his head towards Austin. "Is this true, Austin?"

"Why — yes. Of course, sir."

"You hesitated." Amir glared at Austin.

"I was considering, well, answering you with our history of dedication and service."

"Never hesitate, young man. You must always be decisive. And I don't require your resume. I know more of your history than you know yourselves. That is the primary reason that I'm interested in your future."

"Good advice, sir." Austin said.

"It should be the last required."

"Thank you for your confidence, sir," Diana said.

"I wish to spend more time with the two of you. However, now is not the time. Go enjoy your evening, but carefully consider what I've asked of you. What are you prepared to do?"

Gates quickly stood. "Carey, why don't you show these Citizens how hard we play. They will learn how hard we work — tomorrow." Then turning to Amir. "Director Amir and I have some final details to cover before he leaves."

"Perfect. Let's refresh our drinks, meet more people and fully enjoy this evening," Carey said as they walked from the library to the bar.

"Director Amir doesn't beat around the bush. Does he?" Austin said quietly over his shoulder to Carey.

"You'll find him to be a fair man. He's very sharp and to the point. The faster you learn about him and the other Senior Directors the better."

"I understand."

"Not completely — but you will," Carey said sternly. He stepped in front of the bar and stared at the UA Service girl leaning against the rail. "Do you see these two Citizens?"

"Yes sir," said the young redhead.

"They are the guests of honor. This is their new home. For the remainder of the evening, do not let them out of your sight. You will be closer to them than their own shadows. When their glasses are half empty, you are to bring them a fresh glass."

"Of course, sir."

"Oh — and get the best looking UA Service Fellow to help you. I repeat, you two will be closer than their shadows — if you catch my drift. Whatever these two want tonight — and I mean anything — you will provide. Understood?"

"It will be our pleasure, sir."

Turning to Austin and Diana. "Once we've met a few people you two need to know, we should take our drinks to the hot tub and relax."

"We didn't bring our bathing suits, Carey." Austin remarked casually.

Carey half chuckled. "That's OK — no one else did either."

Diana smiled at Austin and shrugged her shoulders.

The evening was one of the most enjoyable Austin and Diana had experienced. In fact, the entire day had been a uniquely enjoyable experience from beginning to end. It may even have served as a turning point — certainly, one that would be long remembered. The majority of their conversations the remainder of the evening were the typical "meet and greet" variety with little talk of ideology or politics.

Gates joined them, and a few others, soaking in the large patio hot tub late in the evening. The cool summer nights of Colorado favored time spent in the hot swirling water. It was conducive to reflection, creative thinking and more pleasurable activities depending on one's frame of mind and company. But, shortly before midnight Mountain Time, the relaxing, euphoric spell would be broken by a shattering report. A top UA Safety officer walked to the edge of the steaming hot tub. He looked down cautiously and cleared his throat. "Excuse me, Mister President."

"Yes?" Gates looked up sternly. "This had better be good."

"No, sir. I'm afraid it isn't."

"What could possibly be so important to disturb me . . .?"

"There's been a terrible accident, sir."

"What kind of accident?" Gates asked still looking up at the stone-faced UA Safety officer.

"Sir, Director Deimos asked me to inform you that the Austin Lab is gone."

* * * * * *

"Now there's a sight for sore eyes," Alex exclaimed to Gabby as she drove the van out of the thickly wooded entrance and into the farm's open pasture.

Sitting on the pier, fishing pole in hand was Alexander Conall. The old man smiled and waved as the two drove on top of and around the circumference of the pond's levee to the foot of the pier. Alex cut the engine and they slowly walked to the end of the pier where Conall was dangling his feet.

"Looks like we're having catfish for dinner." Gabby licked her lips. "Yummy."

"And a couple for the freezer too, since I got lucky."

"Man — are we glad to see you." Alex broke into a big smile and wrapping his arms around Conall.

"Back atcha. Did you have a good time in Austin, kids?"

"Loads."

"And the rest of the crew?"

"The party was a success. Carlos and gang headed south and should be crossing the Rio Grande shortly. It helps that there's no longer border guards at the river."

"Excuse me gentlemen. First I need a kiss and a hug from the wolfman. Then I need to drive up to the house and freshen up. Happily, we weren't expecting company today. I'm sure I look a mess. It's about time for lunch, too."

Conall set his fishing pole down and did his best to stand without moaning or loosing his balance and falling into the pond.

"Let me squeeze this pretty young thing. Gabby gets younger looking every time I see her. You're the only reason I came to visit, don't cha know. And you're beautiful without freshen' up."

"And I love your eyes." She smiled while kissing his cheek.

"Don't go to a lot of trouble now. I'm family — not company. And, I want to hear a story or two during lunch."

"We can swap more stories later," Gabby said as she walked down the pier.

Conall turned to Alex as she walked away. "Tell me about Austin — any problems?"

"Everything went as planned as best we could tell. Needless to say, we didn't stick around to see the final results. But if the initial explosion was any indication..."

"Nice fireworks?"

"Let's just say, I don't know how much could be left. I'm sure it will be considered a terrible accident caused by a faulty gas line. The security video is stored on-site and isn't fire protected. The candles we used were small. If any survived the blast and ensuing fire, they would be all but impossible to detect. We were listening to the Com-Set in the truck on our way back. As of yet, it's still being considered an accident and no one is claiming responsibility of course. They will be scratching their heads for awhile at least."

"It may not stop the 'Spider' program, but it should slow them down some." Conall put his hand on Alex's shoulder. "You make your old man proud."

"We do our best. We just need to keep the pressure on. This will be considered a huge set back for the UA. Not to mention, it's just another thorn in their side." Alex smiled.

"What about the guards?"

"Carlos will see to them in Mexico. Of course, Sam has been with us all along. Butch, on the other hand, may require a degree of reconditioning therapy.

Needless to say, they are both having their sensors surgically removed ASAP. Dr. Norm will take care of that little procedure once they arrive in Monterey. Both should be full-fledged Plebeians by the end of tomorrow."

"Another step in the right direction." Conall wiped the sweat from his forehead.

"For sure. Now bring *me* up to date. Where have you been? And, how have you been getting along? You're looking good — but a little tired."

"Not bad for one of the older models. Let's talk back at the house. I could use a drink and Gabby needs to hear of my exploits too."

Conall slowly bent over and pulled his catch-line from the water exposing three, fat catfish. They walked up to the house chatting about the Austin trip details. Conall wanted to hear the blow-by-blow. The devil was always in the details.

"Let me get an ice chest and some ice for the fish," Alex said as they stepped onto the front porch. "We can clean them after lunch."

"Sounds like a plan. While you're in there, would you bring your old man a cold drink?" Conall said as he planted his tired body on the porch swing.

Alex quickly returned with a bag of ice in one hand and a drink in the other.

"Here. Try this on for size."

Conall took one sip — licked his lips, then took a long slow drink. "Texas sweet tea — how I've missed that. Thanks. This hits the spot. And do I detect just a hint of chicory?"

"It's a little something my pappy taught me." Alex smiled.

"Are you gentlemen ready for some lunch?" Gabby poked her head from the screened door.

"Thought you'd never ask," Conall rubbed his stomach. "What's on the menu? I'm as hungry as a horse."

"Nothing special — just something quick. We're having huevos rancheros, fried rice and black beans with some fresh pico de gallo. Get it while it's hot."

After lunch they all pitched in to clean the dishes and tidy the kitchen. Gabby suggested that they refresh their drinks and go out to continue their conversation on the wooden bench swings hanging from the pecan trees in the front yard.

"Excellent idea — and an excellent lunch I might add. Thanks, Gabby."

"So — please continue." Alex said. "You left Shiprock and made your way to California."

"I did. Haven't been to the coast for many years. Eugene joined me there and he continued his education. The kid is smart. And he's devoted to our success."

"Very good."

"I also spent some time with your brother and Diana — for the first and sadly the last time."

"Don't say that, dad." Gabby frowned.

"No worries. I'm tired. My time has passed. I'm ready to retire."

"Perfect. So now you will be able to spend even more time with Austin and us." Gabby raised her glass as to salute.

"I wish it were so. But my body tells me otherwise. I may have this one last summer and maybe a beautiful fall in Durango. We'll see." *I'm not sure I would want to live forever anyway, but I'm really going to miss so many things. I suppose, in reality, I won't be missing them completely though.*

"You *will* be with us for the Fourth of July, won't you?" Gabby asked.

"Sure. I'll stay till then. I always enjoy celebrating our former independence."

* * * * * *

"Cleaning catfish was never one of my favorite activities," Gabby said, as she continued to slice each section of fish into measured steaks.

"These are some of the fattest cats we've pulled from the pond in quite some time," Alex said. "They will be perfect on the grill with a little mesquite smoke."

"It just doesn't get much better than this," Conall added. "What's your favorite grilling recipe?"

"Sometimes we'll lather them in our homemade barbeque sauce — the one you taught me. Other times, we soak them in fresh lime juice and baste them with thinly sliced jalapenos and honey."

They spent the remainder of the afternoon in the hot Texas shade of the pecan trees, sipping iced sweet tea, cleaning catfish and planning the future. There were a number of details to finalize before July 4th, just three weeks away. Plus, Conall felt compelled to impart to Alex and Gabby the knowledge they needed to continue in his absence and his ultimate vision of the future. He felt that the next few weeks might very well be his last opportunity to do so.

"What direction do you think my brother will take?"

"Not sure."

"There's a chance that we could become mortal enemies," Alex said sternly.

"True — History has certainly taught us that. My hope is that he is enough a part of me that . . ."

"That his environment has not changed him?"

"Exactly."

"Will you see him again, dad?" Gabby asked.

"It's unlikely."

"How will we learn of his decision?"

"That may well be up to you two."

"I will find a way if need be . . ."

"Take your time," Conall said wiping the sweat from his forehead.

"Are you OK?" Gabby said leaning forward.

"Fine, fine — I'm just tired and feeling a little warm. Now, let's see. What was I saying?"

"You said I should take my time and to be careful approaching Austin."

"Right. Be very cautious when you do. There could be multiple dangers."

"Understood — but, I hope you have the opportunity to live long and bring us together." Alex frowned.

"Nothing would please me more." *Trust me, If only . . .well . . .* "That said — my greatest pleasure would be to have lived long enough to not only bring my family together, but to bring our country together as well."

"We've made real progress of late." Alex stood and placed the remaining catfish steaks in the ice chest.

"True, but there's so much more to do."

"Couldn't the 4th be the final tipping point?"

"Possibly but unlikely. We may know more based on the reaction of the people — conversely, the government's reaction to them. It's like the Chinese philosopher Lao Tse wrote, 'No disaster is greater than underestimating the enemy.' Even so, change will not come rapidly. However, it could accelerate the metamorphosis. You two understand that the country, the people, didn't come to this point overnight."

"Of course we know that."

"And I know you should. Countries and their people have only lost their freedoms, seemingly overnight, as the result of armed and violent coups or wars. The takeover of this country, on the other hand, began many generations ago with the slow, methodical conditioning of the population. People were educated, some might say indoctrinated, and lulled into the belief of entitlements. It was easy in the beginning because those in power targeted the poor — the so called underprivileged."

"But poor people have no power."

"Correct. But they were empowered. They were led to believe they deserved as good of a life as those who had earned it, even though they had not worked for those rewards. The larger middle class was shamed into believing they were responsible for the underprivileged."

"That makes no sense."

"Correct again. Here's where it gets interesting. The people in power not only shamed but also convinced a large enough majority of the middle and upper classes into giving the underprivileged parity. After all, paying just a few more taxes made the higher classes feel good about helping the lesser privileged. Unfortunately, the more you give to people, the less they need to achieve and earn on their own."

"And the less they appreciate it," Gabby spoke up.

"They come to expect it," Alex added.

"Those are the facts. Over time, more and more people chose to receive. Fewer people chose achievement because it was no longer necessary. It was a gradual erosion of values and ethics. We can't change overnight that which took years to create. If I can remember the quote by Henry David Thoreau, 'The finest workers of stone are not copper or steel tools, but the gentle touches of air and water working at their leisure with a liberal allowance of time.'"

"Erosion is corrosive."

"My point exactly. Given time, erosion can work as the common detriment — or hopefully for the common good."

* * * * * *

"Mister President, I'm in Austin, Texas and it's not a pretty sight." Deimos said speaking into his secure Tel-Card.

"How bad is it, Hector?"

"There isn't a lot left — just a large hole in the ground. It looks like a deep crater filled with scrap metal, bricks and debris. This will take some time for forensics to investigate."

"Any initial thoughts as to the cause?"

"It has all of the appearances of a gas explosion."

"Natural gas?"

"Correct — just a terrible accident — a faulty furnace line possibly. And thank the gods, it happened at night. There were only two security guards on duty. Their bodies have yet to be recovered. So, our research team is safe."

"How about the research itself?"

"Some data were lost. Doctor Gudrun has assured me that most of the daily research was backed up off site. The primary loss was in the human test subjects. They were within days of final animation. Sadly, they are completely gone."

"How much of a set back is that?"

"It will take another year to duplicate the human trials, according to Gudrun."

"Unacceptable!"

"I'm not sure there's a choice."

"Get Gudrun on your jet. I want him here — today."

"I'll try, but he and his team are pretty shook up. You can imagine . . ."

"I can imagine how shook up he'll be if he's not here before the end of the day."

"Understood, Mr. President."

"In fact, just how many researchers are on that team?"

"About forty."

"Tell Gudrun to bring his key people with him. Tell him I expect a written report by the time he lands in the Springs on just how his team will rebuild and expedite the completion of this project. I don't care if they have to jerk some Plebes off the street and experiment on them in his garage. Whatever they have to do to make this work quickly. Another year is completely unacceptable. Got it?"

"Understood completely, sir."

Gates squeezed the Tel-Card in his hand to the point of pain. He reached back and threw it into the fireplace with all of his power. Dunstan watched it explode into a hundred pieces turning the orange flames to blue.

"You've got to stop destroying your Tel-Cards, Bill. That's three this month." He smiled.

"Son — of — a — bitch!"

"The 'Wolf?'"

"No — it appears to have been an accident. A *fucking* accident!"

"There's some solace, I suppose. It's good the 'Wolf' wasn't involved. Bill, the truth is if it weren't for bad luck, we wouldn't have much these days. What are the details?"

Gates rubbed his temples while pacing around the Oval Office. "Get me some aspirin."

* * * * * *

Their flight back to California seemed short and almost anticlimactic. After their gourmet in-flight meal, Austin and Diana slept until the aircraft's tires hit the runway at LAX. The week had been an experience of a lifetime, from the euphoria of their new home to the mostly productive, albeit intensive, week of work. In so many ways it seemed as though it may have all been a dream.

"Austin — We must decide on our reality," Diana said as they walked to the parking garage.

"Our lives seem to have taken on an imaginary reality, dear."

"I'm not sure what to think or believe anymore," She said as she opened the car door.

"It's either real — or it's a dream . . ."

"There's nothing that is in between. I've heard that somewhere before," she said with a puzzled look on her face.

They drove back to Redondo from the airport in virtual silence. Both were in deep thought. Uniquely, or possibly not, their thoughts were identical. After parking underground at their condo and taking the lethargic elevator to the third floor, they walked down the short hall and Austin pressed his thumb to the door sensor.

"Look at this," Diana said as she entered.

"What?"

"I almost forgot how small our condo was — is — I mean."

"Cozy."

"Yes. That's the word." She smiled. "In an odd way, it's good to be home."

"Funny," Austin sighed. "I think you're right."

"You realize — the next few weeks could be the last time we will stay here."

Austin sank down onto their worn couch. "Regardless of our choice — you're right."

"Since our nap on the plane I feel wide awake. Why don't we strip down, pour a drink, or two, sit on the patio, watch the surf and enjoy the twilight?" Diana suggested.

"Splendid idea. I'm glad I thought of it," he joked. "We can unpack in the morning."

"Do you think we could close the balcony doors and talk about . . . ?

"Diana!"

* * * * *

Carey Dunstan and Director General Gunther Borghild walked from the entry of Senior Director Amir's estate to their waiting limo. Their meeting was rather brief — to the point one might say. The complete Senior Board had met in private at the end of the week following the Austin lab explosion. It was on the same day they learned that the destruction was not by accident — quite possibly a tipping point. By the end of that day's meeting, the consensus was that a major change would be required. It wasn't the first time the Board had made a terminal decision. They expressed to Dunstan and Borghild their sincere confidence that it would be the last time this decision would be required.

Upon entering the limo, Dunstan asked his driver to take his time driving back to the White House. "As a matter of fact, Enrico, I haven't been to the top of Pike's Peak in quite a while. Why don't you take us for a drive?"

"Yes sir."

"Care for a single-malt, General?"

"Why Carey — I thought you'd never ask." Borghild smiled in rare humor.

"It appears we have some serious planning ahead of us." Dunstan reached over and handed the General his drink.

"Serious, but simple."

"I've known for some time there was friction between you and Gates, General."

"That obvious?"

"No doubt. But you've been a good soldier."

"I've always believed in the chain of command, Carey."

"It has been observed. However, you understand that the chain is only as strong as it's weakest link."

The drive to the top of the mountain was spent considering a variety of scenarios. Each of their options required exact timing, skillful execution and plausible circumstance. It was an exercise that Dunstan and Borghild excelled in. Each was an experienced chess master. At the end of the approximate two-hour drive to the top they stepped from the limo and walked to an observation platform. The sky was a deep and perfect Colorado blue with a formation of cumulous clouds in the distance over the eastern plains.

"A little more than fourteen thousand feet," Dunstan remarked.

"Tallest in the state?"

"One of several fourteen thousand foot peaks, but not the tallest. Mount Elbert is fourteen thousand four hundred and thirty-three."

"I understand there was a time when people would race cars to the top of this mountain. That must have been a challenge to behold, Carey."

"True. I've heard those stories as well, General. That was a period when so many people wasted their time on even more dangerous and frivolous adventures. It doesn't make any sense to me — all in the name of sport — fun — go figure."

"It was a different time, Carey. Believe it or not, war even had a degree of pleasure, in the past."

"I once knew an old man, a professor, whose life-long dream, his challenge, was to climb to the top of every fourteen thousand foot peak in Colorado."

"And? Did he make it?"

"He did. He had photos to prove it. It's fascinating how people enjoy challenging themselves — like technical rock climbing or extreme downhill skiing."

"The President takes pleasure in that — doesn't he?" Borghild suggested.

"Skiing — Yes."

"I thought so." Borghild rubbed his chin as if calculating in his mind.

"Why do you ask?"

"Do you think he could be challenged to hang glide from here — from fourteen thousand feet?"

* * * * * *

The day began not unlike any other Tuesday. Citizens were working. Traffic in the cities was as light as usual. The day was mostly unremarkable. There seemed to be fewer Plebeians gathering in their usual locations, however. Not that anyone would notice. The weather was mostly mild across the country. Almost no one gave a second thought to the fact that it was the Fourth of July. Why should they?

From coast to coast, southern to northern border, Citizens would not fully realize that just one day could impact their future lives so dramatically. Yet, the Fourth of July would once again be a day long remembered. For on July the fourth, 2084, before the day was over, every Credit from the United Authority's Central Bank would completely vanish.

Wolf Cubs

19

"Sometimes in the winds of change we find our true direction." — Unknown

* * * * * *

"What do you mean there are no Credits? I have thousands of Credits in my account!" The Citizen complained to the cashier. "I just bought lunch a few hours ago. I know exactly what's in my account."

"You don't understand, sir. There are no credits because the UA Central Bank's system is down. We've already contacted the bank and they have assured us they will be back online shortly."

"Great. What time do you close?"

"At six — just like all of the other pharmacies."

"But that's five minutes from now."

"Four, sir."

"Right. I just returned from the clinic with this prescription. You see, I need this medication for my six-year old daughter tonight. It's critical. She is very sick."

"I understand, sir. But there's really nothing I can do. UA regulation requires that we maintain these hours. You'll just have to return tomorrow."

"You're joking."

"No, sir. Your situation is much too serious for levity."

"But, what am I suppose to do?"

"I really don't know. I'm not a doctor."

"Let's try this. I'll give you my Citizen's information. I'll take the medicine and return tomorrow with the payment?"

"I'm sorry sir, that's against store policy. You are welcome to stay until six."

"Is there a manager I can speak with?"

"I'm sorry, sir, but the manager cannot be disturbed during the closing sequence."

"It would only take a minute of his time."

"Her time."

"Whatever."

"Impossible."

"Unbelievable! OK — Is there another pharmacy close by — at least one that stays open a little later than . . . ?

"Sir — as I said, UA regulations requires all pharmacies to close at six. And it is six now. Have a nice evening."

* * * * * *

Citizens and businesses alike found themselves in similar circumstances as they had faced in the recent power outage. When there is no power, there is no access to Credits. At least the bright side this go around was that there was no electrical outage. There was light. There was power. There were simply no Credits. Having power was little consolation for the inconvenience, the pressing need for Credits, or if, the gods forbid, an emergency arose.

Tens of thousands of Citizens stood in lines for hours waiting to make their purchases. Others sat captured at their restaurant tables, unable to leave until they could pay for their meals, or closing time, whichever came first. The majority resigned themselves to patiently accepting this annoyance — while a few others took full advantage of the situation.

By the end of the second day, Citizens grew increasingly more concerned. No one was prepared for extended periods without the necessities. Even so, it wasn't so much the two-day abstinence, but rather the unknown. How long before Credits could be accessed? The President, no one of authority communicated what the problem was, how it was being addressed or more importantly, when Credits would become available. The lack of substantive response from their leaders was most disconcerting.

* * * * * *

"Bill — Senior Director Sheng-Li is calling for you on my secure Tel-Card. He said yours isn't working." Dunstan handed the card to Gates. *And it will never work again — at least until the old one is replaced — if it's replaced.*

"Huang — Gates here. What are we looking at?"

Sheng-Li was not only a Senior Director; he was the Director of the UA Central Bank. It was arguably one of the most powerful positions held in the United Authority. All financial institutions including the former Federal Reserve had been merged after the near collapse of the currency in 2055. The UA warned that if immediate actions weren't taken, the country would experience a similar or worse collapse than the "Great Deflation" of 2026. The Citizens were assured that the only fail-safe measure would be to enact the "Monetary Credits Security Act," thus bringing together the control of all personal, business and national Credits under one UA Central Bank. Huang was but the second person to hold the position — his father Xing was the first. He had been groomed from birth to become the obvious successor.

"What we are looking at Bill is the complete and total eradication of the UA's financial records."

"Thank the gods for backups."

"Needless to say, it was our first thought as well. It hasn't worked out so well though — at least, not so far. No sooner do we begin to download the backups then they too become corrupted and the data rapidly starts to disappear. The virus has corrupted the operating systems. It is what our people are calling an 'infinity strain.' The only consolation is that the original records remain safe in Albuquerque at the main data bank. The problem is that they are inaccessible to the UA Central Bank systems while they are stored in that data bank. The data are impossible to access while in storage — at least from a practical standpoint."

"What are our options?"

"At this time, we can only come up with one — the installation of all new operating systems."

"All of them?"

"Correct. We can't take a chance that even one remaining system could begin the cycle again. It will be a massive system replacement not only here at the main bank in Denver, but system software in all of the thousands of branches as well."

"But that could take . . ."

"Correct again. It will take weeks — maybe more. I assure you, our people are working 24/7."

"In the mean time, people, businesses, Citizens have no ability to . . ."

"Exactly — There are no accounts. There are no Credits — period."

"This is going to create chaos. What are we going to do to maintain . . ."

"What are *we* going to do? What are *you* going to do? That is the question. You are the President."

"I'll handle it. No worries. I will — I'll outline an action plan immediately. Do we know what or should I say who is culpable?"

"Bill — There is no doubt. Your renegade anarchists are definitely responsible."

"Respectfully, Huang, they aren't my . . ."

"They are *your* responsibility. And they are an incubus, I might add that you have failed to control."

"Look, we have diligently worked . . ."

"Don't try and spread the blame of your incompetence in this matter by saying 'we.'"

"You're right. And I will take complete and full responsibility for . . ."

"Full responsibility doesn't cut it anymore. This situation is more serious than you can imagine. These are the seeds of social unrest. Control is fragile. Within the last few months our power grid came under attack, we later learn that the Austin lab was sabotaged, and now this. It quite possibly could jeopardize our entire structure."

"I understand and will expedite a plan." *Even though I have no ability to print money, I'll just pull something out of my ass. You're the guy whose suppose to be guarding our Credits. And now this is my fault? Right.*

"The sooner the better — I just spoke with Amir and we're calling a special meeting of the Senior Board tonight."

* * * * * *

Pressure built by the day. Every class of Citizen was affected. Even those in the highest echelons of business and government were impacted. By the end of the second week without Credits, many otherwise peaceful Citizens were resorting to any means possible to feed themselves and their families. Looting was initially covert and under the cover of darkness. But as the crisis continued, people became more desperate and aggressive in their efforts.

Signs appeared throughout the country. And although they seemed spontaneous their message was uniform:

THERE IS NO SAFETY AND SECURITY

THE UA CANNOT PROTECT YOU

NO CREDITS — NO SECURITY
UA — NO WAY

UA Safety forces fired tear gas to chase off thousands of demonstrating Citizens in the Capitol.

"We pay our taxes and now you keep all of our Credits!" Angry crowds chanted. "Where is our security?"

Protesters threw rocks and bricks at UA Security Guards in riot gear when they moved to disband a mob outside of the White House main gates. Similar scenes were played out at UA Central Bank buildings in cities from coast to coast. Complete sections of communities were ablaze to a scale beyond the control of firefighters. Hospitals were overwhelmed with the numbers of injured and suffering. UA Safety troops were completely outnumbered and feared the only resort may be lethal force.

President Gates finally appealed to Citizens on Com-Centers in the third week. He demanded Citizens to remain calm. It was the first appearance of any government official since the crisis began. Gates proudly reported, "I have been involved since day one. A committee was appointed to determine the cause and extent of the issue. It was only today that I could report our findings." He assured them the situation was merely a technical problem and only temporary. Their Credits and accounts were safe. Gates placed the blame on "The Wolf" and "Los Salvadores."

"It is each and every Citizen's responsibility to understand who has taken away your safety and security," Gates announced during his address, "I assure you, the United Authority hasn't taken away your Credits. *Criminals* have stolen your hard earned Credits. Their actions are an attempt to destabilize this government. Instead — they have taken away your very survival. Why do they attempt to harm you? You have caused them no misfortune."

"Let me be clear, 'The Wolf' and the so called 'Salvadores' live among you. They may be your neighbors. It is your duty as loyal Citizens to report those individuals you know, or those whom you suspect may be involved with this group of dissidents. *They* are your enemy. Route your anger to those responsible for your suffering."

"It is to that end, I am offering one million Credits to every Citizen who turns over to us a member of this renegade group — and ten million for their leader — Alexander Conall — the infamous and dangerous 'Wolf.'"

"I assure you, the United Authority will protect you. Make no mistake — you must remain calm. UA Safety teams will be distributing food and water in most cities. Help your neighbors if and when you can. The government is not culpable. Remember — *you* are the United Authority — and each and every one of you must stay united during this period of inconvenience."

"I can also assure you that in short order, your accounts will be restored. Please remain calm. Nothing can be solved with violence. Stay vigilant. Help us root out those responsible. Help us to keep the peace and we will reestablish your Credits with interest. And I — will restore your safety and security."

* * * * * *

Conall witnessed much of the unrest as he began his travel across the state from east Texas to what was once the old-west border city of El Paso. His plan was to make one last trip to the coast. He felt that his heart required a final farewell to Austin and Diana. After a brief visit he would return to Durango — his end of the line. He also hoped to visit his Navajo family, along the way, before witnessing the fall color change of the mountain scrub oak and aspens one last time.

City after city on his voyage bore the battle scars of a civilization in revolt. Smoldering hulks of buildings dotted the cityscapes. UA armored cruisers and Safety Forces patrolled the streets. They were sad sights — ones he never thought he would witness in his country. Sights and events he had hoped could have been avoided. Now, his only desire was that this event would serve as the final catalyst to change the course of the future.

Conall prayed that more of the Citizens would finally be awakened to the reality of self-determined responsibility. Sadly, he also understood human nature. Within short order, possibly weeks after Credits being restored, he perceived that the majority of Citizens might begin to slide back into submission once again. *Why do so many have such short memories? Why is it that people accept the illusory safety and security of their government?* They were but a couple of the rhetorical questions Conall had repeated in his head his entire life. Those thoughts and many others of like nature were always followed by thoughts of his parents and their teachings. He remembered his mother repeating over the years, "If it is to be, it's up to me."

It seemed to Conall that toward the end of his trip to the coast, with rumors circulating the cities like a virus and the omnipresent UA Forces patrolling, there was little hope. Ultimately, Citizens abdicated. Their ultimate response to the hideous issues of the day — at least those outside the power elite — would be resignation. Too many would finally sink into the slough of denial. Most surrendered themselves back to their false sense of security once Credits were restored. It was their corollary to fend off the paralyzing anxiety. He remembered Edmund Burke, the British Statesman who once said, "For evil to flourish, all that is needed is for good people to do nothing." The majority simply felt helpless. Just as Conall had feared, they hadn't the capacity to change, to take charge. In addition, there were far too many who actually believed in their own subordination. It was an addiction in which they would always remain dependent.

If only a few seeds of doubt might continue to grow, Conall thought. *Would there be enough of those who could continue to nurture and cultivate a crop of free thinkers? Freedom, after all, is the capacity for self-determination.* Instinctively he knew this was but the latest conflict in a very long future struggle. And, deep down, he understood that this would be his final battle.

* * * * * *

It was yet another perfect Southern California Sunday — at least for the weather. This was the day of the week for Austin and Diana's routine walk on the beach. They were within a few short days of making the final decision that would change the remainder of their lives. And either choice they made would end their private moments on the beach.

"Time is running out," Diana said while she wiggled her toes in the cold wet sand.

"We're still young. We have plenty of time," Austin gently touched his toes to hers.

"Very funny. You know what I mean, Austin."

"I do."

"So." *We have to stop avoiding the inevitable.* "Austin, it's time to face our future reality."

"I understand. We've gone over the pros and cons of either choice so many times."

"And never a conclusion — a resolution."

"We should wait until the last possible moment," Austin smiled and kissed her cheek.

"You're joking. Why?"

"Because we both work well on deadline." He smiled.

Diana turned and looked directly into his eyes. "Right. What you really mean is that we both procrastinate."

"OK — maybe we should put off procrastinating for awhile."

"Austin — be serious."

"You're right. Let me think." They continued their walk allowing the cold Pacific water to splash over their bare legs. "Here's an idea. I should have thought of it sooner. Why don't we create an imaginary two-column ledger?"

"One column for either choice?"

Austin gave her thumbs up. "Correct. Then we put a value to each item placed in either of those two columns."

"Add them up," she smiled.

"And the decision will be made for us."

"Brilliant."

"In a way — yes. It's a very old concept I learned from my father — or from my former self — whichever."

"Well, it is an excellent idea and I believe you're both brilliant. Even if you are the same person — of sorts."

"Thank you from the both of us," he stopped and bowed.

Diana thought for a moment. "I have a question."

"And that would be?"

"What if we don't like the results of the tally?"

Austin wrapped his arms around her and whispered sweetly, "Tough."

They continued their barefoot walk in the chilled sand — itemizing their line- items along the way. It was decided that Diana would be responsible for remembering the reasons for staying with the United Authority and their corresponding values. Austin would maintain the column for leaving.

"I'm going to miss our walks on the beach," she said.

"They will be pleasant memories to keep."

"Memory is the mother of all wisdom."

"Why Diana, how poetic."

"I know. I wish I originated it," she laughed.

Both were completely unaware of the additional scrutiny of their actions for the past few days. Alexander Conall had watched them from a distance noticing some occasional, covert observers. He couldn't afford to let his guard down at this late date. On his fourth day back at the coast he finally deemed it safe to make his approach.

Austin and Diana recognized the image of an old Plebeian walking barefoot toward them at the edge of the shallow surf. Before they came together, however Conall looked up and noticed, what he perceived to be, two UA Security Agents standing at the edge of the cliff above.

"Good morning," he said as he approached Austin. And in almost a whisper, "Don't stop. Keep walking. Meet me by the Redondo marina at about noon." He continued to walk past at his same pace. Austin and Diana continued a few yards down the beach to find a place to sit and talk.

"What was that all about?" Diana asked.

"Instinct."

* * * * * *

Conall slowly walked around the Redondo pier casually looking from his left to his right and occasionally behind. Without being obvious, he carefully observed everyone coming and going. He was keenly aware of his environment — a survival skill he had honed to perfection through the years. He observed two non-Citizens fishing at the far end of the pier. Walking in their direction, he stopped for a moment beside the door of Polly's Coffee Café near the pier's end. A couple of Citizens also approached the door shortly there after.

"Excuse me, gentlemen?"

"Are you talking to us, old man?" A large hulk of a Citizen stopped and stared at Conall.

"Why yes. I am. It's tiresome talking to one's self all day. Wouldn't you agree?" He smiled. "Would you help an old man get a cup of Coca-Coffee?"

"What's in it for us?" the shorter of the two asked.

"Well now — " he paused, "I'm glad you asked." — as he reached into his pocket.

A few minutes later, the larger Citizen opened the café door and exchanged the hot cup for his strangely interesting reward. Conall thanked the Citizen and walked to the end of the pier holding his steaming brew.

"Good afternoon, gents. Having any luck?"

"Take a look," The older of the two said as he stooped down and opened the lid of a beat up cooler.

"Marvelous. You two fish here often?"

"Every day," he said as he closed the lid, then cast back into the sea below.

"I see you have a crab string too."

"Yep."

"Any good?"

"When they're biten'."

Conall placed both elbows on the rail and gazed far out to sea. He inhaled the sight and the sea breeze, taking it all in for what he knew would be his last time. His desire was to make it last much longer, but it was close to noon and he needed to scout around the marina before meeting with Austin and Diana. He walked back and around to the north side of the pier. Looking down to the slips below. Conall noticed that Austin and Diana were already waiting. They had chosen an inconspicuous corner of the mostly vacant marina with a couple of benches and potted palms. There were no suspicious appearing individuals as far as he could see. Everything seemed quite safe and hopefully normal. After a precautionary period, Conall deemed it safe to take the closest stairs down.

"Good afternoon again, you two."

"Hello," they said almost in unison.

"It's a sad sight."

"You are referring to . . .?"

"The marina. There was a time when these slips were filled with beautiful yachts and boats of all descriptions. Sadly — no more."

"It must have been long ago," Diana said.

"My, yes — very long ago. It seems like a lifetime or more." *Come to think about it, it was my lifetime.*

"What happened?" she asked.

"People — excuse me — regular Citizens can no longer afford such luxuries."

"And they could before?"

"Oh my, yes — yes they could. In fact, I dare say a majority could if they chose to. Those who chose not had other diversions of equal value to choose from."

"That's hard to believe. Yet — deep in my memory I seem to . . ."

"There are many items stored in your deep memory that only require the right resources to bring to your conscious mind, Austin — you as well Diana. But enough of the past — we need to speak of the future. Have you chosen yours?"

"We are getting closer," Austin said quickly. "Have you decided yours?"

"Mine was chosen many years ago. It was only a matter of timing. And the time is now."

"When now?" Diana asked.

"Not today or tomorrow. I will make my final day within a few short weeks."

"You will make your final day?" Austin asked.

"Of course. I choose to be in control of my last decision if at all possible. It will be my final act."

"Speaking of acts by the way, your Act Three, was very impressive — and a pain in the ass I might add." Austin frowned.

"Overall, I think it met my expectation. It accomplished most of the impact I desired. I understood it would not accomplish my final intention. Just as significant, however, what about *your* resolution?"

"To begin with," Diana started, "we believe you. We believe in you and your objective."

"Alex will be very pleased to learn this. I will get a message to him quickly. I know he will look forward to meeting the two of you as soon as circumstances permit."

"Our dilemma," Austin began, "is — well, the direction we should take. There are so many impediments in either alternative."

"I understand. But remember, when obstacles arise, you change your direction to reach your goal, you do not change your decision to get there."

*****

"Good morning, Katy."

"Good morning, sir. It's going to be a busy day. I'll bring you coffee to your office right away."

"Take your time. I'm in no hurry."

"You don't understand. The Director has been in his office for an hour already and he's in a bit of a huff. He asked that you see him as soon as you arrive."

"Any idea what . . .?"

"No. I even asked Randi. She doesn't know either — only that the Director was in a tear when she arrived."

"I guess I'll take that coffee to go."

Austin took the short walk to Akakios' office stopping for a brief moment at Randi's desk.

"Have you heard?"

"Nothing. But it isn't good whatever it is," she frowned.

The door had barely closed behind Austin when Akakios pressed his Tel-Com button. "Randi — no interruptions except from the White House."

"Yes, sir."

Klaud looked up sternly. "Austin — I'm afraid there's been some very bad news. President Gates is dead."

Austin's face turned pale flush and he came close to falling backwards into the chair in front of Klaud's desk. He was all but in a minor state of shock. *Great. Just when Diana and I thought we had chosen a direction. This news may throw us into a redirection.* For a moment he was unable to force enough air from his lungs to speak. "What? — When? — How?

"Late yesterday afternoon . . ."

"Why didn't you call me?"

"Because it was Sunday and I was on my boat. I was exhausted. I sailed in late and didn't check my Tel-Card until I got up this morning. I'm waiting for a call-back from the White House for details and orders."

"This is disastrous. What happened?"

"It seems there was an accident. He was hang gliding off Pikes Peak."

* * * * * *

Conall was pleased that his journey home to Durango was mostly uneventful. His trip began with the knowledge of Austin and Diana's decision. He would have made it to Durango two days sooner had he not stopped to say goodbye to his Navajo brother, Peter Begay. Margaret prepared a wonderful dinner as usual. She sensed it would be the last she would prepare for Alexander.

"Margaret — I must say, you have outdone yourself once again. This meal will be in my final dreams."

"This may have been the last supper I prepare for you. But, it will not be your last. We all return," she sadly spoke as they cleared the table. "We will miss you. The people will miss you. There will be many good memories. Many good stories to tell our grandchildren before we go to our next life."

"Come, my brother. We will have our last talk for a long while and drink our favorite whiskey."

"Margaret is right. We all will return," Conall sighed. "And my hope is that we will be reunited."

"We return — not always can we speak though. The great spirit returns us in many forms."

"Then, I will speak now. You have taught me so very much. My life has been greatly rewarded by our friendship. I feel that I haven't fully repaid you for the gifts you have given me." Conall sighed.

"It's not true. Your gift has also been our friendship. I have learned much from you as well. You have also given your life as a gift to our country. My dreams tell me our world is healing. There have been pains. But the pains are good. They are the healthy signs of the curing process. And, you leave behind a wolf cub — maybe two."

"I hope your dreams come true, Peter."

"My dreams are the truth. Have you chosen your final path?"

"I have. My rest will come as the mountain men of the earlier centuries. Once the colors change, I will wait for the snows to drop to eight thousand feet. My favorite hiking trail is northwest of Durango, high up the La Plata Canyon. About five miles into the forest there is a clearing and a narrow spring. The

Ponderosa Pines rise to the clouds. I will choose a tree and sit at its base watching the sky fill with stars as the light fades. That night will be my final dream. By morning, my body will be frozen."

Peter placed his hand on Conall's shoulder. "Another wolf will find you by the next morning — and feast. At that time my brother, you will become a true wolf."

The End

A part of the trilogy

Made in the USA
Lexington, KY
11 June 2013